Bookmarked
CLUB PICK

Dear Bookmarked Reader,

I'm so happy to hear that my novel *Lost and Found* has been chosen for the Target Bookmarked Club. I'm honored by the recognition, and grateful for the opportunity to bring my work to a larger audience.

Lost and Found follows several two-person teams as they compete in a global scavenger hunt as part of a reality-TV show. I chose to set the novel in the world of reality television for a bunch of reasons. One is that I genuinely like TV, and I was interested in taking a closer look at the role it plays in our lives, for better or for worse. I also liked the drama that a game like this provided—Who will be eliminated? Which team will implode first?—and the built-in structure that it gave the story. Putting my characters in the unreal, constantly televised environment of a reality show allowed me to stick them into a pressure cooker from the first page onward. All I had to do was sit back and see how they'd react.

And the characters are really what the novel is about. The TV show gave me a backbone to hang the story on, but it's my hope that this is a novel you can enjoy whether you love reality shows or hate them. It is, in many ways, a novel about the devastation that can come from keeping things hidden. Each character starts out with a secret, something that haunts them and that they'd like to keep out of the public eye, and each one finds that the scrutiny of being on the show brings the most private details of their lives to the forefront in ways they hadn't imagined.

Laura and her daughter Cassie are trying to rebuild their relationship following the shattering revelation that Cassie has hidden her entire pregnancy from her mother. Abby and Justin, a married couple who met in a Christian "ex-gay" group, find that it's not so easy to pick and choose which pieces of themselves they want to keep. Juliet and Dallas, former child stars, consider how far they'd go to put themselves back in the spotlight. And Barbara Fox, the host of the show, observes it all from the surreal comfort of an air-conditioned glass booth.

Thanks for picking up *Lost and Found*. If you'd like to contact me, or to read more about this book or my first novel, *The Dogs of Babel,* you can check out my Web site at www.carolynparkhurst.com.

I hope you enjoy the book!

All the best,

Carolyn Parkhurst

For more information on Carolyn Parkhurst and *Lost and Found,* go to www.target.com/bookmarked.

Carolyn Parkhurst is the author of one previous novel, the national bestseller *The Dogs of Babel*, which has been translated into twenty languages. She lives in Washington, D.C.

Praise for Carolyn Parkhurst's

LOST AND FOUND

"A delightfully complex and deliciously fast-paced novel. . . . Bestselling author Parkhurst has crafted a deceptively lighthearted romp that eventually pits daughter against mother and husband against wife. . . . A thoroughly enjoyable journey from its enticing start to its completely satisfying ending. Highly recommended."
— Kellie Gillespie, *Library Journal*

"What really interests Parkhurst is quiet, private agonies of love and shame, and on this score she delivers several surprisingly moving stories. . . . Parkhurst catches us again and again with moments of real tenderness. Long before the end, the million dollars doesn't matter; other things, far more important, are found here. And that's reason enough to tune in."
— Ron Charles, *Washington Post Book World*

"Parkhurst endows each character with complexity and pathos . . . and it's soon clear that what they're chasing after will lead not only to prize money but to a deeper understanding of their own failures and desires. . . . What emerges is less a satire than a straightforward character study – one that we're reluctant to put down even after the last contestant crosses the finish line."
— Rebecca Marx, *Elle*

"One of the summer's best reads. . . . Parkhurst's stories and her characters' voices – perfectly pitched to deliver insight without cheap sentiment – soar above the setting. . . . Parkhurst's surefooted, eloquent prose reveals everything in its proper time, and treats the unspoken fears of her questing, broken characters with uncommon grace." — Donna Bowman, *The Onion*

"Entertaining.... *Lost and Found* is a kaleidoscope that is funny and edgy."

— Robin Vidimos, *Denver Post*

"There is plenty of material in reality TV for a vicious satire, but Parkhurst takes a gentler approach, allowing earnestness to trump savage commentary. Catching a plane, you see, is not the most difficult connection to make. The contestants solve puzzles and lug around baggage literal and emotional. Couple by couple, they're knocked off the show, but what makes this lightweight literary fling fun is not the suspense of who wins but the eventual adaptation of the players to the real game – life."

— Connie Ogle, *Miami Herald*

"Parkhurst's chief gift as a novelist is her ability to seize the innermost thoughts of her characters, then convey them with meticulous craft."

— Kimberly Marlowe Hartnett, *Seattle Times*

"*Lost and Found* has all the guilty pleasure of an actual reality show, plus the popcorn indulgence of learning the story behind the backstory each contestant comes packaged with."   — Sherryl Connelly, *New York Daily News*

"*Lost and Found* pulls us by the hand to witness the inexpressible tenderness and cruelty of real emotion in the last place we would expect to find it. Sly and sage, it . . . entertains as surely as it beguiles."

— Jacquelyn Mitchard, author of *The Deep End of the Ocean* and *Cage of Stars*

"A spectacular soap opera.... The novel is about the journey, not the destination. . . . Parkhurst's fictional reality show is better than the semireal real thing. For one, her tale can be devoured in one easy gulp. . . . For another, her cast is impeccable – not a dud in the bunch."

— Joal Ryan, *Los Angeles Times*

"Humorous and touching. . . . Thoroughly original and inventive, peopled with engaging characters, and just plain fun, this novel deserves to be as big a hit as the reality shows it genially pokes fun at."

— Kristine Huntley, *Booklist*

"Parkhurst writes about something much deeper than the surface topic. . . . She has a delicate touch. She enlists us in her characters' struggle to forge honest connections with others despite the obvious distractions of money, fame, religious dogma, and societal expectations. As her broader message is universal to human readers, it is hard to dismiss."

— Chris Wiegard, *Richmond Times Dispatch*

"In her new pop culture–saturated novel, the author of *The Dogs of Babel* goes behind the scenes and imagines what TV reality show participants are really like. . . . You think the bickering is bad on TV? Just wait until you hear what Parkhurst imagines they're really thinking and saying off-camera."

— Carol Memmott, *USA Today*

"*Lost and Found* tickles the idea of what is real and what is fake in the most delicious way. . . . This fast-paced novel handles so many themes so wisely: the desire for intimacy and recognition, showing up in a distorted form on reality TV; the folly of trying to straitjacket sexuality; the loveliness of the moments when we transcend our lonely selves."

— Jeffrey Ann Goudie, *Kansas City Star*

"Employing a constantly shifting perspective, Parkhurst admirably juggles a large cast of characters. . . . She treats the game show as an opportunity for the contestants to decide, as the producer asks of them, 'What have you found?' The answer for readers: heart and wit to spare."

— *Publishers Weekly*

LOST

AND

FOUND

CAROLYN PARKHURST

BACK BAY BOOKS
Little, Brown and Company
New York   Boston   London

Also by Carolyn Parkhurst

The Dogs of Babel

Back Bay Books / Little, Brown and Company
Hachette Book Group USA
237 Park Avenue, New York, NY 10017
Visit our Web site at www.HachetteBookGroupUSA.com

Orginally published in hardcover by Little, Brown and Company, June 2006
First Back Bay paperback edition, July 2007

The characters and events in this book are fictitious. Any similarity to real persons, living or dead, is coincidental and not intended by the author.

Library of Congress Cataloging-in-Publication Data
Parkhurst, Carolyn.
    Lost and found / Carolyn Parkhurst. — 1st ed.
        p.   cm.
    HC ISBN 0-316-15638-8 / 978-0-316-15638-7
    PB ISBN 0-316-06639-7 / 978-0-316-06639-6 / 978-0-316-02362-7 (Target ed.)
    1. Contests — Fiction.   2. Mothers and daughters — Fiction.   I. Title.
PS3616.A754L67 2006
813'.6 — dc22   2005029741

10 9 8 7 6 5 4 3 2 1

Q-MART

Printed in the United States of America

To my mother, with love

LOST

AND

FOUND

ONE

Laura

By the sixth leg of the game, we have accumulated the following objects: a ski pole, a bishop from a crystal chess set, a sheet of rice paper, a trilobite fossil, an aviator's helmet, and a live parrot.

Our backpacks are overflowing. I drop the chess piece into a sock to keep it from bumping against anything and chipping. I fold the rice paper into a guidebook. The helmet I put on my head.

I hand the ski pole to Cassie. "Ready?" I ask, picking up the parrot's cage.

"Like I have a choice," she says. Our cameraman, Brendan, grins. I know he thinks Cassie makes for great footage.

"Okay, then," I say. "We're off."

We leave our hotel room and walk down the hall, Brendan walking backward so he can film us; our sound guy trails behind. In the elevator, the parrot squawks.

"We should give this guy a name," I say to Cassie, holding up the cage.

"How about Drumstick?" Brendan smiles behind his camera. He's loving this.

"How about Milton?" I try. "He looks kind of like a Milton, don't you think?"

"Fine, Mom," Cassie says, staring up at the lighted numbers. "Whatever."

The doors open onto the lobby, and we step out. There are only seven teams left, and the other six are already here. I pretty much hate them all by this point. Wendy and Jillian, the middle-aged flight attendants from Milwaukee, are sitting on a sofa, feeding little bits of bread to their parrot, while Carl and Jeff, the funny brothers from Boston, sit next to them, poring over a guidebook. Justin and Abby, whom a few people have dubbed Team Brimstone (or, occasionally, Team Shut-Up-Already) because they won't stop talking about how the power of the Lord rescued them from homosexuality and delivered them into the loving grace of Christian marriage, are praying. Juliet and Dallas, the former child stars, who are standing (not coincidentally, I think) next to a large mirror, are staring at them with naked malice. Riley and Trent, the young millionaire inventors (they're wild cards – brilliant, but not so good with the everyday stuff, and everyone wonders what they're doing here anyway, since they don't need the money), smile at Cassie as we walk past, but she turns away from them and goes to sit next to Wendy. Wendy says something to her, and Cassie actually smiles and reaches out to touch the feathers on their parrot's head.

The only seat left is next to Betsy and Jason, the former high school sweethearts who have recently been reunited after twenty years apart. They seem to be having a fight; they're sitting beside each other, but his arms are crossed, and their commitment to not looking at each other is very strong. I sit down next to Betsy, balancing Milton's cage on my lap.

"Morning," Betsy says, turning her whole body away from Jason. "Did your parrot keep you guys up all night, too?"

"No, we just put a towel over his cage and he went right to sleep."

"Lucky," she says. "We tried that, but it didn't work. Ours was freaking out all night. I think we got a defective one."

"A defective parrot. I wonder if there's any provision for that in the rules."

"Yeah, maybe they'll let us trade it in. Otherwise, I'm gonna put it in Barbara's room tonight."

There are two camerapeople filming this conversation.

One of the producers, Eli, steps to the middle of the room and claps his hands. "Quiet, everyone," he says. "Here comes Barbara."

The front door opens and the host of the show, Barbara Fox, walks in with an entourage of makeup artists and even more camerapeople. She's small and rigid with short blond hair and a frosty smile. She's one of the most unnatural people I've ever met. I don't know how she got a job on TV. We're not allowed to approach her.

"Good morning, everybody," she says, turning her glassy smile to each of us in turn.

"Good morning," we say like schoolchildren, except less in unison.

Her crew sets her up in front of a large mural of the Sphinx. Filming begins. "I'm Barbara Fox," she says, "and I'm standing in a hotel in Aswan, the southernmost city in Egypt, with the seven remaining teams in a scavenger hunt that will cover all the corners of the earth. Ladies and gentlemen, this . . ." – dramatic pause here, and a strange little roll of her head – "is *Lost and Found*."

Throughout this process, auditioning for the show, going through rounds of interviews with the producers, providing background for the viewers, we've been asked over and over again to "tell our story." The story I've told them goes something like this: I raised Cassie mostly on my own; it hasn't always been easy. She'll be leaving for college next year, and I wanted a chance to travel the world with her before she's gone. Cassie's version is considerably terser. We tell the story like that's all there is, like we're any old mother and daughter doing our little dance of separation and reconciliation. Oldest story in the world.

The story that doesn't get told begins like this: Four months ago, on a warm and airless night, I woke up to find Cassie standing over my bed. I couldn't see her very well in the dark, and for a moment it was like all the other nights, scattered through her childhood, when she'd come to get me because she was sick or scared. I'm a sound sleeper – I guess it's important to say that – and it took her a few minutes to wake me.

"Mom," she was saying. "Mom."

"What is it?" I said. "What time is it?"

"Mom, could you come to my room for a minute?"

"What's the matter? Are you sick?"

"Could you just come to my room?"

"Okay," I said. I got out of bed and followed her down the hall. She'd moved her bedroom into the attic the previous year, and as we climbed the stairs, I could see that the light was on and the bedclothes were rumpled. I noticed a funny smell, an odor of heat and sweat and something like blood. There were towels everywhere – it seemed like every towel we owned was piled on the floor or the bed. Most of them were wet, and some of them were stained with something dark.

"Is that blood?" I said.

"Mom, look," she said. "On the bed."

I looked at the tangle of linens, and it took me a minute before I saw it. Saw her, I should say. There, in the center of the bed, lay a baby wrapped in a yellow beach towel.

"What . . ." I said, but I didn't know how to finish the sentence. "Cassie . . ."

"It's a girl," Cassie said.

"I don't understand," I said. My mind seemed to have stopped working. The baby looked very still. "Is she . . . okay?"

"I think so," Cassie said. "She was awake at first, and then she went to sleep."

"But . . ." I said, and then I didn't say any more. I reached out and unwrapped the baby. She lay naked and sleeping, her body smudged with creamy smears of vernix. Several inches of umbilical cord, tied at the end with a shoelace, grew out of her belly like a vine.

I looked her over, this child, my granddaughter. Tiny. Tiny. There is no new way to say it. If you could have seen her. The translucent eyelids, the little fingers curled into fists. The knees bent like she hadn't learned how to stretch them yet. The feet wrinkled from their long soak. You forget how small they can be. Tiny.

I picked her up, and she stirred. She opened her eyes and looked up at me. A lurch inside me, and I loved her, just like that. It didn't even happen that way with my own daughter, not quite. I held her close to my chest and wrapped the towel around her again.

"I didn't know how to tell you," Cassie said.

"I don't understand," I said again. "You had this baby?"

"Yeah. About half an hour ago, I guess."

"But you weren't pregnant."

She gave me a look. "Well, obviously, I was," she said.

"And you didn't tell me? For nine whole months you didn't tell me? Who's the father? Dan? Does he know?"

"Can we talk about this later?" she said. "I think maybe I should see a doctor." She lowered her voice and looked downward. "I'm bleeding," she said, her voice like a little girl's.

I wish I had said, "My poor baby." I wish I had said, "I'm so sorry you had to go through this alone." But I was tired and bewildered, and I was beginning to get angry. What I said was, "Yeah, that'll happen when you give birth." And I didn't say it very nicely.

Cassie turned away from me and balled her hands into fists. "Well, you don't have to be so mean," she said, and I could hear that she was trying not to cry. "I've been through a lot tonight. It hurt a lot, you know, really, really *a lot.*"

I took a deep breath and tried to calm myself down. "Okay, Cassie," I said. "I'm sorry. This is just kind of a shock." I reached out to take her arm, but she shook me away. "You're right," I said. "We should go to the hospital."

I looked at the baby, who was lying quietly in my arms. "We have to wrap her better," I said. "This towel is wet."

"I think she peed," said Cassie. "I didn't have any diapers. I didn't know they could pee so soon."

"Well, they can," I said. "Let me go get some blankets."

With great care, I put the baby down on the bed and went down the stairs to the linen closet. My mind felt thick, as if my head were filled with clay. I tried to understand this new information, to lay it on top of the things I already knew and to read my memories through it. She'd been wearing loose clothes lately, I'd noticed that much. I thought she'd been gaining weight, but I didn't want to upset her by bringing it up. She'd been sleeping a lot and she was moody, but so what? It's not like that's exactly earth-shattering behavior for a seventeen-year-old.

I opened the linen closet and looked inside. I picked out a quilt that my grandmother had given me when Cassie was born; her own mother had made it for her as a wedding gift. It had been Cassie's favorite blanket in childhood, and she'd kept it on her bed until she reached adolescence.

As I picked it up, I was already imagining the things I would say to this baby one day. I would tell her, You were born under extraordinary circumstances. I would tell her, We wrapped you in a quilt that was older than our house.

I brought the blanket into Cassie's room and spread it on the bed.

"But that's my blanket from Nana," she said. Her voice rose like a child's. "What if she pees again?"

I laid the baby on the quilt, the small, miraculous lump of her, and swaddled her as well as I could. "If she pees, she pees," I said.

"Do you think we should bring this to the hospital?" Cassie asked, picking up the wastebasket by her desk. I looked inside at what it held. It was the placenta, dark and slick as a piece of raw liver.

"I don't think we need that," I said. I tried to think back to the books I had read before Cassie was born. "Wait, maybe we do. I think they need to check it to make sure the whole thing came out. I don't know."

"I'll just bring it," she said.

The baby started to cry, a high, pure kitten-screech of a sound. We both looked down at her.

"She's probably hungry," I said. "I wonder if you should try to breastfeed her."

"No," she said, and her voice was hard and steady. "I don't want to." And I think that was when I knew we'd be giving her up.

*   *   *

The rules of the game are simple. For each segment, they fly us to a new city where we follow a trail of clues through various exotic (and, presumably, photogenic) locations until we're able to decipher what item we're looking for. Then each team sets out to find an object that qualifies. Every item we find has to remain with us until the end of the game, so the items are usually heavy or fragile or unwieldy; it adds to the drama. Losing or breaking a found object is grounds for disqualification. The last team to find the required object and make it to the finish line gets sent home.

At the end of each leg, Barbara interviews the team that's been eliminated, and she asks the following question: "You've lost the game, but what have you found?" I know the producers are looking for cheesy answers like "I found my inner strength," or "I found the true meaning of friendship," but that's not always what they get. The first ones eliminated were Mariah and Brian, a brother-and-sister team from San Francisco. Brian began acting strangely almost immediately; we found out later that he was schizophrenic – he was fine while he was taking his medication, but he'd stopped at some point during the game. (So much for all the producers' elaborate background checks.) The race ended for them in a museum of natural history in Quebec. We were looking for trilobites, but Brian became very agitated by a giant dinosaur skeleton that was on display, and he began to pelt it with trash from a nearby garbage can. He had to be forcibly removed from the premises. Afterward, Barbara found the two of them outside, sitting on the ground like children. Mariah was cradling Brian in her arms as he rocked back and forth unhappily. Barbara walked up to them – you have to give her credit for determination – and asked them her question. Brian looked up at Barbara, his face a frieze of misery. "I've found out you're a motherless dog," he said before Mariah waved the cameras away. I'd like to see how they're going to edit that.

I don't think there's much of a chance Cassie and I will win the game, but I don't really care. Secretly, this is the moment I'm looking forward to most, the moment when Cassie and I stand before Barbara, and she asks me what I've found. Cassie and I will look at each other and smile; I'll reach out and touch her arm, or her hair, and she won't move away. I'll turn back to Barbara, and the cameras, and all the TV viewers of the world. I found my daughter, I'll say. I found my little girl.

Cassie

S o today we're in Egypt, which I guess would be kind of cool if I weren't here with my mom, and we weren't on a fucking game show. It's not like we have time to explore all these different countries; we just rush through and do the stupid game stuff. We got to Aswan last night and Mom made us come straight to the hotel, so pretty much all I've seen of Egypt is an episode of *The Love Boat* dubbed into Arabic.

Barbara's finishing up her little spiel and giving out the clues. They come in white envelopes sealed with gold wax. We all open them at the same time. There's a little poem inside, written in nice calligraphy:

> *A great king toppled in the sand,*
> *Three others looming higher,*
> *Contain a monument less grand –*
> *The name of Godfrey Wire.*

Each of the teams start whispering among themselves, trying to guess what the clue might mean without giving away any hints to anyone else.

"I think I have an idea about this," Mom says softly, flipping quickly through her guidebook. "I know I saw something in here about a temple with four statues, but one of them has lost some pieces. I'm trying to remember what it's called."

"Godfrey Wire doesn't sound very Egyptian," I say.

"No, it doesn't. Maybe it has to do with the keyword." The first part of every segment is called the Keyword Round. Once you get wherever you're going, you have to use the clue to figure out what word the judges are looking for. Then you're supposed to go over to Barbara, who's standing in this stupid-looking soundproof glass box, and tell her what you think it is. If you guess wrong, you get a ten-minute penalty before you're allowed to guess again, which can give the other teams a chance to get ahead.

Riley and Trent (inventor weirdos) have gone to consult with the concierge; Juliet and Dallas (TV babies) are making a phone call. Justin and Abby (freaks) have already figured everything out, apparently, and are heading for the door. Everyone else is looking through books like we are.

"Here it is," Mom says. She leans close and whispers in my ear – we're miked, so they'll be able to pick it up anyway – "The temple of Abu Simbel." She shows me a picture of a giant cliff with these four big pharaoh guys carved into it. One of them is missing his head and chest; the broken pieces lie in front of him on the sand. Brendan leans in to get a shot of the guidebook.

"That's got to be it, don't you think?" she says.

"Yeah, I guess so." I pick up the parrot's cage, and he lets out this annoying squawk. "All right," I say, "let's get on with it."

Over the past four months, my mom has said "We've got to talk about this" so many times that she probably repeats it in her sleep, but every time we do, she doesn't have the slightest clue what to say. And I guess I don't really feel like helping her out. So she doesn't know my side of the story at all.

I got pregnant at Greenstone Village – it's one of those lame "ye olde" places where everyone pretends it's the 1700s, and they act like making candles is the most fascinating thing in the world. We were on a field trip for AP history, which was fun, because once you're in high school, they don't do those much anymore. It made us feel like kids again, handing in our permission slips, getting on the school bus. We were all doing silly stuff like putting our heads and arms into the stocks and trying to get the people who worked there to admit they knew what television was. ("A box with pictures that move? I know of no such sinful appurtenance." Yeah, yeah, we get it, you're so authentic.)

We had this handout we were supposed to fill out, and the teachers were pretty much letting us wander around on our own. My friend Mia and I were walking around together, with a couple of other friends; our boyfriends, Reece and Dan, were trailing behind us. It was September, and there was a crackly feeling to the air. I was saying something that was making Mia laugh, and I couldn't stop looking at her. It was a little bit chilly, and her cheeks were pink, and her dark hair was blowing around her face. All I wanted for the rest of my life was to keep making her laugh like that. Sometimes our arms brushed against each other as we walked, and it was like I could feel the touch for minutes after it happened.

Then Reece stepped up between us and put his arm around her, and she reached around and curled her hand to fit the shape of his waist. I looked at her hand there, her long fingers resting on his side, her silver fingernails, which I'd helped her paint on the bus, shimmering like coins on the dark fabric of his jacket. I felt like someone was squeezing me from the inside.

Dan took my arm and held me back a little, so there was some distance between us and everyone else.

"Come on," he said.

"Where?"

He gestured with his head to the woods that ran along one edge of the village. "Over there."

"Dan," I said. "We can't. What if we get caught?"

"We won't."

"What if the teachers see us go back there?"

"Are you kidding? They're all sitting in the bus, smoking and talking about what they *meant* to do with their lives."

I smiled. I liked Dan, I really did. I looked at the group of our friends walking down the muddy road ahead of us. I looked at Mia in her big gray coat, her dark hair blowing in the wind. She was laughing and talking to Reece; they were holding hands. She hadn't even noticed I was gone.

"Okay, but we have to be quick."

He raised his eyebrows. "Sorry, babe," he said in a fake-macho voice. "Quick is not in my repertoire."

We walked back into the woods until we could no longer see the buildings of the settlement or hear the voices of the other students.

"How's here?" Dan asked, pointing to an empty patch of ground.

"Fine," I said.

We sat down, and Dan leaned over to kiss me. I could feel the dampness from the dirt seeping into my jeans.

Dan moved his lips to my neck and ran his tongue along my collarbone. "I've been thinking about doing this all day," he whispered.

"Me too," I said. It didn't sound very convincing, but he didn't seem to notice. I put my hand under his shirt and ran it over his chest. I moved downward and reached into his pants. He was already hard.

"Let's lie down," he said.

He unzipped my jacket and reached under my shirt. He stroked my nipples through my bra. I closed my eyes and thought about Mia. I imagined that we were in her bedroom, trying on clothes. I pictured her in a slinky black dress, cut low in front so that the tops of her breasts were visible. "My bra is showing," she was saying to me. "Could you help me take it off?"

Dan had unzipped my jeans and was reaching into my panties. "God," he said. "You're so into it today."

I imagined slipping my hands beneath Mia's dress and touching her soft skin. I imagined that as I unhooked her bra, she spun around so that my hands were cupping her bare breasts.

Dan was taking off his pants. I reached over and pulled his penis out.

"Wait," he said, and reached into his pocket. "Ye olde condom." He opened the packet and put the condom on, then climbed on top of me, pressing me into the damp ground. My hands were on Mia's breasts, and our faces were close enough to touch. "Kiss me," she said.

"Kiss me," I said to Dan.

He put his mouth on mine and I plunged my tongue inside. Mia and I were kissing, and she was letting her dress fall to the floor. "You're so beautiful," she was whispering, and she was pulling my clothes off, and we were both naked on the floor of the bedroom . . .

Dan pulled out and looked down. "Shit," he said. "It broke."

I sat up. "It broke?"

"Yeah." There was panic in his voice.

We both stared at the latex wreckage on his penis for a long moment.

"What do we do?" I said.

"I don't know."

We were silent. I glanced down at myself and saw what I looked like; I was wearing a down jacket and no pants. I suddenly felt cold and ridiculous. I began to put on my clothes.

"Probably nothing will happen," I said finally.

He nodded. "Probably not."

I tried to remember when my last period had been. I didn't know for sure. "I don't think it's even the right part of my cycle."

"Okay," he said. He didn't sound convinced. "Good."

We stood up and adjusted our clothing. We started to walk back to the village. I could smell smoke from the blacksmith's shop through the cold air.

"If anything does happen," Dan said, "I'll be there for you."

"I know," I said. He took my hand, and we walked out of the woods toward the low-slung buildings.

It's a four-hour bus ride to the temple, and there's no air conditioning on the bus. Every time I move, I have to peel myself away from the vinyl, and then I start thinking about how many layers of dried sweat are probably festering away on this seat. I'm so hot I feel sick; it reminds me of morning sickness, which makes me think of all kinds of stuff I don't want to think about. On our way out of the city, we get to drive past all the things we're not going to get to do; we see sailboats floating down the Nile, and guys on the street selling falafel, and people in a bazaar buying . . . I don't know, whatever they buy there. We're not allowed to go. It really kind of sucks that all we get to do is ride on a bus with a bunch of screaming parrots.

Then we're in the desert. It's flat and sandy; just your basic desert, I guess. Kind of cool in theory, but it gets boring pretty fast. Every now and then we pass a car, and once we actually see a guy riding a camel, but mostly there's not much to look at. There are two teams who aren't on the bus with us – Abby and Justin, and Carl and Jeff – and everyone's talking about what happened to them.

"Maybe they're going to some other temple," Jason says.

"Or maybe we're all wrong, and it's not a temple at all," Trent says. "Maybe there's some symbolism we're missing. Four kings – maybe we're supposed to find a deck of playing cards." I roll my eyes, which nobody can see because I'm wearing sunglasses. These guys are supposed to be smart; they invented some kind of important cell phone technology that they sold for a bazillion dollars, and now apparently everyone uses it. But they're always coming out with stupid shit like this.

"Watch out, my friend," Riley tells Trent. "I do believe you're overthinking this one."

"Maybe they teamed up to share a cab," Betsy says, and everyone looks nervous. We only have a certain amount of money to use in the course of the game, so you have to be careful about what you spend, but if they've decided to splurge on a cab, they could easily be there before the rest of us.

The two former child stars, Juliet and Dallas, are sitting across from me and Mom, not taking part in the conversation. It's still so weird to see them here, hanging around like they're these normal people. There's not a single person in the world who knows it, but Juliet Jansen is the first girl I ever loved. I used to watch the sitcom she was on, *Best Friends.* Juliet played this girl named Tracy, and she had a friend named Amber. I forget who played the other girl. It was supposed to be that Amber was the pretty one, and Tracy was the smart, funny one, but really they were both pretty, just in different ways. And of course, it was a sitcom, and they both got the same number of jokes, so it wasn't really like one of them was funnier, either. It was definitely a show aimed at kids – there were no parents in the show at all, which seemed cool to me at the time.

Every episode would start with Tracy and Amber on the phone with each other, talking about what happened at school that day, and then there'd be flashbacks to the scenes they were talking about. They'd always show two versions of what happened, Tracy's version and Amber's version, and they were always totally different, which is where most of the humor came from. And, of course, there would be some misunderstanding, and then it would all get cleared up, and the show would end with some disembodied mom voice yelling "Amber, get off the phone" or something like that, and then the girls would say good night, and then Tracy would sneak in one last joke before they hung up. Okay, maybe it wasn't a great show, but I was only twelve when it went on the air, and back then, I didn't really know that there were good shows and bad shows. I sort of thought that everything on TV must be equally good from some neutral, universal standpoint.

I remember Dallas McKinley's show, too, although I didn't watch it as much. It was called *President Scooter,* and it was about a ten-year-old boy who gets elected president. I forget how it happens exactly – I think he gets nominated by mistake, but when people see how corrupt the grown-up candidates are, they start thinking it's not such a bad idea. So the whole show was about how his parents tried to make him a good little president, and he had this power-hungry uncle who kept trying to get him to do evil things.

I had a history teacher who really hated this show; he was always going off about how inaccurate it was, and how there's a minimum age requirement, blah, blah, blah, as if we were all sitting there taking this absurd sitcom seriously. The show was on Wednesday nights, and every Thursday, someone in the class would say, "Hey, Mr. Manning, did you see *President Scooter* last night?" and he'd waste half the class ranting about how TV shows were giving kids an unrealistic view of government. At the end of the year, this really disturbed kid in the class, Tom Symansky, gave Mr. Manning this picture he'd made called "The Assassination of President Scooter," which showed Dallas McKinley getting his head blown off. The artwork was pretty well done, actually, but Mr. Manning sent Tom to the principal's office and gave the rest of us a lecture about how too much TV makes kids violent.

The two shows were on at about the same time, and I remember that Mia had a crush on Dallas McKinley. For a moment so short it almost doesn't exist, I think that I can't wait to tell her I've met him — I can picture exactly what the scene will be like, I can even see the look on her face — but then I remember that Mia and I don't tell each other anything anymore.

Mom leans over to talk to me. "So, let's discuss strategy," she says.

I bend down and rummage through my backpack for my Walkman. "Let's not," I say, putting the headphones on.

One more thing my mom doesn't know: the *Lost and Found* people know about the baby. She certainly didn't tell them about it; I think she's just embarrassed by the whole thing. And it probably didn't occur to her that I'd tell them — I mean, I kept it a secret for nine months, right? But during the screening interview, this woman was asking me if I had any conflicts with my mother and stuff like that, and it just kind of floated out of me. I guess I wanted to tell someone. The interviewer woman thought she'd struck gold. She said, "Could you wait here for just a minute?" and she went and got these two men, who turned out to be like the head guys. "Could you tell them what you just told me?" she asked. And I did. It was even easier the second time.

When we got the call saying we were going to be on the show, Mom went nuts. She kept saying, "I knew they'd pick us!" It was kind of sad — does she think they chose us because we're so fascinating? But I know the truth. They picked us because they think we're this big mother-daughter bomb ticking away with secrets, and they're just waiting for us to explode.

Mom is looking at me like she wants to say something, but doesn't know if I can hear her. I turn toward the window and focus on the sand and the road and the shimmering heat until they're the only things in my mind.

THREE

Carl

I'd be lying if I said I didn't want to kick my brother in the teeth when he suggested we share a cab with Team Brimstone – I've got nothing against God, I just don't want to talk about Him all the time – but they're really not so bad, and if it puts us in the lead, it'll be worth it. We're riding through the desert. It's like a giant beach, but without the good part. Our cab is an ancient black-and-white Fiat with a missing side panel and a rear bumper held on with bungee cord. Our driver seems to hate us, and I can tell you it doesn't smell good in here. The four of us are squished in the back, and Justin and Abby's camera and sound guys are packed in the front with the driver. Since there wasn't enough room for everyone, our camera crew got to take a separate cab all by themselves. I would give a year of my life – well, okay, maybe not a year, but definitely a week – to be riding in that cab instead.

"I've been having the weirdest dreams," Jeff says. "Last night I dreamed we were all in this comedy contest, and we had to do five minutes of stand-up on whatever topic they assigned us. Guess what my topic was."

"What?" we all say.

"Toast."

I crack up. Justin and Abby smile politely. "Toast?" I say.

"Yeah, toast. I was going nuts trying to come up with jokes about toast."

"Did you come up with any?" Justin asks.

"Yeah, I got kind of a riff going. I started out by saying, 'Did you ever notice how pointy the corners of toast are? I burned a piece of whole wheat last week, I swear I could've robbed a bank with it.'"

"Yeah, that's a real knee-slapper," I say, but I'm smiling.

"Well, it was funny in the dream. Then I went into 'How many lawyers does it take to butter a piece of toast?'"

"How many?" asks Abby.

"Four, but I forget why. No one was laughing. I lost the contest to this kid I went to grade school with." He turns to me. "You remember Phil Marks?"

I shrug. "Not really."

"Well, it was him. His topic was underwear."

"Well, that's a lot easier to joke about," Justin says.

"Classic anxiety dream," I say.

"You think?"

"Definitely."

"So what am I anxious about?"

I make a gesture that includes the cab, the desert, the cameraman, the parrots sitting in our laps. "Hello? You're on TV, you're trying to win a million bucks, you're in a strange country. I think we're all a little anxious."

Jeff shrugs. "It beats working," he says. It takes just about a month to film this thing — if you don't make it to the end, you have to spend the remaining time in a sequester location — and Jeff and I are both using a combination of vacation time and unpaid leave. I think that's what most people are doing, although the millionaires are obviously their own bosses, and this one guy, Jason, from the "high school sweethearts" team, actually quit his job. That's some nice, rational decision making there, Jason; if you don't win the million bucks, that's really going to look great on your résumé. Nothing impresses potential employers like a willingness to give it all up for a get-rich-quick scheme.

"So," says Justin. He's youngish, maybe in his early thirties. He's this weird combination of earnest and smug. "What made you guys decide to try out for the show?"

"Uh oh," I say. "You're gonna make him sing."

"D-I-V-O-R-C-E," yodels Jeff.

"Both of us," I say. "Born a year apart, married a year apart, divorced a year apart."

"I'm always following in his footsteps," says Jeff.

"What a shame," says Abby. She's about the same age as Justin, pretty, kind of serious-looking. A lot less vocal about the God thing.

"It is a shame," I say, seriously.

"Well, it may be a shame," says Jeff, "but we're having a lot more fun now."

"How about you two?" I ask.

"It sounded like fun," Abby says. "Travel to all these great places."

"And we wanted to get our message out," says Justin. "TV is a great medium for that."

"What message is that?" asks Jeff, wide-eyed. He knows what message it is; he's just being a pain in the ass.

"That people can change," Justin says. "With God's help. That you don't have to live the gay lifestyle if you don't want to."

"So you wouldn't recommend the gay lifestyle?" Jeff says. "'Cause I've been shopping around for a new lifestyle, and that's the only one I ever hear anyone talk about."

"It's not a joke," Justin says. "It's a sad, sad thing."

"He's just kidding," I say, jabbing Jeff sharply with my elbow. "Bet you didn't know what you were getting into when you decided to share a cab with us."

"So what do you know about this temple?" asks Abby.

I find the page in my guidebook. "It's really interesting," I say. "It was discovered in 1813 by this Swiss guy. It was almost completely covered in sand. It could have been lost forever."

"Wow," says Jeff. "Imagine all the things that get covered up and never get discovered."

"There could be whole cities," Abby says. "Cities underneath the sand."

I skim over the entry in the book. "And, listen to this, the whole thing was moved, piece by piece, when they built the Aswan Dam in the sixties, so the temple wouldn't be covered with water."

"Hmm," says Justin. "Sounds like someone wants this temple covered up."

"Is that 'Someone' with a capital *S*?" asks Jeff.

Justin smiles serenely. "Who's to say?"

I don't know what went wrong with my marriage. There were a lot of things that happened – there always are – but basically, we reached a point where we just weren't nice to each other anymore. I think it started around the time my son was born. Everyone says that having a kid puts a strain on a marriage, but you just don't believe it. You think, how can this do anything but bring us closer? But then there's this new little guy who splits your allegiances, and nobody's sleeping, and all of a sudden there's all this chaos, and the two of you are on opposite sides of it. You can't get mad at the baby, so who's left to get mad at?

My son's name is Benjamin, and he just turned three. Jackie and I separated right around his second birthday. Divorce is a terrible thing to do to a kid. His favorite thing in the whole world is having the two of us in one room, and that's something he doesn't get to see much anymore. Sometimes when he was maybe one, one and a half, we'd bring him into bed with us in the mornings, to try to coax a little more sleep out of him. It never worked. He'd stand between us on top of the covers, towering over us like Godzilla in a blanket sleeper. "Mama, Dada!" he'd yell, pointing down at us with both hands. It was like he was claiming us as his, naming us like Adam in Eden.

I get to see him a lot; Jackie's good about that. She knows he needs his dad around. But there's still so much I miss. I don't always know what his new favorite books are, or what songs he knows, or how he's sleeping. For a while when we were all still together, Benjamin didn't like to sleep with a blanket, so I wouldn't use one, either. It was the only way I could make sure I knew how he was feeling. How could I sleep if he was cold? He was my little guy. Sometimes, if it was chilly enough to wake me up, I'd sneak into his room and cover him while he slept. I remember standing in the dark, not able to see where he was in the crib, and feeling around until my fingers brushed the top of his head or the soles of his feet. Sometimes I'd put my hand on his back, on the soft flannel of his pajamas, and feel him breathe up and down. I'd stand there until he moved or made a little sucking sound and then I'd get the hell out of there, because one thing you do not want to do is wake a sleeping baby. But now his nighttimes are generally daddy-free. And as much as I don't want to denigrate the mother of my child, I can tell you she's not sleeping without a blanket.

It was, no surprise, Jeff's idea to come on this show. This kind of thing is right up his alley. This is actually his third attempt at self-improvement via reality television: he tried out for *Survivor,* with no luck, which is probably just as well – Jeff for a month on nothing but rice is not a Jeff anyone wants to be with. And then he talked me into sending in a tape for *The Amazing Race,* but we weren't welcome there, either. I wasn't that enthusiastic about continuing the effort, but it soon became clear that Jeff wasn't going to give me any peace till we'd been rejected by every show on the airwaves. Okay, I said, we'll give it one more try; how about that scavenger hunt thing we caught a few episodes of? And here we are.

I'm having a great time, though. Jeff's always been a goofball, and one of the things I like best about him is that he makes me into a little bit of a goofball, too. We have fun together every single day, and how many people can you say that about?

When we finally get to the temple, there are no other teams in evidence. A small cheer goes up among the four of us. We know we're in the right place, because at the edge of the parking lot we can see a blue-and-white banner marked with the *Lost and Found* logo – an old-fashioned suitcase, covered with travel stickers, bursting open to release a flock of stars into the air. We get out and unload our stuff.

There's a little bit of a scuffle when it comes time to pay the cab driver; we'd neglected to negotiate a price up front, which is a mistake I won't be making the next time I'm in Egypt. We hand over what seems like a million of those pretty Egyptian pounds, but I figure it's probably not that much money when you do all the math. Jeff points out that the one-pound note actually has a picture of the damned temple on it, and we could've just sat around looking at our money and saved ourselves a trip. We get out of the cab, reunite with our camera crew, and head for the entrance.

It turns out there are actually two temples: a big one dedicated to Ramses II, who built the place, and a smaller one dedicated to his favorite wife, Nefertari. Based on our clue, I think we want the big one. It's pretty imposing, I've got to say. There are four giant statues of Ramses cut into the cliff face, two sitting on each side of the doorway. The second one from the left is damaged, the head and chest broken off. The pieces lie in front of it as if they just fell off and landed there this morning. And off to the side, the TV crew is setting up the ridiculous soundproof booth that Barbara stands in to listen to our keywords.

"Four statues of himself," I say to Jeff. "A little impressed with ourselves, are we?"

"I'm thinking I might build myself one of these babies. Can you picture it? Four giant Jeffs looking down at you?"

"Oh, yeah," I say. "Four of you sitting on a bar stool, holding a beer. We can call it the Temple at Chuck's Bar and Grille."

Justin and Abby have already headed inside. "So what are we looking for?" Jeff asks.

"I have no idea. 'The name of Godfrey Wire,' I guess."

"Well, let's go on in."

We walk into a long hall lined with more statues. "Oh, look," says Jeff. "It's Ramses again." He counts the statues. "Eight more."

"Poor guy. He really didn't have much self-confidence, did he?"

"It's a sad, sad thing," Jeff says, imitating Justin.

The walls and ceiling are covered with elaborate murals. There are all kinds of battle scenes, with guys in chariots shooting arrows, and scenes with Ramses making offerings to gods with animal heads. "Look," I say, pointing to what looks like a pharaoh wielding a sword. "I think Ramses is smiting some people here."

We look at the pictures for a while. We haven't got a clue. "Some of these guys are gods, right?" Jeff says. "Like *God*frey Wire?"

"I think that's pushing it."

At the end of the first hall is a second, narrower hall, and at the end of that is the inner sanctuary, a small room with an altar and four more statues.

"Only one of those guys is Ramses," I tell Jeff, looking at my book. "The rest are gods."

"Is there a difference?" asks Jeff.

Justin and Abby are back here, too, looking closely at the walls. We hear voices coming through the hallway. The other teams have arrived.

"Damn," says Jeff. "There goes our lead."

The tiny room fills up with people carrying ski poles and aviator helmets and birdcages.

"I'll bet this is the most parrots that have ever been in this room," I say to Jeff. The squawking echoes off the walls.

We spend twenty minutes or so milling around, looking at the statues, trying to find anything that looks like it might be what we're looking for, but we're not having any luck. It doesn't look like anyone else is, either. Riley and Trent have some kind of shtick going about pharaohs and flapjacks; it doesn't make any sense to me until I realize they're quoting some movie I've never seen, which makes me feel old. Laura whispers something to Cassie, who says, "No, Mom, that's dumb." Betsy's studying the walls very closely and making notes about the hieroglyphics, while Jason tries to engage her in a discussion about whether or not Ramses looks like their old math teacher. I'm starting to feel claustrophobic.

"Let's go get some air," I say to Jeff. "Who says the clue is in here, anyway?"

We walk back outside and stand looking at the giant pharaohs.

"Hey, look at this," Jeff says. "This one has something carved on his leg. 'Simon Ecclestone, 1820.'"

"Holy shit," I say. "It's graffiti. How rude. I thought people back then had better manners than that."

Jeff and I look at each other, and we both start smiling. "That's it," I say. "That's what we're looking for."

We scan the names carved into the statues' legs. It only takes us a few minutes to find it. Godfrey Wire, 1819. The rest of the teams are still inside. Jeff gives me a high five.

"Okay, so what's the keyword?" I say. "*Graffiti?* Or *1819?*"

"Let's go with *1819. Graffiti* sounds like a guess."

We approach Barbara, who's standing in her glass box. She smiles icily and beckons us inside. The box is air-conditioned, and the cold air feels incredible. The cameras are running.

"Carl and Jeff," she says. "You believe you have solved the riddle and found the keyword?"

"Yes," I say, as solemnly as I can, given that we're standing in an air-conditioned phone booth with a TV star in the middle of Egypt.

"And what is your answer?"

Jeff and I look at each other. "1819?" I say.

She looks at us for a long moment, her face as blank as paper. We wait for her pronouncement.

"You're right," she says, and Jeff lets out a whoop. "You have earned your next clue." She hands us two envelopes, one silver, one gold; the silver one's for now, and the gold one we have to save for later. We thank her and step out of the box onto the bright, hot sand.

FOUR

Juliet

I can't believe how long it took us to figure out we were looking for graffiti. We were the last ones to get it, and the heat was so intense it was like a physical weight. I've been guzzling water ever since, but I'm still a little dizzy. I've always said, someday someone's going to die on one of these shows, and that will be the end of reality TV.

I can't stand it when we do badly on the mental games. I'm sure that when they edit the show, they're going to try to paint us as the stupid team, the bratty child stars who grew up in la-la land and never even went to a real school, and I'd love to avoid that label. It matters how I come across. Most of these people are never going to be on TV again, once the series airs and the initial flurry of talk shows is over. But I certainly hope I will; it's my whole reason for being here. I try to float through the game, to appear as good-natured and down-to-earth as I can. I'm aware this is a competition, and I'm as liable as anyone else to stab someone in the back in order to win, but I've got to be likable while I'm doing it. This is as much of an acting job as anything I've ever done.

As arrogant as it sounds, there's a bit of a sense of hobnobbing with the little people, showing them how ordinary celebrities can be. Look – Juliet Jansen has to lug the ski pole around, just like everyone else! I try to keep perspective, but the fact is, my life *has* been different from theirs. There hasn't really been a time in my life when I haven't been famous. Well, *famous* is a relative term, and the thing about being a star when you're a kid is that people don't necessarily recognize you when you get older and don't look the same. But I've been to the Oscars. There are whole Web sites devoted to me. I'm not bragging; it's just the way my life is.

Dallas and I are on a plane now, on our way to Cairo for the Found Objects round. That's the part where we have to look for whatever thing they're going to make us carry for the rest of the game. Let's hope this one's not alive.

We're the only team on the plane; everyone else caught an earlier one. We'd be in last place if it weren't for those stewardesses. They were almost as slow as we were in figuring out the keyword thing, and then their cab broke down on the way to the airport. I tried not to look too excited when we passed them standing by the side of the road, with all their stuff spread out around them. It was pretty pathetic. So we got to the airport first, and we got a flight right away, but they're going to have to wait another two hours. Looks like they're the ones who're going to get the boot. I'll try to be sad.

"So, Lady Juliet," says Dallas. He's always on; it's starting to bug me. Our camera guy isn't even filming right now. "Shall we try to figure out this clue?" He holds up the paper. It says:

> *In Cairo's nightclubs, women dance,*
> *They spin in every corner.*
> *Find one and you'll find perchance*
> *Three sparkles that adorn her.*

"Well, it seems pretty straightforward. Go to a nightclub, find a dancer, get some . . . sparkles."

"But just, like, any dancer in all of Cairo?"

"I don't know. Maybe we should ask someone."

There's a guy who looks American sitting across the aisle from me. I take the clue from Dallas and lean over to him.

"Excuse me," I say. He looks over, and I smile expansively. I wait to see if he recognizes me.

He smiles politely. "Yes?" he says. "Can I help you with something?" He has a British accent. I don't think my show was ever on in England, but it doesn't matter. I've been told I have an ethereal quality that makes people want to help me.

"I'm so sorry to bother you," I say. "But we're filming an American TV show." I gesture to our cameraman, who's perked up and begun filming again. "And we have to figure out what this clue means. Do you think you could help us?"

As I hand him the slip of paper, I twitch my lips into the tiniest of smiles, not at all flirty, just inviting him to join me in the absurdity of this situation. He smiles back; he's happy to come along.

He reads over the clue. "Well, you know, belly dancers are very popular in Cairo," he says. He pronounces it 'dahncers.' "I expect that's what they're referring to."

Dallas leans over me. "Do they wear anything sparkly?" he asks. I discreetly elbow him back into his seat. This is my scene.

"I don't suppose you have any idea where we might go to find these belly dancers?" I ask. "Not that I'm implying . . ." I trail off and laugh softly.

He laughs, too. "Well, I've never been myself, but . . ." He leans over and pulls a guidebook out of his seat back. He flips through the index. "Here you go," he says.

He passes it over; I let our hands touch briefly. There's a box on the page with a whole list of clubs and hotels that feature belly dancers.

"Oh, that's great!" I say. "We'll just have to write some of these down." I make a show of patting myself down, looking for a pen.

"Oh, just rip out the page," my new friend says. "I don't really fancy belly dancers."

"That's so nice of you," I say. I tear out the page and hand it to Dallas. "Thanks so much for your help. We're so grateful." I lean back into my seat and leave him with a thankful little sign-off glance.

Dallas is looking over the list. "All right," he says happily. "Belly dancers."

"Try to maintain your composure," I say. "Just ask yourself, WWPSD?"

He looks at me, blank and kind of furrowed.

"What would President Scooter do?" I say. He gives me a nasty look. He hates it when I rag on *President Scooter.*

He's looking at the other side of the belly dancing page. "Check this out," he says. "There's a place in Cairo called the Mosque of Mohammed Ali. Do you think it's named after that boxer guy?"

I don't answer, I just shake my head and give the camera a look, like "Can you believe this guy?" I remember one time I was in Washington, DC, for a special we did called *Best Friends in the Nation's Capital,* and we drove past a sign for Chevy Chase, Maryland. I said I couldn't believe they'd named their city after a comedian, and everyone made fun of me for a week. But I was twelve. Dallas is twenty-three.

"We'd better see some mummies," Dallas says. "I'm gonna be pissed if we leave Egypt without seeing a mummy."

And I think about how I can play this. Maybe we can be, not the stupid team, but the team where Dallas McKinley is an idiot and Juliet Jansen is refreshingly clever and down-to-earth but saddled with a dud of a partner. I can see the write-ups already; I can hear the jokes in Letterman's monologue. I can make this work.

"All right, Dallas," I say. "We'll try to find you some mummies." Over his head, I look at the camera and give a collusive smile. Come on, America, laugh with me. We're in this together.

FIVE

Abby

My father, I barely remember. He left early, leaving Mama to raise the boys and me alone on the farm. And some of those winters were mighty cold.

No, just kidding. This isn't that kind of story. See, that's the weird thing about being on television: I could tell you anything, and you'd have to believe me. You'd have no reason not to. I've heard celebrities say that when you're on TV, people think they know you; they walk right up to you and hug you, they act as if you're their best friend, when you've never even met. Perhaps you'll think you know me, but you don't. So, no. No dusty roads, no hardscrabble winters. Just another tale of love and betrayal underneath the sun.

But for now, what you see is this: Justin and I (and our cameraman Sam and sound technician Ethan) are walking in Cairo, looking for a club that has belly dancers. This is a strange thing for us to be doing. Justin is convinced the producers added this challenge just for us, to see how the stuffy Christians would respond to scantily clad women. I tell him that scantily clad women have a long and vivid history in the world of television, and that the producers probably just wanted to have something juicy to put in their promos.

We're a little bit lost. The city is vast and dense, and the club we picked out of our guidebook — one of the few where the book said women visitors could go without being harassed – wasn't where it was supposed to be. Now we're trying to hunt down a second one. Even though it's almost midnight, the streets are full of people, even small children. The traffic is incredible; the streets are packed not only with cars and buses, but also with carts pulled by horses and donkeys. No one seems to obey the red lights, and the honking never stops. I like it, though. It's been a long time since I've been in a place where life goes on so late.

I've always wanted to go to Egypt. In school, I loved the unit we did on Egyptian mythology, especially all the stories about what happens after you die. I remember particularly liking the story of Anubis. Anubis was the Guardian of the Necropolis, and he had the head of a jackal. Egyptians believed that after you died, you would be sent to Anubis to determine whether you deserved eternal life. To decide, he would weigh your heart against the feather of truth. If your heart was light, you would move on to the underworld and live there forever. But if it was too heavy, it would be devoured by a monster, and that would be the end of you. I learned that in the fourth grade, and it's stuck with me ever since. That, and the fact that when the ancient Egyptians mummified people, they pulled their brains out through the nose.

We pass a line of men sitting outside a coffeehouse, smoking from tall water pipes; the rich smell of tobacco soaked in molasses fills the night. It reminds me of the cherry tobacco my dad used to smoke when I was a little girl. You wouldn't believe how smoggy and smoke-clogged this city is; I read somewhere that breathing the air here is like smoking thirty cigarettes a day. Justin stops to look at his map.

"I think if we make a right at the next corner, we'll be able to find this place," he says. We walk past street vendors selling food and souvenirs and turn the corner underneath a row of billboards painted with the faces of what I assume are Egyptian film stars. One of the signs shows a man holding a gun; another shows a man and a woman kissing. I think for a moment that it would be nice to sit in a dark theater and watch a movie in a language I don't understand.

Just to sit back and let the images wash over me, to piece together the story on my own. It sounds like it would be peaceful.

We walk down the block, trying to find street numbers. Finally, we come to the Hotel Barona, a fairly respectable-looking building with a placard outside announcing BELLY DANCING TONIGHT!

"This is it," I say. I start to open the door, but Justin holds me back.

"Give me a minute," he says. He looks genuinely nervous about what we might find inside, and I wonder if he's praying for guidance. Justin has a real sense of the precariousness of our souls; I think a place like this must seem truly perilous to him.

"All right," he says after a moment, though he doesn't look any more resolved. "I guess I'm ready." He opens the door for me, and I walk before him into the club.

I met Justin through Redemption, the ex-gay ministry I joined three years ago. It was a surprise to everyone I knew when I joined. I'd never been particularly religious before; that sets me apart from most of the other members. Most of them are there because they believe that being gay means relinquishing the God they've walked next to all their lives, and they can't stand the thought of His absence. I didn't grow up like that, and some of the churchy details still seem strange to me. But I did believe in God, and I knew I needed to find some help. I was lost – the language we use in Redemption is big, it's as hyperbolic as a hymn, but all of it is true – I was lost, I was in pieces, I was sick, and I was sad. No matter how hard I tried to be happy with the person I was, I always felt like I was fighting an undertow, the vast storm swell of my shame. Finally, I reached a point where I couldn't keep my head above the surface anymore. And then I found Redemption, with a big and little *R*. And then I was redeemed.

When I went to my first meeting, I was afraid to go in. It was held in a city church, not far from where I lived, and I was terrified that someone I knew would see me. It reminded me of the first time I went to a gay bar – it was that much of a transgression. I wasn't sure I should be there at all. But then I went inside, and I saw that there was a room full of people who wanted to welcome me. They had struggled the way I had and emerged happier. They had found a way to love themselves. When everyone held hands and recited a prayer about leaving the darkness of shame for the light of God's love, I was surprised to find myself crying. I felt, for the first time in so long, that I'd found a place I belonged. I felt I had come home.

It was on that first evening that I met Justin. He's not like anyone I've ever known before. He's dynamic; he's convincing. He used to be an atheist, a vehement one, until he got into an argument with a Christian and the Christian won. An atheist and a believer walk into a room, and two believers walk out. This is Justin's myth of origin, the legend that shapes his life. This, I think, is why we're on TV.

I like the way I feel when I'm with Justin. There's a sense of letting go, a surrender that I find restful. Not like, oh, he's the man, so he'll make all our decisions and I'll stay in the kitchen and cook. It's more subtle than that. When I'm with him, I know exactly where I stand. When we walk down the street together, there's not a person in the world who doesn't understand what we are to each other. It's easy. I don't have to think about it at all.

I know people wonder about us when they hear our story. They wonder, crass people that we all are in our own heads, if we have sex. Of course we do. We're married. We do it maybe once a week, sometimes more, sometimes less. The same as a lot of couples, I'm sure. And I start it just as often as he does. He works at it, I can tell. It takes him a little while. But, oh, he's enthusiastic. I've never seen such vigor. He works hard and it pays off. I come from the sheer thoroughness of his effort. I jerk, I spasm like a car in the wrong gear, and when I'm through, he rises triumphant from between my legs, salt on his skin, his beard matted and tangled, like a sea monster surfacing from the deep. Then it's my turn, and I'm happy to repay the favor. I use my hands and my mouth, and between the two of us, we get him hard. In the beginning, if he was having trouble, I'd whisper things that I thought might help, but that seemed like a dangerous land to inhabit. Fantasies are a place we'd rather not venture. Better to stay anchored to the here and now, the clean white sheets, this man, this woman, this marriage bed. When we get where we're headed – and we always do – he gets on top, or I do, and we rock together, one flesh. He doesn't close his eyes. I wonder if he's afraid to. He looks into my face the whole time, and we cling together like we're fighting fierce winds.

In Redemption, they tell us that when we have a lustful thought, a thought that threatens to drag us back to our old, sinful ways, we must surrender the thought to Jesus. We're supposed to put a hand to our heads and pull the shameful thing right out; we're supposed to throw the idea to the ground like the garbage it is. I do this every single day; so far in this race, I've littered six different countries with my unholy thoughts. I manage to do it discreetly, just a brush across the forehead, a hand opened toward the earth. I don't think anyone else has noticed me doing it. But Justin knows. When Justin sees me make the motion, he smiles as if he's bestowing grace. He squeezes my arm and says, "Good work." But I've never seen him do it, not even once. When I ask him about it, he tells me he doesn't need to. He says that he still has attractions to men, but they present themselves in more acceptable ways. When he meets a man he likes, he wants to be his friend. He wants to do manly things with him, sports and conversation and worship. Not sex. He says that it turns out that what he wanted from men wasn't sex but healthy male affection. Now that he understands that, he's free from those yearnings. This isn't the way it's been for me.

I remember that on the day of our wedding, I was getting dressed beforehand in a hotel room, with my mother and my bridesmaids all around me. I remember watching my bridesmaids – my friends and my sisters and Justin's sisters – putting on their dresses, and I felt ashamed before them. I was ashamed that they *knew* about me; they knew I had looked upon other women's bodies with lust. That I had touched other women's bodies like a man might do. Were they shy getting dressed around me, worrying that I would look at them the wrong way? I couldn't tell. But who could blame them if they were? They were all laughing and smiling, zipping each other up, repositioning errant bra straps. To them, it was a simple thing to be naked before another woman. It was the most natural thing in the world. For me, it was something else, and I felt ungainly with the difference, like a hulking beast walking through a city of china dolls.

They helped me into my wedding gown, and I was stunned at how I looked. I looked like any bride, ready to walk down the aisle to meet the man she loves. I could have been anyone. My dress was beautiful. I've always liked wearing girly clothes, putting on pretty, feminine things. But for a while, when I was lost, I put all that aside. I wore clothes that were practical, clothes that identified me as the kind of woman I was. When I first joined Redemption, it was a revelation to me that I could go back so easily to wearing dresses and makeup. I felt like I'd been missing this for years, this girlishness, this dressing up. This was what I thought I had to relinquish. And here, at the end of this long road, here I was in my wedding gown. I loved the way I looked that day. Sometimes, even now, I'll go to the closet when Justin isn't home and take my wedding dress out of its heavy plastic bag. I'll put it on, just to see myself in it. Just to see once more what I am capable of being.

Later, when I stood at the altar with Justin and said my vows, my eyes wandered for a moment to my family, my parents and my grandparents, my aunts and uncles, sitting in the front pews. I thought I might cry when I saw them. The happiness in their faces, the relief. All the people in the church, nearly all the people I had ever loved, were sitting there wishing us their best. I could feel their joy, their loving sanction. I felt bathed by it. And whatever I might have lost, it seemed like it was worth it for this.

There are two acrobats performing when we enter the club. We sit down at a table near the stage. I see that Laura and Cassie are here, too, but none of the other teams. It doesn't mean anything — there must be a dozen belly-dancing clubs in Cairo.

There's an English-language drink menu on our table, with pictures of all the offerings. I order something called *karkaday*, which is translated as "traditional hibiscus drink." Justin orders a Coke. Our plan is that when the dancer comes on, we'll keep a close eye on the stage for fallen spangles, and if we don't find any, we'll approach the dancer after her act and see if she'll oblige us. I take a sip of my drink. It's sweet and flowery and delicious; I drink it all at once until it's gone.

The acrobats finish, and the dancer appears onstage. She has long dark hair, and she's wearing a lot of makeup. She's older than I would have expected, maybe forty. Her costume consists of a black bra, heavily beaded in silver, and a long, sheer skirt sprinkled with sequins. Her belly is covered with black mesh. She begins to dance, slowly at first, then faster. She turns every which way, and the music matches her every move. Her hips snap back and forth. She raises her hands above her head, and her breasts swell over the top of her bra. She moves past our table, close enough to touch. I look at Justin's face. There is no desire there at all.

I cast my eyes downward toward the stage. I am looking for sequins; that's what I'm here to do. I spot one, a tiny speck of brightness fallen to the ground. As I reach out for it, the dancer's skirt brushes my forearm. I look up at her luminous body. The curve of her neck reminds me of someone I have left behind.

I have to stop watching her. I'm afraid of what the camera will find when it looks at my face. I turn my eyes and see Cassie; she's looking at the dancer with an intensity I wasn't expecting, almost – am I reading this right? – a longing. I feel a jolt, palpable as electricity moving through my body. For a moment, my mind reels, and I see them moving together, the young girl and the belly dancer. I imagine Cassie undressing the dancer, moving the straps of her glittering bra over the woman's shoulders, revealing her breasts in a slow, languorous motion. I imagine a kiss, the dancer's hand moving up Cassie's thigh. I feel myself responding in ways I know I shouldn't. I force myself back to this night, this game, this hot smoky room. My husband's arm is around my shoulders, right where it's supposed to be. If you could weigh my heart at this moment, you'd find it's heavy as a stone.

In my mind, Cassie and the belly dancer writhe and writhe. I look down at the floor and touch my hand to my forehead. I take the thought and throw it on the ground.

SIX

Laura

Three sequins are not going to be easy to keep track of. Outside the nightclub, I open up my backpack on the sidewalk, trying to find a safe place for them. Finally, I pull out a plastic Baggie containing my toothbrush and toothpaste; I take the toiletries out and put the sequins in. While I'm wrestling everything back into place, I jam my finger hard against the trilobite fossil. It hurts quite a bit.

"Damn it," I say loudly.

"Damn it," squawks Milton from his cage.

Cassie and I look at each other, and we both start laughing. I can't remember the last time we laughed together. I look at my girl laughing, her face bright and unguarded, and I imagine reaching out and touching her gently on the cheek. But I don't want to ruin it.

"Nice, Mom," Cassie says. "You've corrupted our parrot." But she's still smiling.

"It's like having a toddler," I say. "I'll never forget the time we were in the supermarket when you were two or three, and I dropped a jar of spaghetti sauce, and it broke and splattered all over me. Without even thinking about it, I said 'Shit,' and you started yelling over and over again, all through the store: 'Why you say "shit," Mommy? Why you say "shit"?' Everyone was staring. I've never been so embarrassed."

Cassie smiles. She's heard the story a thousand times, and the fact that she let me tell it without interrupting me feels like a small gift. "You can't say that on TV," she says. "They're going to have to bleep you."

"So let them bleep me," I say, picking up the ski pole and the parrot cage. "Okay, we've got the sequins. What's next?"

Cassie pulls out the gold envelope Barbara gave us at the temple. There won't be a riddle in this one, only a destination. The last team to get there will be out of the game.

Cassie opens the envelope. It says,

Mosque of Qaitbey
Cities of the Dead

"Cheery," says Cassie.
"Damn it," says Milton.

Of course, the big question, the question even I don't quite know the answer to, is, How could I have missed it? There are so many intersecting avenues of "Where did I go wrong" that it's hard to know where to begin. Not so much the birth itself; I understand, I guess, how that happened. Her room is in the attic, mine's on the first floor; I sleep soundly; I use a white noise machine to block out street sounds. I should have heard something, I should have been there, yes; but I take some solace in knowing that for this failure, the blame rests solely on my ears.

But a whole pregnancy: morning sickness, fatigue, mood swings. You'd think I'd at least have noticed she was peeing more than usual. And, of course, the obvious: the big belly, the swollen breasts. Is it really possible that I didn't look at her in profile once during those last few months? I realized long ago that there's no such thing as "perfect" when it comes to parenting, that we all make mistakes, that we do things wrong every single day. But, my God, on the scale of maternal lapses, this one ranks pretty high.

In retrospect, of course there were signs. Like I said, I thought she'd gained weight, but I figured it had to do with her breakup with Dan. But there were other things, too. I remember a night when we'd gone out to a restaurant Cassie likes, a chain place with lots of greasy teen food – nachos, mozzarella sticks, chicken in wing and nugget form. When Cassie's order of chicken strips came, piled high on the plate with their little vat of honey mustard glistening beside them, Cassie recoiled from them as if she'd seen them come to life. She said she thought she was coming down with something. In fact, there were several days last fall when she stayed home from school with a lingering stomach flu. And one time – okay, this seems like a big one – she burst into tears after seeing a diaper commercial on TV. Yeah, I know, what was I thinking? Somehow it just didn't click.

Would it help if I said I was preoccupied? Would it help if I said that, while all this was going on, I was in the middle of making some pretty phenomenal mistakes of my own? Here's my excuse, for whatever it's worth: while my daughter was hiding in her room, watching her skin stretch and thinking up ways to get out of gym class, I was busy nearly marrying a man I didn't know at all.

His name was Curtis, and I met him through an online dating service. Not an auspicious beginning, I know, but I'd just lost a lot of weight, and I wanted to try something new. I may as well be up-front about this: I'd recently lost more than a hundred pounds. I don't like to talk about it. I don't even like to hear people say how great I look, because of the inherent implication. (I knew it, I always think, going over every past compliment, every reassurance. You were lying all along.) People are amazed by what I've done. They want to know how I did it (through hard, hard work – how does anyone do it?), like I've performed some magic trick, the Illusion of the Disappearing Flesh. And most of all, they want to talk about how bad I looked before. It's like people think I'm someone else now, like I've broken free from the woman I used to be, and now I'm free to bad-mouth her: "Gee, I'm glad that fat lady's gone – now I can tell you what I really thought of her."

(Could this have been another reason I didn't bring it up when I noticed Cassie putting on weight? She's always been heavy, though not as heavy as I was at my worst. I'd always felt guilty about giving her those bad genes, those bad eating habits. When I finally succeeded at getting thinner, she seemed happy for me, but her own weight was a topic we studiously avoided. I didn't want to add to her adolescent self-esteem issues, or whatever it was the magazine articles I read were telling me to be careful about. It got to the point where I wouldn't even let my eyes wander to her midsection. Still. Not an excuse.)

But back to Curtis: I had this new body, and I wanted to take it out for a spin and see what it could do. That's when I found Curtis. His online ad was funny, sweet, and self-deprecating, and he looked nice from his picture. We started e-mailing each other, and it all came together so quickly. I felt like I'd known him for years. We lived a couple hundred miles apart, close enough for a few crazy, intense weekends together. And before I could catch my breath, he'd told me he loved me, and I – why? Because I thought this was the best I could do? Because I wanted to avoid an awkward pause in the conversation?–I had said it back.

I knew it wasn't true, but I said it anyway. I thought, wouldn't it be great if it could be this easy? I'd spent most of Cassie's life alone. My husband, Jim – Cassie's father – died in a car accident when she was only a year old. I was a widow at twenty-six. It had never been a great marriage; if I'm honest, I doubt it would have lasted much longer. Two days before he died, I had opened the phone book to "Attorneys, divorce," and this, I think, more than anything, kept me from looking for someone else once he was gone. There are all kinds of widows. I was a guilty one. I hung back and ate more than I should have and prepared to live my life alone.

But now I'd finally decided my penance was over, and here was this great guy . . . well, here was this guy. It should have been clear very early that he wasn't perfect, but as you might have noticed, I tend to miss things. To tell the truth, I've never been good at courtship. I'm not good at reading signals; when I was in college, three different boyfriends broke up with me without my being aware of it. Subtlety isn't my strong point. That's probably why I didn't pick up on Curtis's strangeness, his *creepiness*. To say he was a little bit needy would be like saying that . . . oh, I don't know, I've never been good at this kind of wordplay. That Ramses II had a little bit of an ego problem? That King Tut is a little bit dead? Anyway, my point is, he was needy. He sent me e-mail cards twice a day. When we were together, he couldn't get enough of washing my hair and painting my toenails. Gross, right? But I thought it was sweet. I couldn't remember the last time anyone had held my feet in their hands, the last time anyone had treated my body as an object worthy of examination.

The first time I introduced him to Cassie — we'd been dating for all of two months — he took her hand and smiled beatifically. "I'm a father now," he said. Cassie, bless her sullen, deceiving little heart (she must have been four months pregnant by then), pulled her hand away and said, "Are you *trying* to make me puke, or is that just gonna be a coincidence?"

We were already making wedding plans — a beach in the Bahamas, barefoot in the sand, just the two of us and Cassie (God, what a scene that would have been) — when I finally jerked myself back to reality. Curtis had come to visit for the weekend, and we were cooking dinner together.

"You know what I find myself doing these days?" he asked.

"What?"

"I find myself comparing you to everything I see." He smiled at me in a childlike way he had that was just starting to strike me as the tiniest bit icky.

"Um," I said. "Really?"

"You bet," he said. He gestured to the salad I was tossing. "Laura is like lettuce," he said. "She is vibrant, and she is good for me."

"Huh," I said.

He picked up a tomato. "Laura is like a tomato," he said. "She is juicy and just the tiniest bit acidic. And she reminds me of summer."

"Well, that's nice, I guess." If you have a salad fetish.

He looked around the kitchen for inspiration. Oh my God, I thought. If he does "Laura is like a chicken breast," I'm going to have to stab him with this wooden fork.

"Maybe I'm not like food," I said.

"Oh, you are," he said soulfully. "You are my sustenance." He picked up a baguette and waved it in the air like a sword. "Laura is like bread," he said. "She is crusty on the outside and soft on the inside. She . . ." He faltered.

She what? I thought. She is covered with a fine dusting of flour? She makes a lovely light meal if you pair her with a bowl of soup?

Curtis smiled as he landed on his answer. He looked deep into my eyes and said, "She rises warm and yeasty and she fills me up."

I couldn't help it. I burst out laughing. I laughed and laughed, while poor Curtis stood there looking like I'd run over something furry. It was like I had suddenly woken up. *This man is a fucking lunatic*, I thought. *Get him out of my kitchen.*

"I'm sorry, Curtis," I said, when I could breathe again. "I don't think this is going to work out."

So that's my story. Except it isn't. None of this lets me off the hook. I have let my daughter down in unimaginable ways. I can't stand to think of it now, my girl suffering all alone. . . . I should have been there, that's all there is to say. I'm not sure how either of us will forgive me; I expect I'll be counting my regrets till the day I die. Which, if my daughter had anything to say about it, would be as soon as possible.

The Cities of the Dead comprise Cairo's two ancient cemeteries; tens of thousands of people live there, maybe more. After consulting our book, Cassie and I hail a taxi and load all our stuff inside. Brendan sits up front, facing backward, with his camera turned on us; it's amazing he never gets carsick. Our sound guy, Louie, is in back with us. I tell the driver we're going to the Northern Cemetery, and I show him the page in the guidebook. He turns around to look at us curiously.

"Not nighttime," he says. "You want nightclub, hotel, café. I take you someplace you like."

"No," I say. "This is where we have to go. And we have to get there as fast as we can."

He shakes his head, but begins driving.

"Do you think we'll be safe there at night?" I ask Cassie.

"Of course, Mom," she says sardonically. "We're on *television*. Nothing can hurt us."

We drive through streets that feel increasingly decrepit. There are whole neighborhoods of squatters living in makeshift dwellings scattered among the tombs and mausoleums. We pass rows and rows of open-air shanties with laundry strung colorfully outside.

"Look," says Cassie, pointing at one on our left; it's divided into two rooms, with a narrow strip of corrugated metal slung across the top. "They have a gravestone in their living room." I look, and she's right; a slab of marble rises from the dirt, a couple of chairs on each side of it. I can see a family asleep in the other room: a man, a woman, and two children. There's a TV, too; who would have thought they'd have electricity?

"Weird," I say. I sound like Cassie. "Can you imagine having a dead person buried in your house?"

"Mom," she says, and I can tell I've annoyed her again. "Just because they have a different culture doesn't make them weird."

"Hey, you're the one who pointed." She looks away, but I can see her smile.

Now that I look, most of the houses are built around tombs. It's an eerie thing to see. But there's beauty here, too. Alongside the hovels and the laundry and the skinny cats prowling through garbage, there are ornately filigreed tombs and mosques with minarets rising into the sky. For a minute, I wish I had a camera, and then I see Brendan and Louie and I remember that when we get home, we'll be able to turn on the TV and see the whole trip over again.

Another cab passes us and speeds on ahead. "It's Carl and Jeff," Cassie says.

"Can you go faster?" I say to the driver, a pulse of adrenaline moving through me. This is where it starts to feel like a race, although different teams often arrive at the finish line hours apart. You just never know until you get there whether you're going to be the first team or the last. If everyone else is already there, then we sure as hell better beat Carl and Jeff.

The driver speeds up, but then there's a sound like a gunshot, and he slams on the brakes. I duck down and, in the same motion, reach out toward Cassie and push her head down toward her lap. At least some of my maternal instincts are still intact.

"Mom," Cassie says, sitting up again. "I think it's a flat tire."

The driver swears in Arabic — at least, I assume that's what he's doing — and gets out of the car. I open my door and stick my head out. The back tire has collapsed into itself; it barely seems to be attached to the wheel rim.

"Shit," I say. "Cassie, get out; we'll have to run the rest of the way."

We jump out of the cab and pull our stuff out after us. I grunt as I hoist up my backpack, heavy with the booty of six different countries. I pull out some money — I'm not sure how much, but the driver takes it and nods — and I ask, "How far to the mosque?"

"Not far," he says. He's crouching on the ground, gently touching the tire as if it's a truculent pet that needs to be convinced to go just a little farther. He stands and points up, over some nearby buildings. "See tower?" I nod. "That is mosque. Go that way, then turn."

"Thank you," I say, and begin to lumber away. It's not easy to run while carrying a ski pole and a birdcage. Poor Milton is jostled till his feathers fly. "Damn it," he protests. "Damn it."

Cassie and I run — Brendan keeping pace with us, Louie right behind — until we reach the corner. "There it is," Cassie yells as we turn. She's holding the aviator helmet on her head with one hand. The mosque rises ahead of us, illuminated brilliantly against the night; clearly, the lighting crew has been here already. It's a vast, majestic building, crowned with intricately carved domes and spires. As we get closer, I can see Barbara standing outside, a group of contestants arranged in a semicircle behind her. I try to count who's there, but I can't do the math while I'm running. We sprint the last fifty yards or so, and finally we're standing in front of Barbara.

"Congratulations, Laura and Cassie," she says. "You're still in the game."

We let out a cheer, and I put down the objects in my arms, so I can give Cassie a hug. She doesn't hug me back, but so what? We'll live to fight another day.

We join the other teams behind Barbara – Carl and Jeff, Riley and Trent, Betsy and Jason. Justin and Abby arrive a few minutes later. Jeremy, one of the producers, has gotten word that the other two teams are quite a ways behind us, so we all sit down to wait. The rules say everyone has to stay here until the last team arrives; we all say we hate it, and we'd rather be sleeping, but actually, these times are some of the nicest in the game. The competition's over for a while, and we can share our stories of battle: Betsy and Jason nearly missed their plane from Aswan; Riley and Trent gave the wrong keyword (*graffiti*, rather than *1819*) and were penalized for ten minutes, which allowed Justin and Abby to get ahead; Jeff sweet-talked a belly dancer into letting him pluck three sequins from the curviest part of her bodice. We sit on the steps of the mosque, sipping water in the hot night. Jeremy takes people aside one by one for quick interviews about the day. After a while, Cassie and a few of the others stretch out and sleep.

Betsy's sitting a few feet away from me; Jason's slumped over next to her, snoring softly against her arm. They're a strange couple; she's a lawyer, very smart, very together, and he strikes me as kind of immature. The first time we met, he said, "I'm Jason, but I go by Hippo." Maybe they were a good match once, but it's clear they aren't anymore.

I watch as Betsy carefully disentangles herself, rearranging Jason so his head falls to the other side, and slides over until there's no contact between them. She rubs the spot on her arm where his face was.

"Drool," she says, seeing that I'm watching.

I make a sympathetic face. There's a certain level of intimacy you need before you can tolerate another person's drool, and I don't think Betsy and Jason are currently in that place.

She yawns. "I'm just going to try to look at this as one big research project," she says. "It's one of life's big mysteries, right — would I be better off with my first love? And I'm one of the lucky few who can tell you the answer. No."

"Sorry to hear it," I say.

She shrugs; she looks tired. "Let me ask you a question," she says suddenly. She gestures toward the sleeping lump of Jason. "Did he ask you to call him Hippo?"

I nod. "Yeah. But no one else was calling him that, so I didn't, either."

"Thank God it didn't catch on," she says. "It was his high school nickname, and he wanted to use it on the show, but I wouldn't let him. I just kept picturing the opening credits of the show, with our smiling faces on the screen, and what does it say underneath — Betsy and Jason, like a normal couple who might actually have a chance of relating to each other on an adult level? No. Betsy and Hippo."

I smile. "Why was he called Hippo?" I ask. "Do I want to know?"

"Oh, it was just because he ate a lot, and there was that game, Hungry Hungry Hippos. That's the whole fascinating story right there."

"I guess there are worse nicknames," I say.

"I guess," she says doubtfully. "At least I learned my lesson before I started ordering 'Betsy and Hippo' wedding napkins."

She leans back against the stone steps and closes her eyes. It's hard to make a relationship like that work; people change, I guess, or one does and one doesn't. I imagine for a moment a scenario twenty years in the future, Cassie and Dan rediscovering each other. I always liked Dan; I'm still not clear on the specifics of why they broke up. I guess I thought maybe a good mom wouldn't pry too much; I thought I was respecting her privacy. It's clear now that a little bit of prying might have been exactly what she needed.

After another half hour or so, Juliet and Dallas arrive in a foul mood, which means poor Wendy and Jillian are going to get the boot. When they finally arrive, looking more bedraggled than any flight attendants I've ever seen, we all stand behind Barbara and put on our most sympathetic faces, trying not to look too happy that it's not us.

"You've lost the race," Barbara says to them, and I practically want to mouth the words with her. "But what have you found?"

Wendy puts on a brave smile. "I've found that I'm a lot stronger than I ever thought I was," she says.

Jillian nods. "I've found that Wendy and I make a great team," she says.

Barbara smiles. Perfect answers. She turns to face the camera. "Tune in next week," she says, "when our six remaining teams find themselves in a new corner of the world. Until next time, this is . . . *Lost and Found.*"

The cameras turn off at last. We all say good-bye to Wendy and Jillian. They look exhausted; honestly, I think they're glad to be going home. Cassie and I start walking away from the mosque. When we get to the street, there will be cars to take us to our hotel. It's pitch-black out, and I don't see any stars. Too much smog, I guess. I remember when Cassie was a little girl, not even two years old, she had a love of lights. She wasn't afraid of the dark; she just liked to see things shine. She'd walk through the rooms of our house, day and night, pointing at lamps and light fixtures, yelling "On! Mama do it! On!" (Eventually, I got her to add "please"– her toddler equivalent was "pease"–which made the demands a little more palatable.) One evening, we were out past dark, and as I lifted Cassie out of her car seat to bring her into the house, she turned her head upward and pointed at the dark sky. "On, pease, on, pease," she said, pointing up at the night. "Mama do it."

No one else ever loves you the way your children do when they're young. No one else will ever cry when you leave the room. I try not to spend too much time thinking about those days, because I know they're perfect only in memory, and I know I need to focus on the girl I've got in front of me right now. But sometimes I can't help but give in to it, to live inside the warm hues I've colored those moments with. To remember what it was like, back when she smiled just to see me, when she needed my help to move a spoon to her mouth or to walk down a flight of steps. Back when she had to reach up to hold my hand. Back when she thought I could turn on the sky.

SEVEN

Cassie

I didn't set out to hide my pregnancy. The first few months, I just kept hoping it wasn't true, and by the time I finally hauled my ass to a local clinic, it was too late to have a regular abortion. I would've had to get myself to this one doctor who lived over an hour away, and it would've been a more complicated procedure, all of which seemed totally insurmountable to me at the time. By then, I'd broken up with Dan, and Mia and I . . . well, we weren't friends anymore. My mom was busy with the new guy. Some days it seemed like I barely said two words to anyone. I actually counted one day; it was like a game, "How few words can Cassie say today?" I did it in twenty-one. I started with "morning" and "bye" to my mom, who didn't seem to notice anything. At school, I got by with eight: "X to the ninth," "Rose of Sharon," and "lasagna." At dinner with Mom, there were seven more: "fine," "nothing," "I don't know," and "B plus." And after dinner, just four: "I've got homework" and "'night." I was proud of that number, twenty-one. I wanted to tell someone about it, but I guess that would've defeated the purpose, and anyway, who was there to tell? It was that night, when I added up my grand total, that I decided not to tell anybody I was pregnant. *Okay,* I thought. *Let's see how long it takes them to notice.* And I just kept waiting.

Today we're in Japan. Yesterday was a totally wasted travel day —

it took thirteen hours to get from Cairo to Osaka, then another flight to get to this place called Beppu. They don't always film us constantly when we're traveling; they just do a couple of shots here and there. It's obviously not the most thrilling thing in the world to watch someone sitting on an airplane, although I'm sure if they start running low on material, they'll find a way to use it. (I can just hear Barbara's phony-ass voiceover: "Cassie has been hoping for pretzels; when the flight attendant hands her peanuts, her disappointment is palpable.")

On the flight to Osaka, I was sitting across the aisle from Juliet, and she started talking to me. She's really nice, and she has all these great Hollywood stories. She knows a lot of movie stars, and she was telling me how short they all are in person and stuff like that. And apparently, the other girl on *Best Friends*, the one who played Amber, was a total loser. She could never remember her lines, and she used to cry all the time whenever she messed up. Her mom was always butting in and yelling at the director, saying things like "This is a *child*; can't you make some allowances?" And the director would say, "Well, Juliet's a *child*, and she doesn't need any allowances." I don't know, it probably doesn't sound that funny, but the way she was telling it, it was hilarious. We were laughing really hard, and my mom leaned over and said, "What's so funny?" and I just wanted to die. I mean, why am I the only person on this show who has to hang around with her *mother*?

There was this one moment, though, when I was like, "I can't believe I'm talking to Juliet Jansen." It's not as if I still have a crush on her or anything – I mean, I was twelve – but there was just this moment when I looked at her, and I started thinking about this dream I had about her once, back when her show was on the air. In the dream, Juliet and I were sitting on the couch in my living room, and we were watching *Best Friends* on TV, and then she just leaned over and kissed me. That was it, nothing big; trust me, I've had better dreams than that. But when I woke up, everything was different. It was like this tiny little pinhole had opened up in the air, and I could see through it to this whole other place I never knew was there. That day in homeroom, I just started looking around the room at all the girls in my class, and I imagined kissing all of them. It was, I don't know, *thrilling*. It was like I knew a secret. All these girls thinking about guys, wondering what guys looked like naked, and I got to see girls in their underwear every time we had gym class. It was like I'd only been seeing half the picture up till then. It didn't freak me out or anything, not until later. It was just a fun diversion to have, something to think about whenever class got too boring. I thought, it's not like this matters, it's not like it means anything for the rest of my life. I'm just a kid, and I've got all these hormones, and I can point them at whoever I want. No one even needed to know. It was just this funny game I was playing.

And then I fell in love with Mia. And that's when things got hard.

We're staying at a *ryokan*, which is like a really traditional kind of Japanese inn. Usually they put us in more normal hotels, but I guess they thought they could get some good shots of us roughing it Japanese-style. It's kind of funky; the rooms have straw mats on the floor, and when you first walk in, it looks like there aren't any beds, but it turns out there are futons rolled up in the closet. There are all these shoe rules that are hard to keep straight: take off your shoes when you come in, put on these slippers they give you, but don't wear the slippers on the straw mats, blah, blah, blah. You even have to put on a special pair of "toilet slippers" when you go to the bathroom. That's just gross. And last night, the innkeeper woman took Dallas aside and told him that he had his robe tied the wrong way; apparently, if you put the right side over the left side, it means you're a corpse.

Producer Eli rounds us all up in the entryway. "There's a bus waiting outside to take you to our first location," he says. Everyone groans; we know what this means. It means we're doing a Daredevil Round. The Daredevil Round is this thing they throw in every third country or so to shake things up. They make us do some kind of crazy, dangerous thing, and whichever team does it the best gets a head start for the next leg. We've had two so far; in Canada, we had to go hang gliding, and in Brazil, they made us milk the venom out of a poisonous snake. I'm sure it'll look exciting on TV, but I don't think we were ever in any danger either time. With the hang-gliding thing, we were all strapped to professional guys, and for the snake thing, we were all wearing gloves. So far, Mom and I suck at these. Riley and Trent surprised everyone by winning the hang-gliding round, and Betsy and Jason did the most snakes in the shortest time.

Eli shushes us and keeps talking. "But before we go, we're going to do a quick spot check and make sure everyone still has all their found objects. Line up all your objects on the floor; I'll be coming around with a checklist."

"Oh, God," I say. This is always a pain, having to empty out your backpack and then stuff everything back in.

"It's all part of the game," Eli says.

Mom and I start laying everything out. Helmet, sequins, trilo-bite, paper, chess piece, ski pole, parrot. Our new camera guy, Dave, stands by with his camera trained on our pile of stuff, just in case there's anything missing. They give us new camera crews every leg; I guess it's so we don't get too attached to them and they don't start helping us or anything. They switch out the parrots, too; on the first parrot-inclusive leg, one of the birds got kind of sick in the cargo hold, and the show people decided they'd rather not deal with all the customs problems and potential animal-rights issues. So now we get a new parrot in each country. They try to make sure they all look the same, though; the viewers aren't supposed to know that it's not just one continuous parrot.

I bend down, array our objects so they're all clearly visible. Our latest parrot, named Milton like the last one for continuity reasons, looks at me with his bright little eyes and makes a noise that sounds like a question. I kind of like him, actually. We got the last one to say "damn it"; I wonder what I can teach this one. I lean over toward the cage. "Bite me," I say softly. He just looks at me.

Eli and his fellow producer Kate go through and check off everyone's items. There's a little bit of an uproar when Carl and Jeff can only find two of their sequins, but then they find the third one stuck to the bottom of a sock. Looks like everyone's still in the game.

"Okay, folks," he calls out. "Everybody on the bus."

We take off the little house-slipper things they gave us and put on our shoes. Outside, there's a big blue-and-white bus waiting for us. It's kind of disappointing; it looks just like an American bus. We all climb aboard and find seats. Mom kind of gestures for me to sit with her, but there are plenty of empty seats, so I take a row by myself.

"So did everyone enjoy their fish?" Carl asks the bus at large. Breakfast was bizarre: fish, rice, soup, and a raw egg that no one knew what to do with. "Nothing better, first thing in the morning."

"I was not a big fan of the pickled things," Trent says.

"I kind of liked it," Mom says. "It felt very authentic."

"Man, I would pay a thousand dollars for a short stack," says Dallas.

"Remind me to invite you over for breakfast sometime," says Jeff.

I look out the window. There's a woman walking down the street, leading a little girl by the hand. The girl must be about two. She's wearing red pants and a little white T-shirt, and her black hair is pulled into two little ponytails that stick straight out from the back of her head. They're walking really slowly, and the mother's trying to hurry her along, but then the little girl stops and crouches down to look at something on the sidewalk, and she looks up at her mother with the biggest smile on her face, like whatever she's found there is the best thing in the world. I look up at the sky, and the bus keeps going, we're past them now, but it's too late because I saw them. I saw them. And now my chest feels tight and my insides are all crumpled up and I won't cry, I won't cry, but how the hell am I supposed to concentrate on playing a stupid game?

I focus on the landscape until the feeling's gone. We're driving along a ridge, and down below us I can see the city, all built around a harbor with dark green mountains in the background. It's really pretty, but the way the mountains look makes me feel a little lonely. They sort of remind me of the opening scenes of *M*A*S*H*, which Mom and I used to watch reruns of when I was home sick from school. That theme song always sounded so sad.

"So what do you think they're going to make us do today?" Trent asks.

"Gotta be something Japanese," Carl says.

"Maybe it's that paper-folding stuff," Dallas says.

"Yeah," says Juliet. "That can be really dangerous. Extreme origami."

I try to get back in the spirit of things. "You could get a nasty paper cut," I say. Juliet smiles at me, and it makes everything better. I smile back. It's like I can't even help it.

"Something in the water, maybe," says Abby. "Parasailing or something."

My mom's looking at the guidebook we bought in the Osaka airport. "It's a good thing we're not in Tokyo," she says. "There's a parasite museum there."

"Hey, I've got it," says Jeff. "Sumo. They're gonna put us in diapers and make us fight with our bellies. I could kick ass at that." He stands in the aisle and lifts his T-shirt to shows us his flabby, hairy belly. He bangs it against one of the seats, and everything jiggles. It's repulsive.

"Oh, yeah, that'd be good for ratings," Carl says. "It could be the opposite of sweeps week – how many viewers can we lose in a single episode?"

"Maybe they'll make us do karaoke," Jason says. He's from the high school sweethearts team. They hate each other. (I could've told them it was a bad idea; I can't wait to get away from most of the people at my high school.) "What do you think, Betsy? Think we could win that? You could do 'Papa Don't Preach,' just like that time at the talent show. That was a memorable performance."

"Go to hell," she says.

The bus travels down a long, steep road into the city, toward the water, and finally stops across the street from a beach. There's a small building off to the side, and down by the edge of the water, there's a big square of flat sand, marked off by wooden posts. The sand is dark, almost like mud, and there's steam coming out of it. There are six red parasols standing in a row. Barbara's off to the side, getting her makeup touched up.

"Okay, everyone," Eli says. "Gather around Barbara. She's already done the intro, so we're going to get right down to business."

The cameras roll. Barbara straightens herself as tall as she'll go and arranges her mouth in a teeny little smile. "We're in the city of Beppu, Japan," she says, "home to almost three thousand hot springs. This is the setting for a Daredevil Round our teams won't soon forget."

She holds up a stack of red envelopes trimmed in black. There's a devil printed on the front; he looks like he's doing a little dance with his pitchfork. "Here is your assignment," she says.

She hands the stack to Justin, who takes one and passes the rest. The envelopes make their way around the circle. When Barbara gives us a little jerky nod, we all tear them open. The card inside says,

> *Buried in hot sand*
> *Ancient steam envelops you*
> *Who will be the last?*

"It's a haiku," says Mom. She sounds genuinely delighted. I shake my head.

Barbara talks to the camera. "The hot sand bath, or *suna yu*, has long been a Japanese means of relaxation. Contestants will be buried up to their necks in volcanic sand that has been warmed by the natural hot springs. The temperature of the sand is one hundred and twenty degrees Fahrenheit. The recommended length of a sand bath is ten minutes. Our contestants will stay buried for as long as they possibly can; whichever team lasts the longest will receive a one-hour head start on the next assignment."

No one says anything, but we all kind of look at each other — this is it? This is what they've come up with? We have to lie in the sand. I thought we'd have to swallow live eels or something.

"One member of each team will participate," Barbara says. "Decide among yourselves which of you can stand the heat." She emphasizes the last three words; I think she's trying to make them sound scary, but they just sound louder.

"I'll do it if you want, honey," Mom says. "Unless you'd like to. Either way." She's trying so hard it makes me feel a little sad.

"I'll do it," I say. "I don't mind." I make myself smile a little bit, and she beams like I've just told her I love her or something.

After a series of charades between Eli and a middle-aged woman who seems to work there, the six of us who are going to be buried – me, Justin, Jeff, Dallas, Betsy, and Trent – are taken inside the building to locker rooms. No cameras for this, at least. Betsy and I are the only ones in the women's locker room; we undress and put on some white cotton robes they've left for us.

"So we actually get buried in the robes?" I ask Betsy.

"I guess," she says. She points to a sign posted on the wall: "Apparently, 'It is right and traditional to take off all belongings and wear only robe for sand bathing.'"

"Attractive," I say, checking out the effect in the mirror. It's kind of like wearing a hospital gown.

"The guys'll look cute in these," she says. "On national TV. Jason would've liked it, though, if he were doing this one; he has this thing about his legs."

"What kind of thing?"

"He thinks he has shapely calves. Or at least he thought he did in high school. We haven't discussed it recently."

She looks in the mirror, brushes a hand through her hair, then smiles in a slightly evil way. "'Shapely calves,'" she says. "That's his phrase, not mine. I'll have to weave that in later somehow, when we're on camera. His friends will be merciless about that."

We head back outside and walk over to the big square of sand. Betsy's right; the guys look kind of funny, with their pasty legs and bulbous knees sticking out. They look all different levels of embarrassed, except for Jeff, who's grinning like an idiot. I sneak a look at Jason, standing with the onlookers. He's wearing shorts; his calves look pretty ordinary to me. He catches me looking and raises his eyebrows at me. Gross.

There are long hollow areas dug out in the sand underneath each umbrella, like shallow graves. There are six old Japanese women waiting for us; they're wearing these white bonnets and blue jackets and pants. They all have shovels. One of them comes over to me and bows. Bowing is very big here; in the airport, I actually saw a guy on a cell phone bowing to the person he was talking to. The woman takes me by the arm and gestures for me to lie down in one of the hollows. Once everyone's in place, they start burying us.

The sand is wet and heavy. It feels good, hot but not too hot. I feel the heat soaking into my muscles. The woman shovels sand over me until everything's covered but my head. She smoothes the surface into a little mound. I like this, the heat, the weight. It's like I'm being pushed down into the earth, deep down to a place where I don't have to think about anything.

"I could do this all day," Trent says. Or maybe it's Jeff. My eyes are closed.

"You picked the wrong challenge to do, Jason," says Betsy. "This is way better than the snakes."

Barbara calls out the minutes as they pass, and all the people who aren't buried are yelling out encouraging things, but I kind of tune them all out. My mind is all over the place. It's like having a fever, or being in the womb or something. I start thinking about Mia, but about the good times, the times I still like to remember. There was this one time last year when we'd been studying SAT words, all the synonyms and antonyms. We were at lunch, and Reece and Dan were making stupid jokes, coming up with names for bands. Neither of them had any musical talent, but they were always talking about starting a band, mostly so they could come up with a funny name. So they were throwing around names – I remember that Flesh-Eating Cafeteria was a contender, and so was You've Got Badass Shoes.

When they got to Peepee Shack, Mia looked at me and said, "There's a real dearth of maturity at this table." Dan said, "What's a dearth?" and Mia and I said, in unison, like we'd planned it, "A paucity." And then we both looked at each other and started laughing so hard, it was like we were the only ones there.

Reece and Dan just stared at us. "What," Reece said, "is it some kind of big vocab secret?"

"Yeah," Mia said. "It's a secret." She leaned over to me and put her lips right up to my ear. "A scarcity," she whispered.

I could feel her breath on my neck. I smiled like she'd told me the best secret in the world. I leaned toward her. My lips were almost touching her skin and I could feel her hair brushing against my face. I closed my eyes, and my whisper was no louder than a breath. "A lack," I said. I inhaled; I drew the scent of her into my body. "A want."

She turned her head and smiled at me. She spoke so softly only I could hear her. "An absence," she said.

Then someone dropped a plate across the room, and everyone clapped and yelled, and the moment was over. But later, in class, I was brushing my hair away from my face, and I ran my finger along the edge of my ear and remembered what it was like to have her lips almost on me.

"Nine minutes," says Barbara. It's starting to get a little less comfortable. Little needles of heat start prickling me, making me want to move around.

"Oh, man," says Dallas. "I've got an itch."

"Don't scratch," yells Juliet. She's laughing, but I can tell she's completely serious. "Don't you dare scratch."

He groans in this irritating way. He makes it till Barbara announces "Ten minutes," then he says, "That's it, I'm out." He pulls himself out of the sand and jumps up, brushing himself off and scratching everywhere.

"We're down to five teams," Barbara booms. Dallas jumps into the water in his little kimono and goes, "Ahhh."

"Good try," Juliet says in the most annoyed voice I've ever heard.

Trent makes it to thirteen minutes, Betsy to fifteen. It's really starting to burn. I try to distract myself by looking up at the clouds in the sky. There's one in the shape of England, or maybe a Maltese dog.

"You're doing great, sweetie," Mom calls to me.

I count the spokes on the parasol. There are ten. I close my eyes and listen to the sounds of the sea, to Trent and Dallas and Betsy splashing around. I have this floaty, dizzy feeling. I see weird, random pictures in my head: a stack of green apples in a supermarket, the playground I used to go to when I was a kid. Maybe I'm frying my brain. I see the willow tree in our yard at home, I see a bathtub filled with cool water. I see a baby girl wrapped in my grandmother's quilt.

Suddenly, I have to get up. I can't stand it for one second more. I burst out of the hot little cocoon and feel the air on my skin.

"Good job, Cassie," Mom yells. "You did great."

"Eighteen minutes," says Barbara. "We have two teams left."

I walk into the water. It's warm; I wish it were colder. I want it so cold it makes me numb. Trent, Dallas, and Betsy are standing farther ahead, the water to their knees.

"Welcome to the loser zone," says Dallas. "Didn't that just suck?"

I shrug and keep going. I wade until I'm up to my neck. I hold my breath and duck under. It's quiet and cool. My cotton robe floats up around me so I'm almost naked. I keep my eyes closed and sway with the water. Soon I'll have to come up for breath. I'll have to go back to shore and listen to my mom tell me how well I did, and I'll have to keep on playing the game. But for now, I just kind of hover here underneath the surface, invisible, floating, alone.

EIGHT

Justin

L ying in the sand, I know I'm going to win. The heat is uncomfortable, and there's sweat in my eyes, but I've grown quite good at ignoring the fickle needs of the body. This is nothing to me, this physical shell, with all of its tumult and want. I keep my mind on the goal, and I pray to the Lord to keep me still. When Jeff finally succumbs at twenty-one minutes, and Barbara announces that I am the winner, I don't even get up right away. I can do this for longer; I could do this all day.

Finally, with Jeff making jokes at my expense ("What, is he going for extra credit?"), I dig myself out and go down to wash myself in the cool water. I feel dizzy but ebullient. I walk back to the crowd and give my wife a kiss on the lips.

Abby has done me more good than I can say. She's the reason I hold my head high. I'm a man with a wife. I can stand beside her and say, This is me. Not a day goes by when I don't thank God for bringing her to me.

I go back to the locker room to change, along with Jeff, Dallas, and Trent. There was a time when the thought of undressing in a room with three men, two of them young and one quite handsome, would have meant something different to me. But now I just don't look. I see men as my brothers now, not as objects for a stunted lust. If, for a moment, a wiggling fish of a thought should happen to skim the surface of my mind (as happens when Dallas amuses himself by stretching his naked Hollywood body directly in my line of sight), I simply stop it in its path. I scoop it up and hold it in the air until it suffocates.

Here's the way I see it: God understands that we are frail creatures. He understands that we walk in darkness as often as we walk in light. We fail, and we pray, and we fail again; it's just the way we're made. As long as we keep repenting, there's no need for shame. The ones who get into trouble are the ones who think they don't have to follow the rules. The ones who think it's okay to build their whole lives around a sin of the flesh. Those are the ones I pity. Those are the ones who need my help.

Back outside, Barbara banishes the rest of the teams and takes me and Abby aside. Our cameraman today is a guy named Ken. The cameramen are an interesting bunch. Most of them have traveled all over the world; I've noticed that they all carry laminated cards with their frequent flyer information, so they can rake in the miles wherever their jobs take them. They're used to working in war zones and in areas of great political unrest. They're tough and rugged; they're exactly the kind of man I want to be. Ken's a quiet guy, but nice. He's tall and blond, very muscular; I mention it because anyone would.

"Justin and Abby," Barbara says, once the cameras are rolling, "you have won the Daredevil Round. You will have a one-hour head start on the Keyword Round. Your time begins as soon as you open your clue."

She hands us the white-and-gold envelope. I open it up.

> *An American icon twice displayed,*
> *In two theme parks they pose.*
> *One in a miniworld and one*
> *Not far from Lincoln's nose.*

"There are special instructions for this round," Barbara says. "Because there are two sites you need to visit, you'll have to split up.

I have for you cell phones provided by"– and here she inserts the name of the telecommunications company that's obviously sponsoring this episode. I feel no need to further promote them. "Each of you should go to one of the locations described in the clue; once there, you will work together by phone to determine the keyword. There will be camera crews at both locations."

Abby and I consult briefly. "Let's just head toward the airport," she says, "and we'll try to figure out where we're going along the way."

I agree; wherever we're supposed to go, I don't think it's likely to be here in Beppu. We gather up our stuff and take off running, with Ken and our sound guy Stefan running alongside us, leaving the other teams to while away an hour on the beach. We manage to hail a cab pretty quickly, despite the fact that we're carrying a parrot and a ski pole, and I'm wearing an aviator's helmet. We load our things in the trunk and I reach for the handle on the rear door, but the door swings open by itself.

"Look at that," I say. "We should have these back home." We get inside with our parrot; he's the third one we've had and, like the others, his name is Noah. Ken sits in the front, Stefan with us. The back doors close by themselves.

"*Hijouku*," I say to the driver with a little bow. This is the Japanese word for *airport;* I memorized it last night, in anticipation of a moment like this. I think it pays to be respectful. I can't stand to see the way some of the other contestants act toward the people of the different countries we've visited. Jason assumes everyone speaks English; when he finds someone who doesn't, he just speaks it louder and in monosyllables. And Jeff is such a buffoon, he just adds an *o* to the end of every word, no matter what country we're in. I can just imagine him getting into a cab an hour from now, yelling, "Airporto, my good man. Quicko! Quicko!"

It takes forty-five minutes to get to the airport, which is most of our lead, but I remind myself that the other teams will have to make the same trip. On the way, Abby goes through the list of Japanese theme parks in the index of our guidebook. It makes me nauseous to read in a moving vehicle, but it doesn't bother Abby at all. Just another example of the beautiful symmetry that exists between the two of us. We complement each other perfectly, in the way that only a man and a woman can. I'm filled with a sense of rightness, an awareness of how deeply we've been blessed.

I know that people often don't believe me when I say that I've been healed of my homosexuality. But don't people make choices every day of their lives? Don't we, all of us, make a choice to live in the way that we think is right? I was not happy with the life I was leading. I felt empty; I didn't like the man I saw when I looked in the mirror. And one dark day, when I'd reached the very bottom of my life, I decided I had to change.

Which is not to say it's been easy. If you give up smoking, does it mean you'll never crave a cigarette again as long as you live? No. But is it possible to start each day determined that you won't lift a cigarette to your lips, that you won't light a match and start it smoldering, that you won't inhale poison smoke into your lungs? Of course it is.

Abby fills me in on what she's been reading. Theme parks seem to be popular in Japan; in addition to Tokyo Disneyland and Universal Studios Japan, there's a Space World, a Sea Paradise, and an Adventure World. There are parks where visitors can pretend they're in Germany, Spain, and Denmark. There's a ramen museum, a curry museum, and a pot sticker "stadium," all with their own food-related attractions. The frivolity of it bothers me; there's something excessive about an amusement park based on dumplings.

"Okay, here's something," Abby says. "Tobu World Square in Nikko. It's all miniature models of famous world monuments. The Empire State Building, the Taj Mahal."

"Do they have a Lincoln Memorial?" I ask.

"It doesn't say. But Lincoln's nose has to be the other place, right?"

"Oh, right. Well, whatever the other park is, it has to be nearby, don't you think? I can't imagine they'd send us to different cities. Not unless they can cut Ken in half." That line will definitely be edited out; we're not supposed to make any reference to the cameras.

"Let's see, there are two other theme parks in Nikko," Abby says. "Nikko Edo Mura Village: 'See what life was like in the time of the Samurai.' No, probably not. And Nikko Western Village: 'A Japanese take on the American Wild West.' Oh, this is obviously it; they've got a replica of Mount Rushmore."

"Four presidential noses coming right up. We're set. Good job, baby." Abby smiles, but I feel embarrassed. No matter what term of endearment I use for Abby, it never sounds quite right. "So where's Nikko?"

She turns the pages. "About two hours from Tokyo. I don't think there's an airport; it says to take the train."

"Tokyo it is." When I take Abby's hand, I'm aware of Ken zooming in on the image, capturing the shot. A man and a woman, in love, on an adventure. Sin and darkness banished, a union consecrated by the word of God. I can think of no better picture for the people of America to see.

NINE

Juliet

Our cab driver doesn't speak any English, so he's not much help in figuring out the clue. Dallas and I sit in the backseat of the cab with our camera guy — I can't remember the names of either member of our film crew, and there's no good way to ask — sitting in the front, filming us. I flip through our guidebook, trying to find something about theme parks. I can't find a list of parks, but I do come across a few pages about Tokyo Disneyland. I read aloud:

"'Many favorite rides and attractions from the American parks are reproduced here, including Space Mountain . . . blah, blah, blah . . . It's a Small World.' That sounds right, doesn't it? A 'mini-world'?"

"Sounds good to me, babe," Dallas says. He's leaning back against the seat with his eyes closed. "Wake me up when we get there, okay?"

"No," I say. "Don't be stupid. Help me figure this out."

He stretches, but doesn't open his eyes. "Sounds like you've got it figured out. I mean, how many theme parks can there be in Japan?"

"Well, what about this 'Lincoln's nose' stuff?"

He shrugs. "Don't they have some boring-ass thing about Lincoln at Disneyland?"

"Yeah, I think so." I look at the guidebook entry again. "But it doesn't say whether they have that one here or not."

"I'm sure they do. The Japanese are fascinated by American stuff like that."

That sounds dubious to me, but the fact remains that *somewhere* in Japan there's a theme park with Lincoln's nose in it, so maybe the moron is right.

"Well, wait," I say, looking at the clue again. "It says we have to go to two different parks."

With a great show of reluctance, Dallas sits up and takes the book from me. He reads for a minute, then turns the page. "Right here, genius," he says. "'A new Disney park, Tokyo Disney Sea, opened in 2001. Themed seaports throughout the park include Mediterranean Harbor, Lost River Delta, and American Waterfront.' I told you they like American stuff. They probably stuck the Lincoln thing there."

"Maybe. What do you think this American icon is that we're looking for?"

He smiles big. He's not bad-looking, but so generic. "It's obvious," he says. "Who's the leader of the band that's made for you and me? M-I-C . . ." He trails off; I think he's waiting for me to finish the line, but I'm not going to do it. I just look at him coolly. It kills me that he's figured this out.

"K-E-Y?" he says. He gives me another high-wattage smile, but I'm not some *President Scooter* groupie. I've slept with two Golden Globe winners.

"M . . . O . . ."

I cut him off. "You know, they'll probably cut that," I say curtly. "Otherwise, they'll have to pay for permission to use it."

When we get to the airport, I'm relieved to see that everyone else is buying tickets to Tokyo, too. We're in line behind Carl and Jeff, and most of the other teams are somewhere behind us. Justin and Abby are nowhere in sight, so I guess they used their extra time to get on an earlier flight. I see two flights to Tokyo listed; one leaves in a half hour and the other in an hour and a half. If we don't all get on the first one, then that could make a serious difference in the outcome of this round. I've got to admit, I kind of love this part of it, rushing to get ahead, scheming against the other teams. I'm a pretty competitive person. And I've been trying to get on a reality show for as long as they've been doing them. The whole idea was just made for me. A whole life lived on television, that's what I'd be good at.

I've been in TV forever. My first job was a commercial for all-purpose cleaner when I was thirteen months old; my role was to draw on the wall with a crayon, then the woman playing my mom came and cleaned it off. After that, I did commercials for diapers and oatmeal, and when I was three, I landed an ongoing role on the sitcom *Partners in Crime*. It was about a married couple who are both cat burglars. I played the youngest daughter, the one that they had unexpectedly when the ratings started to drop. It was one of those things where they spend like a year and a half on the pregnancy, and then the baby mysteriously jumps from four months old to three and a half because toddlers are more interesting on-screen. I played the toddler, not the baby; some of my earliest memories are from filming that show. I remember standing offstage with my mom, waiting for my cue, and I remember how good I felt when I got my line right. When I see the show now, I always think I look a little lost, like I don't really know what's going on, but I know I liked being there. And I have nothing bad to say about the actor who played my dad; he turned out to have a huge drug problem, and he was eventually convicted of murdering a hooker, but he was always a sweetheart to me. The show was canceled three months after I joined the cast, which is too bad. I've got to say, I was an adorable kid.

After that, I had a bunch of guest shots and small roles in kids' movies, but it was when I was cast in *Best Friends* that I really came into my own as an actress. Yeah, it was a stupid show — I don't know where they found those writers — but I acted my ass off. There were problems on the set from the beginning; Celia Bagley-Boone, who played Amber, was so wooden she attracted termites, and there was that lighting guy who died. Total freak accident, but it cast a shadow. Also, I think Celia made up that whole thing about the director touching her; she loved attention, and she loved getting other people in trouble. But even if it was true . . . well, just grow up, that's all I have to say. We had a TV show; we were the *stars*. That doesn't happen to too many people in this world.

After *Best Friends,* I went through kind of a rough time. It's really hard to find good parts once you're past "cute kid" but you're still too young to pull off "fuckable." And I got some bad press for that whole lawsuit thing. To clarify, it's not accurate to say that I *sued* my parents; or maybe it's accurate in a strictly legal sense, but it doesn't convey what really happened. We had a slight dispute over the handling of the money I'd earned, and we asked the courts to help us settle it. There are no bad feelings. As I told *People* magazine, my family is more important to me than anything.

Between that and the coverage about the drugs – yes, I grew up too fast, and I spent my share of time in rehab; it takes a lot for a fifteen-year-old to admit she has a problem – for a while, it seemed like no one would touch me. But I paid my dues, I did the soft-porn cable movies and the straight-to-video splatter films, and it's made me a better person. More humble, more hungry. Believe me, I am primed for a comeback. I'm so ready to be back on top, and I think this show is going to get me there.

It's almost too easy. The rest of these people don't know television the way I do. You have to fight for face time, especially on a show like this. What you need to understand is that reality shows don't show reality at all. Reality is boring; no one wants to watch someone brushing their teeth or paying their phone bill. It's all in the editing; they've got hundreds of hours of footage, and they've got to chop it down into something worth watching. What they're looking for is stories; you have to give them a story, or zip, they're moving on to someone else. I did the math yesterday, sitting on the plane: they're going to take all that footage and chop it down to eleven episodes, forty-four minutes each. (Sixteen minutes of commercials is sixteen minutes you're not on the air. These are the things you need to understand.) So altogether, we're talking about 484 minutes of screen time. How many of those minutes are going to be mine?

I've got a few options. I could get hurt; that'd get me some sympathy, but it might also slow us down and get us kicked off the show. I could start a romance with Dallas – that'd test my acting skills – but that's risky. We might end up looking pathetic; we're not America's fresh-faced darlings anymore, we're a couple of where-are-they-nows. It's a tough call whether we'd pull the public's heartstrings or become a walking punch line.

Romance is not a bad idea, though. It would make people stop thinking of me as a "child star" and place me firmly in the world of adults, once and for all. (I'm imagining cover stories in *Elle, Cosmo, Entertainment Weekly* – "Juliet Jansen, All Grown Up!" But I'm getting ahead of myself.) I've looked around at the other guys on the show, but there's not a lot to choose from. I don't want anyone who's already involved or married – certainly not anyone who's gay *and* married – and no one who's over thirty-five. Basically, my only choices are Riley and Trent, and they're kind of nerdy. In this business, who you choose to date is a kind of currency, and the exchange rate for fashion-challenged computer geeks (even successful ones) is not very high.

When I was talking to Cassie the other day, I was getting a definite vibe from her; that might be an interesting direction to go in. It's a little bit of a risk; it's edgy, and I might not get offered any family shows for a while. But if I play it right, it could be very intriguing. I wouldn't go so far as to kiss her – not that I couldn't; I'm sure I could. I almost got cast for this Lifetime movie once about a teenage lesbian whose parents kick her out of the house; she ends up moving in with a kindly teacher, but then of course the teacher gets fired because everyone thinks they're doing it. I didn't get the part, but I spent enough time getting into the mind-set that I know I could pull it off. Still, a kiss might be a little much; you don't want to start alienating people. But a little friendly girl-on-girl flirtation? Who doesn't like that?

*   *   *

Up ahead, I can hear Carl and Jeff talking to a ticket agent. Jeff says, "So how many seats are left on this flight after we buy our tickets?"

The woman says, "Only eight."

Dallas and I look at each other. Each team has to buy tickets for their sound and camera crew, so there's really only room for two more teams. We're going to make it, but not everyone is. I see Cassie and her mom running through the airport; they've just gotten here. "Cassie," I call out. "Over here."

Dallas leans over. "What are you doing?" he says in my ear.

"I think this could be a good team to join up with."

"No way," he says. "How about Riley and Trent? They're smart, and they're not in bad shape."

"I think these two could be an asset. Just trust me on this."

He looks doubtful, but he's learned by now that it's best not to get in my way. Cassie and Laura are heading toward us, lugging their stuff. I hear Riley and Trent yelling at us from farther back, but I just ignore them and sweep Cassie and Laura in line with us. I lean close and rest my hand on Cassie's shoulder. "Come with us," I say. "There are only four more tickets."

"I don't think so, Juliet," Laura says. "This isn't really fair."

I shrug, but I keep my hand on Cassie. She looks at me, then at the teams behind us in line.

"Come on, Mom," she says. "Did you come here to win the game or to make friends?"

I smile and stretch, languorous as a cat. "Whatever. I just thought it might be fun to team up. Get you guys out of last place."

"I think we should do it," Cassie says. "I don't want to go home yet. Do you?"

Cassie looks at her mom in this little-kid-please-can-we-have-ice-cream way, and that seems to do it. Whatever "moral mom/evil cheater" switch Laura has in her brain, Cassie just flipped it.

"Okay, let's do it," she says.

"Great," I say. My voice is like sugar. I give Cassie the lightest of hugs. "This is going to be fun."

TEN

Carl

There's a lot more downtime to a game like this than you might imagine. All that time in the airport and on planes and trains, where we're all just kind of hanging out. Not to mention getting through security with all our junk. We have to check some of it – the airlines don't seem to welcome passengers brandishing ski poles – but the parrots are equipped with cages that actually fit under the seats, so for short flights within a single country, they come on board with us. Every airport, we have to produce a health certificate stating that Polly isn't carrying any diseases, and then we have to take the parrot out and hold it – this is nobody's favorite moment, least of all the bird's – while the airport officials search the cage for explosive perches and radioactive birdseed.

On the way to Tokyo, we end up sitting toward the back of the plane, right near Laura and Cassie; Juliet and Dallas are someplace else, up near the front. Guess that means they'll have the lead in being the first ones off the plane, but it doesn't worry me too much. They're not the sharpest Ginsus in the drawer.

Jeff and Laura have struck up a conversation. I think he's kind of flirting with her, which is always a treat. Jeff tends to come on a little strong with women; he tries a bit too hard to be funny, and it usually doesn't go well.

"So do you have any kids?" Laura asks him.

"Nope," he says, a little too jovially. "I'm lucky if I remember to feed my dog." He slaps his head. "*That's* what I meant to do before I went away."

Laura smiles politely. It's true, Jeff's never wanted kids; in fact, that was part of the reason he and Michelle got divorced. He's great with Benjamin, the best, goofiest kind of uncle. He's the guy who'll get down on the floor and make ear-splitting elephant noises until Benjamin feeds him peanuts made of Play-Doh. I don't have that kind of energy. But he says he doesn't want any of his own. That's one of the few things I don't understand about him. Having a kid . . . it unlocks something inside you, like one of those dreams where you find a secret room in your house that you never knew was there. It's not that parenthood is all good; a lot of it's really hard, and some of it's just kind of boring – can someone please explain to me, what is the appeal of those goddamned Berenstain bears? – but it's just more than you ever knew there was. In the months after Benjamin was born, I felt like I was finding out there was a whole new set of colors I'd never seen before. Why wouldn't you want that?

"What kind of dog do you have?" Laura asks.

I know what's coming before he even says it. "Well, she's a cross between a Labrador retriever and . . . another Labrador retriever."

Laura smiles. She's nice to listen to his ramblings. Plus, she's kind of a captive audience.

"You know who I've always felt bad for," Jeff says, "is presidential speechwriters."

Laura looks a little bewildered. "Why?"

"Well, they don't get any credit. They write these great lines, but the president gets all the credit. 'Ask not what your country can do for you' – one of the most famous quotes ever, but JFK didn't actually write it. It was written by a guy called Theodore Sorenson."

"Really?" Laura says. She's managing to look interested.

"And JFK gets all this credit for something he didn't even come up with. I mean, I'm sure he meant it when he said it, but it's like buying a greeting card; even if you agree with the sentiment, it doesn't mean you wrote the poem."

I decide to intervene. I know that if I don't, Jeff will use this last bit as a springboard for a whole greeting card routine; he's recently been trying out some material about a line of cards for reality show contestants. He's got actual poems.

"So, Laura, what do you do?" I ask. "When you're not being televised."

"I'm an office administrator," she says. "At an elementary school."

"Is that interesting work?" What a lame question.

"Well, sort of. But I like being around the kids. It's the same school Cassie went to. I originally took the job so I could be close to her during the day. "

"Keep an eye on her," I say.

"Yeah." She sounds wistful. "Maybe just catch a glimpse of her on her way to the lunchroom."

I look at Cassie; she has her headphones on, doing that adolescent tuning-out thing. I have a lot of sympathy for teenagers. It's not an easy time, at least not for most people. Sometimes I hear parents of little kids, kids Benjamin's age, talking about how they're already dreading the teenage years, but I don't see it that way. It's all part of the deal; you sign up for the whole package when you have a kid. Your job is to adjust to them along the way, to give them what they need at every stage. Sometimes when I'm at the playground with Benjamin, I look around at all those kids, and I think about what's going to happen to them. I mean, yeah, one of them could grow up to be president, or an astronaut, or the person who cures cancer. But mostly, they're going to be like us. Those of them – this is the effect of my newfound parental morbidity, the worry I can never entirely extinguish – those of them who have the chance to grow up at all, they're going to have broken hearts and jobs they sometimes hate, they're going to have happy days and sad days and days where nothing happens at all. They're going to have *lives*. And we've got to prepare them to live those lives and be as happy as they can.

"You have a son, right?" Laura asks.

"Yup. Three years old." I undo my seat belt, reach into my pocket for my wallet.

"Oh, he's gorgeous," Laura says. She looks at the picture for exactly the right amount of time before handing it back to me. "You must miss him."

"Every minute." I look at the picture for a minute before putting it away, try to soak it up to keep it inside me, the big eyes, the curly hair, the smile. He has a fire engine on his shirt. "But, you know, he's the one I'm doing this for. Money for his future, his education, all that. Plus he'll get to see his dad on TV. He'll get a kick out of that."

This is all true, but if I'm being honest, I feel a little guilty about being away from him for so long. A month is an eternity to a three-year-old. And of course, there's always risk involved in doing something like this. There was a moment when I was signing the waiver for the show — it was this scary document that relieves the producers of responsibility in the case of everything from dismemberment to terrorism to dysentery — where I thought, what the hell am I doing? I've got a kid; I can't be putting myself in danger. But in the end, I decided it was worth the risk. A half million bucks would make a world of difference to us. And I want to teach Benjamin that adventure isn't just something in movies. I want to show him that adventure can be a part of life.

"Three's a great age," says Laura. "They're just figuring things out, exploring the world. I miss that age."

"Yeah, we have a lot of fun." I look at Cassie over in her seat, practically a grown-up. "Well, just think: it may not be too many years before you have yourself some grandchildren. I've heard they're a lot easier."

I can tell right away that I've said something wrong. Laura looks stunned; she sinks back in her seat like I've hit her. God, what a stupid thing to say — Laura's probably my age, early forties. She's certainly not ready to put on a shawl and start knitting doilies. And Cassie's only eighteen; I'm sure Laura hopes it'll be a good long while before she starts having kids of her own.

"I'm sorry," I say, but it sounds kind of hollow, and I'm not sure what else to say.

This time, Jeff jumps in to save me. "You'll have to excuse my brother," he says. "He almost never talks to women. You're like the second one this year."

Laura smiles weakly. "It's okay, really."

"It's true," says Jeff. "There's a researcher at the University of Idaho who's determined that Carl's more likely to be run over by a garbage truck than get a woman's phone number. He wants to write a book about it."

Laura looks at me, and this time her smile is genuine. "Is he always this mean to you?" she asks.

"What can I say?" We look at each other for a long moment, and I try to send out rays of kindness, of apology. "You can't argue with science."

In the Tokyo airport, just like in every airport we've been in, the teams scatter, and it's a hurried dash through the terminal toward baggage claim, then a rush to figure out the best route to get where we're going. I was worried about the fact that we don't even know the alphabet here, but there are a surprising number of signs in English. As soon as we get off the plane, we're confronted with the word *Starbucks* written in giant letters, which prompts Jeff to start humming "The Star-Spangled Banner" under his breath until I hit him in the arm.

We stop at an information kiosk, where a very nice woman, who speaks better English than half the Americans I know, advises us to take the train to Kinugawa, just outside Nikko; from there, we can get buses to the theme parks.

The trains are modern and spacious, and very organized. I read in the guidebook that during rush hour, they hire these guys with white gloves to push people into the crowded cars. (Jeff, of course, finds this hilarious: "Do you think these people were always interested in the field of butt-pushing? Did their guidance counselors recommend butt-pushing as a promising career path?") But now it's early afternoon, and we don't have any trouble getting on, lugging all our junk. We don't get that many strange looks, even with Jeff wearing the aviator helmet; either everyone's too polite, or they're used to odd fashion trends. I'm leaning toward the latter; among the other passengers on the train, I see a couple of grown women in schoolgirl dresses, a group of teenagers dressed like surfer chicks with bleached blond hair, and a guy wearing a T-shirt that says "Let me be your sugar dentist."

The camera draws some attention, though, and a few of the other passengers come over to try out their English skills on us. Jeff spends a while chatting up a young woman with platform boots and hair dyed reddish-brown, but she doesn't seem to get any of his jokes. I just sit back and relax. There's nice scenery out the windows, and I'm eating a box lunch we got on the train platform. There are all these little compartments with different tidbits in them: a single dumpling, a few pieces of sushi, a carrot cut into the shape of a flower. It's almost too pretty to eat. At one point, someone comes through the train car with a little cart, selling sake, and I practically have to hold Jeff down to keep him from buying one. I mean, come on, we're playing a game here. We need our wits about us.

In Kinugawa, Jeff gets on a bus to go to Western Village, and I head off to Tobu World Square. Our camera guy goes with Jeff; I'll meet up with another cameraman at the park. As I sit on the bus, I realize this is the first time I've been completely alone in almost three weeks. No cameras, no other teams, no Jeff. It's exhilarating to realize – how pathetic is this?– that if I wanted to, I could scratch my butt without worrying about all of America seeing me do it. (I probably won't give it a try, though, given the disgusted looks I get from the other passengers after I blow my nose. Do they not get colds in this country?) I'm enjoying the freedom, but when we pull up to the park and I see Barbara getting into her little booth at the entrance – she's dressed in "TV Hostess Casual" today, wearing tight jeans and what appears to be a leather halter top – I wish Jeff were here to make one of his smart-ass comments. I can't believe it, but I miss the jerk already.

ELEVEN

Abby

Standing in front of a miniature model of the Taj Mahal, I feel a little balloon of lightness rise in my chest, and I have to admit that I'm happy to have a break from Justin. He's an intense man, to say the least, and if I don't get some time on my own now and then, I start to feel like my edges are blurring, like I'm made of a much softer substance than he is, and his very presence leaves an impression. Not to mention that he was starting to get on my nerves, the way he spends every flight memorizing foreign phrases from our guidebook, the way he puts his arm around me whenever he remembers the cameras are there. Really, no married couple should be together twenty-four hours a day. This is why people fight when they're on vacation.

I've been wandering around Tobu World Square for about a half hour now, backpack on my back, parrot cage in hand, trailed by a cameraman named Stu and a local sound technician named Hiro – Ken and Stefan went to Western Village with Justin – looking for American icons. I love it here. I've got the whole world spread out before me in 1/25 scale. Here I am in New York, standing almost as tall as the Flatiron Building; I take a short walk, and here are the pyramids, here's Versailles, here's the Great Wall of China. It's like being in a trompe l'oeil painting; the perspective is all wrong. I walk past the Eiffel Tower, turn a corner, and I'm face-to-face with the

Temple of Abu Simbel, for the second time in three days. But this time I tower over all four Ramses.

The park was designed by the same company who did the sets for the original Godzilla movies, and they've taken great care with each scene, adding bonsai trees and crowds of tiny people. They've got hot dog vendors in Central Park and tourists eating ice cream on the steps of the Parthenon. There are miniature bank robbers and miniature traffic accidents. I don't know what Justin has been seeing at the cowboy park, but I'm willing to bet I got the better end of the deal.

My cell phone rings, and I give myself a minute before I answer it. "It's me," Justin says. I do like the intimacy of that, having someone in my life who can say "it's me," and I don't even have to think about who it is.

"How's the Wild West?" I ask.

"Corny as all get out," he says. That's such a Justin-ism, "as all get out." My impulse would be to say "corny as hell," but of course Justin would never say that. Hell is not an abstraction to Justin; it's a place he's hoping to avoid by the very narrowest of margins.

"Really?" I ask.

"Yeah, definitely," he says. "It's just bizarre. There's a huge Mount Rushmore with a gift shop inside, and all these Japanese guys walking around dressed like cowboys. I just saw a shoot-out at a saloon, with bad guys and a sheriff, and a horse who kept sticking his nose into people's shopping bags. And of course, the whole thing's in Japanese."

"Wow."

"So . . . what are we trying to do here?" he asks. "We try to find some American icon that appears in both theme parks, and that'll be the keyword?"

"I guess," I say. "It's a little confusing."

"Well, what've you got on your icon list?" he asks.

"Let's see . . . there's the Statue of Liberty, the Empire State Building, the Chrysler Building, the White House. Have you seen any of those?"

"Nope. I've got cowboys, obviously, and Mount Rushmore . . ."

"Which I guess contains four American icons."

"Right. Plus I've seen a stagecoach, a steam engine, a picture of Jesse James, and some robots that are supposed to be Marilyn Monroe, John Wayne, and Abe Lincoln."

"Which, I would hope, includes his nose?"

"Oh, we've got three different copies of Lincoln's nose here. One on the robot, one on Mount Rushmore, and a huge, full-scale version in the gift shop."

"Full-scale? Lincoln's nose wasn't *that* big, was it?"

"No, it's full-scale to the nose on Mount Rushmore. It goes from the floor to the ceiling. You can actually go inside it."

"Well, that's just wrong. No one should be able to go inside Lincoln's nose." I add Justin's items to my list. "Well, let me take another look around, and see if I can find any of those. They've got all these miniature people at all the exhibits; I should probably take a closer look at them. Maybe Teddy Roosevelt is hidden among them or something."

"Okay," he says. "I'll keep looking, too. Call me if you find anything. Sweetie." He always adds the pet names at the last possible moment. (But he uses them, right? That's what's important.)

We hang up, and I head back to the America Zone section of the park. Standing next to New York Harbor, I see a young Italian couple who were on the bus from Kinugawa with me. They were kissing then, and they're kissing now, their bodies coiled tight, wrapped around each other against the vista of boats and skyscrapers, with the World Trade Center rising behind them, untouched and pristine. The Japanese visitors are studiously ignoring them; I don't think public displays of affection are very welcome here. But I can't help watching them for just a minute. There's such relish in the way they hold each other, such pleasure. I can't imagine a moment like this in my own life, a moment when Justin and I feel such urgency for each other that we have to press our bodies together immediately, touch every surface we can, not caring who might see.

Maybe I'm just not that kind of person. The first time Justin and I even held hands in public, it was a struggle for me. What does it mean, I thought, for me to walk down the street holding a man's hand? I remember once, during the first week of my first relationship with a woman, she and I were walking down a quiet street, and she slid her hand into mine. For the space of one block, we walked like that, one exhilarating, frightening block. And then we heard a small noise from someone's yard, and we jumped apart like we'd burned each other.

Walking with Justin years later, I thought about that, and I wasn't sure whether I was ready to cross so completely to the other side. I know how it looks. I have been young and desperate, and I have seen men and women walking together, looking as if the whole world was theirs. As if they held all the secrets of the universe inside their clasped hands. And I have felt so sad. I wouldn't want anyone else to feel that way, not on account of me. Still, there I was, with this man I was committing myself to, falling slowly toward love or something not too far from it; wasn't I allowed to show it? Would there never be a time when I could take a person's hand without worrying about how it looked? For other people, it's a simple thing, the linking together of two bodies, the public performance of tenderness. But for me, it will always be a complicated act.

Here is the strange fact of my life as I have come to live it: I feel, at every moment, two completely different kinds of shame. Shame for being the woman I was, and shame for leaving her behind. It's with me always; it inhabits every bit of me. I've lived so long with it curved inside me, pressing against the walls of my body, that I have no idea what shape I would be without it. For a while, before I joined Redemption, I thought that if I could just dig deep enough to find out where all that shame originated, maybe I could pluck it right out. But I don't think it would come out so cleanly. That hard little kernel of mortification and self-hatred – does it really matter where it came from?– has had too much time to germinate. It's sent out its sheer little tendrils and filaments until they cover every surface. If I started pulling at it, I'm afraid it might gut me completely.

The funny thing is, it hasn't been easy to get to this point in my life. I've worked hard at it. The Redemption program is tough. You have to cut yourself off from all your old friends, like a prisoner on parole; you have to sit through prayer meetings and support groups and "gender retraining" cosmetic lessons. You have to learn to censor your thoughts and to angle your desire. It's like teaching a plant to respond to the moon instead of the sun. And this is where it's brought me. I've crawled across deserts to get where I am; I've swum lakes of fire and scaled mountains of ice, all so I can pick up the phone and hear a man's voice say, "It's me."

Members of other teams are starting to filter in — I see Trent over by the miniature White House, and Cassie's kneeling by the Empire State Building. (I feel a twinge when I see her, a new little fiber of shame snaking through me, when I remember the thoughts I had about her in the Cairo nightclub. She's practically a child, and I . . . well, I have no right to be thinking about anyone other than my husband.) In any case, now that other contestants are arriving, it looks like our head start is over; Justin's big macho performance in the sand hasn't amounted to much. The kissing couple are still going at it, and my mood has reached a very dark place. I walk around examining the exhibits, crouching down to look at all the details. Cameraman Stu crouches with me; he's top-heavy with his camera, and I imagine for a moment that if I were to push him gently, he might simply roll backward and lie on the ground, stranded on his back like a beetle. I'm no longer charmed by the tiny people in the exhibits, the happy little bodies throwing Frisbees and waiting for trains. Their lives look absurdly simple. Until such time as I can shrink down and join them in their happy little landscape, I want no part of it.

So it is that when I find what I've been looking for, when I peer into the window of the miniature Hanover Trust Building and I see Marilyn Monroe standing there, her skirt flying up around her, I don't even care. For one dangerous moment, I want to leave everything: Justin, the TV show, the Italian couple with their tongues down each other's throats. For one dangerous moment, I wonder if I might be happier someplace else.

I close my eyes. This has happened before, and I know what to do. I stand very still until the feeling passes, breathing deeply and trying to clear my mind. I dial my cell phone and wait to hear my husband's voice; I tell him I've found the answer we're looking for. I walk back through the world and all its treasures, back to the entrance of the park, to whisper the name of a movie star to a woman in a glass booth. And every step I take makes me more relieved to be staying where I am.

I have heard that if you look at the remains of a woman born in an earlier era, back when bodies were hidden and fine ladies couldn't take their clothes off by themselves, you'll see that her bones have bent themselves to the shape of her corset. You'll see that after all those years of stricture and compression, the constant embrace of whalebone and satin and steel, her body has changed its very form. It's barbaric, we think now; we live in an age of looseness, and we can hardly imagine submitting to such constraint. I wonder, though, whether those women could have given up the corset if they'd wanted to. I wonder if, after a lifetime of being bound and held, it was something of a comfort to be laced in tight. Without it, their bodies must have felt wrong – the wobbly flesh, the ungainly freedom. I wonder if they missed the pressure when they loosed their stays at night. I wonder if they even knew how to breathe.

TWELVE

Laura

In the litany of family stories that I've heard through my life — the time my uncle started the car at the age of four, the moving day when my parents' dog walked five miles back to their old house — one story in particular won't leave me alone. Once, somewhere down the path of my lineage, there was a baby who drowned in a washtub while his mother was hanging out clothes. The mother was an aunt of my grandmother's, a figure wedged so deep in our family past that I don't even know her name. But I think about her sometimes; I imagine her standing in the sun in the moment before she has realized what has happened. The cold water on her hands, the smell of soap and wet cotton. The white sheets blowing in the breeze. It haunts me. "She was never the same after that," my grandmother would always say when she told the story. As if there could be any question at all.

My granddaughter, whatever her name is, is not lost to me in quite the same way. She has gone on living in this world, sleeping and sighing and kicking her chubby legs. The fact that I'm not there to fasten her diapers and kiss her toes is irrelevant in the big scheme of things. The important part is that somewhere out there, she lives.

The night she was born, after Cassie woke me and presented me with the head-spinning news of this child, I drove to the hospital very slowly. Cassie sat in the backseat, holding the baby. The trash can with the placenta in it was on the passenger-side floor; as it turned out, we would forget to bring it in to the ER, and I would find it waiting for me when I left the hospital many hours later. It would be weeks before the smell of blood and birth would be gone from the car.

It was the middle of the night, and we didn't see many other cars. There was a time, when I was young, when driving on roads this empty might have meant I was coming home from a party or a late-night tryst with a boyfriend, but for most of my adult life, the only time I see streets like this is when I'm on the way to the hospital. I have three memories of doing this. The worst involves freezing rain, a late-night phone call, and getting my sleepy, cranky girl out of bed, so that we could drive to the ER and sit in the waiting room while her father died on a table behind a curtain. Another one – not fun, but not nearly as bad – is from Cassie's ninth birthday; she had a slumber party and one of the girls became ill with what turned out to be appendicitis. I arranged to meet her parents at the hospital; I packed all six kids into the car, and while the sick girl sat in the backseat, vomiting bile into my spaghetti pot, the other five chirped away like little parakeets, thrilled to be traveling through the world at that time of night.

The third memory, which is really the first, is of the night Cassie was born. It was a clear, frigid night, and Jim – still on this earth for another thirteen months – was so keyed up he nearly drove into a parked car. My water had broken, and my contractions were starting to get strong, but there was a sense of jubilation that passed between the two of us that's unequaled in any of my other memories of our marriage. It was, I think, our happiest hour. It felt momentous: *this is a night that will change our lives forever.* Before dawn broke, I would bleed and sweat and throb and roar. And then, in an instant that felt strangely sudden, there would be a *whoosh,* and the pain would stop, and my slippery little girl would open her eyes to the light.

But on *this* night, with *this* baby, it was a different sort of ride. There was no rush; the drama of this baby's birth had already taken place, humbly, in an attic room, on a pile of terry cloth. She was fussing a little when we got in the car, but I suggested Cassie put a finger in her mouth, and that, combined with the motion of the ride, seemed to settle her. For a while, we were all quiet.

I've learned with Cassie that you have to be careful about the questions you ask. We've been playing good cop/sullen cop for long enough that I know that when she feels attacked, she just closes herself up completely. And I suppose it occurred to me that when a woman has just given birth, no matter what the circumstances, she deserves a little courtesy; at the very least, you shouldn't pull the car over, grab her by the shoulders, and scream, "What the hell were you thinking?" which is what I felt like doing. So I did some careful sifting of the questions that were jumping around in my brain. I rejected "How could you do this?" and "Did I not teach you about birth control?" and "You're lucky that baby's alive." Instead, I asked, "How's she doing back there?"

"She's okay," Cassie said. I looked at her in the rearview mirror. She was looking down at the baby. I couldn't read her face.

"What do you think of her?" I asked.

She was quiet for a minute. She turned her face to the window and looked out at the murky landscape. Then she leaned back against the seat and closed her eyes, the baby slumped against her chest. "Her head's kind of pointy," she said finally.

A little puff of laughter escaped my lungs. I don't know what kind of pronouncement I was expecting her to make, but that wasn't it. "That's normal," I said. "It'll go away in a couple of days."

We were almost at the hospital. I wanted to say *something* before we got there. "I'm having a little trouble with this," I said.

Cassie yawned. "I'm sure you are," she said.

"You could have told me," I said. I tried not to sound critical.

The baby started to cry again, and Cassie lifted her up to her shoulder. For some reason, that gesture affected me strongly; *she's a mother,* I thought, and felt something in me contract.

Cassie looked down at the top of the baby's head. When she spoke, her voice was careful and even.

"You could have noticed," she said.

*   *   *

Back here in TV-land, I've spent about an hour and a half wandering around Western Village, having curt phone conversations with Cassie and trying to dodge Japanese cowboys who I feel certain are calling me some equivalent of "little lady," before I realize that the blowsy blond robot in the saloon is supposed to be Marilyn Monroe. (Why is Marilyn Monroe present in a re-creation of the Old West? I have no idea. I guess maybe she did a few westerns during her career. Or maybe it's just that the creators of the park couldn't imagine an America *without* Marilyn Monroe.) I don't think our slowness has cost us too much; I know Justin from the ex-gay team has already left, but I still see Jeff-the-goofy-brother, Riley-the-inventor, and Jason-the-erstwhile-high-school-sweetheart. Neither of the child stars is anywhere in sight.

So Cassie goes to talk to Barbara in her booth, with me present via cell phone – cameraman Dave suggests that I pose with the phone to my ear in front of Mount Rushmore, so he can get some inspiring reaction shots – and I hear Barbara's voice coming through, loud and brittle.

"Laura and Cassie," she says, and I have to hold the handset away from my ear. "I have some news that may surprise you both. The two of you will not be reuniting for the Found Objects Round. For this portion of the game, it's every contestant for himself." She pauses dramatically, then adds, "Or herself" in a way that I guess is supposed to sound meaningful, but doesn't really add anything at all.

She seems to be waiting for a reaction. "Wow," I say. It is a little bit strange for them to be messing with the rules of the game this way – and who knows why they want us to end up with two found objects – but it doesn't seem like too much of a shock. Reality shows thrive on twists and surprises, and this seems like a fairly mild one. I worry about Cassie, though, having to do this on her own.

Barbara goes on. "If the two of you should happen to run into each other on the way, you may not talk or communicate in any way. Cassie, here's your clue for the next round; Laura, if you'll look to your left, you'll see President Lincoln approaching you with yours."

I look, and there he is — an extremely short Abe Lincoln with Asian features and a surprisingly bushy beard. He bows to me gravely and hands me two envelopes: one silver, one gold.

"You'll need to return your phones now," Barbara says. "Cassie, I'll take yours; Laura, please hand your cell phone to our sixteenth president." I hear Cassie let out a laugh on the other end, and for a minute I really miss her. I realize that this is what I have to look forward to: a lifetime of listening to her voice on the other end of the line.

"Good luck," Barbara says. "And one more thing — you'll want to get to the Meeting Point as quickly as you can. If you don't . . . the consequences may be dire." How dire could they be? Besides sending us home, what can they do to us? I'm assuming they don't have FCC clearance to cut off our limbs or anything.

I switch off my phone and hand it to the ersatz Lincoln. He bows again and heads off, presumably to a busy schedule of translating the Gettysburg address and getting shot by the Japanese version of John Wilkes Booth.

I open the silver envelope.

> *Head to Tokyo's Kitchen Town,*
> *Walk through the streets and prowl*
> *For sushi that you can't gulp down,*
> *Fish that won't turn foul.*

Underneath, in italics, it says, *"Your assignment is: futomaki roll."*

I gather my stuff — somehow when Cassie and I divided our Found Objects, I wound up with most of the bulky ones, although luckily she got the parrot — and head toward the exit of the park with my camera crew in tow. Cassie ended up with the guidebook, so I guess I'll get a train back to Tokyo and try to figure out on the way what "kitchen town" refers to. I hope Cassie can do this. She's eighteen, but she's kind of a young eighteen. She's a little bit sheltered, which is probably my fault. So much of parenting is haphazard, and you can only hope that when the smoke clears you haven't done too bad a job. So far I'm not exactly batting a thousand.

I get a bus back to Kinugawa, and there's Cassie at the train station. I smile at her, but she turns away. Right — no communication of any kind. Maybe that's the reason Cassie's been practicing this skill for the last year: she knew it might come in handy if we were ever on a reality show.

I go up to the ticket window and question the agent as well as I can about the best way to get to Tokyo. The Japanese train system is really confusing; Cassie and I changed trains twice on the way here, and I'm sure there must be a better way to get back. The man behind the counter takes out a map and shows me several different routes, but he doesn't speak English, so it's all pantomime. He points to a few different stations in Tokyo, but I don't really know which one I need to go to.

"Kitchen town?" I ask, but he shakes his head. Finally, I settle on a route that looks pretty straightforward and buy a ticket; I figure I'll try to ask someone on the train where I should get off.

Cassie and I both go to the same platform, so I figure we must be on the same page. There aren't too many other people waiting, but as usual, we cause a stir with our TV cameras and our outrageous gear. A couple of kids come and stand behind me to wave at the camera. Finally, Dave puts the camera down; all I'm doing is sitting there anyway.

After a while, first Carl, then Jeff arrive from the theme parks. No matter how much of a lead you think you have in this game, the travel schedules always bunch everyone up. Carl and Jeff make quite a show of ignoring each other, so much so that I think it actually crosses over into a form of communication. Finally, Carl comes over with his parrot and sits next to me on my bench. Dave's filming me again by this point; Carl's been teamed up with Brendan, but he puts his camera down once he sees Dave is getting it. My sound guy, Dennis, hovers with a boom mic. Several benches down, I see Jeff approach Cassie, but she's talking to a young Japanese guy, and he moves on to another bench. It's nice to see Cassie reaching out to someone. I can't tell from here if she's flirting, but I hope she is.

"So what's with the divide-and-conquer, do you think?" Carl asks me.

"I have no idea. Do you know what 'kitchen town' is?"

"I assume it's an area of Tokyo where the citizens are terrorized by giant egg beaters."

"Right," I say. "Or maybe everybody there lives in big refrigerated houses, and the cars all have rolling pins instead of wheels." That's really stupid. I'm not good at this. For so long, my weight was an easy excuse for not flirting with anyone; now it's suddenly clear I'm just inept.

"We could make some inquiries together," Carl says.

"I don't know," I say. "I understand that for this portion of the game, it's"— I do my best to imitate Barbara's clipped tones —"every contestant for himself."

"Or herself," Carl adds. His Barbara is better. "No really, I think I'm starting to get the hang of this Japanese stuff." He turns to the two kids who have come back to stand behind us. They're maybe seven and eight. "*Donde esta* kitchen town?" Carl asks. The boys smile and shrug.

"You want to be on TV?" he asks. They look blank. "Well, if you want to be on TV, then you have to make a face like this." He sticks out his tongue and rolls his eyes back in his head. The boys dissolve into laughter. Carl points to the camera and gestures to the boys to do what he's doing. Somehow he gets his point across, and the three of them stand there, making grotesque faces, until we hear the train and the boys' mother calls them back. Brendan runs after them; he needs to get the mom's signature for the boys to appear on camera.

The train is sleek and modern looking. I drag my stuff on, nearly impaling the woman in front of me with my ski pole. It's crowded, and there don't seem to be two seats together, so Carl and I split up. It's not until I've shoved the ski pole and helmet in the overhead rack and stuffed my backpack under my seat that I look around for Cassie. I don't see her, but I figure maybe she's on another car.

Then, as the doors close and the train begins to pull away, I look out the window and see Cassie standing on the platform. Her camera guy, Austin, has pulled back for a long shot. Cassie searches for me in the windows, finally catches my eye. She holds up the parrot and smiles. And then she's gone.

THIRTEEN

Cassie

I couldn't resist seeing the look on my mom's face when she realized I wasn't going with her. Pure shock; her mouth even dropped open a little bit. She probably thinks I'm running away or something, like I'm going to just disappear into the Japanese landscape with the cameraman and the parrot. She doesn't trust me for a minute; she doesn't believe I'm capable of finding my way around in a foreign country, or reading a map, or following a stupid clue written by a bunch of production assistants. She certainly doesn't believe I'm capable of finding someone who speaks English and figuring out that she and the Loser Brothers are all on the wrong train.

Okay, it's not the *wrong* train, exactly; it'll still get them to Tokyo. Eventually. But after consulting my handy guidebook and asking a few questions, I've figured out that if I wait another ten minutes, I can get a direct train to Asakusa, which is the closest station to the famous "kitchen town," while the three of them will all have to transfer. I'll get there a full half hour sooner than they will. It's pathetic how proud this makes me.

Kitchen town, it turns out, is the nickname of Kappabashi, which is the restaurant supply section of Tokyo. The guy I was talking to said that they sell all kinds of fake food – fake noodles, fake dumplings, and (drum roll) fake *sushi* – which restaurants use to show people what kind of food they serve. My assignment is *tako*, which I'm still not entirely clear on – I'm not a big sushi person – but I think it might have something to do with an octopus; when I showed the clue to the guy I was talking to, he started waving his arms around wildly and saying, "Eight, eight."

I manage to get on the right train, with parrot, backpack, and cameraman, before any other teams show up. I haven't seen Juliet and Dallas since the airplane; I wonder if they're really ahead or really behind. My money's on behind. I look out the window and yawn. It's been a long day; the hot sand bath this morning in Beppu seems like a million years ago. The camera guy, Austin, is sitting across the aisle from me, next to the sound guy, Randy, who's dozing. Austin's turned his camera off, and he's reading a sci-fi novel; I lean over and tap his arm.

"If I fall asleep, would you wake me up when we get to Asakusa?" I ask.

He smiles and shakes his head. "If you fell asleep and missed your stop, it would be the most exciting shot I've gotten all day," he says. "No offense."

"That's okay. I wouldn't want to follow me around all day, either."

Austin laughs and goes back to his book. The tech guys are polite, but they don't really want to interact too much. After a few minutes, a woman with a little cart comes through the train, selling all kinds of weird-looking drinks and snacks. When she stops near me, I see that there's a kind of drink called Pocari Sweat – it says it in English right on the can – and I have to try it. After some fumbling with the money, she gives me the drink and I open it. I take a sip and spit it back immediately; it's disgusting, thick and kind of salty-sweet. The can is hilarious, though; if my backpack weren't already totally packed, I'd take it home with me.

My ex-boyfriend Dan, buyer of shoddy condoms, likes to collect strange food products. One of his cousins went to Hawaii and brought him back some chocolate-covered cuttlefish, and he has a can of something called "President Oat" that he found at an Asian market. I'd kind of like to send this to him; he's a nice guy, and I feel bad about the way things worked out. I don't think I treated him particularly well. The last time I saw him was right after the baby was born – I needed his consent for the adoption papers, so I had to tell him what had happened. It was a bad scene. My mom was there, and his parents, too, and everyone was pretty much in a state of shock, as you might imagine. He ended up signing, but from the moment he put the pen to the paper, he wouldn't look at me, and he wouldn't say a word. *I'm sorry,* I wanted to say, but what good would that have done? And anyway, there were too many things going on inside of me: partly I felt like apologizing, but partly I felt like screaming and crying and telling everyone that this wasn't easy on me, either. And part of me just wanted everyone to stop speaking in hushed tones and acting like I'd done something unforgivable. So somehow "I'm sorry" never made its way to my lips.

The truth is, I only really started going out with Dan because Mia was dating Reece, and the two of them were friends. I figured we could all hang out together. Plus, I was flattered that he liked me; there haven't been that many guys who have been interested in me. I've always been kind of heavy – I mean, I don't think a lot of skinny girls get pregnant without anybody noticing – but I'm not dumpy the way my mom was when she was fat. On days when I'm actually feeling okay about myself, I think I fall more on the side of sexy fat – curvy, voluptuous. Rubenesque. I know all the words.

Still, you don't find a lot of teenage boys who are looking for Rubenesque, so the attention was kind of nice. And I didn't hate the physical stuff. It was kind of exciting to see the effect I could have on him – with guys, it's just all right out there, isn't it? And given what I've heard about most teenage boys, he was really pretty good about making sure I was enjoying myself. I think he'd probably read some books or something.

I liked Dan. But, you know. Obviously. He wasn't Mia.

Even knowing how things worked out with Mia, or didn't, it still gives me a little thrill inside to think about the time when I had those feelings, and it didn't seem impossible, and nobody knew about it but me. For so long, it was just my secret. It burned inside me, and I felt like I was carrying something important, something that made me who I was and made me different from everybody else. I took it with me everywhere, and there was never a moment when I wasn't aware of it. It was like I was totally *awake*, like I could feel every nerve ending in my body. Sometimes my skin would almost hurt from the force of it, that's how strong it was. Like my whole body was buzzing or something. I felt almost, I don't know, *noble*, like a medieval knight or something, carrying this secret love around with me. I'd walk through the halls at school, and I'd think, this is it. This is what it means to be young and alive. These days that are just filled with yearning . . . I don't think adults have that very much.

At the same time, though, it was kind of hellish, spending so much time with Mia without being able to tell her what was going on. I used to imagine that she and I were in a play together, and for some reason I had to play a boy, so that we'd have to kiss. I used to imagine that some lunatic came into the school and held a gun to my head and forced me to say how I felt about her in front of everyone. One night, she slept over at my house, and we were sitting there talking. It was late, and there was a quiet moment, and I said, "Tell me something about you that I don't know." I thought she'd say some little stupid thing and then ask me the same question, and I'd be able to tell her. But instead she told me about this time she was at the library, and this old guy started talking to her and tried to get her to go to his house to see some magazines he had there. It was such a creepy story that I couldn't exactly follow it up with a declaration of love, but it's not like I ever had the opportunity, because she never even asked.

When I look at Justin and Abby, part of me thinks they're total freaks, and I just want to roll my eyes and say, You're gay already, get over it. But the thing is, when I hear Justin going on and on about how homosexuality is wrong, or when I hear someone make a stupid gay joke, there's some little piece of me that feels a twinge. There's some little part of me, deep in some ragged place, that can't help but wonder if they're right. It's not like I think it's a terrible thing to be gay, or that I even know if that's what I am. But when I think about it, it's like I'm standing on the top of a skyscraper, right at the very edge, and it's just such a fucking long way down.

*　　*　　*

When the train gets to Asakusa, I get off with my little entourage of bird and camera crew, and push my way through the rush-hour crowds until I find an escalator.

The station turns out to be in the basement of a department store, which is a little disconcerting. Suddenly, I'm in the middle of a big food hall with lots of little stalls all over the place. Some of them have big bins of dried beans and spices; some are selling little cakes or dumplings or bottles of sake. I check out a display of sushi, but it appears to be the edible kind, so I wander up through the women's clothing section and finally make my way out to the hot rush of the street.

I stop a woman in a business suit and say "Kappabashi?" and she points me in the right direction. I love this, being here in a strange city, almost by myself. It makes me feel optimistic, like everything's opening up, and my life is just beginning. I could live here if I wanted to, someday; I could go anywhere I want.

Kappabashi isn't hard to find. It's not so much a district as it is a long street lined with restaurant supply shops; at the entrance to the street, there's a building with a huge chef's head on top of it, smiling benevolently into the distance. Across the street, there's another building where each balcony is shaped like a teacup. Oh, and there's a big sign that says, in English, KAPPABASHI–TOKYO'S ONLY KITCHENWARE AND RESTAURANT SUPPLY DISTRICT. So, yeah, I'm pretty sure I'm in the right place.

I walk down the street and look into the open storefronts. It's amazing how specific each shop is; there's one selling nothing but chopsticks, stacked in plastic bags, and another with nothing but paper lanterns. There are shops with tables and tables full of tiny soy-sauce dishes and others specializing in utensils, cash registers, order pads, chef's uniforms. Austin has me stop for a minute so he can get a shot of a giant stir-fry pan. And finally – ta-da! – I see a window displaying a bowl of fake noodle soup, with slices of pork floating in the broth and chopsticks hovering in midair, and I've found what I'm looking for.

We go inside the store. It's pretty breathtaking. Everywhere I look, there's amazingly realistic food, all of it made of wax and plastic. Some of it's Japanese food, but a lot of it isn't. There are bowls of fried rice and platters of grilled fish, steins of beer and pizzas and a giant red crab splayed across a plate. I'm suddenly incredibly hungry.

I walk up to the sushi display. There's a lot of it, all different kinds, but I don't really know what I'm looking for. As I'm standing there, I notice that I'm not the only American in the store; there's a young married couple walking around looking at the food, and the woman has a baby in one of those carriers on her chest. The baby's mostly hidden, but I can tell it's a girl because she's wearing pink socks, and I can see the top of her head, which is so fuzzy I want to reach out and touch it.

I pick up a piece of sushi with some little orange balls on top of it – some kind of caviar, I guess – but I'm not really looking at it. The baby starts to make some little noises, and her mother speaks to her in a voice that's almost like singing.

"What's wrong, sweet girl?" she says. "Do you want to look around?"

Her husband helps her to unhook the carrier, and she lifts the baby out into the air. The baby's wearing a little romper with purple flowers on it. She's so pretty I think I could cry. I almost can't look at her all at once.

I turn away and walk up to the man behind the counter. "Tako?" I say. I pronounce it like the Mexican snack; I don't know if that's right or not. I'm about to show him my clue, so he can read it himself, when I realize it's in a different alphabet. "Sushi," I say by way of clarification.

The man smiles and says, "Yes, yes." It's amazing how many people here speak English. He leads me back to the sushi display and picks up one of the pieces. It's a strip of rice with white "fish" on top of it. The white pieces have brown edges and what appear to be little round suckers. So, yeah. Octopus.

"Tako?" I ask again, just to make sure, and the man nods. He rings me up, and I pay what I think is about fifteen bucks. That's a pricey souvenir; it comes out of my show money, but I guess everyone will have to pay for one. It's pretty cool, though. I hope I get to keep it.

I open my gold envelope to find out the Meeting Point for this round:

Sensoji Temple
Tokyo

I turn around to leave. The couple with the baby are looking at the desserts. The father's holding the baby now; she's sitting up in the crook of his elbow, and he's naming all the treats for her. He shows her little cakes and fruit parfaits and golden tarts topped with strawberries. I force myself to look at the baby, force myself to smile at her parents. There are going to be babies in the world. I've got to get used to it. The mom sees me looking at the baby and smiles.

"How old is she?" I ask.

"Five months," they say, answering together.

I nod and keep my mouth shut. There's so much I could say, but really nothing. Nothing that would be okay.

"What are you filming?" the woman asks me. The baby looks at me with a stony, wide-eyed stare. She opens her mouth and tries to insert her entire fist. "Is it an American show?" the mother asks.

I don't want to talk to them anymore. "Yeah," I say. "It's a really stupid show." And that sense of possibility I felt walking down the street ten minutes ago is gone, because I can't go anyplace where this won't follow me, and I can't do anything to change the fact that somewhere out there, there's a baby who's no longer mine. Walking out of the store with my parrot and my sushi, I feel hideous, like everything I've done must be written on my skin. I walk through the streets of Tokyo with my cameraman behind me, knowing that anyone who looks at me will be able to see my shame, my sorrow, my regrets as ugly as scars.

FOURTEEN

Justin

This is merely an interlude, a wrong turn of the kind that we all make from time to time. Regrettable, certainly, but merely part of being human. We walk a precarious path – who among us can say he's never stumbled? Soon enough, the camera will be turned on, and I'll be back in my life, walking up the steps of a temple to take my beautiful wife in my arms. But for now, for one bare and feeble moment, I'm going to close my eyes and fall.

Ken is leading me through a network of alleys filled with neon. We pass noodle shops and pachinko parlors, yakitori stands and movie houses and stalls selling watches and tea. We pass a fugu restaurant with a tank of live blowfish at the entrance. I'm aware of the risk I'm taking. I'll be late buying my sushi, late getting to the Meeting Point, but I don't care. Abby and I are in the lead. I lay in burning sand for this; this time is my reward.

"Are we almost there?" I ask Ken.

"Almost," he says. We turn a corner. "This is Ni-Chome," he says. "There are supposedly more gay bars per block here than any-where else in the world."

"It's Sodom," I say, and for a moment I believe it.

Ken gives me a level stare. He shakes his head. "Too late for that," he says.

*   *   *

It began on the train, sitting with Ken, with his camera turned off and no other contestants in sight. Our sound guy Stefan wasn't with us; he'd gotten ill at the theme park, and we hadn't met up with his replacement yet. So it was just the two of us. In a moment I'm sure I'll return to in my more desperate hours, Ken opened up his camera bag to find a new battery pack, and what I saw inside there made my stomach drop. A magazine was tucked inside among the equipment; the lettering was in Japanese, but it was clear what kind of magazine it was. It was not unlike certain magazines I've held in my own hands, back in my weaker days. The man on the cover was young and lithe; his eyes were very dark. I felt a key turn in my gut.

I averted my gaze, but not quickly enough. Ken saw where I'd been looking; he laughed and said, "Well, that's indiscreet. Sorry about that."

I looked down at my hands. "It's none of my business," I said.

I'm sure my discomfort was apparent. Ken seemed to find it funny. "I guess you don't subscribe to that one," he said, smiling at me.

"I do not." I tried to keep my tone cool.

Ken pulled the magazine out of the bag and held it out to me. I didn't take it, but I let my parched eyes drink it in. "I bought it here in Japan," he said. "Obviously. I had a few others – I thought, you know, a little souvenir from each place they send us." He laughs. "But I ended up throwing them out before we got to Egypt. God knows what the penalty is for bringing that kind of stuff into a Muslim country."

His arm was touching mine. I looked out the window at the sky and the earth. All of God's fine work laid before me, and still it wasn't enough to divert me from the closeness of his body.

He leaned in toward me and opened up the magazine; he turned his body so that the other people on the train wouldn't see what we were looking at. It created an intimacy I didn't want, but I couldn't seem to say anything. The magazine was very thick. All those pages of pictures. Sin and vice and the bodies of men. Why did it feel like he was showing me treasure?

"It's kind of funny," he said. "They blur out the actual sex organs. But it's pretty clear what they're doing."

It was abundantly clear. Few things have ever been clearer to me. *Stop it*, I thought. I closed my eyes for a long moment and tried to quiet my roiling mind.

"So aren't you going to say anything?" asked Ken. I could feel his breath on my cheek. "Try to save my soul?"

"Maybe another time," I said. I was having trouble speaking. His arm — did I say it? — was touching mine. From shoulder to elbow, I could feel him against me.

"I thought you were on a mission," he said. "Stamp out sin? Spread the Word?"

I looked him in the eyes, and immediately wished I hadn't. A rope of desire snaked through my body. "Even missionaries get tired," I said.

Ken laid the magazine in my lap. "Well, you should at least confiscate this," he said. "For my own good."

I looked down at the profane object. The man on the cover looked up at me. "You can burn it," Ken said. "Unless . . ."

Unless. I traced the cover of the magazine lightly. I let my fingers rest on the glossy chest of the man made of paper.

"What do you think?" he asked. "Do you think you'll burn it?" I hesitated, then shook my head.

The train was pulling into the station. There were pictures of naked men in my lap. My hands were trembling. I looked at Ken and knew I was undone.

Ken nodded. There was something in his face like victory; I can only imagine what he saw in mine. "I've been to Tokyo before," he said. "I know a place."

"Here we are," says Ken. We're standing outside a white building with the words *Hotel Coco* written across the front; it's designed to look like a medieval castle, although it's laughably small. Ken opens the door and waits for me to step across the threshold.

"You go first," I say, nervous, though nobody seems to be looking at us, and in this corner of the world, who would care? But old habits are hard to break. "I'll come in a minute."

He shrugs and goes in ahead of me; I walk up and down the sidewalk, look in shopwindows without seeing a thing. After I've had time to count to sixty twice, I return to the hotel and open the door.

There's no one else in the lobby, just Ken standing in front of a large lighted display with five rows of photographs. Each picture shows a hotel room; each one is decorated in a different theme. Some are lit up, and some are dark.

"Choose one of the lighted ones," Ken says. "What are you in the mood for? Outer space?" He points to a room with shooting stars painted on the walls and glittery planets hanging from the ceilings. "Grotto?" He shows me a room filled with rocks and pools of water. "Christmas?" He points to a garish room decorated in red and green, dripping in tinsel. A huge, grinning Santa looms over the bed.

"I don't care," I say. I reach out and run my hand down his bare arm. I am aching and hollow and I need him to touch me.

"How about this one?" he says. He selects a room draped in red velvet. It looks like a whorehouse. He presses a button; the machine spits out a key and a card with a room number: 17.

"Do you want me to go up first?" he asks. His voice is gentle. I nod; I know it's foolish, but it's the way I've always done it. It helps tamp the fear down a little.

"Okay," he says. "Wait five minutes and then come up."

I pace the lobby. I can't keep myself still. It's like this every time. I should leave. How many times can I falter and still hope God will welcome me back?

But this is why I need some extra time. A moment to clear my mind; a moment to let myself imagine I'm someone else. I take a deep breath, then I ring for the elevator, go up to the second floor. Walking down the narrow hallway, I feel exhilarated and terrified and sick.

I tap on the door and it opens inward. I step in to find Ken waiting. This is me, I think, as I kiss this man, this wondrous vessel, and feel an ecstasy so sharp it hurts. This is me, this is me, this is me.

FIFTEEN

Abby

I read once that, while he was president, Abraham Lincoln suffered from an intense fear that he would die if he went to bed without turning his shoes so that their toes pointed to the east. The night before his assassination, a new White House chambermaid misunderstood the instructions and turned them to the west. The president dismissed her the next morning, but the damage was already done.

That's not true, of course. I just made it up. But you wanted to believe it, didn't you, just for a minute? We crave stories like that; we love the idea that there's a web of meaning underneath everything that happens, holding together the bones of human experience like a ligament. We love stories that make us shiver; we want our lives to hold some mystery within them. Why do we dare to hope there's a heaven? Why do we close our eyes when we kiss?

Okay, enough of that. I get like this when I spend too much time by myself. Justin is good at helping me get outside my head and back into the world, but for the last several hours, I've been on my own, and my ruminative nature has gotten the best of me. Enough.

I had to go to two different model food stores before I found the abalone sushi I needed, but I'm still the first to arrive at Sensoji Temple. I pass through a gate marked with an enormous lantern and walk through an alley full of shops selling souvenirs and religious artifacts. Inside, there's a complex of six or seven different shrines and temples surrounding a central courtyard. There's a five-story pagoda and a large incense burner, surrounded by people waving smoke over their bodies. I overhear a tour guide say that the smoke is supposed to have healing powers.

I find Barbara standing in the middle of the courtyard with the producers and the crew. It seems that we're doing things a bit differently this round, since the teams have been separated. We film Barbara greeting me and checking to make sure I've bought the right kind of sushi, but instead of telling me I'm in first place, she says, "Make yourself comfortable. Once the other contestants have arrived, you'll be gathering to hear a rather shocking announcement. And remember, there's still no communication allowed between you and your partner."

While I'm waiting, I take a look around the temple grounds. According to legend, the temple was founded in the seventh century, after two fishermen found a statue of Kannon, the goddess of mercy, in their nets. Although the statue remains here to this day, it's hidden in a golden shrine; it's considered too holy to look upon.

I spend some time watching visitors go about their prayers. I'm fascinated by the rituals. It all seems so simple, so concrete. Bathe yourself in the smoke from the incense; rinse your mouth with holy water. Throw a coin in a box; clap your hands to make sure the gods are listening. Make your wish and bow.

Wandering around the courtyard, I come upon a little booth where you can pay to have your fortune told. There's a large bank of wooden drawers, each marked with a different character; it looks like a giant apothecary chest. I find some coins in my pocket and drop one hundred yen into a slot. There's a monk standing nearby, draped in yellow robes; his job seems to be to help the foreigners. He indicates that I should pick up a tin box and shake it; when I do, a bamboo stick emerges. It has a Japanese character on it, and with a little help, I locate the drawer that's marked with the same symbol. I open the drawer and pull out a slip of paper.

"If you don't like," says the monk, "tie it there." He points to a wooden rack with several rows of wire strung across it; each one is covered with tiny strips of paper. "Then the bad fortune blow away."

I look down at the paper. The fortune is written in both Japanese and English. I read it out loud so Stu can get it on camera: "Number 23 Good Fortune. The cloudy sky will get more and more clear and the moon will appear. The linen robe turns into a green one. What you've been troubled for a long time will soon begin to fade away. Your virtue and happiness will reveal themselves." Underneath, it says, "The person you wait for will come. Building a new house and removal are good. Marriage and employment are all good. Making a trip is all right."

The monk is watching me. He gestures to the rack, littered with unhappy fortunes, and shrugs. I smile and shake my head. "I think I'll take it with me," I say. I walk away and look for a bench, so I can sit and rest and think about my linen robe turning green.

Cassie's the second to arrive; I can't imagine what's keeping Justin. After checking in with Barbara and getting her fortune told, she comes to sit next to me.

"Well, this sucks," Cassie says, handing me her fortune. It reads, "No. 17 Bad Fortune. You did not study yet, the way how to make things perfect. Everything don't come out as you expected. All what you try, get too complicated, and then you suffered from them, and get annoyed. Everything comes back to the beginning start and the progress turns around without any proceed." At the bottom, it reads, "Your request will not be granted. The patient keeps bed long. The lost article will not be found. The person you wait for will not come over. Stop to start a trip. Building a new house and removal, marriage of any kind, and employment are all bad."

"I don't even understand it," Cassie says, "but it doesn't sound good."

"You should go tie it to that thing over there. Supposedly, that means the bad things won't happen."

She shrugs. "It's kind of a funny souvenir," she says. "It matches my state of mind perfectly."

"I'm sorry to hear that," I say.

She looks at me for a minute, like she's weighing whether or not to say something. It makes me a little nervous. "Are you and Justin going to have kids?" she asks finally.

The question takes me by surprise. The truth is, Justin and I are not using birth control. It's like a dare. But this is not something I want to discuss with Cassie or the American viewing public. "Probably," I say.

She nods and busies herself with her backpack. Her parrot makes some noise, and Noah responds; I wonder what the two of them are saying to each other. I lift Noah's cage onto my lap and reach a finger through the bars. I stroke his feathery head.

"Do you miss it?" Cassie asks suddenly.

"What?"

She looks me in the face. "Women," she says.

It feels like a blow. My stomach twists, and my face gets hot. I'm very aware of Austin, kneeling in front of us with his camera.

What can I say to her? I think of Justin tuning in to watch this show when it airs, I think of my parents and my sisters and all our friends from Redemption. But then I think about why she might be asking, and I wonder how important my answer is. I don't want to steer her wrong. Her whole life is stretched before her, and I hope she'll find a way to live it the way she wants. I couldn't do it, but maybe she can.

"Sometimes," I say. It's the best answer I can give. Even in Redemption, we admit that it's not something that just goes away. No one could possibly object.

I'm afraid she'll ask more questions, but she just nods and goes back to looking at her fortune. I try to remember what it's like to be Cassie's age, when love and sex are still surprising and full of possibility. There's a feeling that you've finally begun to live in the world, like until now you've just been marking time. Like you've been waiting your whole life to find out what it feels like to hold someone in the dark. To turn underneath the covers and find someone there. Such a substantial thing.

I was Cassie's age the first time I kissed a woman, and I was shocked at how normal it felt. I was shocked that it didn't make the clocks stop ticking and the sun turn dark. It was just what it was; it was flesh against flesh, a mouth and a mouth and nothing more. It was sweet, and it thrilled me as deeply as anything has, but in the end it was just a kiss. The ground didn't crumble, and the oceans didn't dry. The world spun on its axis just the same.

As for why I couldn't hang on to that feeling, that sense of rightness . . . I don't know. It's complicated – is there any life that isn't? – and at this point it hardly seems worth thinking about. I look up and see Justin coming through the temple gates. He looks ruddy and imperious, like a warrior returning from battle, complacent and well fed. I've made my choices, but there's more than one way to live a life. I stand up and begin to gather my things. As I reach down to the ground for my ski pole, I lean in close to Cassie and clap a hand over my microphone. I whisper softly, so the cameras won't hear. "Every single day," I say, and it's no more than a breath. As cowardly as I know I am, it feels like an act of bravery. Cassie smiles faintly, and I know she's heard me, and I'm glad.

Justin and I don't speak, as per Barbara's instructions, but I notice him looking at me a few times with a kind of searching, imploring expression I don't quite understand. The other contestants continue to trickle in; next comes Carl, then Laura, then Jeff. Everyone mills around, avoiding their partners, gathering fortunes and buying skewers of chicken from a little stall. Eventually, the inventors show up, but Riley's brought the wrong kind of sushi – he's wound up with *makajiki* instead of *mekajiki* – and he's sent back to Kappabashi. The high school sweethearts arrive, then Riley returns and this time his sushi is approved. After he's been checked in, he sits down next to me on my bench.

"Damn," he says. "I love sushi, too. I really thought I had this one covered."

"Oh, well," I say. I'm snacking on some chocolate-dipped cookie sticks called Pocky, which I picked up at the train station. The newsstand where I bought them also had something called Men's Pocky, which looked almost exactly the same; I almost bought some just to be perverse, but then I wondered what Justin would have to say about it. I hold the package out toward Riley, and he slides one out and takes a bite. "You should still be okay," I say. "Dallas and Juliet aren't here yet."

He nods. "Maybe they've been mobbed by adoring fans. Wait, I can't remember — are we in Japan or 1995?"

I smile. He seems like a nice enough guy, but I'm not sure what to say next. This is the first conversation I've had with Riley; really, I've barely spoken to anyone but Justin in the last few weeks. People stick close to their partners in this game; looking around, I can see that everyone's mingling more now that they've separated us. Do the rest of them feel as lost as I do, to find themselves suddenly on their own? I realize how guarded I've been, walled up in my little two-person fortress. *What an unnatural situation we've signed on for,* I think.

"So what made you guys decide to do this?" I ask finally. It's a question everyone's wondered about; their whole hook is that they're these computer-genius-entrepreneur-millionaires, so they don't need the prize money. And once you remove the money from the equation, the whole reality TV formula kind of loses its equilibrium.

He gives me a shrewd, squinty look. "Ah, the *Gilligan's Island* conundrum: why were the Howells on a crappy three-hour excursion cruise in the first place, when they could've been on their diamond-encrusted yacht? And why did they bring so many clothes?"

"Uh, right," I say. "I guess."

"That's what we're trying to figure out, too. I'll get back to you when I know the answer." And with that, he stands up and bows from the waist. "Thank you for the chocolate-dipped confection. Good evening to you, ma'am," he says, tipping an imaginary hat. And I'm alone on my bench once more.

Finally, more than three hours after I arrive, Juliet walks through the gates, followed a little while later by Dallas. Juliet looks flawless —

I think she's taken the time to reapply her makeup, which is not a choice most contestants would make in the course of a race. She strides over to Cassie with her arms outstretched. I hear her say, "You would not believe what we've been though; Dallas insisted we were supposed to go to Tokyo Disneyland." Looks like they're out; I can't say I'll really miss them.

Barbara gathers us in the middle of the courtyard and asks us to line up according to the order in which we arrived. It's long past dark by now, and the temple is officially closed; I guess they've gotten permission for us to stay late. But the lighting crew has been hard at work, and where we're standing is dazzlingly bright.

Eli, one of the three producers, motions for us to be quiet, and Barbara begins to talk. "Welcome to Sensoji Temple," she says. "Tonight, we have a few surprises for you." She pauses, as if waiting for a rumble of astonishment to move through the crowd, but we all just want to go to bed.

"First of all," she says, "the last two contestants to arrive will not necessarily be the contestants asked to leave. That's good news for Juliet and Dallas." She smiles insincerely at them, and they smile insincerely back.

"Secondly . . ." She pauses again. When she speaks, her syllables are crisp. "The teams as you know them no longer exist. Your partner is no longer your partner."

Now there *is* a noticeable reaction. Nobody says anything, but there's a definite change in the energy of the group. There's a general straightening of posture, and we all glance around at each other's faces. People look alarmed, or surprised, or confused. Barbara looks gratified.

"Or, I should say, your partner is no longer *necessarily* your partner. Starting with Abby, the first contestant to cross the finish line today, and moving on down in the order of arrival, each of you will be asked to choose the partner you want to work with for the duration of the game. You may choose to stay with the person you've been with up till now, or you may choose to team up with someone else entirely."

Everyone seems to relax a little bit. If everyone can just stay with the same person, then what's the point? I think this is a misjudgment on the part of the producers; if we all decide to keep our original teams, they're going to look stupid.

"The cash prize remains the same," Barbara says. "Whichever team wins the game – whether it's an existing pair or a new combination – will split the prize of one million dollars. As for your found objects, you will keep whichever ones you brought with you from Nikko."

Well, at least if I choose Justin, I won't end up with two parrots.

Barbara continues. "The person you choose has the option of saying yes or no; if they decline your offer, you may choose someone else. However, if you receive two rejections, you'll be forced to move to the end of the line."

She pauses for effect. "Choose well; the last two people to be chosen will be going home tonight. If no one chooses either Juliet or Dallas, then they will be the ones who are disqualified. Are there any questions?"

People generally look a little confused; it's late, and these are annoyingly convoluted rules. But no one speaks up.

"Good," says Barbara. "Abby, who do you choose to play the rest of the game with?"

For just a moment, I imagine what it would be like not to pick Justin. I imagine sitting on a plane with Laura, figuring out clues with Carl, racing toward the finish line with Jeff. And for just a minute, it feels like a relief.

Then I'm ashamed of myself. He's my husband; we're in this together. "Justin," I say, loud and clear. Justin gives me a smile so warm, so dazzling, that I can't believe I ever thought about betraying him.

Barbara says, "Justin, do you accept Abby's invitation?"

"I do," he says, and I'm back on my wedding day, a bride wrapped in her husband's arms.

"Very well," says Barbara. "Justin and Abby, please step out of line. Next is Cassie."

I watch Laura's face. She looks nervous, but so hopeful it breaks my heart. Cassie only glances at her for a minute, then looks all the way down to the end of the line. "I choose Juliet," she says.

Oh, God. Dallas slumps, Juliet beams. Laura closes her eyes; I don't think she's entirely surprised. Carl, however, looks stricken. He shakes his head like he can't believe what he's just seen.

"Very good," says Barbara. She looks gleeful about this turn of events. "Juliet, do you accept Cassie's invitation?"

"Absolutely," says Juliet. She smiles warmly; she looks as if she thinks that if she tries hard enough, she might actually be able to make light pour out of her body.

"Step out of line," says Barbara. "Carl, you're next."

Carl looks at Jeff, and I see something pass between them. Carl mouths something I can't quite make out. It might be "I'm sorry" or it might be something else entirely.

"Laura," he says. He sounds resolute.

Laura smiles just a little; Jeff makes a show of shrugging as though it makes no difference to him.

"Laura, do you accept Carl's invitation?"

"Yes," she says. "Thank you." They step out of line.

"Now Jeff," says Barbara.

Jeff looks at who's left. It's the inventors, Riley and Trent; high school sweethearts Jason and Betsy; and Dallas McKinley, TV's President Scooter. There aren't a lot of great choices.

"Well," he says, "my brother chose someone prettier than me, but I think I'm going to choose brains over beauty. Trent?" He glances in Trent's general direction, but I'm not sure Jeff actually knows which one is which.

"Trent, do you accept?" asks Barbara.

Trent looks pained. "Sorry to disappoint, but I'm going to have to say no. Riley and I are just such a good team."

Jeff nods amiably, but I can see this isn't turning out to be a great night for him.

"Very well," says Barbara. "Jeff, you get one more pick; if this one is rejected, you'll move to the end of the line."

"Um," says Jeff. He scans the group. "Okay, Dallas."

Dallas lets out a whoop. I was sure he'd be going home; I guess he was, too.

"Shall I take that to mean you accept?" asks Barbara.

"Yes," says Dallas. He straightens up and smiles like he's accepting a People's Choice Award. "I accept."

Next comes Trent; of course, he chooses Riley. And that's it. "You've made some very interesting choices," says Barbara. "Betsy and Jason, you're the last ones left. I'm afraid you'll be going back home."

Jason and Betsy look a little stunned. They arrived almost an hour before Juliet and Dallas; they were sure they were safe.

Barbara walks over and stands between the two of them. "You've lost the game," she says. "But what have you found?"

Betsy goes first. "I've found out you can't go back to high school," she says. "I've found out I have better taste now than I did then. And I've found out that Jason's calves are not nearly as shapely as he thinks they are."

Barbara smiles; I guess she figures that if they're not going to say something inspirational, cattiness works just as well.

"And you, Jason?" she asks. "What have you found?"

Jason summons a misty look. "I've found that it's an amazing world out there," he says, "but we live in the very best country of all."

Oh, Jesus. (Sorry.) I hear Cassie snort. Jason looks pleased with himself, though. I guess it'll play well, if that's the kind of thing you're concerned about; maybe it will get him a few talk show appearances, or a guest shot on a sitcom. Fifteen minutes starting now.

Barbara turns to the camera. "Tune in next week," she says, "when our five new teams find themselves in a new corner of the world. Until next time, this is . . . *Lost and Found.*"

The spotlights turn off, and all hell breaks loose. Carl calls out to Jeff, who ignores him and starts to walk away. Laura says, "Cassie, I'd like to talk to you," and Cassie just says, "Later." The cameras stay on for all of it.

A crew member starts coming around with info about where

we're staying. Justin puts his arm around me and kisses me tentatively on the lips.

"You had me worried," he says. I can tell he means it by the way his voice cracks a little; he's usually very careful about modulating his tone. "You took long enough to answer the question."

"Just adding some drama," I say. I rub his neck; he seems to need some kind of reassurance. "Hey, what took you so long with the sushi?"

"Ken had camera trouble, and our sound guy got sick," he says. He busies himself with our found objects. "And then I got lost on my way to Kappabashi."

"Ah. Sounds like fun. I'm sure I'll get to see all the exciting details in a few months."

He doesn't answer right away. He picks up the ski pole; I put the aviator helmet on and pick up Noah's cage. "Maybe," he says, finally. He's working on deepening his voice. "You never know what they'll put in, and what they'll edit out."

We walk through the temple gates and out onto the street. Tokyo is lit up like a carousel. I'm thrilled to be here, thrilled to find myself in a part of the world I never thought I'd see. Justin hails a cab and helps me inside; he speaks his few words of Japanese to the driver, and I'm happy he's taken the time to do it right. We settle into the backseat, surrounded by all our crazy gear. He knows me. He knows all about me. I rest my head on his shoulder.

SIXTEEN

Barbara Fox

One a.m., Tokyo time. The contestants have all gone to their rooms, and the cameramen have left them at the door like polite suitors. They'll have a few hours to try to sleep and to deal privately with the aftermath of the choices they've made tonight. The ones who have new partners are learning how to share their living quarters with a near stranger – one of the switch details we didn't mention on air; if we're going to stay on budget, we can't start paying for a whole extra set of hotel rooms. Plus this is a good way to ratchet up the tension. And the ones who stayed together are wondering if they'd have done better with someone else. I wouldn't want to be in any of those rooms tonight.

Here at the production hotel, which isn't luxurious but is marginally nicer than the one where the contestants are tossing and dreaming, nobody's sleeping. I'm sitting on a sofa in the suite that we're using as a makeshift control room. The cameramen have come in one by one to check in their tape, and have gone off for a few hours of rest, as mandated by their contracts; they're not union, but they are guaranteed a certain number of hours off every twenty-four-hour period, so the clock's running until we can start up again.

Now the production crew is going through the footage and logging what's on the tapes. Most of the editing work will be done after we get back to the States – that's where the stories will really start to take shape – but the producers like to go through it every night to get a sense of what we've got. There are three producers, Eli, Jeremy, and Kate, who go out on the road with the teams, as well as an associate director, a handful of production assistants, and a network rep. Not to mention Oliver, who's the executive producer and creator of the show; he oversees everything. (Right now, he's on the phone with a member of the advance team in our next location, who are getting things ready for our arrival tomorrow; apparently, one of the challenges we had planned violates some kind of local law.) This show is a huge operation. Once you add in the camera and sound guys, the hair-and-makeup person who travels with me, the parrot tender, the segment producers, and the rest of the field crew, we're quite a merry little band of travelers.

Everyone's happy with the outcome of tonight's contestant scramble. We were all a little afraid that everyone would just pick the same partner. No backstabbing? No betrayal? Where's the fun in that? But it worked out perfectly. The remaining contestants sleep the sleep of the troubled, while Jason and Betsy, sweethearts no more, are on their way to Belize, which is where we're putting up the eliminated contestants until filming ends. We do this for confidentiality reasons; if we sent teams home one by one, it wouldn't be too hard for the media to guess the winner. So we hole them up someplace till the end of the game; they can't contact their loved ones, but at least they can relax on the beach. The contestants call it Reject Rendezvous. Fare thee well, Betsy and Jason. You'll get a daily stipend and phone interviews with a shrink if you need them; sometimes, people have a little trouble dealing with the emotional fallout of being on a show like this. But there are worse things in life than a free vacation. Hell, maybe you'll fall back in love.

Jeremy, Kate, and Eli have three different monitors going; they've got headphones on, and they're simultaneously watching footage of Juliet and Dallas, Carl and Jeff, and Cassie and Laura. There are room service trays on the dressers and coffee table, and one of the PAs, a skinny guy with red hair who may or may not be named Zachary, is going around picking up empty water and soda bottles.

I'm sitting back and watching it all, enjoying a cup of sake. I should go to bed – it's not like they need me for anything here – but I like this part of the day. The contestants are tucked away for the night, sequestered safely in their rooms, and now the real work begins. I don't have children, but I imagine this is what it feels like when you finally get the kids to bed and the adults have some time alone.

"You guys've got to see this," says Jeremy. He's paused Juliet and Dallas. Juliet's got her mouth open and her eyes squeezed shut; it's quite an unflattering pause. Jeremy unplugs his headphones and turns up the sound. A group of us gather around the monitor.

The video starts up. The camera pulls back to reveal that our two hapless subjects are standing in front of the ticket gate at Tokyo Disneyland.

"Didn't they split up?" Kate asks. "I thought the clue was pretty clear."

"Later on they did," Jeremy says. "Eventually, they figured everything out and completed the task, but here they're still a little confused."

On screen, Dallas looks baffled; Juliet looks like realization is beginning to set in.

"Do you see a *Lost and Found* sign anywhere?" asks Dallas.

"No," says Juliet. Her voice is tight. There's laughter in the room around me. "I don't."

"Aren't we supposed to meet another cameraman here?" Dallas is asking on the screen. He really isn't getting it.

"Yes," says Juliet. She starts out sounding angry, then revises her voice to weary. "And there were supposed to be other teams here, and production people, and just basically *something* to suggest that someone might be filming a TV show here."

We all erupt into laughter. It'll be a tough call whether to edit that last part out. The producers don't like the contestants referring to the show as a "show"; they tell them to say "game" or "scavenger hunt" instead. They want to keep that fourth wall firmly in place. But it's such perfect characterization, what with Juliet's carefully controlled rage and Dallas's struggle to understand what's going on. It's a beautiful moment.

"Wait for it," Jeremy says. "It gets better."

"Well, do you think we should go inside?" Dallas asks. Juliet's mouth drops open. She gives the camera a "do you believe this guy?" look.

"Yes, Dallas," she says. She sounds like she's talking to a child, or maybe a non-English-speaking puppy. "That's a great idea. Let's pay . . ."– she looks over at the ticket signs –"Let's pay seven thousand yen so that we can go inside and see if maybe they're all just hiding from us. What the hell, let's get a two-day pass so we can really do a thorough search."

Fresh laughter all around. "This is fine television," says Eli.

"You think we're in the wrong place?" asks Dallas.

Juliet closes her eyes, gathers her strength. "Yes, Dallas," she says. Her words are bricks. "I think we're in the wrong place."

Jeremy pauses the tape again, and a few people applaud. "Excellent," says Oliver. "Nice," says one of the PAs. This one's a woman with deliberately tangled hair and chunky glasses. They all look like such babies to me.

"Beautiful casting," says Kate. "You know I was a little apprehensive about throwing celebrities into the mix, but is it ever paying off."

"Well, 'celebrity' is a matter of degree," Eli says. Everyone laughs, but I feel a shift in the room. I'm the only one here who could possibly be called a celebrity, but I'm aware that my place on the Hollywood ladder is somewhere in between "game show jiggle girl" and "parking valet to Mr. Leno." Even my position on this show isn't ironclad; I'm the second host they've had, and if audiences are lukewarm, I'm sure they'll go looking for a third. The room's gotten quiet, or maybe it's my imagination. Best to address it head-on.

"I hope you'll all think of me someday when you're casting *Lost and Found: Washed-Up Hosts Edition,*" I say in what I hope is a genial tone. I mean it as a joke, but the laughter is uncertain.

"Don't be silly, sweetness," says Oliver, in a voice scarred by cigar smoke and yelling. It's his show, so it's his job to make a statement here, and maybe that was what I wanted all along. "You'll be here long after the rest of us are gone."

"Are we all out of water?" asks Kate, holding up an empty bottle, and the room is back in motion. Her question strikes me as funny, though the only one who responds is a PA, who picks up the phone to order more. How will we survive? We're on an island, we're filming a reality show, and we've drunk all the water there is.

I'm not unaware of what the contestants think of me; how could I be when I watch footage of them talking about me every night? They think I'm icy and brittle; in one of the clips we won't be airing, a contestant who was weeded out early on said that he'd screw me if he weren't afraid of getting frostbite on his dick. It was a pleasure to send him packing. His answer to the money question ("You've lost the game," etc., etc.) was a grammatical revelation; it contained four different uses of the word *fuck*, and each one was a different part of speech. The techs whose job it is to add bleeps will be buying new swimming pools with all the overtime they'll be putting in on that guy.

It surprises me that the contestants (and to some degree, even the crew) don't understand it's a persona. Not that I'm the warmest person in the world, or the most natural with people, but the way I am on camera isn't me, not by a long shot. Before I auditioned, I had to decide how I was going to put myself forward. You have to choose your archetype, decide which idiom you're working in. I'm forty-three, which is, of course, ancient in television, and I'm a woman. Not that I'm saying it's harder to succeed as a woman — that's an excuse; whine, whine. But the rules are different, there's no question about it. For a man doing this kind of work, amiable is the way to go. You need to be good-looking (preferably rugged, but it's not a deal breaker), and you need to be likable. But amiable doesn't work for a woman unless she's also going for cute, and I knew that wasn't going to work. I couldn't do corn-fed homecoming princess, and I couldn't do tits-and-ass lingerie model. So I picked mature ice-queen sophisticate, and what can I say? It got me the job.

This show could potentially be very big for me, but I've had so many almost-breaks that I've stopped attributing any meaning to them. I've done a bit of acting, mostly when I was younger, including a yearlong stint on a soap opera, which didn't turn out to be as star-making as I'd been led to expect. (My character didn't even die a colorful death; she succumbed to an asthma attack after her villainous sister hid her inhaler.) I did a bunch of one-off roles on sitcoms and prime-time dramas, and I was cast in a film that went on to win three Academy Awards, but my scenes didn't make the final cut. I spent three months as an anchor on an LA morning program, and two years as a field reporter on an entertainment magazine show. The result is that I've got a list of credits longer than half the Oscar winners in Hollywood, but nobody knows who I am. You might recognize my face, but you sure as hell don't know my name.

Lost and Found may do it for me or it may not. We're filming the second season right now; the first got respectable ratings, but didn't really make much of a splash. (Exit the former host, an amiable man who erred on the side of goofiness; enter me.) Now we're back, with a little restructuring and a few surprises – more interesting teams, new twists like tonight's partner reshuffling – and I think this time we really have the potential to develop a following. It's a good show, if we can just get people to watch. Oliver's original concept, which admittedly has evolved a little bit over time, was to create an adventure show where intelligence counted as much as physical prowess. Sure, we throw in the occasional bungee jump or snowboarding challenge, but the real meat of the game lies in how well you read the clues, keep track of your objects, weather the confusion of travel, navigate foreign cities. And, of course, how well you work with your partner.

"Check this out," says Kate. She's running a scene of Cassie standing in the fake sushi store. Cassie stops to talk to an American couple with a baby, and the camera zooms in for a beautiful close-up of her tortured face.

"Thank you, Austin," says Jeremy.

"Money shot," says Eli.

Oliver booms in. "Well," he says. "Only if we can get her to talk about the baby she gave up. Otherwise, the audience will find her response a little mystifying."

"We ought to start planting babies," says Eli. "Hire people to parade their kids past Cassie until she cracks." We laugh. He's joking, but only just.

There are many gray areas in putting together a show like this. We can't do anything that will be perceived as influencing the outcome of the game, but there's manipulation; of course there is. And there are aspects of game play that the viewers will never see. In one of the early rounds, for example, there was a clue none of the contestants could figure out. Maybe the writers made it too hard, or maybe these people are just stupider than we thought; in any case, time was running short. We had to be out of the location in an hour, and if we didn't hurry it up, the cameramen were going to have to go on overtime; it was going to be a mess. So the producers held a quick powwow and decided that in cases like this, we could swoop in and give everyone a hint. We've done similar things a couple of other times as well, subtle direction when everyone seems to be lost. None of this will make the final cut – it messes too much with the format of the show – but if everyone's getting the same information, I don't see how it matters. What airs on TV will not be an accurate representation of the competition that took place that day, but the outcome will be the same. And that's what disclaimers are for, right?

Since filming began, we've all been holding our breath on a number of counts. Will we get everyone into and out of each country without running into trouble with visas or customs? Will we come in on schedule and under budget? Will there be injuries? Which team will implode first? Will the challenges prove as dramatic as the writers have imagined them to be? (People are always surprised to hear there are writers for a show like this, but what exactly do they think happens? We get to Japan and someone says over breakfast, "I know – why don't we have them lie in hot sand today"?) But our most crucial concern, and the one we have the least control over, is this: Will the contestants give us the stories we want them to give us?

Everyone's here for a reason. When the producers are screening applicants, they cast for conflict – you want some teams that get along well together, but it's not going to be a very interesting show if everyone does – but they also cast for story. They look for questions that audiences will want answered. Can you change your sexual orientation? What happens to child stars after they grow up? Wouldn't we all be better off if we tracked down our first loves? Then we cross our fingers and hope that the answers will emerge on camera. We film the contestants constantly, we do interviews with and without their partners, and we gather sound bites that can be woven together in postproduction to give the show some narrative flow. But a few of the contestants have been reluctant to expose themselves too fully. We do our part: in the on-the-fly interviews during game play and the longer sit-downs at the end of each segment, we try to lead the conversation in the directions we want. But we can't force it. That's why we're hoping that today's shake-up will loosen some tongues. After all, if we can't get Cassie to talk about her baby, Abby to talk about her hidden desires, Carl to talk about his sick kid, then what have we got to work with?

Jeremy screens some footage of Riley and Trent in the cab on the way to the Beppu airport; they're having a wide-ranging debate I can't quite follow, involving everything from black holes to comic-book characters. They're going to play well, I think; they're cerebral but entertaining, weird but not too weird. Audiences might root against them at first, because of the money factor, but in the end, likability is a lot more important. On the other hand, of course, villainy is just as crucial for viewers; what you want is a healthy mix.

"Holy shit," Eli says suddenly. He's been watching Justin's footage; he stops the tape and rewinds. He presses play, and we see a hotel room, garishly decorated in tones of red and gold. Justin is nowhere in sight. The camera shakes, then steadies as it's apparently set down, and the camera guy steps out into the frame.

"My name is Ken Sutphen," he says. His voice is hushed, and

he's speaking quickly. "I'm a camera operator for *Lost and Found*. I'm a gay man, and I'm about to reveal that Justin Crawford is a complete and utter hypocrite. There's no such thing as ex-gay."

There's a knock at the door (of the sleazy hotel room on the screen, not the tasteful one we're sitting in), and Ken opens it. Justin walks in, and within a few seconds, we're all being treated to *America's Filthiest Home Videos*.

"Oh my God," says Kate.

"My eyes!" says the redheaded PA in mock horror.

Eli hits fast forward, and we watch the events unfold in superspeed. Even so, it goes on for quite a while.

"Where the hell's the sound guy?" asks Oliver.

"Sudden bout of food poisoning," says Eli. "Ken called in from the train, and we had another one meet them in Asakusa."

"Did Ken say anything when he checked in his film?" asks Kate.

The tousled PA speaks up. "He said, and I quote, 'I got some exciting stuff.'"

Laughter. "That's 'exciting' with three *x*'s," says Eli.

We keep watching; no one looks away. In fast forward, with no sound, the events on the screen take on a slapstick quality.

"Laurel and Hardy: the lost films," I say. I get a few strange looks. I guess it wasn't that funny. I'm a little punchy.

"Were Laurel and Hardy gay?" asks one of the PAs, a wide-eyed waif of a girl whose name I forgot as soon as I learned it.

"No," I say. "Not that I know of."

We watch for a moment in silence. "So much for maintaining the illusion," says Kate. She means the illusion that what you're watching is reality and not a TV show. We like to keep the crew hidden as much as possible. A naked cameraman on the screen is a bit of a faux pas.

"I don't know if we fire him or cross our fingers for an Emmy," says Jeremy.

The action on the screen reaches its expected conclusion, and Eli stops the tape. We all look at one another. We're starting to feel a little giddy.

"This is huge," says Jeremy. "This is more than we ever expected."

"Are we going to be able to use it?" I ask.

"Well, not much of it, obviously," he says. "But, yeah. Don't you think?"

We all look at Oliver. He shrugs. "Of course. Justin has signed all the releases. We're allowed to show whatever we get." He grabs a legal pad and starts making some notes. "We'll need to interview Ken. He's a character now, like it or not. And he needs to sign a release."

"I'll go see him in the morning," says Jeremy.

"He can't continue working on the show," says Oliver. "This clearly goes against the conflict-of-interest clause in his contract. We don't want even the appearance of a crew member contaminating game play. Who's scheduled to leave tomorrow?"

"Austin," says Eli. As the game progresses and the contestant pool shrinks, we have to reshuffle the crew a little bit. Sometimes a camera crew gets reassigned to cover duty — pick up the slack, get location shots — and sometimes the ones with the least seniority get sent home.

"Well, see if he can stay on. But don't get rid of Ken just yet; we may need him. What time is it in LA?"

"Ten a.m.," says the PA who may be Zachary. He looks like a little boy who's been kept up too late. "Ten a.m. yesterday, or whatever."

"Get Legal on the phone for me. I want to get their take on this."

The room swirls into motion around me. I sit back and watch. My sake has gone cool, but I sip at it anyway. It's taken me a long time to get here: this sofa, this makeshift nerve center, this glittering Tokyo night. This is the beginning of something for me, or it's not. Tomorrow, I'll be in another country, watching the game unfold in ways I can't even imagine. But tonight. Tonight, here I am.

SEVENTEEN

Carl

I wake up to a ringing phone and a feeling like I never want to move again. At this point in the game, the cumulative jet lag and stress are really starting to take their toll. I feel stunned with fatigue; opening my eyes feels approximately the same as being punched. I'm coming down with a cold, too. My nose is stuffy, and apparently, I've been sleeping with my mouth open. My tongue feels like it's made of dried mud.

I pick up the phone and croak into it. A polite, accented recording says, "This is your wake-up call. The time is now six-thirty a.m." I hang up and look around for Laura, but the other bed is already empty; I can hear water running in the bathroom. Not much was said between us last night. We rode back to the hotel more or less in silence and got down to the awkward business of sleeping in the same room. We had a fitful night, marked by an overzealous air conditioner and a parrot who found it necessary to undergo some kind of unfathomable avian crisis at 4:39 a.m. I feel like I'm on a very strange honeymoon, one where the bride makes mournful noises in her sleep, and the groom whimpers when he pulls his socks on over his blisters.

I get up and throw on some clothes as quickly as I can, afraid the whole time that Laura will come out of the bathroom and catch me in an inelegant pose: "Middle-Aged Nude with One Foot in the Air" or "Husky Man Bent over His Shoelaces." But she doesn't, and by the time she does appear, looking tired but somehow fresh, I've dressed fully and collapsed back onto the bed under the weight of my own exhaustion.

"Good morning," she says, giving me a resolute smile. "Has the parrot guy come by yet?"

"No," I say. "Not yet." They don't trust us to feed and care for the parrots ourselves, which is probably for the best.

"I forgot to ask," she says. "Does your parrot have a name?"

"Little Ricky," I say, staring up at the ceiling. I feel suddenly melancholy. I don't know how we're going to get through this, any of us. "Jeff's idea."

At breakfast, all the teams are present, sitting in their new configurations. There's a fair amount of tension in the room. If looks could kill – well, if looks could kill, I'm sure we'd all have been dead long before this.

I see Jeff standing at the breakfast buffet and walk up next to him, followed by our new camera crew, with Elliott on camera and Misha on sound. I hope Elliott gets some shots of the buffet; it's pretty spectacular (and kind of a relief after yesterday's fish and pickles). All the food is cut into beautiful shapes and meticulously arranged; they're big on presentation in this country. Jeff is filling his plate with pastries, fruit, and cold cuts. The show pays for all our hotel meals, but not for any food we eat during the course of playing the game, so people tend to load up on breakfast. Across the buffet, I see Trent filling an empty paper coffee cup with miniature croissants. "Stealth," he says to his cameraman, covering the cup and dropping it in his bag. "Stealth is key." Across the room, Riley lets out a strange mooing sound and several people turn to look; Trent takes the opportunity to remove a bouquet of fruit skewers from an artful display shaped like a peacock's tail. He wraps them in a napkin and drops the whole thing into his open backpack. "Stealth and misdirection," he tells the camera, nodding wisely.

"So," I say to Jeff, finally, after Trent moves on to commit bigger acts of larceny at the dessert table. Jeff looks at me, expressionless. I try to think of a point of entry. What I come up with is: "What did you think of those toilets?" They had these crazy toilets in the rooms, with control panels on them. There was a button to heat the seat, one to activate a bidet attachment, and one to blow hot air on your ass. There was also a button that just made a whooshing noise, presumably to cover up any noises the toilet user might be making. It took me ten minutes to figure out how to flush.

"Very nice," Jeff says, with ice in his voice. "I could talk about them for hours." He picks up a fruit tart and walks away. I guess I'm going to have to pay for causing him to end up with Dallas. We'll be fine eventually, but I'll probably have to take a few digs first. Jeff isn't the most mature person. Once when Benjamin was just learning to talk, we let Jeff babysit, and Jeff spent the whole afternoon teaching him the wrong names for fruit. We came home, and Benjamin toddled out of the kitchen, holding an apple. "Lemon," he said, smiling brilliantly, offering the word like a gift. We almost couldn't bring ourselves to correct him.

I'd like to explain to Jeff why I chose Laura – basically, it killed me to see Cassie reject her that way, and I couldn't just leave her standing there like the last kid on the playground – but I think I'll have to give him a little cooling-down time first. I get some breakfast and head back to sit with Laura, who's looking glum. She's watching Cassie, who's deep in conversation with Juliet. Juliet is glowing in a way that somehow manages to look deliberate; she leans over and speaks softly to Cassie, resting her hand on Cassie's arm. Cassie throws back her head and laughs. They're putting on a show.

"You better eat up," I say to Laura. "You never know how long it'll be before we get another chance." She attempts an anemic smile and pierces a piece of cantaloupe with her fork. She doesn't bring it anywhere near her mouth.

I try again. "So how about those toilets?" I say. Why do I keep bringing this up? It's like a tic. But this time she smiles for real.

"Pretty fancy," she says.

I cast about for a suitable follow-up comment, but I'm tired, and it turns out I don't really want to talk about toilets after all. I feel like

I should say something about Cassie, try to make Laura feel better, but I just don't have the energy. "Tough morning," I say instead, and Elliott gets some great footage of us finishing the meal in silence.

We gather in the lobby for an interminable housekeeping session regarding our found objects; the producers need to establish a list of how each team divided their loot when they split up, so they'll know what each team is responsible for. (Laura and I have ended up with only one parrot and one ski pole, but two trilobite fossils and six sequins.) Then they have us hand over all our remaining cash, so they can split it up equitably; Jeff and I each get half of what we had left. Finally, after the usual filmed inventory, which everyone passes, Barbara appears out of nowhere to make our lives hard.

"Good morning," she says crisply. She's smiling brightly, but I see faint circles under her eyes. She was probably up late teasing small children or bleaching her eyeballs or something.

"I trust you're all settling into your new groupings. I'm going to give you your clues for the next Keyword Round, but things are a little different this time." Significant pause, eyebrows raised. "This time, we're not going to tell you the country and city you're going to visit next. You have to figure out for yourselves where in the world you need to go."

Barbara looks triumphant. We all nod and try to look shocked. My head aches.

"For this round of the scavenger hunt," she continues, "you may not collaborate with any other teams. You may not use a guidebook, and you may not buy any special devices to help you. The use of maps is allowed. And this time . . ." She smiles at each of us in turn. "This time, there are two different clues. You have a choice to make: Letters or Numbers?"

She turns to the team on her right. "Riley and Trent," she says. "Which do you choose?"

Riley and Trent look at each other, agree without speaking. "Numbers," Riley says firmly. Barbara hands him an envelope.

She goes around the circle. Cassie and Juliet choose Numbers for some unfathomable reason; Jeff and Dallas choose Letters, and so do Justin and Abby.

"Laura and Carl," says Barbara. "May I have your choice?'

Laura and I look at each other. "Letters?" she whispers.

"We'll take Letters," I say. I reach out for the envelope.

"You may open your clues," she says.

I break the wax seal and pull out the slip of paper inside. It says:

JAWS IV: ASK NUDE JERK

That's all it says; Elliott zooms in for a close-up. I burst out laughing. There's got to be more to it than this.

"The clue you've just opened contains all the information you need to find the site of our next Keyword Round. When you arrive, you'll be given another clue."

Laura and I look at each other; her face displays an emotion somewhere between bemusement and despair. Looking around at the other teams, I see similar expressions from all the other Letters people. Luckily, the teams who chose Numbers look just as baffled.

Barbara claps her hands twice, like she's summoning a house-boy. "Good luck, teams," she says, with a smile like an iceberg. "Get to it."

We disperse to different corners of the lobby to confer with our teammates. Laura and I sit down on a slick gray sofa and stare at the clue. Elliott kneels before us.

"So," I say finally. "What the fuck is this?"

Laura laughs. "I have no idea. *Was* there even a *Jaws IV*?"

"I think there might've been, but it sure as hell wasn't subtitled *Ask Nude Jerk*."

"Right," she says. We look at the words some more. We're sitting close together, our heads bent over the clue; it feels casually intimate, like all the nicest moments of marriage.

"Maybe it's an instruction," I say. "We have to find a nude jerk and look at his jaws."

Laura nods. "Somewhere in Tokyo, there's an obnoxious naked person waiting for us to find him."

I smile. "I suspect that's true of most cities."

Laura slumps back for a moment, dropping the clue to her lap. She rubs her temples and sighs. "Okay," she says, sitting up straight and brushing the hair away from her face. "Let's get serious. What could this mean? How could this be a clue to where we need to go?"

"Do you think it has something to do with sharks?"

"Maybe . . . but no, I bet that's a red herring."

"Okay, Barbara said this is all the information we need. Maybe it's a code; maybe the letters stand for something else."

She nods. "Good idea. How about if we replace each letter with the one that comes after it: change A into B, and so on?"

"Let's see. That would be KBXT . . . well, clearly, that's not right."

I look around the room; everyone's still working. "Maybe we're supposed to rearrange the letters," I say.

"An anagram. I bet that's it." She reaches over to her backpack and pulls a pen from a zippered compartment. "Do you have any paper?"

I think about it. "No, only my Japan guidebook and the found-object rice paper; we're not supposed to write on that."

"I'll go get some," she says. She walks over to the front desk and returns with several sheets with the hotel letterhead and an extra pen. She hands me some supplies. "Let's see what we can find," she says.

I write all the letters at the top of a piece of paper, and start trying to puzzle it out. "There are a hell of a lot of consonants," I say.

"Yeah, but let's give it a try. I don't have any other ideas."

I work with the letters for a while, trying to come up with combinations. Cassie and Juliet get up to leave, looking triumphant. They sweep past us, as well as you can sweep while carrying a parrot cage, a ski pole, and a backpack, and Cassie doesn't even look our way. I glance at Laura; she purses her lips and keeps working.

"Sweden," she whispers to me after a few more minutes. "We've got all the letters for Sweden."

"What does that leave us with?" I ask.

"J-A-I-V-A-S-K-U-J-R-K," she says. She writes the letters out.

"Aha," I say. "Jaivaskujrk, Sweden."

"Well, it might not be that; we probably need to rearrange the letters. But this could be right. Scandinavian languages use lots of *J*'s and *K*'s, don't they?"

"Well, all my information comes from the Swedish chef on *The Muppet Show*, but I'm going to say yes."

"Okay," she says. She's brightened up a bit; she's more animated than she's been all morning. "Let's go find a Swedish map."

This has been the experience of a lifetime for me. Egypt, Japan, Sweden . . . I never would have dreamed it. We'll win the money or we won't; I almost don't care. For me, it's been enough to learn that the world is wider than I knew.

I never expected we'd make it this far. When Jeff and I found out we'd been picked as finalists for the show, I was completely baffled. We'd sent in a tape of the two of us screwing around; our bit was that we were the Barber Brothers, because our dad owned a barbershop, and we both worked there when we were younger. So on the tape, Jeff's giving me a haircut, and we're trading witticisms and doing our little brotherly spiel, and then Jeff says, "And the best thing is, after forty years of being brothers, he still never knows what I've got in store for him." And he shaves a stripe down the middle of my head.

If you pause the tape here and watch the next few minutes in slow-mo, you'll get a good view of my reaction, which the casting people later called "very authentic," and Jeff describes as "fucking hilarious." My face contorts from confused to disbelieving to shocked to outraged, and finally, I grab the clippers from him and shave a chunk out of his own hair. We both ended up having to shave our heads completely; it wasn't my favorite look (and luckily it's grown out a bit), but it was either that or spend the next several weeks walking around looking like patients who'd gotten lost on their way to the electroshock room.

So, I mean, sure – good tape, kind of funny, two brothers goofing around. But I heard there were something like three hundred thousand applicants, and it wasn't *that* funny. I was shocked to hear we had made the finals. We got called out to LA, along with about twenty other teams, all very hush-hush. (Even now, my ex-wife is the only one who knows where I really am; my boss and most of my family think Jeff and I are on an extended road trip. We had to sign a nondisclosure clause; if we tell anyone we're on the show before the network announces it, we're liable for ten million bucks.) We spent a couple of weeks in LA, going through the whole routine – interviews, IQ tests, psych exams, background checks. We weren't supposed to have too much contact with the other finalists, but of course everyone was watching each other, and I've got to say that some of the teams that weren't ultimately chosen seemed a hell of a lot more interesting than us. There were two guys who'd been in combat together – one had saved the other's life, or something like that – and there were twins who had been adopted by two different sets of parents. There was a couple where the husband had disappeared for a while, and it turned out he had some rare form of amnesia; they weren't reunited until the wife went on *Unsolved Mysteries,* and the husband happened to catch the show. There was some pretty serious competition. After we got home, when we got the word we'd been chosen over some of these other teams – amnesia! twins separated at birth, for Christ's sake! – I remember looking at Jeff and saying, "How the hell did this happen?"

But Jeff just shrugged. "We're fun," he said. "The twins had no charisma, and the amnesia guy was unstable, to say the least."

This was true. He didn't shower, and he spent hours every day making meticulous notes in a little notebook he carried with him. I looked over his shoulder once and saw that he was making a list of the locations of the hotel's emergency exits.

"Anyway," Jeff said, almost as an afterthought. "You're a hero with a tragic story. Everyone loves a sad clown."

"Excuse me?" I asked.

"You know," he said. "I told them about Benjamin."

It took me a minute to understand what he meant. When I did, I was appalled.

Benjamin was born with a congenital liver disorder called biliary atresia. It's a problem with the bile ducts; they discovered it when he was three weeks old. I remember that we were very frightened, even before we had a diagnosis. Everything was the wrong color: his skin was yellow, his eyes were yellow; his urine was dark; his bowel movements were strange and pale. He had surgery when he was two months old, the tiniest little tadpole; they did a procedure where they attached part of his small intestine to the liver to help the bile drain. We had great hopes, but ultimately it didn't help. So when he was fourteen months old, just learning to walk – I remember him toddling around the waiting room beforehand, wearing a tiny hospital gown that reached all the way to his ankles – we did what they call a "living donor transplant." They took a piece of my liver and transplanted it into Benjamin.

We both came through it fine. It was harder than I thought it would be – you can't really imagine what pain will be like when you're not feeling it, can you? But I got through it. I was in the hospital for about a week, and out of commission for another five; all in all, my ex-wife contends it wasn't much worse than her C-section, which is not something I can really take a position on.

Benjamin's recovery was worse. For a baby that age, who wants to walk and explore, being confined is torture, and I think that being forced to stay in a hospital bed, his body tied to machines and IV bags, was worse for him than any pain he felt. Or I guess that's what I want to think; how could I possibly know? The only words he could say when we went into the hospital were *duck* and *steps*. I'm selfish enough to be glad I wasn't there for the worst of it; I was recuperating elsewhere, and it was Jackie who had to sit with him and keep watch over him, to keep him still and try to comfort him without dislodging any wires. Pain aside, my part was easy; I saw him briefly after the surgery, and then not again until most of it was over, when the only visible effects were a scar on his downy belly and a vocabulary that had doubled to include *nurse* and *pinch*. The last word confused me until Jackie explained it; it was what they told him it would feel like whenever they stuck him with a needle.

But, see, that's exactly the kind of thing I can't dwell on. Benjamin is three years old now: charming, inquisitive, infuriating. He's everything he's supposed to be. His prognosis is good, although there's always a feeling that this will never entirely leave us, that we'll never quite be out of the woods. I don't have a lot of lingering effects; the liver is very good at regenerating itself, and within a couple of months, mine was back to its normal size and working at full capacity. I'm not a hero, unless your definition of *hero* is a very roomy one. I'm a man who acted out of fear; the way I see it, there wasn't even a choice to be made. There's nothing admirable in it at all.

I don't know why the casting people chose me and Jeff over all the other people who applied. I'd like to think they wanted us for comic relief; maybe they thought we'd travel the world merrily, shaving each other's heads. But I suspect, with something akin to nausea, that their decision was less about the camaraderie of brothers all grown up than about some movie-of-the-week idea about a devoted father giving up a piece of himself for his little pink-cheeked cherub. That's not what it was; it wasn't nobility and sacrifice and easy tears. It was agony and blood and a glimpse of my life without him. It was a horrible, messy time, the strain of which undoubtedly led to the end of my marriage. And I will not let this show turn it into a narrative thread.

I love television, and most of the time, I have faith in this show and in all the people involved in its production. But in my more cynical moments, I think that what they want is to create some new Frankenstein kind of über-TV: soap opera and sitcom and talk show and game show all rolled into one. I think they think they can have it all. But they can't. At least, they're not going to get it from me.

Laura and I are on the way to the airport; we figure it'll save us time in the long run, and we can probably get ahold of some maps there. Elliott's in the front seat of the cab and Misha's in the back with us, which means Laura and I are smushed in pretty close. I've got Little Ricky's cage on my lap, and the ski pole is on the floor, pointing up at a dangerous angle. Laura's going through the letters again, to see if she can come up with any other possible destinations.

"Java," she says. "That could be it."

I think hard, but I've got nothing on Java. One thing about this trip, it's made me realize what an ignorant bastard I am. "What do you know about Java?" I ask.

"Not a lot, but — hey! Isn't that where Jakarta is? That's got *J*'s and *K*'s." She goes through the remaining letters, crossing them off. "Nope, that's not it."

"Okay," I say. "Well, when we get there, we'll pick up maps of both Sweden and Java, and see if we can find anything."

She puts down her paper. "God, the clues are getting tougher, aren't they?"

"Yeah. I wonder how the others are doing with Numbers."

"I don't know. Cassie's okay at math, but it's not her best subject."

"Well, Jeff's best subject is *Flintstones* trivia, but I doubt that's going to come in handy on this one."

Laura leans against the door and kind of folds up into herself. Again, I figure she's thinking about Cassie, and I wonder if I should say something. But we're on camera, as always, and maybe she has her own topics she'd rather not turn into story lines. I look out the window for a neutral subject to talk about.

"Not a lot of vanity plates in Japan," I say. The license plates are white with green lettering, and they contain mostly numbers.

"No, I guess not."

"This one time," I say; I pause until she looks up at me. "I was driving down the highway, and I saw an accident between two cars with vanity plates."

She waits, but I don't say any more. "Really?" she says.

"Yup. It was like found poetry. I swear this is the truth: one of them said 'ATTORNY' and the other said 'BONEHED.'"

"Wow," she says, her face relaxing a little. "Poor Bonehed." We'll get through this. I think we'll make a good team.

"No kidding," I say. "It's not an easy life. Let's pause and have a moment of silence for all the Boneheds of the world."

Finally, finally, she smiles. Misha's giving me a strange look, but I don't care. Outside the car, there is sprawl and glamour and a language I can't begin to understand. We're racing toward a new country. Laura smiles, and my work here is done.

EIGHTEEN

Juliet

Now that I've managed to free myself of the dead weight of Dallas, TV's President Neuter, I feel like I can really concentrate on getting ahead on this show. I must say, whether this gambit with Cassie pays off or not, it's a whole different game when you're partnered with someone who's actually intelligent. When I opened up the Numbers envelope and was confronted with this —

67 50 802
020 36 198

— I got a little panicky, but Cassie figured out in about five minutes that it's the coordinates of the next place we're supposed to go. I don't think Dallas has ever heard the word *coordinates,* except in relation to the sportswear line he "designed" for Sears.

I like Cassie a lot; we had a great time hanging out together last night, even with no cameras around. She's smart and she's funny, and more important, I think audiences are going to like her. I'm still deciding whether flirting with her is the right way to go; she's a little fleshier than I'd like, and I have to think about how that'll look. But she is pretty, and I guess if those plus-size models can make a living, then the public must be getting less choosy. Either way, there's good chemistry between us, and I think she's definitely attracted to me, which is energy I can play off of, no matter what I decide to do.

Is this a great way to treat somebody? No, probably not; give me some credit, I know that much. I try to be so careful about what pieces of me leak through to the public, but the truth is, I don't always know what to think about myself. Some days, it occurs to me, and there's no room for doubt, that I'm hard and cold, and that if you're looking for a way in, a little chink in my armor that reveals a soft, pink heart beating underneath, you'll be looking for a long, long time. And other days, I just think I've done what I've had to do.

But I can't really spend much time on that. It's too important for me to succeed here. I feel like this is kind of my last shot; after this, it's either reinvention and a second chance, or it's a straight slide down into self-parody and invisibility. Sometimes you hear about child stars who go on to live normal, happy lives outside Hollywood – didn't Eddie Haskell from *Leave It to Beaver* end up as a cop or something?–but that's not me. This is all I've ever known; what am I going to do, turn around and go to law school? I barely made it through high school. Answer phones in an office somewhere? I don't think so. This is my life. I have to make it work.

Dallas has a theory – yeah, I know, Dallas with a theory?–that the best way to handle this thing is just to have fun. It's not the kind of gig that wins you acclaim; it's not like there's an Emmy for best performance on a game show. He says we're here to show we're fun and appealing, to remind people they like to watch us. You want to hang back a little, he says, keep yourself a little blank; people have to be able to make you into anything they want. Empty yourself out, be the screen for them to play their fantasies on. Don't screw it up for them. People might think they want to know what we're really like, but they don't. To find out we're as boring as anyone, that we're not so different from anybody else . . . where's the fun in that?

But it's not so easy for me to relax about this. And anyway, there's not a lot that people don't already know about me. Every breakup I've ever had has been reported in the media. I've spoken publicly about my short-lived religious conversion, my taste in music, and my boob job. People know I'm a vegetarian, and they know my birthstone is ruby. When my cat died, I got condolence cards from people I'm never going to meet.

Do you know me? Yes and no. If there are things I've kept for myself, it's less because I have some secret self that I don't want the public to see than because I think that not everything about me will play well. Like the fact that when I was on *Best Friends,* every time I flubbed a bit of dialogue, I would punish myself by scratching a line in my belly with a safety pin. Or the fact that after the show was canceled, I had to restrain my mother from making death threats against my costar Celia Bagley-Boone. Or this: that the thing I'm most scared of in all the world is living the rest of my life in private.

So self-preservation is key. I understand that the world I've grown up in may be a very skewed one, but it's the only one I know. And – can it possibly be a surprise?–it's where I want to stay.

Cassie and I are the first ones to arrive at the airport, and, believe me, first place is somewhere I'm very happy to be. We're standing in front of the airport directory, trying to determine our next move. We still don't have all the information we need; assuming Cassie's right that these are coordinates, they're missing the north/south and east/west information, so there are four different places on Earth these numbers could refer to. (Look at me – I'm learning geography! Wouldn't the studio tutors be proud?)

We're looking over the list of airport services, while our new crew – Garrett on camera, Akil on sound – stand over us, waiting for something interesting to happen.

"Well," says Cassie. "They've got a dental clinic, a lottery ticket counter, and a reflexology center, but no 'Let Us Look Up Your Global Coordinates' desk."

"Can we just go buy a GPS thing?" I ask.

"No, that was one of the rules, remember? 'You may not buy any special devices to help you.'"

"Okay, can we *borrow* one?"

Cassie looks at me like I'm a little bit slow. "Um," she says. "I think we're making this too complicated. I think we can figure it out by looking at a map?" She points at a listing on the directory. "Like at this bookstore here?" She's not exactly being sarcastic, but I don't like her tone.

"Fine," I say. I can freeze her out in a minute if I want to; I can make her desperate to feel the warmth of my smile. "I just thought we could move into the twenty-first century."

If I'm expecting her to fall over herself to get back in my good graces, it's not working. "Right," she says. "And I just thought we could do something easy."

She turns and starts walking in the direction of the bookstore, and somehow I'm the one following her. Maybe I've made a miscalculation. This is only our first day together; I should be trying to build a connection.

Running after her seems undignified, so I don't catch up to her until we reach the bookstore. She's talking to the clerk, an earnest young man who seems to be trying very hard to understand her.

"Atlas," she's saying, making indistinct hand motions. How exactly does she think she's going to convey the word *atlas* with her hands? "World map."

"Map," says the man, nodding. He's immensely relieved. "Map . . . Tokyo?"

Garrett's got the camera trained on Cassie. My turn. "No," I say, stepping into the frame. I look deep into the salesman's eyes and smile appealingly. "World," I say. I make a sphere with my hands, right at the level of my breasts. Are the Japanese big on boobs? Should I be showing my legs instead, or trying for some kind of schoolgirl thing? But it seems to be working; no one's looking at Cassie now. "Earth. World." I make my words long and soft. "Whole world."

He's got it now – he's beaming – but it takes him a minute to drag his eyes away from mine. "Yes," he says. "Whole world." He stands up tall and leads us to the right section. Cassie may know how to read a clue, but I've got my own assets to contribute to this team.

Cassie picks up an atlas. She looks annoyed with me, but I can soften her up. I lean over the book with her, so that my hair is brushing her shoulder. "I'm hopeless at reading maps," I say softly. "Show me what we need to do."

And, believe it or not, that's all it takes.

NINETEEN

Cassie

God, could I be more pathetic? After picking a fight with me and shaking her boobs at the bookstore guy, all Juliet has to do is brush against me, and I'm all, "Oh, please, let me teach you how to read a map." What do I think, that my extreme hotness is going to cause her to have some kind of lesbian awakening, and that we're going to run off together to open a bed-and-breakfast? No. But here I am in Narita Airport, explaining the principles of latitude and longitude to a TV star whose picture I kept in my diary for a year and a half. And I can't help it, the way she's looking at me makes my skin prickle.

It looks like we're going to Scandinavia; at least, I'm pretty sure we are. The map's in Japanese, and I'm not absolutely sure I'm doing it right. But I think I'm on the right track.

"See," I say to Juliet. We're leaning over the atlas together. "If you look at 67 degrees north and 20 degrees west, it puts us in the water off the coast of Iceland." I point at the blue paper; she puts her finger next to mine and taps the map. "So that's not right. And if it's 67 degrees south, we're practically in Antarctica." I slide my hand down the map, and she follows. "It doesn't matter whether it's 20 degrees east or 20 degrees west, because they're both in the water. So . . ." I look up; I'm surprised to see how close our faces are. She looks very intent, like she's soaking up every word I say. I look down at the map again and move my finger to just above the Arctic Circle. "So it has to be 67 degrees north and 20 degrees east, which is up here in . . ." The name of the country is written in Japanese. "Sweden? Norway? I never got all those countries straight."

"Don't ask me," she says. She smiles at me; *Juliet Jansen* smiles at me. (Jesus Christ, get ahold of yourself. Enough with the starstruck thing. I take a step backward, put the atlas on the shelf.) "Someplace cold," she says. Then, as an afterthought: "I hope it's Sweden; I'm really popular in Sweden."

I almost start laughing, it sounds like such a ridiculous thing to say. Maybe it's just my lack of worldliness; I mean, no one I know has ever been "really popular" in any part of the world. I guess it's impressive. But what does she think, that we're going to touch down in Stockholm and be mobbed by huge contingents of screaming blond fans?

I see Garrett's got the camera on me, and I try to compose my face. "We need a more detailed map," I say. "One in English." I browse the shelf for a map of Scandinavia, but there isn't one; at least, I don't think there is. It's hard to tell since I can't read Japanese.

"Well," I say. "How about we go find an airline that flies to Scandinavia? Maybe they'll have a better map. At least now we have some idea of where we're going."

Juliet sweeps the air with her arm, inviting me to lead the way. "I'm right behind you, Cassie," she says, and I don't know, she may be full of herself, she may be a total diva, but I love the way my name sounds on her lips. "Take me away."

I'm not so sure it was a good idea to choose Juliet over my mom. I know my mom was hurt by it, and that's something I'll have to deal with eventually. And, adolescent crushes aside, it's starting to occur to me that choosing a partner based on, say, intelligence, rather than number of appearances in *Teen People*, might have been a good way to go.

But there's something else. Last night in the hotel room with

Juliet, hanging out and talking, I started to feel like I might be making a friend. And I'm not sure that's a good idea. I haven't had a friend in quite a while. I'm scared of what I might say.

After all these months of silence, I'm suddenly afraid of opening my mouth. Three different times last night, I almost told Juliet about the baby. It's pathetic; give me the tiniest bit of intimacy, and I feel like pouring my heart out. I didn't do it; this show isn't the place to let your guard down, even when the cameras aren't around. And for all I know, Juliet has her own reasons for being so nice to me. I'm not an idiot. But there was this slumber party feeling, the two of us lying in our beds after the lights were out, each of us thinking of new things to say each time we were about to drift off. The urge to confide in her, to let the words slip through my lips and dissolve into the darkened air . . . it was very, very strong.

Right now, somewhere in this world, the baby I gave birth to lives with some random people I know nothing about. They're her family now. She has a mother who isn't me; when she's eight years old, or sixteen, or thirty-five, she'll say something about "my mom," and I won't be the one she's talking about.

I guess I can't really complain about the "random people" part of it, because I could have done things differently, and I didn't. I found this Web site when I was about seven months pregnant, and it had all these profiles of couples who wanted to adopt; for a while I thought I would pick one of them, and then at least I'd know something about where she was going to end up. I looked through all the possibilities, and I spent a whole weekend making lists and charts and trying to narrow it all down. A bunch of them I dismissed right away: some of the people had bad haircuts; some of them used too many exclamation points. Some of them seemed kind of old, and maybe that shouldn't matter to me, but it did. And you know what? Spelling counts. At least, it does when you're trying to convince someone to give you their baby.

Several of the couples seemed really nice; I'm sure any one of them would have been a good choice. But in the end, the whole thing kind of freaked me out. It made it so specific; I'd be giving my baby not just to some generic "kind and loving couple," but to *these* people who like to cut down their own tree at Christmastime or *these* people who have a motorboat, or *these* people who breed Weimaraners for a living. It brought up way too many questions about fate. I mean, right there in front of me were twenty different possible lives for my baby, and what if I chose the wrong one? What if the couple that loves gardening and goes to the theater all the time is going to get divorced in two years? What if the computer programmer with the acne scars is going to drown in his swimming pool next summer, and my baby will be raised alone by his wife who's a "self-proclaimed 'neat freak'" and is wearing those ugly leggings? It just made me aware of all these factors I hadn't even considered, like what part of the country she'll grow up in, and how many cousins she'll have. Is upstate New York a good place for her to grow up, or should I pick Florida?

I tried to picture this child, this little baby I knew only from the strength of her kicks, and I wondered what she would want me to choose. Would she like to have a dog or a cat? Would she rather live in the mountains or near the beach? Would she like to have an older brother? Should her father have a mustache? Would she like a mother who speaks French? And who's to say that any of these people would be better for her than me, a mother with no job and no education and probably not nearly enough maturity, but the only person who loved her before she was even born?

The woman we talk to at the SAS counter is very nice; she's tall and blond, and she speaks both English and Japanese, in addition to Swedish or Finnish or whatever her native language is. Her name is Elin. After a few minutes of explaining what we're looking for and why we're being filmed, she pulls out an English-language map of Scandinavia and pinpoints the coordinates we're looking for.

"Jukkasjärvi," she says, although it's completely unintelligible to me until she shows us the listing on the map. The way she says it, I would have thought it started with a *Y*. "It's here, see? In Swedish Lapland, in the north. You will need to fly into Kiruna."

"Okay," I say, copying down "Jukkasjärvi." I notice that I'm the one who seems to be in charge here. Juliet just leaves everything up to me, which is a big change from being with my mom. "How fast can we get there?"

Elin taps her keyboard. "There is a flight to Copenhagen at twelve forty this afternoon." I look at the clock; it's almost eleven. "From there, you will need to fly to either Stockholm or Göteborg. Let me see what will get you there soonest." More tapping; Juliet yawns behind her hand. "Yes, Stockholm is better, I think. Let me check the flights to Kiruna." After another moment, "Yes, I think I have found the best route for you. You will fly to Copenhagen, then Stockholm, and you will arrive in Kiruna at nine twenty-five this evening, local time."

"What time will that be, Tokyo time?" I ask. I'm not sure this is the right question; basically, I want to understand how long we'll be traveling.

"Tokyo is eight hours ahead of Sweden. This means that you will be arriving at what would be five o'clock tomorrow morning."

I think I must look horrified; Elin laughs. "It's not so bad," she says. "The flight to Copenhagen will take not quite eleven hours, and the other two flights are much shorter; one is an hour, the other an hour and a half."

Whatever; I can sleep on the plane. "Okay," I say. "We'll take four tickets." I hold out my hand to Garrett, who gives me the credit card we use to charge our flights to the show.

We hand Elin our passports. When she looks at Juliet's, she suddenly smiles very big. "I knew this," she says. "You are Tracy, yes? From *Best Friends?*"

Juliet's been slumping against the counter, but now she springs to life. "Yes, I am," she says, all twinkly and humble. "I can't believe you recognized me."

"Your show was very big in Sweden," says Elin. "I enjoyed it very much."

"Thank you," says Juliet. She's glimmering like the dawn. I guess she wasn't just blowing smoke up my ass about Sweden. "That's so sweet."

Elin processes our tickets, and Juliet signs a ticket folder for her, making sure Garrett captures the moment on camera. We gather up our baggage — I seem to get most of the heavy stuff — and we're off on our long journey together: Juliet Jansen, star of stage and screen, and Cassie Gardner, celebrity whore.

TWENTY

Justin

It's not uncommon for me to be swallowed up by a tide of unrest following a slip like the one I made yesterday, but the depth of my agitation today has taken me by surprise. I feel fidgety and wired; I feel like every joint, every sinew, is twitching beneath my skin. I was awake before dawn, movies playing in my mind, my body in flames. *Redirect,* I thought. *Cast it away.* I plucked the thoughts from my mind, tossed them to the floor beneath the bed with all the force I could muster; I reached out to my wife in the dark, ran my hands over her soft body and imagined that I might find something less yielding there. She turned to me with a hushed breath of an "oh," and I plunged and dove as though I wanted her more than anything in the world. Afterward, in the shower, I knelt in the spray and rocked back and forth in a desperate pantomime of prayer, and hoped that, for just a few minutes, God was watching but not listening in.

It was, of course, a relief (the base tug of my disappointment notwithstanding) to find that Ken was nowhere in sight when we gathered in the lobby for the assigning of camera crews. I don't know if he's been sent home or reassigned to more general camera duty; either way, it looks like my future contact with him will be limited. Our cameraman for this segment is a thick, unappealing man named Stu, and our sound tech is the much-dreaded, foul-smelling Raymond, so maybe someone's looking out for me after all.

Abby and I are both good at word games, so it didn't take us very long to determine that the clue was an anagram and to tease the word *Sweden* out of the mishmash of letters. Finding a non-Japanese map of Sweden seemed to be a trickier task, but we got lucky: we talked to the concierge, hoping he might be able to point us toward an English-language bookstore, and when we told him what we were looking for, he mentioned that the Swedish Embassy was only two blocks away. Clearly, the producers must have known this – they must have chosen the hotel with this in mind – but I'm not sure it would have occurred to us to ask, and I'm willing to bet it didn't occur to too many of the other teams. The people at the embassy were very helpful, and within twenty minutes we were in a cab speeding to the airport, the word *Jukkasjärvi* scrawled on a piece of paper in my lap, while the Japanese landscape passed us by. I didn't even want to look out the window. I couldn't wait to put that country behind me.

We're now on a plane to Copenhagen, on a flight that seems it will never end. Cassie and Juliet are here as well, and so are Carl and Laura; I'm not sure how far behind or ahead the other two teams are. Abby's just waking up after a long doze, but I've been staring straight ahead for seven hours, praying to God to deaden the nerves I've reawakened. There's something wrong with me, something very, very wrong.

"Hi, snoozy," I say to Abby. I'm amazed at the nonchalance of my voice. I sound like anyone, anybody's husband.

"Hi," she says, sleepy, sweet. I imagine a knife that could cut me in two. I imagine a life where I'm everything she deserves.

"How much longer?" she asks.

I look at my watch; I've already set it to Copenhagen time. I won't need to reset it for Sweden. "Four hours," I say. "It'll be nice to be in a Christian country again,"

"Mm-hmm," she says, but she looks down as she says it. I worry sometimes about her relationship with the Lord. I'm not sure she's given herself as completely as she could. I'll need to talk to her about it sometime, but right now I can't muster the energy to be a mentor.

I shift in my seat; there's not a lot of legroom. I'm so sick of sitting on planes. The flight attendants are coming through with a snack; we had lunch five hours ago, a cold meal of chicken and salad and a hard brown roll. Now the flight attendant hands us each a white paper bag, and we open them like it's Christmas. A cup of plain yogurt, a sandwich of tuna and pickles, a plastic container of water. And a chocolate bar! My spirits rise for the barest fraction of a moment, and then I think I have no right to feel even such a small joy. The idea of penance descends on me, cool and soothing.

"Here you go, honey," I say, handing Abby the candy. "I want you to have it."

Back when I called myself "gay"— and believe me, there's no sadder irony than the corruption of that happy word to mean something so vulgar – I was a bit of an activist. I marched in parades; I tried to convince myself that *pride* meant something different from what it says in the dictionary. Because pride was never what I felt.

I joined Redemption on a cold, cold morning when I'd sunk myself very low, though honestly it was not so different from a hundred other sordid mornings I'd weathered. The night before, I'd met a man in a bar and gone with him to his home; I'm sorry to say that this was nothing new for me. We'd done things I do not care to recount, and though I'd been able to banish my misgivings for as long as the heat between us lasted, I awoke with a feeling like fire ants under my skin. I needed to get out of there; I needed, more than anything, to leave behind that man who'd been my accomplice in this lustful act, that apartment whose very walls were witnesses to my repugnant behavior. I rose quietly and began to find my clothes with shaking hands, but in my sick haste I stumbled over my own shoes, and the man awoke.

"Where are you going?" he asked. He knelt on the bed and reached up to where I stood; he put his arms around my neck and tried to pull me back down with him. He was naked, and he touched my bare skin, and I nearly weakened. But there was a full-length mirror on his closet door, and as I began to sink into his embrace, I saw the way we looked, as an outsider might see us. It was the expression on my own face that got me: hesitant and frightened and so very, very eager. I have never felt more disgusted. In that moment, my life narrowed to the angle of that reflection: a pinpoint of light caught in a piece of glass, two men bound by an unholy hunger. And I found the strength to break away.

In Redemption, the first thing they do when you join is to try to get to the root of your homosexuality. It's a bit of a puzzle. For a man, it could be the result of an uncaring mother or an absent father, or it could be the opposite: a mother who hovers, a father who gets too close. In my particular case, it wasn't clear-cut. I grew up in a Christian home, and I was certainly taught that homosexuality was wrong. My parents are still married, and I believe my father was a good male role model; I'm not aware of ever feeling abandoned by either of my parents. There was never any abuse, at least none that I remember, though I don't rule out the possibility that I've repressed something crucial. I had an older brother, but there was no sexual play between us. I never wished to be a girl; my parents dressed me the same way other parents dressed their little boys. But clearly, somewhere along the line, something went wrong; perfectly normal families don't produce homosexual children. I sifted, and I prayed, because I knew that until I located the origin of my deviance, the exact moment my development was derailed, I would never live a full life.

In the end, my Redemption mentor and I came up with several theories, and I'm not sure I'll ever know which one is the true source of my pain. There was a girl I dated for a few months in the ninth grade, who left me for a better-looking boy; perhaps the emasculating nature of this betrayal led to some confusion about my own gender identity. (Certainly, in my subsequent ruminations about what the two of them might be doing together, she was the one I imagined changing places with.) And then, also, I had an elderly aunt who lived with another woman. Though no one in my family ever hinted at any impropriety in their relationship, I think it must have been clear to the adults that these two women were not living a natural life. The fact that they were included in all family gatherings,

Aunt Evie and her "friend," makes me question my parents' judgment, to say the least; to bring that kind of influence into a house with growing children seems like the most dangerous kind of folly. I have to wonder if perhaps my parents' tacit approval of that lifestyle, their refusal to stand up for righteousness and reject sin when they found it in their very family, made me feel that such perversion was acceptable.

I don't know. There are too many threads to untangle, too many different times in my life when an unhealthy idea might have taken root inside me and begun to bloom. All I know is, every time I have ever touched a man, every time I have lusted after a man, I have felt ashamed. I'm certain that the remorse I feel, the guilt, the self-hatred . . . I believe that those feelings are a message from God, a sign that what I'm doing isn't right. I try to see these desires as a disability, as a challenge that God has set for me. I try to rise above it like a man. And all I can do is believe that, sooner or later, I will be victorious.

Abby and I play Hangman on cocktail napkins. Our camera crew come over to get some quick shots, then move back to their seats to rest. We do TV phrases ("Lovely parting gifts," "And now a word from our sponsors"), hymn titles ("Morn of Morns, and Day of Days," "Since Jesus Came Into My Heart"), and foods we want to eat when we get back home ("blueberry pancakes," "barbecue," "chili dog").

"It's nice to have some time together," I say. "I feel like we're never alone these days."

"Mm-hmm," she says. She's bent over her tray table, embellishing the hangman from the last round. She gives him curly hair and a bowler hat. "I guess we should have known that 'reality show' and 'romantic getaway' aren't synonymous."

I look at the top of her head, her shiny brown hair. I think about kissing her, but I don't. "I hope we have a baby soon," I say.

She takes a deep breath, lets it out. "Well, I don't think it's going to happen on this trip," she says. "The times have been all wrong, and all this stress . . ."

"Oh, I know," I say. "I didn't mean it had to be right this minute. God has a plan; we just do our part."

Abby looks up at me, suddenly. She looks intent but wary. "But even when we get home," she says. "Do you really think it's a good idea? I know at some point I'll be past this, but right now I still . . ." She looks down; I can see her blushing.

"You need to say it," I say. "Admit it out loud."

"I still have so many . . . thoughts that I wish I weren't having." She closes her eyes.

I put my hand on her shoulder. "It's okay, sweetie," I say. "It's okay. It's a struggle, I know it is. But you have to fight it. It gets better, I promise." I'm at my best in this role: adviser, comforter, giver of strength. It's moments like this when I feel most like a husband.

She nods, puts on a smile, but she looks like she's trying not to cry. "I know," she says. "I'm sorry."

"Would you like to pray?" I ask.

"All right," she says. Her voice is small.

I take her hand and bow my head. I begin to speak, words that will soothe us both. The comfort we're looking for is right here, inside the knot of our hands, if only we know how to claim it. We soar through the air, above the earth, below the solace of heaven.

TWENTY-ONE

Abby

The first time I heard the word *gay* was on an episode of *Three's Company.* I was about six. Whenever I try to get to the bottom of things, to figure out where my first ideas about homosexuality came from, this is where I always start. I don't remember the exact wording; it was a joke, one of many, about the character Jack Tripper, who had to pretend he was gay in order to share an apartment with two women. I was watching the show alone – it was on in reruns in the hour before my family ate dinner; there was a good deal of background bustle, but I was in the room by myself – and that word, borne on air, traveled out of the TV set and into my life. A tiny moment, but a crucial one; I imagine the word floating there above my head, a drop of rain about to break the surface of the ocean. Bend in close, look at the reflection on the watery surface; you'll see it contains my entire life.

Later, at dinner, I asked what the word meant; there was only the barest moment of silence, the smallest glance passed between the adults, before my father gave an answer. He was not a prejudiced man, and his answer was not a bad one. He said, "It's a man who likes men instead of women or a woman who likes women instead of men." Some of the people I've met in Redemption have their own stories like this, and theirs are invariably worse: lectures on abomination, graphic misinformation, mouths washed out with soap. I cannot say how it is that my father's explanation, so tame by comparison, so innocuous, came to form the center of such a tight and painful knot. But somewhere between the sitcom laugh track and the word *instead,* I learned everything I know.

I was eighteen when I came out to my parents. It's still hard for me to think about. I think I'd sort of imagined they'd be okay with it; honestly, I hadn't given it a lot of thought. I was a freshman in college, home for spring break; parents, beware your children when they come home from college! They will find a bomb and they will drop it on you; or so it probably seems. In any case, my parents took me out to dinner, and during the course of the meal, my mother asked me if I was seeing anyone. I took a breath and told them that I was.

Their reaction stunned me. They were hurt; they seemed battered by this news. For the next two years, every conversation we had was fraught, overladen with emotion. I have cried in more restaurants than I can count. My parents were sad and disappointed and furious. They suggested counseling; they assigned blame to a hundred different sources. They grieved; they actually grieved.

It was a bad time for them; I understand that. But to me, it felt as if I had found a hole in the bottom of the earth, and I'm not sure I've ever recovered. I hadn't known there was anything I could do that would create a chasm this big, yet I'd broken us apart with a handful of words about something I hadn't even done on purpose. It seemed I had found a place where their love stretched thin. I pictured it as a membrane, tough but taut. For a while, it was pulled so tight you could shine a light straight through.

By the time Justin and I arrive in Kiruna, we're exhausted. We've been traveling for twenty hours. I don't think Justin slept at all; I had a couple of unsatisfying catnaps that barely skimmed the surface of sleep. I've gone through several levels of fatigue — I've been grumpy and punchy and faintly ill — but now I just feel kind of disoriented. I feel cushioned from the world, and somehow slanted . . . am I even making sense?

Justin and I, Laura and Carl, and Cassie and Juliet all get our bigger items from baggage claim; luckily, we went through customs in Copenhagen, so we don't have to do it now. There's a customs process called carnet that the camera crews have to go through with their equipment; I don't fully understand it, but it always takes a while. I'm sure that by the time the show is edited and put together, they'll make it look like we're always just jumping out planes and zipping out the door. If only that were the case.

By the time we leave the airport, it's almost ten p.m. local time, but it's not even close to being dark. We're above the Arctic Circle and although we've missed the midnight sun by a matter of weeks, in August there are still about eighteen hours of daylight. I read all about it in the in-flight magazine. Twice. Kiruna has a population of twenty-six thousand; it's home to the world's largest underground iron mine, a space center, and a church that was once named the most beautiful building in all of Sweden. Outside the city, members of Lapland's native Sami population herd reindeer. The region is untouched and picturesque. Not far from here, there's a mountain where you can ski at midnight in June in full daylight. Oh, I know all about Kiruna; too bad it's already time to move on.

I see the other two teams heading for white Volvo taxis, but it seems that while I was in the ladies' room, Justin has made friends with a middle-aged Swedish couple who have agreed to drive us to Jukkasjärvi. I'm not quite sure how this happened, but it doesn't surprise me; Justin is, as I have said, nothing if not dynamic. And people are eager to help when you have your own camera crew.

Justin introduces me to our new friends; their names, as I understand them, are Bengt and Nanna. They are pleasant, ruddy, vigorous; I'll bet they lead lives that are easy and satisfying. (No, stop it — every life is complex. What is it about me that makes me think no one else has any troubles?) Bengt takes the parrot cage and the ski pole from me and leads us to the parking lot.

"You have not skis?" he asks. "Only a pole?"

I nod. "Only a pole," I say. It seems too hard to explain. I'm not in the mood to chat with strangers; honestly, I'd rather have taken a cab.

But Justin is smooth and jovial as ever. "Only a pole," he says, his voice booming through the strange, bright night. "We like a challenge."

Bengt and Nanna smile politely. We reach their car, a beige sedan. I don't see how we're all going to fit. Justin and Bengt load everything into the trunk, and Justin and I cram into the backseat with Stu and Raymond. Nanna graciously offers to take the birdcage. I wind up sitting on Justin's lap, which embarrasses me somehow; I have a glimpse of a girlhood I didn't have, a car crowded with friends, a tiny slip of a cheerleader perched on her boyfriend's knee. Whatever Justin and I are to one another, this isn't a part of it.

"So then," says Bengt as we leave the airport. I look out the window; Kiruna appears, a low city against an enormous sky. "How is it that you come to be on a television show like this?"

I sink a little. There are many possible answers to this, but I know which one Justin will choose.

"My wife and I have a message we want to spread." He speaks slowly so they'll understand. "We have both left homosexuality, and we're eager to spread the word."

I say nothing. Must we bring this up with everyone we meet?

"You have left it?" asks Nanna. "Like you leave a place?"

"That's right," says Justin. "Like you leave a place you know you shouldn't be."

"I have not hear of this," says Bengt. "It is common in United States, to change from one to the other?"

Justin smiles broadly. "Oh, yes. It's happening more and more all the time."

Well, let's not spread lies. We are, after all, ambassadors of a sort; maybe we shouldn't be implying that all of gay America is rushing to join the ranks of heterosexuality.

Justin continues, as I knew he would. "But homosexuality is still a crisis; that's why we need to let people know there's an alternative."

Nanna shakes her head. In profile, she looks perplexed. "I do not think we have this here," she says. "Here is not such a crisis, I think."

"In God's eyes," says Justin, "it's always a crisis."

Sometimes I wonder how we can be so sure what it is God sees.

How arrogant we are, I sometimes think, to imagine there's someone watching us every minute. To think our every action matters that much. Perhaps God's eyes are more focused on the landscape outside the windows of this car: these dark forests, this rugged beauty. Perhaps this is where God turns when He needs a rest from all the noise of prayer.

"And this has worked?" asks Bengt. "You are happier now?"

Justin tightens his arms around my ribs. I know he'd like me to answer, but I don't. Who cares what these people think of me? I can be the strange, sullen woman they talk about. The one married to the nice man.

"Absolutely," says Justin. He kisses the back of my head like I'm a big doll, a prop in his one-man show. "I'm filled with God's joy."

"And you, Abby?" asks Nanna. She turns to look at me with a small, questioning smile. "Are you also filled with God's joy, or do you have your own?"

Strange that after all this time, I still find it hard to lie. I look out the window, past the cage of Justin's arms. "Right now," I say, "all I am is tired."

There have been maybe three or four times in my life when I've been certain there's a God. To Justin, this would sound like heresy, to admit that I'm not convinced of God's presence every minute of every day. But to me it's a miracle. Three or four separate occasions when I've known beyond any doubt that there is something greater than me at work in the universe; how many people don't have even that?

The first time, and the one I return to most often, was when I was in college, during that grim time with my parents. It was my sophomore year, and I was home for Christmas. There had been nonstop fighting since I arrived, I was sad to be away from my girlfriend – though things had been a bit rocky between us lately; we would break up less than two months later – and I was feeling very low. Though I did not, at that point, consider myself to be particularly religious, there was one endless, wretched afternoon when I found myself falling into prayer. *Please,* I thought. *Please. Show me that this is not the worst thing in the world.*

About an hour later, I was watching TV with a great-uncle of mine who was visiting for the holidays, an acerbic man who was not known for his tolerance. He seemed to object to most of the things I was interested in watching; at one point, he turned off a Woody Allen movie with the words, "Shut up, you little freak." He settled on a new channel, and all of a sudden, there was Bob Hope, wearing a tuxedo, standing against a blue curtain. My uncle put down the remote; Bob Hope was someone he didn't mind watching.

"I'm proud to live in this great, free country," said Bob Hope, "and I'm proud of our commitment to free speech. And I'm proud of our country's commitment to protecting the rights of its citizens to work and live free from bigotry and violence."

Suddenly, I felt a little nervous. I glanced at my uncle; his face was impassive.

"That's why I was amazed to discover that many people die each year in antigay attacks and thousands more are left scarred, emotionally and physically."

My palms were sweating; my stomach lurched. I'm not sure what, if anything, my uncle knew about me, or about the arguments I'd been having with my parents, but his views on homosexuality were no mystery to me. I braced myself for an attack; I wasn't sure if I could take it.

The monologue continued. "Bigotry has no place in this great nation, and violence has no place in this world, but it happens. Prejudice hurts, kills. Please don't be a part of it." Then white words on a black screen: "GLAAD: Gay and Lesbian Alliance Against Defamation."

For a long minute, I held my breath, waiting for a reaction, but my uncle didn't say a word. Something else came on, he flipped through the channels, and the afternoon continued at a glacial pace. But I felt as though I'd been touched by fire. It was an astonishing moment. I felt as if – and I know how this sounds – God had spoken to me through Bob Hope. I'm not sure I can say why it had such an effect on me; the content about gay bashing was certainly not heartening, and Bob Hope was not someone who mattered to me one way or another. But on that cold day, in that uncertain time of my life, to have a positive message about homosexuality delivered into my home by a well-respected public figure . . . It was wondrous, mysterious, oracular. This was more than a bookend to the *Three's Company* incident of my childhood. This was my moon landing, my Ruby-shooting-Oswald, my Beatles on *Ed Sullivan;* this was the moment I realized that television mattered, that it carried some weight. That under the right circumstances, it could possibly change a life. Even if only for the length of a winter afternoon.

I never saw the ad again. I later learned that Bob Hope had filmed the PSA as an apology for using the word *fag* on *The Tonight Show;* I also learned that, due to lack of funding, the spot aired almost nowhere. The fact that I came across it at all is a wonder.

Like many narratives of grace, this story suffers a little in the retelling. When I called my soon-to-be-ex-girlfriend that night and told her about what I'd felt, she said, "Well, that would be evidence that there's a God, if God's purpose were to creep you out." But faith is a highly personal enterprise; I suspect that God knows that. Flowers in the desert, a bush in flames, succor in the form of a TV commercial; can you say for sure that any one of those isn't real?

It's starting to get stuffy in the car; we're packed in tight, and our sound guy's hygiene isn't all it could be. I find the window button on the armrest, buzz it down; the air that comes in is moist and cool. There's a lake on our left, surrounded by pines. The sky is tinged with pink. Try to remember this, I think; this is Sweden in the summer. I may never be back here again.

"Where in Jukkasjärvi do you need to go?" asks Bengt.

I look down at Justin; he raises his eyebrows and shrugs. "I'm not sure," I say. "All we know is the name of the town."

"Well, we are almost to town. I suppose we drive around a bit. Jukkasjärvi is not so big."

"Look for a blue-and-white sign," says Justin. "And a woman in a glass booth."

"This show," says Nanna. "It sounds very unusual."

"Perhaps they will be at the church," says Bengt. "The church here is very famous. It is Lapland's only wooden church. The altarpiece is by Bror Hjort."

In the backseat, glances are exchanged. We don't have the slightest idea who that is. Bengt turns onto a quiet road. Ahead of us, I see the church, which appears to be two buildings, a squat brick-red tower in front, and a larger meetinghouse behind. And, yes, there's the sign and there's Barbara sealed inside her box. Someone must have alerted her that we were almost here; at least, I hope that's the case. It would be a little sad to think of her standing there for hours at a time, like Snow White with her casket turned on its end.

"This is it," says Justin. Bengt stops the car; as far as I can tell, we've beat the teams who took cabs. Justin was right again, as usual.

"Thanks so much for driving us," I say. Justin opens the door, and the two of us extricate ourselves. Stu and Raymond get out the other side, and Bengt opens the trunk for our luggage. Nanna hands the birdcage through an open window.

"It is our pleasure," she says.

"Can you stay just another minute?" asks Justin. "You may be able to help us with our next clue."

"Yes, of course," says Bengt. He's bent over a release that Stu has handed him to sign. I've never met such agreeable people.

A white Volvo rounds the corner; it's Carl and Laura. Justin and I hurry to beat them to the church. Barbara, stone-faced, watches us run toward her. She might as well be made of wax. On the side of her box, there's a little Lucite cubby filled with envelopes; I grab one and rip it open. Inside, in calligraphy pretty enough for a wedding invitation, there are two words: "What's missing?"

Carl and Laura brush past us. I hold the paper up to the camera, read it aloud, then Justin takes it from me and brings it back to Bengt and Nanna in their car. He hands it to Bengt through the window.

"Do you have any idea what this might mean?" asks Justin. He's whispering, so Laura and Carl won't overhear. "Do you know anything that's missing here in Jukkasjärvi?"

"Missing," says Bengt. He shakes his head.

Behind us, I hear Carl let out a yell when he reads the clue. I turn around and see the two of them step into the Barbara box. Apparently, they already know what's missing.

I turn back to Bengt and Nanna with renewed urgency. "Is there something that used to be here that's gone?" I ask.

"Well," says Nanna, as if it's too obvious to be the answer. "Perhaps they mean the Ice Hotel?"

Laura and Carl have gotten their next clue; they run back to their waiting cab.

"The Ice Hotel?" says Justin. "Maybe – what happened to it?"

Bengt and Nanna share a smile. Bengt shrugs extravagantly. "It melted."

A second cab pulls up; it's Cassie and Juliet.

"It melted?" asks Justin. "It was *made* of ice?"

"Yes," says Bengt. "They build every year. They build in November, it is gone by May."

"Everything is made of ice," says Nanna. "You drink some vodka, the glass is made of ice. You eat your meal, the plate is made of ice. Even your bed is made of ice."

Cassie and Juliet get out of their cab. As they run past us, Nanna says, "That girl – the one with blond hair. She is very familiar to me."

"Let's go," I say to Justin. We take off toward Barbara. As we leave the car, I hear Bengt speaking excitedly in Swedish; I can make out the word *Tracy*, and a word that sounds like *best*. I guess they've recognized Juliet.

"Don't tell them anything," I yell back toward Bengt and Nanna, but I don't think they'll listen. They've gotten out of the car, and Nanna is searching through her purse; I hear her say something that sounds an awful lot like *autograph*.

We overtake the girls, and step into the glass booth. Barbara smiles coldly. I don't think she's going to last on this show.

"Justin and Abby," she says. "You believe you have solved the riddle and found the keyword?"

"Yes," we say in unison.

"And what is your answer?"

I let Justin speak for us. "Hotel," he says. He sounds like he's never been surer of anything.

She lets us hang for a second. "You're right," she says with a smile that doesn't reach any farther than her lips. "You've earned your next clue." She hands me a red envelope with black trim; this means Daredevil Round. It's an unwelcome surprise. How long do they expect us to keep going? My eyeballs ache; if the task is anything harder than extreme cocoa drinking, I'm going to be in trouble.

"Thank you," says Justin. We step out of the booth, and Cassie and Juliet step in after us; they look giddy. Thanks, Bengt and Nanna.

I open the clue. It says:

> *Head to the grounds of the Ice Hotel for an eye-opening challenge!*

> *You've wrestled snakes and learned to sweat*
> *In hot sand buried deep.*
> *But now your toughest struggle yet:*
> *A soft bed, but no sleep.*

"Uh oh," I say.

"I was expecting dog sledding or something," says Justin. "But this sounds harder."

We walk back toward Bengt and Nanna, standing by their car. They've unloaded our luggage onto the grass, and they're bent over a piece of paper, smiling. When we get close, I can see it's Juliet's signature.

"Hi," says Justin. "Thanks so much for waiting. I know it's late, but do you think you could possibly drive us to the Ice Hotel grounds?"

"I am so sorry," says Nanna. "We have agreed to drive Miss Jansen and her friend. You can take their taxicab."

Unbelievable. We're in the most remote corner of Lapland, and we're being dumped for a B-list sitcom star.

"It was a pleasure to meet you," says Bengt, looking beyond us.

He waves to Juliet and Cassie, who are running toward the car. "Good luck with your metamorphosis."

"Uh, thanks," I say, confused for a moment by his statement. "Let's go." Justin and I gather our belongings and lug them to the cab as quickly as we can. Bengt and Nanna's car takes off ahead of us; they must have loaded Juliet and Cassie's luggage while we were still in the booth. Justin and I climb into the backseat of the cab; Raymond piles in with us, and Stu gets in front next to the driver. The driver is a young man, maybe twenty-five; he's slim, with a faint scraggle of yellow beard. He's smoking a cigarette.

"Can you take us to the Ice Hotel?" I ask.

He nods and starts the car.

"What can you tell us about the Ice Hotel?" asks Justin.

"Ja, Ice Hotel," says the driver, and nothing more. He doesn't seem to speak English.

It's finally getting dark. I close my eyes, just for a minute, and try to imagine an entire hotel made of ice. In my current state, even a frozen bed sounds restful. I think about all that work, year after year: a winter barn-raising, carving beams from ice and packing snow into bricks. A house made of the weather. I don't know what it looks like when they're done, but I picture it like a castle, tall and transparent and glistening like gossamer. And every spring, the sun shines; every spring, the ceilings start to drip. Nothing is permanent, I think, as I slip into a space between sleep and waking. Everything melts. And in my half-dreaming state, this thought carries the weight of epiphany.

I let my head fall onto my husband's shoulder. Are we in a cab or on a boat, I wonder, my mind stretching wide. I feel like we're skimming the water. We're above the Arctic Circle, and the waves are edged in white. Together we sail through the darkness, Justin and me and our marriage made of ice.

TWENTY-TWO

Laura

We got lucky; on the way to Jukkasjärvi, our cab driver told us all about the Ice Hotel, so as soon as we saw the clue, we knew what the answer was. Even though there won't be any prizes till after the Daredevil Round is over, it's nice to be in first place, if only for a matter of minutes.

It's eleven o'clock at night, and the sun has almost set; the sky is hung in pink and blue like a baby shower. Our cab lets us off outside a complex of wooden cabins surrounding a large expanse of green grass. I suppose that this empty space is where the Ice Hotel will be built when winter comes again. I work on figuring out the money to pay the fare — we changed our money in Stockholm, though I doubt that's footage anyone will see — while Carl unloads the trunk. I have to say, as much as I'd like to be doing this with Cassie, it's a lot easier with Carl. He makes it fun; for the first time, I feel like I'm free to enjoy myself, rather than trying to conduct a monthlong therapy session, which wasn't working anyway. Cassie and I didn't really talk on the plane — we weren't seated near each other — but we did end up waiting for the bathroom at the same time, and she actually gave me a smile, which I chose to read as conciliatory. Maybe this time apart will be good for us. In the meantime, I can relax a little bit, see the sights, laugh at Carl's jokes. Let him help me with my bags. Have an adventure. What do you think about that?

We stand on the grass and look around to get our bearings. There's a smell of pine needles in the air, and the cabins glow with light. I'm suddenly in the middle of a swarm of mosquitoes thick as fog. Somewhere, just beyond what I can see, a river rushes through the twilight.

"There's the sign," says Carl. I see it, the blue-and-white *Lost and Found* sign; it's hanging outside a wooden building with a sloped red roof marked RECEPTION. Is that English, I wonder, or are the words just the same? As Carl picks up the birdcage, our latest Little Ricky cries out in annoyance or confusion or joy. I'm sure this isn't the way he imagined his evening going.

"Come on," I say. I slap at a mosquito. The other two teams arrive in quick succession as we're heading toward the building. They seem to have switched places – now Justin and Abby are in the cab and Cassie and Juliet are in the beige car. How did that happen?

Carl and I speed up to get inside first. Even with the parrot and the ski pole in his hands, he manages to open the door for me. We enter a large, open room, brightly lit, with white walls and a beige tiled floor. The room is empty except for a small group of production people and, incongruously, three guys in blue scrubs. There's a reception desk along one wall and a big round-bellied stove sleeping in the corner. I see that some chairs have been arranged in front of a giant TV; on the screen, Barbara stands frozen in front of the church where we just left her. Out of range of the cameras filming us, one of the producers – Eli, I think – pushes a button on a remote, and Barbara springs to life.

"Welcome to the Ice Hotel," she cries, as if she can see us, too. She's standing in daylight; clearly, this was taped earlier. She looks better on TV than in person, I notice. Younger, smoother.

"Thank you very much," Carl says to the television. "I *feel* welcome."

"I guess we're supposed to sit?" I ask. We drop our bags and settle ourselves in big, red, cocoonlike swivel chairs that seem somehow, satisfyingly, *Swedish*. The other two teams rush in with a clatter of ski poles, a banging of birdcages, and after a few moments of load-lightening, they take seats next to us. I sneak a glance at Cassie; I can't read anything from her face. What else is new?

"You are sitting in the reception building of Jukkasjärvi's famous Ice Hotel," says Barbara. She pronounces *Jukkasjärvi* carefully and with great relish; she's probably been practicing all day. "Right now, the Ice Hotel itself doesn't exist. Once winter comes, thousands of tons of snow and ice will be formed and sculpted into the world's most unique resort." I sigh under my breath; this is a pet peeve of mine. Something is unique or it's not; it can't be *more* unique than something else. Out of the corner of my eye, I catch Cassie looking at me, a faint smile on her face. She knows what I'm thinking; she's heard the "unique" lecture about a thousand times. I smile back at her and feel renewed. See? Things aren't so bad between us; we still have this. No matter what else happens in our lives, we'll always know the things that piss each other off.

Barbara's still going on about the building process; pictures of past ice hotels, now melted away, flash on the screen. "In addition to beautiful guest rooms and suites, the hotel will contain a restaurant, a bar, and a replica of Shakespeare's Globe Theatre, all constructed entirely from ice. There is even an Ice Chapel, consecrated anew each year, where dozens of couples are married every season." I consider that. I'm sure it makes for a pretty wedding – the glimmering icicles, the bride wrapped in white fur – but it sounds wrong to me, an inauspicious way to start a life together. Shouldn't marriage be about warmth?

Carl leans close to me. "What is this," he whispers, "an infomercial? Are we going to be asked to buy a timeshare?"

I try not to giggle. I feel like we're schoolkids, whispering through the filmstrip. "Probably part of the contract," I say. "Good publicity for the hotel."

Barbara pauses and pretends, in her glassed-in, prerecorded way, to look at each of us in turn. Her last glance lands on a pair of empty chairs.

"But until winter," she says dramatically, "the Ice Hotel is no more than a dream."

Empty, heavy pause, then Barbara brightens. "And speaking of dreams . . ." she says.

"Smooth segue," I whisper to Carl. "I see why they pay her the big bucks."

"Here are the details of your next Daredevil Round. There is no small number of summer activities available in Lapland, but you won't be engaging in any of them. We know that at this point in the game, your biggest enemy is fatigue. And so your challenge is this: you'll be given a soft, warm bed, a sanctuary under the stars. We'll make every effort to make you as comfortable as we can. The only catch is, you can't fall asleep."

There are a few murmurs. "Yeah," I hear Cassie say to Juliet. "We got that from the clue."

"We're up for it," Justin calls out cheerfully.

Barbara continues, oblivious. She's probably asleep now herself, unless the other teams are expected in soon. "Perhaps you've heard stories about wartime torture methods involving sleep deprivation. This is nothing like that. We're not monsters." She smiles in a way that can only be described as monstrous. "You *may* go to sleep at any time. But if you want to get ahead in the game, you'd better stay awake.

"Here's how it will work: each of you will have electrodes attached to your scalp, so that you can be hooked up to an EEG machine." Carl and I exchange a look that's somewhere between alarm and annoyance. Electrodes? "It's a harmless procedure," Barbara assures us, "often used in sleep studies, and it will allow us to pinpoint the exact moment when you fall asleep. Next, you will repair to the comfortable beds we have prepared for you; each team will share a bed. You may talk, tell each other stories and jokes, sing songs, or do whatever you want to do to keep each other awake"—here, Carl looks at me with raised eyebrows; I smile, blush, look away—". . . but you must remain on the bed. We'll be timing your progress, and if either member of your team falls asleep, you're out. Teams who arrive after you will also be timed. In the morning, we'll look at the results; the team who has stayed awake the longest will receive a two-hour head start on the next round of the game."

Barbara smiles wickedly, tries again to single us out with her eyes. "Welcome," she says, "to the longest night of your life."

The video is turned off, and Eli gives instructions. "Okay, guys," he says. "We've got some technicians here from the Stockholm Sleep Center." He gestures to the three guys in scrubs, who wave and smile self-consciously. "They're going to do the electrodes. We've also got some comfy pj's for you to change into." One of the PAs, a red-haired guy barely older than Cassie, starts circulating among us with a pile of flannel. He hands me and Carl each a pair of loose-fitting blue pajamas with the *Lost and Found* logo, the suitcase of stars, embroidered on the breast. Another PA follows with fuzzy slippers. They've gone all out for this. I'm surprised we don't have to wear comical nightcaps.

"Snazzy," says Carl.

"Do we get to keep these?" I hear Cassie say.

"There are bathrooms over there," says Eli, pointing. "You can leave all your stuff here; someone will be coming to look after the parrots. After you change your clothes, I'll need you to come over to this table two at a time – first Laura and Carl, then Cassie and Juliet, then Justin and Abby – for the electrodes. When you're all hooked up, I'll take you out to the Theater of Sleep."

Raised eyebrows, glances all around. "Um, excuse me, Eli?" says Carl. "The Theater of Sleep?"

Eli shrugs. "That's what we're calling it," he says. "It's on the site where they're planning to build the ice theater."

I love the drama they attach to everything. The Theater of Sleep, the longest night of your life. All to make us forget what a silly thing it is we're engaged in. This is not going to be the longest night of anyone's life. It's not a night of birth or death; it's not a night for falling in love or having a fight or breaking up. None of us are studying for an exam, or battling an earache or a stomach flu or throat cancer. We're on a game show, and we're going to try to win a million dollars by seeing who can keep their eyes open the longest; they can use flashy language, but they can't make it mean anything more than that.

Carl and I go first to change our clothes and emerge comfortable and slightly sheepish. The pajamas aren't the most flattering garments I've ever worn, but it's still amazing to me that someone can hand me a piece of clothing in an ordinary size and I can just put it on. For years, there were whole neighborhoods I avoided, neighborhoods filled with stores I couldn't even set foot in. I'd cast my eyes down if I had to walk past, not even daring to look in the windows; now I can just go in and shop. It's been over a year, and I'm still not used to it. I still expect someone to take it away.

Our sound guy, Misha, helps us get miked up. We sit in straight-backed chairs, and the two technicians go to work on us. One of them parts my hair and inspects my scalp. He takes an alcohol pad and scrubs at a spot of skin; I try to remember the last time I washed my hair. It was in Japan – was that this morning or yesterday morning?

The other guy is gluing an electrode behind Carl's ear. "Is this the way you imagined your life working out?" Carl asks me.

I smile faintly. It's a joke, but it's not the kind of question I want to contemplate right now. My tech squirts some kind of gel onto my head.

I think about the night ahead of me, lying in bed with a man I hardly know. This would have been a nice one to do with Cassie, I think, the two of us hanging out in our flannel pajamas, with me telling stories to keep her awake. I remember going on long drives with her when she was a little girl; we'd go to visit my parents or my late husband's parents, or sometimes in the summer we'd rent a cabin on a lake. The car trips on the way there were always nice times for us. We'd sing songs and play games, and when she got fidgety and it was too dark to piece together the alphabet from street signs and license plates, I'd start to tell her stories, all the stories of our lives. Tell me about the time when you and Uncle Jake were little, and you took all the food out of the freezer while Grandma was asleep, she'd say, or tell me about how you and Daddy met, and I'd tell her all those worn-out old stories, using exactly the same words I'd used all the times before.

Sometimes, when I think about the birth of Cassie's baby, I

imagine a different way that night could have happened. Of course, if I'd known what was happening, we would have been at the hospital, but in my fantasies, I'm there with her in that attic room, holding a damp cloth to her head, my knuckles sore from her squeezes. In between contractions, I tell her all those stories again. When you were a baby, I'd tell her, I used to call you my wiggle worm. I used to call you my little potato bug. ("Nice," I imagine Cassie saying. "Did you have a thing for invertebrates?" But the sarcasm in her voice would be light, its edges melted smooth by the warmth of nostalgia, because, come on, we're talking about her *babyhood*, and how hard can she be?) You were reading before you were three, I'd tell her. You once told me, out of nowhere, that God's last name was Joyce. And then, as she gripped my hand tighter and I started to lose her again to the pain, I'd tell her the most important ones of all. The first time I heard you cry was the best moment of my life. You were delivered by a doctor named Dr. Lord. You were born on the coldest night of the year, and everyone said you were the most beautiful baby they'd ever seen.

There's more, though, and maybe, if Cassie had wanted to keep the baby, maybe I would have found the strength to tell her some of the stories I've never spoken out loud. The stories someone ought to tell you when you become a mother. For the past four months, I've had a new clock ticking away in my mind, keeping track of my granddaughter's time in this world — how old is she now? what's she learning to do? — and inevitably, I find myself thinking about Cassie's infancy. Not all of the memories are easy ones, even though they represent the very beginning of us, the start of the story we've become. The months after she was born . . . it was a strange, tough, astonishing time for me. There was a feeling like drowning. All rules suspended; time as thick as honey, nights as long as days. The baby's piercing cry; dreaming without sleeping; waking up to find the bed wet with milk.

During the first week after we brought her home, I remember saying to my husband, "I love her, but I don't know if I love her enough." It was a terrifying thing to me to be responsible for this child, unfathomable and fragile, with all her squalling need. I was scared to be alone with her. I didn't know how I was going to carry out this job I'd taken on, the raising of this new person. It seemed too great a task. I was afraid I'd forget to teach her things, like "please" and "thank you," or the words for grass and trees. I don't know what it's like for other women, women with calmer temperaments and vast inner resources; for me, it was very hard. I knew how mothers were supposed to be, and I knew I wasn't holding my own. A mother isn't supposed to cry because the baby keeps kicking off her socks; she's not supposed to feel utterly defeated by the task of clipping minuscule fingernails. She's certainly not supposed to stand over the crib in the middle of the night and say, as I once did when we'd been awakened four different times in three hours, "I hate the fucking baby."

Is this too much to reveal? I feel ashamed even speaking these words. No, I would never say these things to Cassie, at least not quite like this. And maybe, if she ever becomes a mother again, with all the rich and cavernous meaning that word entails, she'll have an easier time than I did. But if she doesn't, I'd want her to know she wasn't alone. I can't be the only one who ever felt this way. Can I?

The other part of the story, the part that's obvious but still needs to be said, is that it was worth it. Abundantly; exquisitely. I made my way through that heightened year, with all of its shock and tumult and, yes, all of its shining moments of joy. Cassie laughing in her sleep when she was three months old. Cassie, nursing, her eyes drooping shut, raising one soft arm and running her fingers over my face like a blind man. The sound of her babbling; the curve of her downy head; a million kisses to the velvet skin of her neck. I struggled and I pushed through, and sometimes I thought I might not make it at all. And on the eve of her first birthday, I lay in bed and wept as though my heart would break to think that this year was over.

This, for me, is the tragedy of giving this new baby up, of letting her be raised by strangers: the minute I looked at her for the first time, I knew I was ready to do it again. I would have done it again, every bit of it. If you haven't raised a child, started in infancy and raised her right up to the teen years, then you might not understand what it is I'm saying here. *I would have done it again.*

By the time the sleep tech is finished with me, fifteen minutes later, I've got two electrodes pasted to my scalp, one on my forehead, and one behind my right ear. A rainbow waterfall of wires spills down the side of my head. There are no mirrors around, but I can feel my hair sticking up in strange ways; Carl, certainly, looks a little less than dashing with his funny pajamas and his head full of cowlicks. As Eli leads us toward the door, on our way at last to the famed Theater of Sleep, I see Cassie looking at me with amusement. "Hey," she says. "It's FrankenMom." And as Eli opens the door and sweeps us out into the balmy northern night, I find I have a lump in my throat because it's the nicest thing she's said to me in a long time.

Walking across the lawn, I can see that the Theater of Sleep is quite lovely; I imagine it will look even better on TV. They've made a kind of fairy bower out here in the summer night: five brass beds, piled with pillows and covered with satin and velvet, under a tent of mosquito netting draped like a bridal veil. There are ropes of flowers and strings of tiny lights. It's like a honeymoon suite for ten.

Carl and I part the filmy curtains and enter the room they've created. I see that there are nameplates on the beds, and I find the one that's been reserved for us. There's a camera set up on a tripod at the end of the bed, but no cameramen in sight; they're giving the crew some time to rest. It'll be strange not to have anyone lunging at me for a while.

"Well, this is intimate," says Carl.

"Do we just climb in?" I say. I notice now that there are carts with medical equipment – these must be the EEG machines – lined up next to each bed. They've managed to camouflage them with tulle and rose petals; it reminds me of those human interest stories you see sometimes where a couple gets married in a hospital because one of them is seriously ill. Those stories always make me cry.

"I guess so," I say. "Which side of the bed do you like?"

"I'll let you choose," he says.

I go around to the far side of the bed and pull down the covers. I leave my slippers on the grass and climb in. It's soft, and the sheets are cool. I pull the covers up to my chin. Carl climbs in next to me, careful not to touch me. One of the sleep technicians comes over to connect our wires to the EEG machines.

"Your time starts now," he says in accented English. He pulls a stopwatch from his pocket and pushes a button on it. He hangs the device from one of the brass curlicues on our headboard and walks away.

"Well, here we are," Carl says.

"Bet you didn't know it would be so easy to get me into bed," I say, and immediately feel embarrassed.

"You call this easy?" Carl says. "I've got to say, this is the weirdest first date I've ever been on."

We both laugh a little awkwardly. This is the first time we've admitted there might be a romantic undertone to any of this. Are we saying we're interested in each other? Or are we just joking around? Like I've said, I'm not so good at reading those cues. And we're not exactly in the most natural environment.

"So," I say. "Time to stay awake." Before I lay down, I'd been thinking that I didn't see how we possibly *could* go to sleep, with battery packs under our pajamas, microphone wires snaking up our chests, and electrodes glued to our heads, but now that I'm here in the bed, I'm starting to feel pretty drowsy.

Cassie and Juliet come in through the filmy doors. I smile at the sight of my girl in her big pj's; she looks so much like a little kid.

"Don't you two look cozy," Juliet calls.

"Ugh," says Cassie. "My mother in bed with a man. I don't even want to look."

They find their bed, which is across the tent from us, and climb in together. "Well," I say, trying for a joking tone. "I never thought I'd see my daughter in bed with another woman."

Juliet makes a joke back—"Oh, Cassie," she says, playing to the camera, making a show of putting her arm around Cassie, of pretending to lean close — but it's my daughter I'm looking at. She's staring at me, and her eyes are wide, and there's something in her expression, an openness, a vulnerability I haven't seen since she was about nine years old. She's searching my face across the space of the tent; she's looking for my reaction. There's a shift inside me, something as subtle and momentous as continental drift. Plate tectonics, is that what it's called? The surface of the earth taking on a new shape, clicking into place in great big puzzle pieces. And suddenly I know, or I think I do, something new about my daughter. For the first time in my life as a parent, and in spite of the apparent illogic of it—*but she had a boyfriend! So how'd she get pregnant, then?*—I understand something about my child without having it all spelled out for me. And what I feel isn't shock or disappointment, or any of the things she might be scared of as she sits over there looking so small in that oversized prop of a brass bed. What I feel is hope, because my daughter needs me, and finally I've got another chance to prove myself to her. And maybe this time I'll be able to do something right.

TWENTY-THREE

Carl

Lying in bed with a woman I like, not touching, just lying in bed and talking. How many women in my life have I had nights like this with? Not many, maybe six or seven. I could count, but that seems obnoxious; or maybe it just seems young. Once you get into your thirties or forties, it feels a little juvenile to be keeping track. Who am I trying to impress? Just myself. What a stud.

The real question, though, isn't how many women; it's how many women since Jackie. It's how many nights like this have I had since I stopped sleeping next to the woman I married, the woman I thought would be the last. None; this is the first. And why that should make me so nervous and sad and hopeful, I have no idea, but I'll tell you this: I'm not in any danger of falling asleep.

Laura seems rejuvenated, too, for reasons that may or may not have anything to do with the proximity of my big manly flannel-covered self. We've been lying here for over an hour, facing each other. The conversation has been, if not exactly sparkling, given the circumstances, extremely pleasant. And the fact that there are no cameramen lends an unexpected intimacy to the situation, perhaps dangerously so; important not to forget that there are still cameras recording us, even if nobody's operating them.

"Do you know any jokes?" Laura asks me now.

"Hmm." I give it some thought. "There's one Jeff likes. It starts, 'There was this guy who inherited a pig farm' . . . no, I think I'm too much of a gentleman to tell it."

She smiles. "Better keep that one in reserve," she says. "We may need it later."

Probably for the best. It's a stupid joke; the pig farmer discovers he doesn't have any male pigs to keep his farm going and concludes he's going to have to inseminate the pigs himself. But the way Jeff tells it, it's hilarious. I hope he and Dallas get here soon; I hate the thought of him coming in last, being sent home without me. The clues have been tough this round, and to be honest, I'm not so sure Jeff's up to the task. I've always been guilty of letting him lean on me a little too much.

"So," I say to Laura, casting about. I'm not sure what's going to come out of my mouth next, but it doesn't matter. We've got all night. "If you were a TV mom, which one would you be?"

She makes a face. "One of the crappy ones," she says. "One of the ones who doesn't make the beds, and feeds the kids frozen waffles for dinner, and doesn't have any idea what's going on in her kids' lives."

"Oh," I say, "one of the realistic ones. I'd like to see that show. I could play the dad who hides the Candyland game because he just doesn't feel like spending three hours saying, 'See, now you move your little guy to the next blue space. No, no, your guy's the *red* guy. *Daddy's* guy is green.'"

Laura laughs a little. I like this idea, a sitcom starring Laura and me. The two of us cheerfully struggling to Brady-Bunch our families, each of us displaying our own well-loved quirks and working through our easy-to-solve problems. Laura and I in a split-level house, smiling wryly as Cassie throws out sullen-teenager one-liners and Benjamin makes all the precocious observations adults would never say out loud. And then I drag myself back to *this* planet, the one where I've only just met this woman, and we live in different cities; the one where teenagers are sullen for real reasons, and ex-wives make things complicated, and small children don't fall into new family structures quite so easily. The one where I don't even *like* split-levels.

"I've actually done that," I say. I'm back on Candyland. "I have actually hidden toys from my three-year-old son."

Laura stretches her arms, folds them behind her head. "Well, if that's the worst thing you ever do as a parent, you're doing pretty well."

"Oh, don't worry," I say, rubbing a sore spot on the back of my neck. "I've got plenty of time to do worse." I'm not sure I actually want to think about what the worst thing I ever do as a parent might be. Most of the time I think I'm doing fine as a dad, but there's a lot of muddling through, and I'm sure there will be a million different times I'll do the wrong thing. I mean, look at him, that shiny-eyed little boy I carry around in my wallet – he's perfect now, and by the time he's grown up, he won't be. Whose fault will that be?

But I get the idea this is a tricky issue for Laura. What can we talk about? I'm starting to feel lulled by the intimacy of the situation and I'd like to go a little deeper, but none of the stories that seem worth telling are worth telling to the cameras. I feel suddenly that I'd like very much to talk to her about Benjamin's surgeries, about the way they gave the shape of my life a different outline, about the tiny details I can't get out of my head. I remember that when he was fourteen months old and the two of us were going in for the transplant, Benjamin's hospital gown was printed with pictures of Daffy Duck and the Tasmanian Devil. I remember waking up afterward, feeling like I'd been hit by a truck, and looking across the room to see the little guy lying behind the rails of his hospital crib, struggling to lift his arm. There was an IV in his wrist, and they'd attached a board to his forearm to keep him from moving it; the whole thing was covered with some kind of elastic stocking. It was awkward for him to try to move it, and it must have been heavy, but he seemed determined, and it took me a minute to understand what he was trying to do. He couldn't talk much yet, but we'd taught him a few signs from a baby sign language book – Jackie was always up on all the latest parenting trends – and he was trying to ask for a sip of water.

Strange that I even feel like sharing these things after so short a time, but I do. I'd like to tell Laura about the most heartbreaking moments of my life — a little boy in a hospital gown covered with cartoon characters, a little boy in an ecstasy of pain asking for water by making the sign for "more." I guess — and the very hopefulness of this thought takes me by surprise — I'll have to tell her after the game is over.

It's the middle of the night when Jeff and Dallas stumble into the tent. Laura and I have kept each other awake for three hours and fourteen minutes, according to the little clock on our bed, but it's getting harder. We've abandoned all pretense of serious conversation — it's just too awkward with that camera standing over us at the foot of the bed — and we've resorted to playing games of the long-car-trip variety. She kicked my ass at some game she used to play with Cassie where you keep adding letters to a word and rearranging it to make a new word, but I beat her at the TV spin-off game I used to play with Jeff. (Can I really imagine a future with a woman who doesn't know that *Mork and Mindy* was a spin-off of *Happy Days*? I give her points, though, for bringing up *Good Times,* which is that rarest of all species: a spin-off of a spin-off.) I'm not sure I'm wowing her with my charm, but we're having a good time; it's just too bad we don't have any Mad Libs.

Justin and Abby are still awake — the last time I tuned in to their little corner of the room, they were having an earnest discussion about the role of women in the Bible, which is a fascinating topic, I'm sure, though not something that would keep *me* awake — but I'm sorry to say that Cassie and Juliet have been disqualified. Despite a spirited tickle fight initiated by Juliet, the two of them drifted off about an hour ago; I'm not sure who fell asleep first, but their EEG equipment made a little ringing noise, and one of the techs came in and pushed a button on their stopwatch. I don't think Juliet's going to be pleased with the subsequent footage; she's over there snoring like a buzz saw.

Then the gauzy curtains part, and the air is filled with my brother's enormous voice. "Good evening, Jukkasjärvi!" he yells, butchering the Swedish. "Let the slumber party begin!"

He and Dallas have customized their pajamas by adding black bow ties and top hats — where the hell did they get those?— and I see with a pang that they're having a great time together.

Jeff stops by our bed on the way to theirs. "Hello there, brother," he says. "Bet you didn't think we'd ever get here."

"I've been counting the minutes," I say drily.

"We had a little trouble with the clue," he says, "but we were lucky enough to meet some lovely Japanese graduate students who helped us figure it out."

"Graduate students of the female variety," adds Dallas, with an inane eyebrow waggle.

"Yeah, I hear they come in both sexes now," I say.

"Do they ever," says Jeff, and nudges Dallas with his elbow. The two of them laugh and high-five in a way that seems just about right for Dallas but ridiculously childish for Jeff. I roll my eyes at Laura.

"Okay, then," says Jeff. "We'll leave you to go back to whatever you were doing." He makes it into an innuendo; I don't even bother responding. I take a deep breath, let it out slowly. So my brother made a friend. Why should that piss me off?

They go and get ready to be hooked up to their machines, with a lot of loud complaining about having to share a bed. I watch, feeling sour. Since the team switch, I've been going on the assumption that if either one of us makes it to the end, we'll share our winnings with each other. But it occurs to me in a bitter little burst that I don't have the slightest idea if that's Jeff's intention or not. He could be planning on keeping it all himself; hell, knowing him, he could probably blow through that kind of money in a weekend.

"I'm here to tell you," says Jeff to the room at large. He's propped up against the pillows, still wearing his top hat. "President Scooter has the coldest feet in America."

"Um, we're in Sweden, bro," says Dallas. "Duh."

I try to tune them out. Okay, I know why it pisses me off; I can be honest about it. It's because all my life, Jeff and I have always been this team, this unit, this duo. It's always been, "Hey, the Tag-gart boys are here — let's get this party started!" and now I see it had nothing to do with me at all. Get rid of one brother to play off of, he finds another. Here I've been sitting around worrying about whether Jeff depends on me too much, whether he'll do okay in this game without me, and it turns out I shouldn't have bothered. I'm more lost without him than he is without me.

"I am starving," Jeff says loudly. "Can we get some room service?"

Cassie stirs in her sleep, pulls the big puff of a comforter over her head. At least they're doing our work for us; they're keeping us all awake.

"He's funnier when he's with you," Laura says to me. "You kind of keep him in check."

"Thanks," I say. Actually, it's nice to hear.

"Is he always on?" she asks. "Have you ever seen him in, like, a somber mood?"

I shrug. My mind skips to a well-worn groove, and we're onto another story I can't tell, at least not right now. It's something that happened when Benjamin was two months old and having his first surgery; Jeff came with us to the hospital. It was a terrible day, all of it kind of surreal in my memory, but there's one moment I'll never forget. It's one of my favorite stories about Jeff, and it doesn't in-volve a single joke.

Right after Benjamin went into surgery, the three of us — me, Jackie, and Jeff — were sitting in the parents' waiting room. It was a sad room to be in; there were about fifteen of us there, holding cups of sour coffee and glancing at the clock, each one of us thinking about a little boy or girl lying unconscious behind a set of double doors. Fifteen of us trying not to think about scalpels and scars and outcomes; fifteen of us holding onto pacifiers and sippy cups and stuffed rabbits that we thought might offer comfort in another hour or two or three. None of us were talking; the room was as hushed and somber as a church. And then these two clowns wandered in.

Let me be clear: I'm talking about *actual clowns*. Wigs made of green yarn, hats with giant daisies; white makeup and red noses and big shoes. It was a children's hospital, and they must have been there to visit the kids; how they wound up on the surgical ward, I really don't know. But the introduction of this festive presence into the grim atmosphere of the waiting room . . . it was not something any of us wanted to see. It was . . . I don't know how to describe it. It was appalling.

They walked in and began their little show. "'Parents' waiting room,'" said the taller of the two, reading the sign outside the door in a loud, theatrical voice. "Is this where I go to get myself some parents?"

There was silence in the room; people looked at the floor and the walls and their cups.

"This must be the place," said the shorter clown, almost yelling. "Do any of you folks know if I can buy myself some parents here? I've got cash money." Here, he reached into his pocket and pulled out a bouquet of paper flowers. He approached one of the mothers, a woman I'd seen earlier in the presurgery room. Her daughter looked to be about five years old; they'd been reading a book together. The little girl was quiet and had big eyes. I have no idea what was wrong with her; I still wonder sometimes if she's okay.

"Do you know where I can buy a mother?" the short clown asked the woman. "I've got a hundred zillion dollars here." He thrust the flowers toward her face; she had to move her face to avoid being brushed by the bright paper. "See?"

The woman didn't say anything. She stood up and gathered her things clumsily; I think she was shaking. She pushed past the clown; her face was pinched and miserable.

"I'm sorry," the other clown, the tall one, yelled after her as she headed toward the door. "I'm going to have to ask you to leave."

The woman made a little choking sound, and put her hand to her face. Jeff was out of his chair in a second. He was very serious. Jeff, serious, is not something you see very often. He approached the two clowns and took each one by an arm. They sputtered in buffoonish outrage as he pulled them toward the door, but Jeff was firm. "You need to leave these people alone," I heard him say in a low voice. "You need to go." I watched my brother the joker, my brother the perpetual cutup, lead the clowns away. I'm not sure I've ever been so grateful for anything in my life.

Around dawn, which starts about six hours after sundown, Laura and I start whispering to each other. Jeff and Dallas are still awake, if slightly subdued, but Justin fell asleep in the darkest part of the night, and after the telltale beep, Abby let herself drift off, too. There's still no sign of Riley and Trent.

Laura's eyes flutter a little bit. I've got to keep her awake. We're not allowed to take off our microphones, but no one's ever said that we can't cover them up. I put one hand over my microphone and one hand over hers. She seems a little surprised by my touch – I do, after all, have my hand between her breasts – but then she sees what I'm doing and puts her hand over mine. I lean in close; my face is in her hair. "So," I say. "Tell me about yourself."

She laughs, then leans into me. "What do you mean?" she whispers softly. Her words vibrate on my skin.

I'm back to the softness of her ear. I want to kiss it but don't. "What would you tell me if the cameras weren't here?"

She looks shy, suddenly. "Well," she whispers back, though not as quietly. "I'd ask you what we were doing in bed together in the middle of Sweden."

But I don't want to let it go at a joke. "I'll start," I say, breathing the words out of one side of my mouth. I'm not entirely sure that what we're saying won't be picked up; I imagine the postproduction crew using all their finest equipment to turn up our voices, to eavesdrop on our bedtime murmurs, as if they mattered to anyone but us. I'd hate to get home and see this scene with subtitles.

"Benjamin," I tell her as softly as I can. I'm not sure what I'm doing here; I just want us to know each other better. "Congenital liver disease; surgery; gave him part of mine. Horrible time."

She looks at me with so much concern I feel guilty. Great date conversation.

"I'm so sorry," she breathes into my ear. "How is he now?"

"Fine," I say, pulling back so she can see my face. "Fingers crossed."

"Good," she says. She hesitates. "My turn, I guess. What should I tell you?"

"Anything," I say. "Start with the easy stuff." Maybe I shouldn't have started so big; I don't want her to think she has to tell me any huge secrets or anything. Hell, we could just play Telephone, as long as it'll keep her whispering in my ear.

"Okay," she says. She reaches out with her free hand and puts it on my chest; now she's pressing each of her hands to mine, covering up our two microphones. She leans in and whispers, "I used to be fat."

I nod. "I used to be a telemarketer," I whisper. Not sure what I'm going for, but it makes her laugh.

"Here's a better one," I say, talking with my lips against her neck. "I talk in my sleep. Really weird things." My ex-wife, who I wish would stop entering my mind as I lie in bed with this lovely woman, tells me that I once sat bolt upright and said, "Wouldn't it be funny if Bob Vila from *This Old House* were a U.S. senator?"

"Not tonight you don't," says Laura. Her voice is soft and intimate, and I'm not thinking about my ex anymore. "Not if I can help it."

"I really like you," I say. I'm not even whispering.

Laura straightens a little and shakes her head. Her face is impenetrable to me. "Here's why you shouldn't," she says in a normal voice. She's let her hands drop; now she presses them harder to mine and leans against me. "I'm messy. I'm oblivious to things that are going on around me. Sometimes I talk about people behind their backs." Yeah, those are deal breakers. Keep it coming, I think. Bring it on. Tell me all the reasons I shouldn't even consider falling for you.

"I've only had one boyfriend since my husband died. He liked to paint my toenails and compare me to food."

I almost laugh, but she sounds so serious I don't. Well, jeez — that one actually works out in my favor. Next to that guy, I sound like an absolute catch.

She pauses, keeps her lips to my ear. "I'm a terrible mother," she whispers. Her voice is matter-of-fact. "Cassie had a baby, and I didn't even know she was pregnant."

Oh, God. That one takes me by surprise. I start to lean back, to see what her face looks like, but she pulls my ear back to her mouth. "We gave the baby up for adoption," she says. She's whispering, but her voice is hard. "I don't think things will ever be right with my daughter again."

She pulls away, folds her arms. Gives me a look that's like a dare. Does she think I'm going to walk away? I'm tied to the bed with wires, for one thing.

"Come here," I whisper. I take hold of her shoulders and pull her close to me. Sometimes you just need someone to take your side. "That must have been so hard," I say.

She sags a little; when she speaks, her voice is strangled. "I know," she says. "I can't imagine making her go through that alone . . ."

"No," I say, interrupting her. My voice is firm. "I mean for you."

She shrugs, doesn't quite believe me. Doesn't matter. The sky's getting lighter; I'm starting to hear the birds. We're going to figure it out.

From across the lawn I hear Jeff's voice rise, jovial, excited. "So his wife says, the pigs aren't in the meadow *or* in the mud; they're all in the pickup truck, and one of them's honking the horn!" Dallas laughs in a way that makes him sound like an overcaffeinated rooster.

I smile at Laura. "That would be the end of the pig farm joke," I say. "I guess I could tell it to you now."

Laura looks up through the mesh ceiling to the pink and purple sky. She shakes her head slowly; she looks sleepy, but not so sad. "I've heard the beginning and I've heard the end," she says. "Let's save the middle for another time."

The sun rises. I reach out across the soft white country of the mattress and take her hand.

TWENTY-FOUR

Cassie

Well, here's one good thing to come out of this whole surreal experience: if I ever get desperate for money, I can always sell my story to the tabloids. *My night in bed with Best Friends star Juliet Jansen! "She kept trying to tickle me!" says confused gal pal.* By the time you figure out nothing interesting happened, you've already gotten up to the front of the grocery line, and you may as well just toss the magazine on top of your pile.

Really, it was kind of boring; we didn't talk about much. It wasn't like the night we spent in the hotel room when the cameras weren't there. (Aha! Puzzle pieces falling into place! It's like my mind is suddenly closed-captioned for the judgment-impaired: "Juliet is not the same when the cameras aren't there!") She was completely *on* the whole time; she made jokes about how dorky we both looked with all the wires sticking out of our heads, and she told pointless stories about being a presenter at the MTV Awards. There wasn't a word that came out of her mouth that wasn't designed to make her look good.

And the tickling thing was just weird. We'd been in bed for about an hour at that point, and I guess she was running out of amusing stories about herself. So she did this big shifting-gears thing — it was like watching someone try to drag themselves away from a mirror — and she turned her attention to me. She turned to face me, and out of nowhere, in this really cheery voice, she said, "So, do you have a girlfriend at home?"

I was blown away. I'm not looking forward to seeing the expression on my face when we get home and this thing finally airs; I'm sure I looked completely panicked. I mean, there'd already been that lame joke that my mom made about seeing me in bed with another woman; I was pretty much ready to be done with the lesbian-insinuation portion of the evening.

Juliet let me sputter away for a minute, and then she said, "Because one of the hard things about being a child star is you don't get a lot of time to make any close girlfriends." And she smiled like it was all just an accident of phrasing.

"Oh, well," I said, sort of recovering. But the truth is, I don't have a good answer for that either.

"So tell me," she said. "What do girls do at slumber parties?"

"Um," I said. I'm sure I'm going to come across as the biggest idiot. But she wasn't really looking for an answer.

"Do they do this?" she asked. And then she started tickling me.

For a minute, when I was just caught up in the surprise of it, the sheer physical experience, it was absolutely thrilling. I mean . . . it just was. She had her hands all over me; I don't need to spell it out. But there were all these wires from the electrodes and the microphones, so it wasn't the most natural thing in the world to be moving around, and then I saw Juliet glancing toward the camera. And suddenly I just had this feeling that she was trying to get something out of me.

"No," I said. I pulled away as well as I could, and arranged the sheets so there was plenty of cotton between us. "I've never been to a slumber party where anyone's done that."

Juliet looked annoyed, but she covered it quickly. And then it was awkward, and the awkwardness led to silence, and eventually the silence led to sleep. I woke up on a sunny morning in a field in Sweden, with a beautiful woman lying next to me, and my first thought was that maybe I should have let her touch me a little longer.

*   *   *

The fact is, I've only kissed one girl, and it didn't go well. It was Mia; of course it was Mia. It happened last December, on the day I found out I was pregnant. Or, at least, the day I took the test; I'd had a pretty good idea for a few weeks before that. By my calculations, I was ten weeks along; that's how long it had been since that field trip to Greenstone Village, so I thought I had a couple more weeks to think about having an abortion. The thing is, and I don't know why they don't teach you this in health class, doctors start counting your pregnancy from the first day of your last period, which makes absolutely no sense. Say you get pregnant the first time you have sex (which was not the case for me, but it could happen) – that means you were actually still a virgin on the day they count as the first day of your pregnancy. Stupid. But, whatever, the point is that when I went to the clinic the following week, they told me I was already too far along for the kind of abortion they could do there, as I've mentioned. And while I spent most of my pregnancy cursing the medical profession and sex-ed books and whoever it was who decided to use the phrase "twelve weeks" in all the books and pamphlets without explaining what it meant, I can't really say now that I wish it had turned out differently. That baby . . . well, it's hard to talk about. But I would never say I'm not glad she's in this world.

Anyway, before I start begging Justin and Abby to take me along on prolife marches or whatever, I want to get back to that day, the day I found out I was pregnant. It was a Saturday; I took the test first thing in the morning and, of course, totally freaked out. I stayed in my room for a while, crying and panicking, and, no surprise, my mom was clueless; I think she was on the Internet, sending love notes to Curtis the Wonder Stalker. He was probably offering to pumice her dead skin or pop her zits or something, and she was probably swooning at the romance of it all. I thought about calling Dan – I mean, he was the father, and he did say after the condom debacle that he'd be there for me if anything happened – but I just couldn't deal with him right then. I'd been less and less interested in being with him lately; it's not so much that I was getting sick of him, as I was getting sick of *us,* this fake couple that everyone (including him) seemed to think was real. I just couldn't deal with being part of this afterschool-special cliché, the frightened boy and girl holding hands in the waiting room of the abortion clinic, which is where I still thought I was headed. So I called Mia.

She could hear right away that I'd been crying, but before I could tell her about the pregnancy test, she kind of took over the conversation. "I was just about to call you," she said. "Reece told me what happened with you and Dan. You must be so upset."

I had to think a minute before I understood what she was talking about. When I realized, I almost laughed. The night before, Dan had called to tell me that his parents were forcing him to take some other girl to a dance; it was the daughter of a friend of his mom's, and she went to a different school, and apparently she needed a date for her winter formal. The two moms arranged it without asking Dan if it was okay. Dan was really apologetic and kept telling me it didn't mean anything, and I sort of pretended to be mildly upset, because that's what he seemed to expect. But the whole time we were talking, I was sitting on my bed, reading the instructions on the pregnancy test, and believe me, the idea of Dan dancing with another girl was not at the top of my list of worries.

But Mia sounded so sympathetic and so concerned, and I just wanted to bask in that for a minute. It seemed like bringing up the pregnancy would kind of shatter the moment, turn it into something bigger and scarier. So I just let her believe that she was right, that I was sitting at home on a Saturday morning crying over the thought of my boyfriend buying a corsage for someone else.

"Yeah," I said. "It really sucks."

"Listen," she said. "Do you want to go shopping this afternoon? It might make you feel better. I want to buy something really nice for the Big Dinner." She said it with capital letters. She and Reece were going to have their one-year anniversary in another week, and he was taking her out to some big fancy restaurant. Gag. But yeah. An afternoon alone with Mia. I'd never say no.

We met up and caught the bus to the mall. I kept thinking I'd be able to find a good moment to bring up the pregnancy, but it was really hard. I could tell her now, I kept thinking, or now, but it was such big news, and I felt shy for some reason. The mall was packed — it was only a few weeks till Christmas — and we had to fight our way in and out of stores. Everything was loud and bright and overheated. Mia seemed to have decided that the best way to console me about Dan was to avoid the subject; she was chattering away about Reece and about what she was going to buy him for an anniversary gift. It was all so *important* to her, and it just made me feel so sad.

We didn't have much luck with the shopping at first. Mia had some very specific ideas about what kind of outfit she was looking for, and nothing seemed right to her. And I had to stop about five times to pee and once to get a snack; I was hungry all the time then, right at the beginning, and I'd noticed that if I didn't eat every couple of hours, I'd start to feel sick. Mia was starting to get annoyed with all the interruptions, and I almost told her why I was acting so strange, but it still didn't feel right. I'm sure there are a lot of people whose biggest moments take place at food courts, but I didn't want to be one of them.

Finally, toward the end of the day, we found a store that had a bunch of dresses that Mia thought were promising. She gathered up an armload of slinky, shiny things and headed for the dressing rooms.

"Do you want to come in with me?" she asked.

"Sure," I said. We'd seen each other undress before. It was no big deal.

We had to wait a couple of minutes for a room to open up; I stepped in with her, and she closed the door. The little white room was filled with cast-off clothes, inside out and falling off their hangers. There were pins scattered on the floor. It was messy and cramped, but it felt intimate somehow. We were alone in there, closing out the chaos of the store.

I pushed aside a pile of clothes to make room on the narrow bench. This was a skinny person's store; the frothy little items I had to move in order to sit down were things I could never wear in a million years.

Mia started to undress. She was wearing some kind of vanilla perfume, or maybe it was body lotion. How do I do this? I thought. How do I say the words? I tried an experiment; as she was pulling her sweater over her head and her ears were covered by the soft wool, I whispered "I'm pregnant" as softly as I could. It was like a fairy tale test, like the pea beneath the princess's mattress. If she could summon some superhuman sense to hear what I needed to tell her, then . . . then what? Then it meant she cared about me and she would help me get through this? Then it meant that, in some small way, I could win out over Reece? I didn't know. But it didn't matter; she didn't hear me, not even enough to say, "What?"

Mia stood in her underwear, trying to decide what to try on first. She was beautiful, and I wished I could touch her, and my day just kept getting worse. She pulled a dress off the hook on the wall and pulled it over her head. It was gorgeous and tight-fitting, made of some stretchy dark red fabric. There were sleeves that were no more than straps; they fell at the tops of her shoulders. It was cut low over her breasts.

"Your bra is showing," I said. "Do you want me to unhook it for you?"

She looked at me strangely. "Um, no," she said. "I've been doing it since I was twelve." She reached behind her and unfastened her bra, then pulled it out through the straps of the dress. Her breasts swelled over the top of the neckline.

"That looks really good," I said. My voice sounded hollow. "Your mom would freak, though."

"Yeah." She appraised herself in the mirror. "Maybe if I got some kind of wrap to wear over it?"

"Only if you wrap it around your boobs."

She looked at herself for a long moment. "I don't care," she said. "I'm getting it. I'm not even going to try on the others." She started to unzip the dress. "We're done. Should we call Reece and see if he wants to pick us up?"

Somehow, that was too much. I saw how the rest of the day

would go: we were going to leave that room and be back in the mall, and then we'd be with Reece, and this whole day would be wasted. And I'd still be pregnant, and I'd still be all by myself.

"Listen," I said. "Can you just wait a minute? There's something I need to tell you."

She stopped and looked at me, full of concern. I had her attention, and it was too late to turn back. For a minute, neither of us said anything. "Do You Hear What I Hear?" was playing over the loudspeaker and for some reason, it made me want to cry.

"What is it?" she said. "Is it about Dan?" Her zipper was half undone, and one side of her dress drooped a little.

I don't know what happened. It was like I finally had the chance to tell her my secret, and it felt like a rare opportunity. A moment that might never come again. She was dressed like she was going to a party. I was desperate and frightened, and at the last minute, I just changed my mind about which secret I wanted to tell. I leaned forward and put my hands on the bare skin of her shoulders, and I kissed her.

Divide time up into the tiniest unit you can imagine – a fraction of a fraction of a breath of a moment. That's how long my lips were on hers. That's how long I soared above everything around me, the clothes on the floor, the wall of shoppers, the swelling music coming from the ceiling. And then she pulled away.

"What are you doing?" she asked. She didn't look mad, just startled and confused. And maybe a little bit hurt.

"I," I said, and no more.

"Cassie," she said. "No. Just . . . no."

She turned away and started once more to work the dress off her body. Then she turned her head back in my direction. "Would you mind waiting outside?" she said.

I gathered up my coat and bag and opened the dressing room door. A tiny blister of panic began to grow inside me. How much, exactly, had I ruined with that one impulsive move? "I wish I hadn't done that"—are there any words that are worse? Fuck all that stuff about "it might have been" being so sad; at that moment, I would have given anything for a life spent imagining that Mia might have kissed me back.

I stood among the racks of sparkling holiday dresses, stony and terrified. Finally, Mia came out of the dressing room and walked past me without looking at me. "Let's go," she said. Her arms were empty.

"You're not buying the dress?"

"No," she said sharply. "I don't want it."

"It looks really nice on you," I said, and stopped myself short.

She gave me a look that made me wither and shrink. "Let's just go," she said.

I followed her through the maze of the mall and out to the stone bench where the bus would come. Inside the strange, sterile environment of the mall, we'd missed the passing of day into night. Outside, it was clear and cold and dark.

We stood and waited. "I'm sorry," I said, finally. Her scarf blew around her in the wind. "I don't know what I was doing."

"I'm not going to talk about it," she said, her voice fiercer than I'd known it could be. "Not here."

Not, as it turned out, anywhere. These moments with Mia, humble as they are, are the very last ones I have. After this, there would be a process of freezing me out in increments until I dropped off cleanly, like a finger exposed to frostbite. And after that, a freezing of my own: without Mia, there was no reason to be with Dan, so I sent him off without even telling him about the baby. And I learned how to be on my own.

But that night outside the mall . . . for some reason, that I hold onto. Isn't it strange, the way something can be painful and precious at the same time? I've never felt sadder or more scared than I did that night, but I treasure every detail. The December stars, the frozen mud. Waiting in the dark to get on the bus. This ache inside. The crispness of the air. Her breath visible to me. These are mine to keep.

Ten months later, in a moment that seems much less real, I'm riding the Stockholm subway with Juliet Jansen, followed by Garrett

and Akil, our camera crew du jour. My mom and Carl were the ones
to win the head start, though it took a while to determine it, since
Riley and Trent didn't arrive until the rest of us were already waking up.
They burst into the mesh tent around noon looking tired and annoyed; apparently, they'd figured out the coordinates wrong and were
in London, waiting for a flight to Iceland, before they double-checked
a map and realized they'd made a mistake. So they're colossal idiots,
but since this was a Daredevil Round and not an elimination point,
they had to finish the leg before the rest of us could move on. The
rest of us had some time off while they did their Theater of Sleep
thing. It was nice – people napped, the Ice Hotel people showed us
their "freeze house," where they have a little ice sculpture museum
during the summer, and we ate a meal of reindeer meat and cloud-
berries, which was better than it sounds. (Well, most of us ate it;
Juliet said she was "detoxing" and couldn't ingest anything but
spring water, but later on I saw her scarfing M&M's from her backpack. Maybe she was put off by Jeff and Dallas's incessant Rudolph
jokes.) And for once, we got to stay someplace for a little while without rushing on to the next task.

As it turned out, Riley and Trent weren't any better at staying
awake than they were at reading a map; they were both asleep within
forty-five minutes, and my mom and Carl got their head start after
all. Two hours later, the rest of us were presented with a manila envelope, an instant camera – gosh, do you think the camera company
might be a sponsor, by any chance? Barbara managed to fit the name
in about fifty times – and our clue for the Found Objects Round:

> *What kind of vacation would it be*
> *Without some holiday pics?*
> *The world's longest art gallery awaits:*
> *Look inside your bag of tricks.*

They must be running out of energy; I swear, the clues are getting
lamer. Inside the envelope (sorry, "bag of tricks") were four photographs of different pieces of artwork, along with further instruc-

tions; apparently, we're supposed to find the art pieces featured in the photos and take new pictures with our cameras. One team member has to be in each photograph; the pictures themselves are our Found Objects. Once we've got all four pictures, we can proceed to the Meeting Point, where one team will be bumped off.

After talking to some people who worked at the hotel, all of whom seemed to hold *Best Friends* in high regard, Juliet and I learned that the Stockholm subway, the Tunnelbana, is sometimes called "the world's longest art gallery" because of all the murals and sculptures it contains. We caught a flight from Kiruna, and we were in Stockholm at the central subway station by 10 p.m. It's Friday, and the trains run till 3:30 a.m.; if we don't find everything we're looking for before then, we'll have to wait till morning.

We've already found one; our taxi driver recognized the art in one of our pictures – a tunnel with giant blue vines climbing a white wall – as being in the T-Centralen station, so that's where he dropped us off. We've got three left to find: a gold-and-copper mural that looks kind of like a cave painting, with two soldiers and two horses approaching each other in battle; a bright green wall painted with dayglo pink and orange flowers; and a statue of a short naked man with red skin and yellow hair. The subway system here is gorgeous. It's very clean, and the walls of the stations are kind of bulbous and curvy, like the walls of a cave; according to a brochure I picked up at the airport, when they were building the later stations, they just blasted the space out of the rocks and left all the contours intact. They're called "grotto stations." And, yes, there's art everywhere.

We're on a blue-line train now, on our way to the Kungsträdgården station to look for our little naked guy, on the advice of a young woman who approached Juliet to tell her how much she'd enjoyed her work. Everywhere we go here, Juliet gets recognized. She's not exactly mobbed by fans asking for autographs, but she gets a lot of interested looks and shy smiles. And she loves it; she's just soaking it up. Not a mopey bone in her body since we got to good old Scandinavia. I think she's going to be sorry to leave Sweden and rejoin the rest of the world, where *Best Friends* is nothing but a corny memory.

"Here we are," I say as the train pulls into the station; we only had to go one stop. Garrett and Akil position themselves by the door.

"Great," says Juliet, speaking just a little louder than necessary and granting a smile to the rest of the people in the train car. "Let's go find that statue!" It's like she thinks she's in a play.

We get off the train, and there's our naked guy, right on the platform. He's got kind of a pygmy-esque look about him. He's not entirely naked; he has a cape knotted around his shoulders and some kind of fig-leaf thing over his apparatus. He has long yellow hair and a beard, and he looks a little concerned about something.

"Do you want to be in this one?" I ask Juliet. I was in the blue-vines picture.

"You know I do," she says. Her voice is kind of flirtatious, but it's not really directed at me. I can't tell if she's flirting with the statue or with the country at large. She steps up to the sculpture and puts her arms around it; the little guy is short, but he's on a pedestal, so her arms only come up to his knees. She turns her head and plants a kiss on his thigh. I'm willing to bet that's not allowed, but it's 11 p.m. on a Friday and I'm sure the transit police have other things to deal with. Anyway, what are they going to do, arrest Juliet Jansen, beloved star of *Best Friends*? I snap the picture as Garrett records me recording the event.

We still don't know where our last two pieces of artwork are, so we approach the man at the ticket booth (who, amazingly, seems not to recognize Juliet). He nods when he sees the two pictures, and he's in the process of pointing out the stations on a map when I hear Juliet swear softly. Akil steps in and adjusts her microphone pack; I guess they didn't pick up her profanity clearly enough.

"Watch out," Juliet says. "Here come the dramatists."

I look at her, a little confused. "I think 'dramatist' means playwright," I say. But without turning around, I hear the loud, theatrical voices of Jeff and Dallas, and I guess I know what she's talking about.

"Hey, buddy!" I hear Jeff yell. I turn back toward the platform and see that he's talking to the statue. "We have been looking for you everywhere."

I take a look at the map and try to figure out where we need to go next. We head back toward the platform, where Jeff and Dallas are making a show of setting up their photograph. They're still wearing their stupid top hats; Jeff takes his off and places it on top of the statue.

A young hipster-type guy, maybe college-aged, approaches them. "Excuse me," he says. He has a British accent. "Aren't you President Scooter?"

Dallas beams. "Why, yes, I am," he says. For some reason, he imitates the guy's accent. "So good of you to notice."

The British guy looks through his pockets, finds some paper. Dallas signs his name, and there are thanks and admiration all around.

"Did you see that, dude?" I hear Dallas say to Jeff after the man has walked away. "I told you, my show was huge in England."

The sour look that settles on Juliet's face is only there for a second; then the train comes, and we take our map and head off to finish our task. But later, after this evening is over – after we locate and photograph the rest of our artwork, open our gold envelope, and find our way to the Meeting Point at the gleaming crystal tower of Sergels Torg; after we learn that my mom and Carl are in first place, and after Riley and Trent earn themselves a one-way ticket to Reject Rendezvous by making the wrong decision about when to conserve their cash (should've taken a cab, guys); after we get a few hours' sleep and wake up to the bustling Stockholm morning – we will open a clue telling us that our next stop is London. And the look on Juliet's face will be one of sheer terror.

TWENTY-FIVE

Juliet

We're getting closer to finding a winner.
Now picture fourteen stonemasons high up in the air,
The site of London's most precarious dinner;
Today only pigeons dine there.

I think I've mentioned that my show never aired in England. Which is fine, right? I'm staying calm, staying centered; nothing to panic about. It's not like anyone knew who I was in Egypt or Japan; I could've been invisible. It's kind of nice to be anonymous for a change, no one bothering me for autographs or wanting to talk about their favorite episodes. *Best Friends* was a long time ago. I should be focusing on my future.

But I need to be pragmatic. Dallas is already getting a lot of camera time, ever since he joined the comedy team of Jackass & Bigger Jackass; if it's true that we're now entering *President Scooter* territory, then I've got to figure out a way to make myself more visible. Obviously, winning the game would be a good idea. Half a million bucks would be nice, and the resulting magazine covers and TV offers would be even nicer. But I can't rely on that; there are other people who are better at playing the game. I'm still wondering if I can make use of Cassie somehow. The flirtation thing hasn't been working exactly the way I thought it would, and now I'm not sure what will put me in the best light. I just have to make sure that the time I have on camera counts.

We're actually driving to London for the Keyword Round; who knew that was even possible? I don't know if they're trying to save money or make things more picturesque, but we were told there was no air travel for this leg of the race. We printed out directions at our hotel; it's a twenty-hour drive (including a few ferries), and we have to go through Denmark, Germany, the Netherlands, Belgium, Luxembourg, and France before we get to England. Seven countries in less than a day, and not a single one where anyone knows who I am.

Cassie's driving this stretch, so I'm sitting in the backseat of the car the show provided us with. Our cameraman, Elliott, is in the passenger seat, and the sound guy, Misha, is sitting next to me. We've been on the road for almost six hours, and we're not even out of Sweden yet.

"Exit 30," Cassie says, looking at a road sign. We're on a four-lane divided highway, but there's lots of greenery around. Very picturesque; I'm sure Elliott's getting some good shots out the window. "Malmö. That's what we want, right?"

I look at the map in my hands. "Yeah," I say. "That's where we get the bridge to Denmark."

"Great. You got any of that Plopp left?" An hour or so ago, we stopped for gas, and we picked up some snacks at the gas station store. "Plopp" is a kind of Swedish chocolate bar with caramel inside; Cassie seems to find the name hilarious. We also got potato chips, some M&M-type things called "Non Stop," and some disgusting licorice candies with hot powder inside. I pass the chocolate up to Cassie.

"So is Cassie short for something?" I ask. Just making conversation; this road trip thing is getting old already.

"Yeah, Cassandra. I hate it."

"Really? I think it's pretty."

"Thanks." She sounds doubtful. "I guess most people don't really like their own names."

I actually do like mine. Sometimes people ask me if Juliet is a stage name, like maybe if you looked deep enough into me, you'd find out that on some cellular level I'm nothing but a boring old Julie or a Jennifer. But Juliet is the name I've had since day one. It helps, I guess, to have a mother who plans for you to be a star before you're even born, who's writing up a schedule of casting calls for diaper commercials before she even goes into labor. My parents have a videotape of my birth – I'm surprised they haven't tried to sell it yet; maybe there'll be a market for it if this show goes well – and the first thing my mom says, when she's holding me in her arms for the very first time, is, "Are those red marks on her face going to fade?" I find it so funny that Cassie and Laura seem to think they have this huge feud going on, when to someone like me their life looks like a fucking sitcom.

But it's not worth dwelling on. Typical showbiz mom, success at all costs – how boring is that story? Can I really say I've been hurt by it? I hate all that talk-show bullshit, everyone whining about how their parents screwed them up. It's over; move on. A lot of people suffer. A happy childhood isn't a right.

"Okay, help me out here, navigatrix," Cassie says. "Is this road going to take us to the bridge, or do I need to turn somewhere?"

"I think we're good. Look, there's a sign that has it in English – Øresund Fixed Link. That's what we want."

Suddenly, up ahead, the bridge comes into view. "Oh, wow, there it is," Cassie says. "Look at that."

"Oh my God," I say. It's pretty dramatic; it's a long, curving stretch of a bridge held up by two tall triangles of cables. It looks kind of impossible, like that can't really be enough to support it. It seems to go on for miles.

We pull up to a tollbooth, and Cassie pays. "Two hundred eighty-five kroners," she says as we pull onto the bridge. "That's a lot, isn't it? What is that, like forty bucks?"

"I don't know," I say. I'm starting to feel a little sick. I've never been a good car traveler; I should've taken some Dramamine. I've been eating all this junk food, and the car has that new-car smell, which everyone else in the world seems to love, but which I always find a little sickening.

"Wow," Cassie says. It is an amazing view – it's like there's no separation between us and the sky, us and the sea – but I'm having trouble concentrating.

"So we haven't really talked about the clue yet," Cassie says. "I don't know anything about stonemasons or a dinner party, but isn't there some place in London that's famous for having a lot of pigeons?"

I don't answer. I'm really starting to feel bad. I roll my window down and wait, hoping it'll pass. And then I know I've waited too long.

"Um, Cassie," I say. My voice is tiny. "I think I need to stop."

She looks at me in the rearview mirror. I've got my hand over my mouth, just in case. "I don't know if I'm allowed to stop here," she says, but she pulls over to the side of the road.

I open the door and step out; there's a narrow walkway that runs the length of the bridge. I move unsteadily to the railing; I hear a door close behind me and realize unhappily that Elliott's coming with me.

It's loud out here. The wind roars, and there are cars rushing past; it occurs to me that some of them must contain Swedes, and I wonder vaguely if anyone will recognize me as they zoom by. Misha's gotten out of the car now, too; I guess he didn't want to miss the fun.

I lean forward and see rough blue water, white flecks, light glimmering on the surface; it's a long way down. I gag, but nothing comes. Elliott's right there with the camera in my face, ready to get every minute of it. And I'm wearing a microphone – are they going to put the noises on TV? This is awful. What can I do, I wonder wildly, to sabotage the show, make sure this never airs? I gag again. Oh, God, I can't stand it, I can't stand to have this happen. I feel completely humiliated.

Suddenly, Cassie's out of the car, and she's standing between me and Elliott. She puts her arm around me and guides me forward so that my head's farther out over the edge.

"It's okay," she says. She pulls my hair back and holds it behind my head. "You'll feel better. Just let it go."

It's like I needed permission; some mechanism in my body releases, and I throw up over the railing. It happens again and again. It's windy, and some of it splatters back onto us. I want to die.

"All done?" Cassie asks when I finally stop.

I look down. We're both going to need to change our clothes.

"I'm sorry," I whisper.

"Don't worry about it." She sounds so – I don't think I've ever used this word – kind. I try to imagine what Dallas would be doing in this situation. Not holding my hair, that's for sure. Cassie finds a tissue in her pocket and hands it to me. "It happens to everyone," she says as I dab at my mouth. "I used to get carsick all the time when I was a kid. We'll wait a few minutes, let you get some air. And if you need to stop again, we will."

I nod. I have a broken feeling, like something's come loose inside me. I realize with horror that I'm going to cry. God, how many ways can I find to lose control on camera?

"Take deep breaths," says Cassie, and I start sobbing, aware of Elliott standing three feet away. I've cried on camera before, pretty, delicate little tears that were easy to start and stop. But now my whole body's shaking, and I'm making horrible noises that are worse than the retching.

"Juliet," Cassie says softly. She puts her hand on my arm, pats me gently. "Really, it's okay. It happens. People throw up."

I nod, but I can't make myself stop. Cassie stands there and waits. The people of Sweden rush by in their cars, and if they take the time to look at me, I'm sure all they see is a sad woman with a red face.

"Okay," I say when I finally manage to get hold of myself. My voice makes a hiccupping noise as I talk. "Let's go."

"All right," Cassie says. "We should probably stop and get cleaned up when we get to the other side. We'll just keep the windows open till then."

I get into the backseat and lean back into the upholstery. I feel emptied out. I open my window and let the wind blow through, chilling me. Cassie starts up the car and we pull back into the traffic lane; the bridge stretches in front of us, seemingly endless. A strange thing happens up ahead: the bridge slopes down to water level and appears to simply stop. It's the entrance to a tunnel; the last few miles of the crossing are made underneath the sea, but the optical illusion of it is dizzying. It looks as though cars are driving down into the water to be swallowed up completely. I imagine a sea creature that lives beneath the surface, waiting for the travelers to come through and pay a different kind of toll. At this moment, it doesn't sound so bad.

"How you doing back there?" Cassie asks.

"Okay," I say, though really, I don't know how I am.

"We're going under in a minute," says Cassie.

I wait for the moment when that happens; I look out the window and wait for us to disappear. I wonder how I'll feel when we come back to the surface again.

TWENTY-SIX

Justin

I'm in very good spirits by the time we get to Trafalgar Square. The long road trip with Abby has been just what I needed – a man and his wife on a journey together, bound by a common purpose. It's an image that fits in perfectly with all my childhood ideas of what it would be like to be an adult; it reminds me of how I want my life to be. I can do this, I think, driving through country after country with the windows open, making easy conversation with Abby; I can make this work. I imagine us taking trips like this someday with a carful of kids making noise in the backseat. Someday we'll have a photo album full of perfect moments like this one.

Only once or twice during the trip did I think about Ken and about the time we spent together in Tokyo. I haven't seen Ken since that day; I assume the producers have finished with him and have sent him home, or on to another job. It's for the best, really, although I have to admit that for the first few days, I found myself looking for him everywhere. And even now, nearly a week after it happened, I can't keep my mind from returning to him once in a while. These thoughts could be described as "fantasies," I suppose, though they're not all of a sexual nature. I've wondered what his life is like, and even whether (God help me) there might be a place for me in it. This kind of reverie is dangerous and wrong-headed, but sometimes I find it hard to drag myself back to the happy reality I've created here and now. It may sound laughable, but during those moments I find it useful to recall not the Bible or any sermon I've ever listened to, but the lessons I learned from watching *Fantasy Island.*

When I was a kid, I spent a lot of Saturday nights watching TV with my mom. It was a nice time for us, staying up late and eating popcorn, although I do have to wonder if it's healthy for a boy's development to spend so much time building this kind of identification with his mother. But we had a good time. She adored *The Love Boat,* which I liked well enough, but for me *Fantasy Island* was the high point of the evening. I loved the lush greenery of the opening, the tropical sophistication of the host's white suit, the guest stars raising colorful cocktails in tribute to him. The interesting thing, though, was the way that no one's fantasy ever turned out the way he or she expected it to. There was always mortal danger, always unforeseen consequences. Every episode was a morality play. It told the viewer, Be careful what you wish for; everything comes with a price. It said, Don't ask for too much – you already have everything you need.

The show went off the air when I was ten or eleven. But in the next few years, as I began to have an awareness of the affliction that plagued me, I returned to this idea more and more often: you can't trust the things you really want. If you had the chance to live your fantasies, you'd learn not to want them at all. I was sure that if I could visit that island, if I could find the strength to whisper to Mr. Roarke some of the things I'd been yearning for (though I must confess that I found this prospect more distracting than I should have), then I'd finally understand why I shouldn't feel the way I felt. I would discover a fatal flaw, some kind of twist that would give me the strength to abandon the messages my body was sending me. In my imaginings, I never could figure out exactly how this reversal would occur, but I knew it would be enough to put an end to all my fruitless wishing.

So last night, in the dark of early morning, as I rested in the backseat while Abby drove us through Belgium, I thought of *Fantasy Island,* and I found the strength to put an end to the feverish thoughts that were invading me. I imagined stepping off a plane into a hot overgrown day; I imagined the safety of lifting a glass to my lips, knowing that someone was there to protect me from what I wanted.

Abby and I made good time driving, and it looks like we're the first ones here, although the other teams aren't far behind; we all got bunched up in Calais, waiting for the first ferry, so everyone else should be here soon. Abby and I came to Trafalgar Square because of the reference to pigeons in the clue, and we do seem to be on the right track; as soon as we arrive, I see Barbara standing in her glass box over by the edge of the fountain. We park our car in a specially marked spot and leave it for a crew member to return for us, and we get out to join the throngs. We still don't know what keyword we're looking for; I assume it has something to do with stonemasons and a "precarious dinner."

"Is there any kind of information booth here?" I say to Abby. Our camera crew today consists of Robert on camera and Joel on sound; Robert's a burly Australian guy, and Joel is a wiry American with leathery skin. They're both hovering nearby. "Someone we could ask?"

"I don't see one," she says. "But there's a tour group. Maybe we can tag along and listen in."

"Good idea, honey."

We join a group of tourists — mostly Americans, from what I can tell — standing around the base of the giant column that dominates the square. The guide is a middle-aged British man with a loud, booming voice. He's holding a red umbrella over his head, even though it's not raining; I suppose it makes him more visible to his group.

"This handsome monument," he's saying, "is Nelson's Column, one of London's most beloved landmarks. It was built to honor the great naval hero Admiral Nelson, who lost his life in the Battle of

Trafalgar in 1805, but not before managing to defeat Napoleon and the French and Spanish fleets. His last words were 'Thank God I have done my duty.'"

Admirable sentiment. It must take a very noble person to think such lofty thoughts at the moment of death. I'm sure my last words will be very mundane.

"The column is a hundred and eighty feet high," the umbrella man says, "and the statue of Nelson on top of it is eighteen feet tall. There's an interesting story about its construction . . ."

Usually, I'm a big fan of these kinds of holiday history lessons. On my own vacations, the ones I've taken with Abby, I'm always seeking out tours like this; I like to feel like I'm edifying myself, and not just giving myself over to leisure. But now my fatigue is starting to catch up with me, and I find my mind starting to wander. I look around at the crowds of tourists filling the square, the pigeons searching out people with snacks. Idly, I turn my gaze to the fountain, and then I'm not listening at all.

Ken is sitting on the concrete edge, with his back to the falling water, and he's looking right at me. He's smiling slightly, and he raises his hand in a casual wave. I turn away, quickly. Just to look upon his face makes me terrified and ashamed, but underneath there's something else: a small, obscene note of buoyancy.

Abby pokes me in the arm. "Did you get that?" she says.

"Sorry, what?"

"He said that before they put the statue on top, all the stonemasons involved in the construction had a dinner party on top of the column."

"Oh . . . right. Good." I'm aware, suddenly, that I'm wearing the aviator helmet on my head, the brown leather straps hanging down foolishly over my ears. I take it off and smooth my hair with my hand.

Abby looks at me, faintly amused. "Where are you, exactly?" she says. "Because I'm here in London, playing a game."

Where am I? I'm in my childhood church, listening to a sermon on Leviticus; I'm in a Tokyo hotel room, in a landscape of red velvet that looks like a whore's Christmas.

"Sorry," I say. Come on, bring yourself back. "I guess I was thinking of something else."

I'm afraid she'll ask me what I was thinking about, and I start to fabricate an answer, but she doesn't. "Well, I guess we've got our answer," she says. "What do you think the keyword is? *Nelson? Column? Statue?*"

"Let me look at the clue again," I say. I'm dying to turn around, to see if Ken's still there, if he's still looking at me. I manage a half turn while unzipping a pocket of my backpack to get the clue. He's still sitting by the fountain, smiling more broadly now; he looks like he's watching a show. He's wearing shorts, and it's hard for me not to let my gaze linger on the muscles of his thighs.

"Okay," I say, pulling the card from my backpack. Concentrate. "'*The site of London's most precarious dinner; / Today only pigeons dine there.*' So it's got to be *column*. Unless they're looking for a more architectural word, like *plinth* or something." My face feels hot; I wonder if I'm blushing.

Abby smiles. "Honey, they wrote this clue with people like Dallas and Jeff in mind. They're not expecting us to come up with *plinth.*"

"Right." Does she hear how unnatural my voice sounds?

"Well, let's go tell Barbara," she says. "We don't have much of a lead; I just saw Laura and Carl a minute ago."

What am I supposed to do here? My place is with my wife; how long will it take me to learn this lesson? I take Abby's free hand — she's got the birdcage in the other — and walk stiffly toward Barbara's box, aware all the time that Ken's eyes are on me. We have to walk right past him. I keep my eyes straight ahead.

Barbara smiles as we open the door to her booth. We step into the cool air.

"Justin and Abby," Barbara says. "You believe you have solved the riddle and found the keyword?"

"We do," I say. I squeeze Abby's hand tight; this is my lifeline. Remember that.

"And what is your answer?"

"Column," I say.

It's very cold in here; I don't know how Barbara stands it. Abby and I stand before her for what seems like a very long time, chilly supplicants awaiting her judgment.

"You're right," she announces triumphantly. "You have earned your next clue."

She hands Abby two envelopes, one silver, one gold, and we step back into the sun and the noise. Abby takes a few steps away from the glass booth and sets down her things. She starts to open the silver envelope. I look around for Ken; with great alarm, I see that he's risen from his seat and is walking toward us.

I drop my backpack near Abby's and lay down the ski pole and the aviator hat.

"You read the clue, and see if you can figure anything out," I say quickly. "I've got to find a bathroom."

"Okay," she says. She's distracted by the sealing wax on the envelope.

I set off toward the column and make an unobtrusive gesture for Ken to follow me. I'm dismayed to find Robert coming after me with his camera.

"I'm just going to the bathroom," I say to him. "You can stay with Abby."

"Sorry," he says. "I've gotten instructions to stay with you."

I was going to go around to the far side of the column, out of Abby's sight, but I change course and head toward the public restrooms near the steps of the terrace. I hope Ken will follow; I don't know how I'm going to manage a private conversation with him, but he clearly has something to say to me, and I can't have him shadowing me and Abby.

Robert and I reach the door of the men's room, and I step inside alone. The cameras generally don't follow us into the bathroom, especially a public restroom where there might be other people who don't want to be caught on film. They do allow us this small measure of privacy. It's busy in here; there are men coming in and out, going about their business. I stand by the sinks and wait.

After a moment, Ken walks in. It embarrasses me to look at him directly. I turn on the water and hold my hands under the cold spray. Ken walks over and stands at the sink next to mine.

"Hi there," he says. "Romantic little spot you've chosen."

The insinuation in his voice infuriates me. "What are you doing here?" I ask as coldly as I can.

"I have a job in London this week," he says. "I heard a rumor you'd be shooting here today."

"And what? You wanted to say hi?"

"No." His voice is suddenly businesslike. "Actually, I just wanted to ask you a question."

"Okay," I say. I find I'm shaking a little. I turn off the water and reach for a paper towel.

"Okay," he says. He fixes his eyes on me in a way I find disconcerting. "I just wanted to know: after what happened between us in Tokyo, are you ready to admit that the whole ex-gay thing is bullshit?"

I stare at him. "Absolutely not," I say. My voice sounds higher than I'd like. This happens sometimes when I get upset; I forget all my Redemption gender retraining and I start to sound like a faggot. I work on modulating my tone. "You must have a very high opinion of yourself," I say, "if you think an afternoon with you would make a man forget God."

He looks disgusted. "I don't think God has a problem with gays," he says. "I think God has a problem with hypocrites."

"Well, I'm not sure what Bible you've been reading," I say, "but I'm not really interested in discussing theology with you." Lower; better. "The fact is, I stumbled in Tokyo. That's all. I stumbled, and now I'm ready to walk the true and upright path." I crumple the damp towel in my hand, I squeeze it with all my might. "And now," I say, trying for dignity, though I'm not sure I manage it, "if we're all done here, I need to get back to my wife."

"We're not quite done," Ken says. He leans forward with a slight smile on his lips, and for a terrible, thrilling moment, I think he might kiss me. "I think you're despicable." He spits the word out like he's been saving it for a long time. "The work you do damages people. The group you're in, the 'message' you're trying to spread . . ." He shakes his head like he can't find words that are strong enough. "It's dangerous. Shame kills. Do you know what the suicide rate is for gay teens?"

I stare at him. It's like he's speaking a different language. We're not teenagers. I don't know what this has to do with us.

"I just want you to know," he says, looking at me with such contempt I feel weak, "that I filmed us that day. I filmed everything that happened in that hotel room. The producers have the tape. When this show airs, the whole world is going to see what a hypocrite you are."

I feel dizzy, and I can't catch my breath. For a moment, I think I might faint or vomit or fall to my knees. I hold on to the edge of the sink to steady myself. Ken watches my reaction. He looks very happy with himself. He looks like destroying a man's life is the most satisfying thing he's ever done.

"Get out," I say, as if I have the right to expel him from this public place, as if I'm the lord of the men's room or something. I'm thinking of my parents sitting down to watch their son on TV, I'm thinking of all the members of the Redemption ministry waiting to hear me spread their message of hope. And Abby. Oh, Abby.

"Yeah, all right," he says. "I'm going." And he does, and how can it be that even in this high moment of crisis and terror, I feel a little stab of grief in my chest when I see him walk away?

I stand by the sink for a few minutes, trying to collect myself. I have to get back out there to Abby; I have to figure out what I'm going to do to keep this situation from ruining me. As I leave the restroom and step out into the sun to see Robert waiting for me, filming my exit, I realize, too late, that I've been wearing a microphone this whole time. I can see the way they'll do it: a shot of the restroom door, my conversation with Ken playing as loud and clear as they can get it. Perhaps they'll caption it on the screen so viewers won't miss a single word. But what does it matter when the very act of my falling has been recorded on film? I catch sight of Abby standing across the square, and she waves to me. She looks concerned; I've been gone a long time. I compose my face, try to stand tall, and make my way toward her. I'm her husband, and I've got to do what I can to protect her. Now, more than ever, I have to be a man.

TWENTY-SEVEN

Abby

Justin looks strangely grim as he walks toward me, and my first reaction, before I can stop myself from thinking it, is *good*. He's been relentlessly cheery all day, and I have not. And he hasn't seemed to notice; he doesn't have the slightest idea what's going on with me. Whatever's happened to upset him — an intestinal disturbance, a rain of pigeon shit on his shirt, a glimpse of a rainbow bumper sticker on a car — it makes me happy to see him for a moment without the triumphant smile on his face.

And here I am blaming him for not being able to read my mind. The marriage counselor we've seen a handful of times (a Christian practitioner recommended to us by Redemption to deal with the unique problems that come up in a marriage like ours) has always stressed the importance of communication, and I know it's my own damn fault that I'm suffering in silence without telling my husband that something's bothering me. I take a deep breath and resolve to be a better partner.

What Justin knows, but what I haven't perhaps discussed in enough detail for him to understand the full impact, is that I spent a year in England when I was in college. When he heard we were coming here, he was happy we were going someplace I was familiar with, where I'd know how to use the subway and the telephones, where I wouldn't be confused by the money or the roadways. He's heard my funny stories about language inconsistencies and culture shock; he's eaten, with some interest, the cheese and pickle sandwiches I made him with savory brown chutney I bought at a shop catering to British expatriates. He knows that during my time here I'll want to pick up a can of Lilt soda and a packet of salt-and-vinegar crisps; he knows that if we had more time, I'd want to take the train down to Brighton and walk along the pebbles by the sea.

What he doesn't know, although it seems to me he could figure it out easily enough if he gave any thought to the dates, is that England is the scene of all my greatest crimes, my most unruly passions. The last time I stood in Trafalgar Square, I was twenty years old and my hair was cut short like the bristles of a shoeshine brush. I was getting ready to march in a parade; I was surrounded by people I thought I belonged with, and I was holding the hand of a woman I loved with all my heart. For the first time, I thought I understood my place in the world. I would have hated this person who stands here today, this woman with shaved legs and lip gloss and a church to pray at every week. I would have scorned every bit of me: these eyes, searching for my husband in the crowd; this hand with a chip of diamond glinting in the sun. I would have felt such pity. Is anything ever as clear as it seems when you're twenty?

Sometimes I try to imagine my life written as a biography. Not that I'm deluded enough to think that anyone would want to read such a book, but it interests me to think about how it would be laid out, where the chapters would begin and end, where the emphasis would lie. That year in England, I imagine, would have to be written in silver ink or printed on special parchment, set apart from the rest of the story with richly printed papers. Not because it was perfect or purely beautiful, but because everything was heightened. It's a time that lives inside me still: a question, a bruise. There is soreness there, and tenderness. Press your finger to it, and you'll see my face change.

What Justin doesn't know is that England, to me, is a place both sacred and profane. It wasn't the first place I ever kissed a woman, or the first place I applied any of those names (so hard for me now to say out loud) to myself. By the time I arrived, I'd already had and lost a girlfriend; I'd already sat through all those tearful dinners with my parents. But England was the first place it ever occurred to me that I might be able to find a way to live in the world, the first place I thought I could craft an identity that encompassed everything I was. That year was unlike anything my life has been before or since. It was a glimpse of something that has never been fulfilled. Here, more than anywhere else on earth, it's clear to me that I'm a fraud.

"Hi," says Justin when he reaches me. His demeanor is very different than it was a few minutes ago. He's somber, all business. "Did you look at the clue?"

"Not yet," I say. "I was waiting for you." Really, I was waiting for Robert and his camera. They like to get a shot of us opening the envelope. I watch Justin for a minute; he seems to be avoiding looking at me directly. "Everything okay?" I ask.

"Fine," he says briskly, finally meeting my eyes. He's completely opaque to me. "Something I ate."

I open the silver envelope and remove the card inside.

> At the Ballydugan Weavers House,
> Someone waits inside a room
> To teach you Ulster's oldest art
> With a shuttle and a loom.
>
> The pretty item that you make
> Will be your Object Found
> So get yourselves there, quick as you can;
> Feel free to leave the ground.

"Two verses this time," Justin says.

"So we're leaving England already," I say. I don't know how I should feel.

"Ulster," he says. "Is that Northern Ireland? Is that safe?"

I shrug. "I think things are better now," I say. I wonder how ignorant we're going to look on camera. I feel suddenly hopeless; there's so much I still don't know about the world.

"Well, let's get to the airport," he says. "We can do some research there, try to figure out where exactly this Weavers House place is."

"No," I say. "Wait a minute." I look around the square wildly, trying to think of a reason we might need to stay a little longer. I spot a snack kiosk nearby and point at it. "Let me just see if they have that soda I like."

Justin forces a smile, but he looks impatient. "Well, hurry it up," he says. "Every second counts."

I leave my gear with Justin and set off, unencumbered. I just want another minute to walk on this pavement, another minute to immerse myself in this air. The woman I held hands with that day, her name was Sara. She is here, somewhere. Not in Trafalgar Square, I'm sure, though that hasn't kept me from looking. But if I could pull back somehow, rise into the air and look down on this island from above, she would be there, a tiny dot moving through her life. What would it mean for me to see her now? What would happen if I could lay my eyes on her just once? Nothing, probably. Nothing.

I reach the snack stall and survey the soft drinks available. No Lilt, but they have Tango, which is practically the same. "One Tango, please," I say to the man when my turn comes. "And one Coke." Coke, I remember, tastes a little different here. I want to see if I've remembered it right.

I pay for the drinks, running my fingers over the coins as if they were relics of some ancient world. I stood in this square with Sara, waiting for everything to begin. We marched in the parade and read the slogans on all the T-shirts; later, we walked around the festival grounds and slow-danced together on the grass. It was June, and school had just ended; my plane would leave two days later. The edges of that day are crisp in my memory, so sharp they could cut like paper if only I could put my hands on them. We had a plan, Sara and I; I would go back to the States for my last year of college, and then I would come back and never leave.

And then . . . and then. Back in my life, my ordinary, constrained life, I began to lose that sense of sureness I'd felt in England. Back at home, where I wasn't anybody new, where I was the same person I'd been since I was born, I couldn't see my future quite so clearly anymore. It seemed I hadn't been free in England at all; I'd simply been on a longer tether than I was used to. Back at home, when there wasn't any more slack, everything seemed murky and frightening, and those little shoots of shame began once again to take root. I told Sara I'd met someone else. I struggled and wandered on my own for longer than I like to remember, and then I joined Redemption and I laid my burden down.

I carry the drinks back to Justin, the metal cool in my hands. "I wanted you to try this," I say, handing him the Coke. "It might settle your stomach. And it's not quite the same as at home."

"I'll drink it in the cab," he says, sticking the can in his backpack. He picks up the ski pole, the pilot's helmet. "We've got to get going. Laura and Carl just left, and Cassie and Juliet are here. Can you get the birdcage?"

I nod, but I don't pick it up. "Justin, I'm having trouble here," I say. It seems urgent that I tell him before we leave. I need his strength, his reassurance; the game can wait. "The last time I was here . . ." I glance at Robert and Joel, recording everything I say. "It was right in the middle of everything. You know . . . everything. It's a little hard for me to be back here." It's a relief to say it, to offer him the opportunity to help me carry this weight.

He sighs; his face doesn't soften at all. "Well, it's a good thing we're leaving, then," he says shortly. "That was, what? Ten years ago? I think it's a little strange that you're still so concerned about it. Clearly, you haven't made as much progress as we thought." He balances the ski pole under his arm and picks up the birdcage himself. He walks away from me toward the street, tall and brisk.

I feel like I've been slapped. Strange to think of it now, but I was elated when Justin and I had our first fight; somehow, I thought it made our marriage more "real." I was happy to see we weren't going to be so careful with one another that we couldn't access any real emotion. My ideas about marriage were very vague, gleaned from watching my parents and peeking into the bedroom closets of families I babysat for, but I thought this was a good sign. But now I just feel alone.

By the time I catch up to him, Justin has already gotten a cab, and he's loading the trunk. I put my things in next to his and get in without a word. Joel climbs in next to me; Robert gets in the front. I will not cry; there's no safe direction for me to turn my face without being seen. I look out the front window as the cab takes off through the streets of London, which I'm afraid I may never see again.

The thing that interests me most about this imaginary biography I'm crafting is the ending. I want more than anything to flip through the pages, to get to the part when I'm old and furrowed, when I can finally see myself at peace. Sometimes I long for that; I can't wait to be seventy, eighty, ninety years old. None of this will matter then. Right?

TWENTY-EIGHT

Laura

This trip has been like a dream, by which I mean it's been fragmented and disorienting, and it's going to take me a long time to make any sense of it. Two hours in London, and we're already on our way out. Can I really say I've been to these places when all I've seen are the airports? At least I've got an interesting story to tell my — well, to tell anyone who wants to listen.

Carl and I were lucky enough to find a very nice (and talkative) older gentleman who was more than willing to help us with our clue. I think he was drawn to the cameras; he told us that he's been campaigning for several years to have himself named "the poet laureate of Trafalgar Square," and he seemed to think this might help his cause. He knew the answer to the stonemasons question right away, but it took us another ten minutes to extricate ourselves from his company; he'd just begun a dramatic recitation of his epic work, "Lord Nelson's Footprints," when we finally got away.

"Do you think we should've given him a few bucks not to talk to anyone else?" Carl asks me once we're in the cab.

"No," I say. "I can't really plot against Cassie."

"Yeah, that's true," he says. "Anyway, he's just as likely to hold up the other teams as he is to help them. Who knows how long that poem goes on for."

"Betwixt," I say, looking out the window. It's a beautiful day, and the streets are filled with pretty young people lit by the sun. "You have to admire a man who uses the word *betwixt* in casual conversation."

"You want me to start saying that? You got it, babe. No more *between* for me."

I smile without even meaning to. The last few days with Carl have been lovely and very fragile. Everything's been slow and tentative; we haven't even kissed yet. A kiss seems like such a leap of faith, with everything so uncertain, so artificial. I feel like we're in some kind of children's race, balancing an egg on a spoon, or hopping with our legs tied together. So far so good, but how long can we keep it up?

And why am I even bothering with this, I wonder, what do I know about romance, anyway? Almost nothing. A few college boyfriends, an unbalanced computer match, and a quiet, lonely stretch of marriage with a very sad ending. I remember sitting with Jim one night, a few months before he died – Cassie was asleep upstairs, though I knew she'd be awake for a feeding in a couple of hours – and I was sorting through our music collection, playing all the love songs I'd listened to as a teenager. I could remember what close attention I'd paid to those lyrics when I was thirteen, fourteen; here, I thought, is what my future will be like, if only I listen hard enough. And now here I was, a grown-up with a child. That, right there, was my husband, sitting on the couch. Reading a book, oblivious.

I wanted something from him then, this man I'd married. I wanted to dance with him in our living room late at night; I wanted to make love on the floor while a song that shaped all my views of love played in the background. If this was love, if this was marriage, then we should have access to everything those songs promised. We should own that romance. I gathered my courage; I walked over and put my hand on his shoulder, pulled him to his feet, but I knew immediately that I couldn't go through with it. We were both too self-conscious. He did a kind of joke dance, swinging me around with jerky movements, and then he went up to bed, leaving me by myself. And how could I complain? That was the man I married; he was wonderful in many ways, but he was never going to dance with me in our living room. He wasn't going to come back down the stairs and take me in his arms. Those were just facts I'd have to face.

I sat on the couch, hugging one of Cassie's teddy bears, and the soft fur on my face, the cottony bulk in my arms, was almost enough. *He loves me,* I thought, *I know he does.* There was no doubt about that, none at all, at least not until this song was playing and I started to wonder what *enough* really meant. I sat on my own, listening to my music, until the feeling passed and I was able to go upstairs and lie beside him, thinking, *Yes. What you have to offer me is enough.*

"Your hair looks nice that way," Carl says. I've pulled it back.

"Unwashed, you mean?" The cab is cavernous, and we're not smashed in as tightly as we usually are in these situations. To compensate, I move a little closer to him, so that our arms are touching. I'd like to think it could work out between us; I really would. But we live a thousand miles apart, and we've met in the strangest environment possible; only a teenager or a romantic or a fool would be naive enough to think that a relationship born in this kind of crucible could last longer than eleven episodes.

"Yeah, unwashed," he says, pushing back gently with his shoulder.

Then again, I find myself thinking in secret hopeful moments, why not? In a year – only a year – Cassie will leave for college and begin, for the first time, to live a life completely separate from mine. The blank slate that will face me then has been, up till now, too frightening to look at except in small glimpses. Maybe . . . especially if we won the money . . . I don't know. Let's just get through the televised portion of our relationship; then we can see where we stand.

"Poor hygiene doesn't work for most people," Carl says, reaching out to brush away a strand that's fallen into my eyes, "but it's a good look for you." He lowers his hand and rests it on my knee; I look at it for a moment, then raise my eyes to the road, the traffic, the brilliance of the day. "Really," he says. "Just betwixt you and me."

* * *

Part of my problem, I think, my reluctance to give myself over to dizzy infatuation, is my awareness that this game is drawing to a close, and that it may end without the life-changing mother-daughter rapprochement I'd been hoping for. I've barely seen Cassie for days, not that seeing each other has ever been a guarantee of meaningful communication for us. What was I thinking – go on TV, get a TV ending?

I'd like to talk to her, but there hasn't been a good opportunity. I'd like to find a way to approach her about this new thing, this sexuality issue, to feel her out and offer support, if I can find a way to do it subtly. And also, I've been thinking about something that I think might help us both with the problems that are dividing us: I think we should write a letter to the baby.

It's within our rights. We ended up with what's known as a semi-open adoption. This means that neither side has access to last names or addresses, but we can communicate with the adoptive family on a limited basis through a third-party mediator. It's been agreed that the baby's new parents will send us a photograph every six months for the first five years, and yearly after that. We've agreed to provide information about our medical history, and any other biographical information that may prove pertinent, and in the future, if both parties agree, there is the possibility of a yearly meeting, supervised by the mediator. It's all carefully negotiated, all very well thought out. It's not what I would call natural or comfortable, but it does have this going for it: it means we haven't necessarily said good-bye to that little girl forever.

The time I had with her was very short. The night she was born, really – that was it. If there has been such a thing as the "longest night of my life," it wasn't that night in Sweden with Carl, though I suspect that's a memory I'll always keep close. It was the marvelous, bittersweet stretch of darkness when I became a grandmother and then went back to being nothing of the kind.

When we arrived at the hospital, in the middle of the night, we went first to the emergency room. "My daughter just gave birth," I told the woman at the desk. "At home."

I was embarrassed saying the words; I expected her to judge me, ask me questions I didn't know the answers to. But she was unimpressed. "Labor and delivery," she said. "Third floor. I'll call for a wheelchair."

I went to retrieve Cassie, who was sitting in a plastic chair with the bundle of baby in her arms. She was staring impassively at a TV that was turned to a news channel. "We have to go upstairs," I said. "Labor and delivery. We have to wait for a wheelchair."

"Labor and delivery," she said, looking down at the baby. "Too late."

Upstairs, our arrival was greeted with more concern. Cassie and the baby were taken away to be examined, and I was given forms to fill out. In the space for doctor's name, I put my own OB/GYN; I'd taken Cassie to see him for yearly checkups, but the last one had been about eleven months earlier. I didn't know if she'd been to see him or anyone else about the pregnancy; I doubted it. The "estimated due date" space I left blank.

In time, Cassie was admitted and taken to a room; she fell asleep almost immediately. I sat in a chair by her bed and waited for news of the baby. After an hour or so, they rolled her back to us in a clear little bin like a vegetable crisper. They'd put a diaper on her and dressed her in a T-shirt and a white knit cap; she was swaddled in a blanket edged in pink and blue.

"Everything looks good," said the nurse who wheeled her in. "The doctor will come by in the morning. Mommy's asleep already?" It took me a moment to realize she meant Cassie.

"Yes," I said.

"Well, just ring if you need anything." It surprised me how casual she was, as if all this were the most normal thing in the world.

After she left, I walked over to the little box and peered inside. The baby was awake but quiet. I unwrapped her carefully, looked over her sweet, mottled little body. Then I folded the blanket back around her, picked her up, and took her to sit in the chair. I held her in my arms, and watched her fall asleep. When the sun rose, and a nurse came in to wake up Cassie and take her vitals, the two of us were sitting there still.

In the light of morning, things began to move very fast. Shortly after breakfast, a social worker came to talk to us, and Cassie told her that she'd decided to give the baby up for adoption. I made some attempt to talk to Cassie about the other options; I told her that if she wanted to keep the baby, we would find a way. I argued with her, I cried; I did not let that baby go without a fight. But Cassie wasn't interested in listening to what I had to say, and really, why should she be? I hadn't been there for any of it, not the early months of nausea and fatigue; not the late, heavy months when every movement is work. Certainly not the attic night with all its bloody towels and deep valleys of pain. I had no right to intervene at this late date; in the end, there was nothing for me to do but stand there and let Cassie make her choices, and I watched as the baby was placed in her crisper and wheeled out of the room.

So far, Cassie's been resistant to the idea of having any contact with the adoptive parents, whose names we know are James and Theresa. But two months more and a picture will land in our mailbox; with any luck, we'll get some kind of brief progress report. We'll even find out what they've named her. Cassie and I are both . . . well, I hesitate to speak for Cassie in any matter at this point, but I think it's fair to say that in our own separate ways, we've both been battered by this loss. And maybe writing a letter would help. Closure, right? Is that what I thought I might find?

We arrive at the airport and do some research to find out exactly where we're going. The Ballydugan Weavers House, it turns out, is part of the Ulster Folk and Transport Museum, a little ways outside Belfast. There are hourly flights.

Justin and Abby arrive shortly after we do, and end up on the same flight; for a while, it looks like we'll be the only two teams. As it turns out, Dallas and Jeff never do show up, but as we're waiting in line to board, I'm delighted to see Cassie and Juliet running toward the gate. Juliet seems uncharacteristically subdued, but Cassie, flushed from the exertion, looks fairly happy.

"Hey, Mom," she says, landing behind me in line. "I met your friend in Trafalgar Square. The poet laureate guy." There's a gentle, teasing note to her voice.

"He was funny," I say.

"You made quite an impression," Cassie says. "He asked if I knew 'the lovely American woman with the green jacket and the parrot,' and when I said you were my mom, he asked me to tell you that if you're ever in London again, he'd love to 'share his supper with you and the pigeons.'"

"No," I say, laughing. "He did not say that."

"He absolutely did," she says. She turns to Juliet. "Didn't he?"

Juliet nods but says nothing. Unusual for her; does she not realize there's a camera on her?

"You better watch out, Carl," Cassie says. "You've got competition."

I blush, but I'm elated by the whole conversation. Not that an eighty-year-old man of questionable sanity finds me attractive, but that my daughter is giving me the time of day.

"I'm not the jealous type," Carl says. "Maybe you should drop him a postcard when you get home. Did you happen to get his address?"

"Yeah," Cassie says. "Wacko Poet, Trafalgar Square."

"Good idea," I say. I beam at Cassie. "That reminds me," I say, buoyed into foolishness by the wave of hopefulness that's washed over me. "I've been thinking that when we get home, or even before, maybe we should write a letter to James and Theresa. For them to give to . . ." I glance at the camera; this is not something I want to reveal to the general public. "You know who," I finish lamely, as if this were a lighthearted matter, as if this little lost baby of ours were the subject of some playful guessing game. "To read in the future," I add, though I can see I've already ruined everything.

Cassie stares at me; her mouth falls open a little. Her face is a picture of hurt and dismay. "You're an idiot, Mom. You know that?"

she says, her voice full of fury, wavering with tears that haven't yet made it to the surface. She leaves the line and storms off with her backpack and her ski pole to stand as far away from me as she can. Yes, I'm an idiot. As a matter of fact, I do know.

Carl puts his hand on my shoulder. "It's a tough situation," he says. "With all this travel stress, and the cameras always around."

I stiffen. That's not it. And what does he know, with his sweet, adorable little three-year-old? But I don't say that; I'm starting to wonder if it would be better if I never said anything at all. Breathe in, breathe out; let's try not to alienate everyone who likes me. I manage a small smile and let him rub my neck. "Yeah," I say. "It's tough."

On the plane, Carl and I are seated a few rows behind Cassie and Juliet, and I spend a lot of time leaning out into the aisle, trying to catch a glimpse of Cassie's face as she turns to watch the seat-belt demonstration or to accept a drink from the beverage cart. I can't see very much; I can't tell how much damage I've done. I watch her interactions with Juliet; the two of them seem to be deep in conversation. I wonder if it's possible there's something going on between them. I worry about Cassie getting too attached to this new celebrity friend; maybe I'm not being fair, but I just can't believe that Juliet's chummy behavior is completely on the level. Cameras and money; let's not forget what this show is really about.

Looking at Cassie, it's impossible for me to see her only as she is now; always, to me, she is everything she's ever been. I look at her and see every moment of her life. This is nothing new; this is simply what it means to be a mother. But I have to wonder now whether all those early moments will cease to matter in the final telling, whether all the stories I have about Cassie and the life we've lived will be eclipsed by this one big story, the great narrative of my failure. I have to wonder whether we'll ever be okay again.

"I don't know if you're finished watching the Cassie and Juliet show," Carl says suddenly. His voice is gentle. "But there's something kind of interesting going on over here."

I turn to look at him, but don't immediately see what he means.

"The plane is snowing on me," he says. And it's true; tiny white flakes of frost are falling from the air vent onto his chest. His blue T-shirt is dotted with icy crystals.

"What is that?" I say, reaching out to touch one of the flakes. It melts between the warmth of my finger and the warmth of his chest.

"No idea," he says. "Signs of the apocalypse?" More specks fall on his shirt, swirl in the air above his body.

A flight attendant is walking by, gathering used cups and napkins. "Excuse me," I say as she passes. "Do you know why this is happening?"

She looks at the peculiar weather event that's taking place in our row and smiles.

"That happens sometimes," she says. Her voice has a lovely Irish lilt. "It's frozen condensation. It has to do with the humidity outside the plane and the air-conditioning inside. Nothing to be concerned about." She picks up the empty cup on my tray and moves on.

"How strange," I say. My own air vent is turned off; I reach over my head and give it a twist. Little bits of snow drift down toward me.

It would be silly to make too much of this, but sometimes things can take you by surprise. Sometimes the most prosaic elements — the ordinary workings of an airplane, a surplus of moisture in the sky — can combine to feel like magic. *Our first kiss was in the snow,* I think, not knowing who it is I'm planning to tell, and I lean forward to touch my lips to his.

TWENTY-NINE

Cassie

I saw a TV show once about these birds called cowbirds. The cowbird is sometimes described as lazy because, rather than building a nest of her own and caring for her babies, she drops her eggs into other birds' nests and abandons them to be raised by a new, unsuspecting mother. The problem is that if these eggs are allowed to hatch, the little cowbirds will take food away from the smaller fledglings of the other breed, causing the original nestlings to die. So it happens that when a mother bird discovers a cowbird egg in with her own, she'll abandon the entire lot and build a new nest on top of the old one, with her own eggs still inside. She sacrifices the eggs she's laid and lays some new ones right on top. She'll do this up to six times, sitting on top of all her little lost babies, trying again and again. I don't know, I just think it's really sad. Something about the mother living like that, with the babies she's given up always underneath her feet. That's kind of how I feel, like no matter what I do for the rest of my life, that little baby is always going to be there underneath it all.

Or, what do I know. Maybe I'm just the cowbird.

Anyway, I'm starting to understand that this thing I've done, having a baby and giving it away, is the messiest, most momentous decision I'll ever make in my life. And even though I think I did the right thing, I'm never going to stop wondering if things could have been different. It hurts and hurts and hurts. And writing a letter isn't going to change a fucking thing.

When we land in Belfast, I grab my stuff as quickly as possible and rush to beat my mom and Carl off the plane. Juliet follows right behind. She's been acting kind of strange ever since she puked in Sweden; she's been quiet and helpful and interested in hearing what I have to say. She's been much less diva-ish; when we were on the ferry from Calais, we saw a group of British high school girls approach Dallas for an autograph, and all Juliet did was smile indulgently, like it was cute that Dallas had fans. I'm kind of afraid I might be witnessing one of those sudden, convenient Hollywood conversions, except that instead of Scientology or Kabbalah, Juliet's chosen some kind of vomit-based religion.

In any case, we move quickly, and we're out of the airport before anyone else. It's cooler here than it was in London, and I pull a jacket from my backpack. On the plane, we enlisted the help of a flight attendant, who told us that the Ulster Folk and Transport Museum is about a half hour away and that there's a bus that stops right outside the museum gates. After checking the timetables, though, we find that the next bus isn't leaving for an hour; we're still doing okay moneywise, so we decide to take a cab. Just as well; I'd like to put some distance between us and my mom.

We load luggage, crap, and entourage into a funky-looking red taxi, and we pull away just as Justin and Abby walk out to the curb. They both look miserable; I guess even Jesus can't make you happy all the time. My mom and Carl are right behind them, but I look the other way. The good news, in terms of the race, is that Dallas and Jeff seem to have missed the plane, so they're most likely the ones who'll be out. We saw them briefly in Trafalgar Square, but they seemed to be on the wrong track; they were stopping random passersby and asking, "Are you a stonemason?"

The driver takes us on a series of narrow highways, bypassing the city of Belfast completely. I look out the window as we go; it's pretty here, green and misty. By the time you get to the tenth or fifteenth country, it's hard to take it all in, but I try to make a note to store the landscape in my mind. When the show finally airs, I'm sure there will be some generic travelogue footage edited in, and it's bound to get all mixed up with my own impressions. Which can I trust, my own memories or the pretty scenes on TV?

"Hey, check that out," I say to Juliet, pointing to a road sign. It shows two hunched-over stick figures walking with a cane; underneath, it says ELDERLY PEOPLE.

"That seems mean," she says.

I shrug. "Not as mean as running them over, I guess."

"So," she says, putting on her "concerned about others" look; she's almost got it down. "Who was your mom saying you should write a letter to?"

In the front seat, Elliott's spun around to fix his camera on me. Do they all know everyone's secrets, I wonder, or are they just trained to look for sources of conflict? Juliet looks like she'd genuinely like to know, but it's not going to happen here.

"No one," I say. We're driving past a field of sheep. "Some people we're related to, sort of." And even that seems like saying too much.

I'm not entirely delighted to discover that the Ulster Folk and Transport Museum is basically an Irish version of Greenstone Village, the historical recreation infotainment park where I got myself knocked up. According to the pamphlet we get at the entrance, "the Museum seeks to cover the whole range of the way of life and traditions of ordinary people living in Northern Ireland in both the past and present." I scan the map – Cruckaclady Farmhouse, Gorticashel Flax Mill, Lisrace Forge – until I find Ballydugan Weavers House. Well, at least they don't appear to be big on candle making.

Juliet and I – just like any other tourists, aside from the parrot, ski pole, and camera crew – walk through the big, grassy field that comprises most of the park. There's a little village on one end; from there, a series of paths leads visitors through a scattering of picturesque cottages with thatched roofs. The Weavers House is one of those buildings.

"There it is," Juliet says, pointing to a low, white house with a *Lost and Found* banner outside. We both break into a run for no apparent strategic reason, given that there are no other teams in sight.

Inside the house, it's cool and dark; the walls and floor appear to be made of mud. We're in a long, narrow room outfitted with four tall wooden machines, which I guess are the looms.

A woman dressed in a rough brown dress, with a droopy white bonnet on her head, approaches us. "Good afternoon," she says, "and welcome to the Ballydugan Weavers House."

"Thank you," we mumble.

"You'll need to decide which one of you will be working the loom; whoever it is will need strong fingers and sharp eyes."

Juliet and I look at each other. "I can do it," she says, but her tone doesn't convince me. I look down at our hands; my fingers are stubbier and less shapely. It's not like either one of us has much experience with manual labor, but somehow I feel that the task falls to me.

"That's okay," I say. "I'll do it. Looks like fun."

The woman points to the loom on the end and indicates that I should sit down on a narrow bench in front of it. "You'll be working on a Jacquard loom," she says. "The Jacquard method was invented in France in the early nineteenth century and was widely used in the Northern Irish linen industry. It uses punch cards to adjust the warp thread as you weave so that a pattern will form in the fabric; this technology was later used in early computers. Weavers could change the pattern simply by changing cards; this was an important development for the textile industry."

I nod, though I have no idea what she's talking about. I'm pretty sure this information is for the benefit of the cameras, but I'll be surprised if it makes the final cut. You throw around phrases like "adjust the warp thread," and people start wondering if they've turned on PBS by accident.

"What you'll need to do," she says, "is move the shuttle back and forth to weave the linen." She demonstrates, showing me the shuttle – a kind of oblong wooden boat with thread spooled inside it – and a pedal I need to step on. As she moves the parts of the loom, some threads lift up and others descend; I see that they're actually starting to weave themselves together.

"We've arranged for a special pattern to appear in the fabric," the woman says. "When you've produced enough cloth for the pattern to be made visible, you'll take it to Drumnahunshin Farm, where a seamstress will be waiting for you to complete your Found Object."

"Okay," I say, annoyed by the tediousness of the whole thing. I'm sure it'll take hours to do all this, and then they'll edit it down to five minutes, because how else can they make weaving seem like a good use of your prime-time viewing?

"Oh," the woman says brightly, as if she's just remembered a tiny detail, "and be careful not to tangle the thread; if you do, you'll have to start over!"

The door opens, and in walk my mom and Carl. I think my mom's trying to catch my eye, but I'm looking studiously at the loom. There's a tall wooden frame, with a bed of white string unspooling flat across and another set of strings hanging down. A chain of thick paper cards with holes punched in them hangs from the top; they look kind of like the rolls on the player piano at this old-timey theme restaurant my mom and I used to go to. I guess these are the punch cards that determine the pattern. I take hold of the shuttle and give it a little push.

At first it seems easy; I move the shuttle back and forth, and step on the pedal, and somehow actual fabric is resulting. I see hooks rise and fall, and the string of punch cards moves forward. It's slow and repetitive, and after a while my arms and back begin to ache a little, but it's not difficult.

"You're doing great," Juliet says from time to time. She's doing her best to sound really encouraging. I'm afraid she might make up a cheer.

I see across the room that my mom's getting started at the loom; after a few minutes, Justin and Abby arrive, and they decide that Abby will do the task. The three of us weave away.

"Damn it," I hear my mother say.

"Hit a snag?" asks Carl.

"Yeah," she says. She sounds dejected. And then, with resolute cheeriness, she begins the corny line I've been expecting from her all along. "Oh, what a tangled web we . . ."

"Mom," I say, cutting her off. "You're on TV. Try not to look like such a dork."

"Sorry," she says. She sounds kind of hurt. I feel a little bad, but really? Not that much.

We continue on weaving for at least an hour. God or whoever punishes me for being mean to my mother, and I tangle my thread twice in a row; Abby messes up once, then my mom again. After a while, Dallas and Jeff barge in, and Jeff makes the same damn tangled web joke. Dallas sits down at the last loom and gets the spiel from Bonnet Lady; when she's finished explaining about the shuttle and everything, she bends close to whisper in his ear, and I'm pretty sure I overhear the words "President Scooter." Way to be historically accurate; I'm sure the Irish peasant weavers were all about American sitcoms.

We work on. It's dim in the little cottage, and my eyes are starting to hurt from focusing on the tiny threads. The air is heavy and moist, and I've been sweating almost from the beginning. Dallas is not having an easy time with his loom; his thread gets tangled four times in the first five minutes. I move my head around to try to release a crick in my neck; this prompts Juliet to stand behind me and rub my shoulders until I tell her it's interfering with my weaving. Finally, a pattern begins to emerge on my fabric; it's the *Lost and Found* logo, the suitcase full of stars. It's actually part of the fabric, white on white. It looks almost classy.

"You got it," Juliet says. "Great job!"

Across the room, my mom laughs suddenly, and Carl says, "There it is," so I know she's got it, too. It annoys me that we're finishing at the same time.

"I'm done," I yell to the humble-countrywoman / Scooter-groupie, who's untangling Dallas's thread again. She comes over and cuts my piece of linen off the loom.

"All right," she says. "You may now take your fabric to Drumnahunshin Farm."

She goes to cut my mom's cloth for her, and I jump off the bench. Juliet's already out the door. We run down the path, looking at the map, until we come to a two-story white house with a black roof. It's bigger than the Weavers House; I'm sure when Irish kids come here on field trips, they learn there's some kind of socioeconomic implication to that fact, but I don't currently care. We go in through a red door outlined in ivy and enter what looks to be the dining room of the farmhouse. The walls are white with light wood paneling running down the bottom half. The ceiling is surprisingly low. Were people shorter back then? We're greeted by another bonnet lady.

"Good afternoon," she says. "Which one of you did the weaving?"

"I did," I say.

"Then you" – here she takes Juliet by the hand and leads her to a seat at the round table in the middle of the room – "will be the one to do the sewing."

Juliet looks a little frightened by this development, but she nods and tries for a determined smile.

"You'll wait in the parlor," the woman says to me. She takes my rectangle of white linen and points me into the adjoining room. As I leave, I hear her talking to Juliet: "The other fabric pieces you need are in this bag, and here's a pattern of the item you'll be creating."

"Okay," Juliet says tentatively. "Are there any instructions on how to . . . you know, sew?"

The woman laughs.

There's already a cameraman stationed in the dining room, so Elliott follows me into the parlor. It's a smallish room with a fireplace and some old-fashioned-looking furniture. I sit down on a threadbare sofa – I assume it's okay to sit here; there aren't any velvet ropes or anything – and wait.

After a couple of minutes, I hear my mom and Carl come in; it occurs to me that since my mom did the weaving, Carl will have to do the sewing. Which means I'll have some quality time with Mom, hanging out in the farmhouse parlor. Let's hope Juliet turns out to be a fast seamstress.

My mom's smiling when she comes in. "This ought to be good," she says. "I don't think Carl's ever held a needle in his life. He told me he once used a stapler to fix the hem on his pants." I'm waiting for her to sit on the sofa next to me, but she sinks into a chair on the opposite side of the room.

"How's Juliet doing?" I ask.

"Not bad, surprisingly," she says. "She'd gotten the needle threaded, and was working on making some stitches. She was even using a thimble, although I don't think she had it on the right finger."

I smile. She looks pretty in this light, but kind of tired. I have this feeling I always have with my mom, like things could be okay between us if she'd just back off a little and relax. If she could just let things sit for like, five minutes.

"So," she says, and I stiffen a little. See, here we go – what bombshell issue is she going to insist we talk about now? But all she says is, "Are you having fun?"

I shrug. "Yeah," I say. "Are you?"

She nods. "I am. I really am."

"Good," I say.

We sit in silence for a minute. We can hear faint snippets of conversation from the other room. It's nice not to have anything to do for a little while. I could practically fall asleep.

"Juliet seems nice," my mom says suddenly. I open my eyes and look at her. Juliet seems a lot of things, but nice isn't one of them. What is she getting at?

"Yeah," I say. "I guess."

"Did I ever tell you," she says, "that when I was a teenager, I kind of had a crush on a girlfriend of mine?"

I sit up straight; across the room, Elliott seems to spring to attention. Oh my God. What the hell does she think she's doing?

"Of course, nothing ever happened, and as it turned out, I really like men . . ." God, this just gets better and better. I stare at her, stunned. "But it made me realize that sexuality is a lot more fluid than . . ."

"Stop," I say. "Just stop."

"I don't mean to make you uncomfortable," she says. Her face has turned faintly pink, but she looks determined to bring this nightmarish conversation to completion. "But I'd really like you to feel you can be open with me. I want you to know I support you, and I would never judge you. But I'm concerned about whether Juliet is the right person . . ."

"Just shut up, okay?" I say. I get up and pace the room. I can't sit in one place; I feel jumpy and faintly sick. We're in a farmhouse in Northern Ireland; we're on a fucking TV show. Why does she think this is a good time? "Just shut your mouth. You don't know anything about me." I mean it. She doesn't know a thing.

The front door opens and Justin and Abby walk in; they head into the dining room. I'm still pacing; I stop by the window and look out at the tall summer grass, the white stone fence that rings the grounds of the farm.

"I'm sorry," my mom says. "I didn't mean to upset you."

Abby appears at the doorway and stops there, held back I guess by the force field of awkwardness and discomfort that's so thick you can practically see it.

"Everything okay in here?" she asks with a small smile.

"Sure," I reply. "It's great." I go back to the sofa and sit down.

"Justin is a little annoyed about having to sew," Abby says. "I know it's kind of silly, but the program we're in has all these rules about men doing men's work and women doing women's work."

"Yeah, he better watch out," I say. I'm feeling very sour. "This could bring on a relapse. Nothing like sewing a hem to make you want to suck a great big cock."

"Cassie," my mother says. She sounds scandalized. So much for openness and fluidity of sexuality.

Abby blushes and looks at the ground. I feel bad; yeah, their program is fucked up, but it's not her fault I'm mad at my mom. "Sorry," I say.

"That's okay." She's still not looking at me. "I know not everyone agrees with our methods."

But the mood in the room is not good, and somehow I'm the one who's ruined everything. I rest my head against the nubby upholstery and close my eyes.

I don't dream about the baby; that's never happened, although sometimes I wish it would. I dream I'm a little girl; I've gotten hurt, and my mom is comforting me. How much more pathetic and obvious can you get? I wake up with tears in my eyes.

There's a noise of excitement from the next room, and Juliet rushes in, her arms filled with white fabric.

"I did it!" she yells. "I actually made a piece of clothing. I mean, some of the pieces had been sewn already, but I put it all together. It wasn't even that hard!"

"Great," I say. "Let's see it."

"Here it is," she says, unfolding the garment in her hands. "Isn't it pretty?"

She shakes it out and holds it up in the air. I breathe in sharply. It's a tiny dress, meant for a baby. It's long and white, with puffed sleeves and a round little collar trimmed in lace. It's a christening gown. The piece I made, with the *Lost and Found* logo etched into it, is the front of the skirt; later, maybe, I'll think about how cheesy it is to put a game show logo on a baby's dress, something that's meant to be used in a religious ritual, but right now I'm stunned and speechless.

Juliet's watching my face. "What's wrong?" she asks, but I don't answer. I'm looking at the empty sleeves, the empty neckline, the tissue of the fabric waiting to be filled with a baby's soft flesh. I feel a pain somewhere in my chest — deeper than my muscles, deeper than my ribs — radiating through me. I walk toward Juliet and take the dress in my hands, touching it gently, as if it held something precious.

The night my daughter was born . . . that phrase, just by itself, is hard for me to say. The night my daughter was born, she was slippery like a fish, and her skin was almost blue. I turned her over and tapped her on the back, and then she drew breath and cried. That sound . . . it went through my whole body. It was like the beginning of the world.

The heat and the mess, the cord and the placenta. The wet, bloody sheets. The dark night through the window. My baby's cry.

I didn't mean for it to happen at home, all by myself. I thought I had more time; I'd heard women talk about being in labor for twenty-four or thirty-six hours, so I didn't think there was any rush to get to the hospital. I thought I could wait until morning at least; I think I had some idea that I could wait till my mom went to work, then go to the hospital on my own. But things got fast and hard, and I stopped being able to think clearly. I called out for my mother once, just once, when the pain got so bad I couldn't do anything but live inside it. But she didn't hear me. I did it all on my own, and I feel like that gives me certain rights. That night is mine. It's got nothing to do with her at all.

My baby arched her back and squalled like a little storm; she was still attached to my body. I put her down, sprawling, on a towel. I could still feel the contractions coming, though they weren't as bad; a few minutes later, the placenta came out, and then the two of us were separate.

I lay back on the pillows until I could breathe normally again; I felt like going to sleep, but I didn't think that was a good idea. I'd been watching all these shows about people having babies, and I remembered something about how if you have the baby at home, you should tie the cord with a clean shoelace before you cut it. It was hard to get up and walk, but I went to the closet and found a pair of sneakers I'd only worn a couple of times. I took them back to the bed with me and undid the laces, then tied them tightly around the cord in two different places. There were scissors on my bedside table; they'd never been used to cut anything tougher than wrapping paper. I cut between the shoelaces; blood spurted for a minute, then stopped.

The baby lay on the towel bow-legged, her arms bent at the elbow, her fists near her ears. I picked her up and laid her on top of me for warmth; I'd seen that on TV, too. I looked at her and looked at her. Her eyes were a color I'd never seen; I couldn't pin it down to brown or blue. "Hi," I whispered. "Hi."

She put her face to the skin of my belly and tried to suck. I moved her up to my breast, and she found the nipple right away. Just that once, I fed her from my body. Just that once, she lay in my arms and was mine.

Afterward, she closed her eyes, and I wrapped her in a beach towel. I set her in the middle of the bed. I knew what was going to come next: I was going to try to stand; I was going to work my way down the stairs. I was going to get my mother, and everything would start to happen. But first I curled myself around her, and tried to contain her within me for just a moment more.

The night my daughter was born, my flesh ripped, and I crept through a chaos of pain.

The night my daughter was born I felt like I was torn in two.

I'm crying and moaning and holding the little dress to my face. I'm sure I'm going to ruin it. Juliet looks horrified; Abby's staring, wide-eyed. My mom comes up behind me and tries to hug me, but I push her away. Suddenly, I'm furious.

"They did this on purpose," I say. My voice is choked and shaky.

"Who did?" my mom asks.

"The show, the producers, whoever. They want me to have a breakdown, they want me to tell everyone. They want me to tell *him*." I point at Elliott, holding the camera steady on my wretched face.

My mom looks confused and a little wary. "But how would they know?" she asks.

"Because I told them, okay?" I'm starting to yell. "During the auditions. You think they picked us because we're so fascinating? They picked us because we're a fucking freak show!" I let out a strangled, frustrated scream. I want to be a little kid again. I want to lie on the floor and kick and yell.

My mother looks hurt and upset. "Why would you do that?" she asks.

I shake my head back and forth. "I don't know. What does it matter?" I turn to Elliott, put my face right up to the lens. "Fine," I say. "Fine. You want me to lose it? You want me to freak out? Here you go."

I pick up the ski pole and try to break it over my knee. It bends but doesn't snap. I throw it to the ground. I look around; the aviator helmet is sitting on the sofa, but I don't know what I can do with that. I open the zipper on my backpack and root around inside until I find the sequins, the rice paper, the crystal chess piece. I throw the chess piece into the fireplace; it bounces, and the little knob on the tippy-top chips off. I toss the sequins to the floor and grind my shoe into them; I tear the rice paper into shreds.

"Is that enough?" I yell. "Does that get me off this show? What else do I have to do?"

My mom is staring at me; she looks like she's going to cry. Carl and Justin have come from the other room and are standing in the doorway with Bonnet Lady, who looks a little frightened.

Juliet steps toward me. She has a strange, intense look on her face; at first, I think she's angry. "I'll help," she says. She opens her own backpack, finds one of the photographs from the Stockholm subway. She holds it up in the air and rips it in two.

For some reason, this deflates me. I sink to the ground and start to cry. I put my face in my hands and rock back and forth. And then someone's beside me, and it's my mother. She puts her arms around me, and this time I don't resist. I sway and weep, and she's right there with me, holding me tight. I'm a little girl, and I'm not, and I want her, and I don't. But I let her hold me, and I rest my head on her shoulder until I'm empty and spilt among the wreckage.

THIRTY

Juliet

When I was on *Best Friends,* I had this acting coach who kept telling me I needed to "be more authentic." I had no idea what he was talking about; I was twelve. But I think maybe now I get it; when I saw Cassie so upset, I just wanted to help her. I didn't think about the cameras, I just did what felt right. It was real; not planned out, not staged. It cost me half a million bucks, and who knows how it'll play. It's a little bit scary. But I'm glad I did it. This same acting coach used to tell me I needed to take more risks. I didn't know what he meant by that, either – how do you take risks while reading lines from a sitcom script? But I think he'll be happy with my performance here today.

After Cassie calms down and the camera guys have got her mother-daughter moment on film, producer Kate steps in to talk to us.

"Okay," she says. We're still in the farmhouse parlor; shooting's been suspended for a few minutes. "Obviously, you guys are going to be eliminated for this. The contracts you signed clearly state that loss or breakage of a found object is grounds for disqualification."

Cassie and I nod. *Will this be a disaster?* I'm thinking. *Will I be doing the talk-show damage-control circuit in three months?* Right here, right now, things seem clear: I have a friend, and I gave her my support. Easy, right? But I know – and this is where I get into trouble, this is where I start to wonder if I can trust myself — that down the line there are going to be plenty of opportunities to spin this episode, to reframe it. To take this one genuine moment and make it into something completely different. I can see myself making my entrance, walking across the set. I can feel the chill of the air conditioning, the heat of the lights. The cameras trained on my every move, the safety of an audience, cheering just because I'm there. I settle down on the sofa, across the desk from the host, and I feel more at home than I have in any house I've ever lived in. Then the questions begin — the teasing tone, *What was the deal with that little incident in Ireland? What exactly happened there?* — and I have a choice to make. It wouldn't take much — a joke about Cassie's weight, an insinuation that she might have had a crush on me. It would be so easy. I can hear the words coming out of my mouth. And it makes me feel sick.

Kate continues with her little scolding. "We also need to check with the museum people to see if you've caused any damage; if you have, you'll be responsible for it. We'll need you to sign waivers saying that your actions were your own, and that you weren't encouraged to do this by anyone connected to the show." We nod again. I look around. We've made a mess, but I don't think we've done anything much to the room itself.

"Okay," Kate says. She doesn't seem angry or anything, just tired like the rest of us. "Here's how we're going to handle this: you two will continue on till the end of the leg, and when you reach the Meeting Point, Barbara will disqualify you there. Since we're so close to the end of the game, we're not going to send you to the sequester location; we're going to need everyone at the finish line, so you'll just continue on with us, traveling with the crew, but you won't be on camera. Got it?"

"Yeah," I say. Cassie murmurs something like a yes. Her face is swollen from all the crying, and she seems quiet and sad. I put an arm around her and squeeze her shoulder for comfort. It seems like the right thing to do, but I don't know. (Can I do this without ruining it? I wonder. Can I change my persona, present myself as someone who doesn't care what people think? Or maybe I can reach someplace where I actually don't. What, exactly – and I know how stupid this sounds, but it's something I really need to understand – what, exactly, is the difference?)

"And we'll need to do exit interviews, explaining why you've acted this way, what made you snap, et cetera. Okay?"

"I guess," Cassie says. "What does it matter now, right?"

"Great," Kate says. "Well, let's get on with it."

The door to the cottage opens, and Dallas and Jeff walk in.

"Man, that took forever," Dallas says, projecting his voice to make sure his presence is noted. "I was not meant to use a loom. This is why I never do historical stuff."

I imagine Dallas dressed up for a costume drama, wearing knee breeches and a tricornered hat, and an ugly little snort of laughter makes its way out of my mouth. I try to cover it with a cough. Yeah, I'm sure the big historical directors are busting down Dallas's door.

"Whoa," Jeff says, catching a glimpse of the parlor. "What the hell happened here?"

Cassie looks at me; she seems like she doesn't know how to answer the question. "We had a little accident," I say. "We're out. Congratulations."

Jeff and Dallas do the whole woo-hoo and high-five thing. "Final three," Jeff screeches. "We're in the final three!"

"Well, we may as well open our last clue," I say to Cassie. "Find out where we're going for our public humiliation."

"Yeah," she says. She leans over her backpack and comes up with the gold envelope. She still seems so down.

"Hey," I say softly. "It's going to be okay. It really is." And I don't know any of the details, I don't know what's making her so sad, but I can do my part not to add to it. This could be something new for me; this is about how to be an adult. Or maybe it's about how to be a normal person.

I take the envelope from her, tear it open. "Drive to the Wishing

Chair at the Giant's Causeway," I read. "There are cars provided outside the museum gates."

"What should we take?" Cassie asks. "All the broken stuff?"

I think about it a minute. "No," I say, making a decision. I'm in charge for a change. "Just the parrot. We're traveling light."

THIRTY-ONE

Carl

In the list of surreal situations I never imagined I might find myself in, sitting in a nineteenth-century Irish farmhouse and sewing little dresses with my brother is very close to the top. Add a disgruntled former homosexual and a couple of cameramen zooming in on my shoddy needlework, and you've got the makings of a very bizarre nightmare. I'm only surprised to find I'm still wearing pants.

Kate has just ushered us back in here to get on with our sewing after Cassie's interruption in the parlor a few minutes ago. Yikes — rough scene back there. I'm sure it's been coming for a while, but this whole pressure-cooker environment can't be helping. Not sure what I can say to Laura — this will pass? I'm certain it will, but I know that having children does strange things to your perspective. The kid's resistant to potty training, and suddenly you're picturing him walking down the aisle in diapers; you miss a little thing like your daughter's pregnancy . . . well, I can only imagine the serial-killer scenarios that must be running through Laura's head. Maybe this was just the kind of thing she was looking for: a chance to be a mother, a chance to get it right. And it's the first time I've seen the two of them in a room together without Cassie trying to get away as fast as she can. That's got to be good for something.

In any case, in spite of all the weirdness of the day, I feel like things are hopeful. It's sunny outside, and I'm learning how to make something with my hands. In a few days, rich or not, I get to go home and see my little boy. And not three hours ago, Laura kissed me of her own accord. I have a sense of the world expanding around me.

My baby dress isn't shaping up into anything special, but I've got to say, it looks a hell of a lot better than Jeff's.

"Did you just sew the armhole shut?" I ask him. He's bent over the fabric, squinting as he moves the needle in and out. He's going to get a lot of grief from his buddies when this segment airs.

"That was intentional," he says. He examines the armhole (which is, indeed, sewn closed), and reaches for a pair of scissors. "No one ever thinks about the poor one-armed babies when they're designing clothes. There could be quite a market for this."

I grin. Can it be that things are back to normal between us? All it ever takes is time; we've never been able to stay mad at each other for long. And I'm glad he's getting along with Dallas. I want him to have fun.

I lean over the table to get a better look at what I'm working on. It's not that hard, really. They've given us all the pieces – the little sleeves are already sewn; the little collar already has a frill of lace around the edge – so all we have to do is put it all together. As far as I can tell, it doesn't even have to look particularly good, as long as everything's in the right place. But Jeff looks completely flummoxed, and Justin is sitting over there grumbling under his breath. The key is speed; I make my stitches big and sloppy. As long as they hold everything together, right?

"Crap," says Jeff. "I stuck myself again." He puts down his needle, sucks on his fingertip for a minute.

"You want a thimble?" I say.

He gives me a sardonic look. "I'm not going to wear a thimble," he says.

"They're just trying to humiliate us," Justin says suddenly. He's been pretty quiet so far, but I get the idea he's continuing a conversation that's been going on in his head. "They want to make us look like something less than men."

Jeff and I look at each other. "Um," I say. "I think they just want to make us look like something less than dressmakers."

"They didn't know it'd be all men," Jeff says. "Juliet did it, right? And if you'd done the loom instead of Abby, you'd be sitting this one out."

Justin shakes his head. "They want to see me emasculated," he says. "They want people to turn on their TVs and see me reduced to a woman's role."

Jeff nods soberly. "You're right," he says. "It's all about you."

I pick up a sleeve, focus on my sewing. I don't really want to be involved.

"First Corinthians," Justin says. He's talking to himself, really. "'But I would have you know that the head of every man is Christ; and the head of the woman is the man; and the head of Christ is God.'"

Jeff leans over to me. "Cool," he whispers. "A woman with the head of a man. She'd probably be feeling herself up all the time."

I shake my head, trying to look serious. I'm not going to make fun of the Bible on national TV, and neither should he. I'm the big brother; I'm back to keeping Jeff in line.

Justin wields his needle with a vengeance, stabbing the fabric, quoting more Bible verses as he goes. I'll give him this – it's a more masculine form of sewing than I've seen before. He's turned it into some kind of warfare.

"What do you think Benjamin's doing right now?" Jeff asks, speaking up to be heard over Justin's mumblings. It's a holdover from a childhood game we used to play on vacation, except we used to ask the question about our dog: "What do you think Jolly's doing right now? Sleeping? Chasing a ball?"

"I don't know – what are we, five hours ahead? He's probably at preschool. I think it's the day the music guy comes to sing with them." I think of Benjamin sitting on the floor in a circle singing "Wheels on the Bus," and a pang goes through me. I sew faster, like it might get me home to him sooner.

"I can't wait to see him," Jeff says, and I smile. It's a nice thing for him to say.

"This cannot go on," Justin says quietly. But he keeps sewing.

Jeff rolls his eyes. "Bad day for Bible Boy," he whispers to me. I shush him. A couple more stitches and I'm done; I finish attaching the sleeve and tie the thread in an unnecessarily big knot.

"Finished," I call out.

The seamstress gets up from her chair in the corner, comes to inspect my work. She holds the dress up and looks at it skeptically. "Lovely," she says finally. Is that sarcasm in her voice? How authentic is that?

"See you guys later," I yell to Justin and Jeff. And then, just to bug them, "Enjoy your sewing circle."

I run to the parlor, where Laura's sitting with Abby and Dallas. "Voilà," I say, holding the dress up with one hand and extending the other to Laura. "Let's get out of here."

"Wow, that looks really nice," she says. She sounds completely genuine, which makes me laugh. The dress looks like crap. She takes my hand, and we walk out into the sunny day, leaving Drumnahunshin Farm, home of emasculating assignments and unexpected breakdowns, behind us forever.

In the car, Laura doesn't seem to want to talk about Cassie; we talk about the money instead. Up till now, I've just been playing the game, trying to stay in it, but all of a sudden winning seems like a real possibility. With Cassie and Juliet out — I talk gingerly around this aspect of it — Laura and I are among the last three teams. There will be one more leg, one more set of tasks for us to complete, and whoever's ahead at the end goes home with a million bucks. Since Justin seems to be unraveling in some unfathomable way, and Jeff (as much as I love him) is Jeff, it looks like we might have a pretty good chance.

"What would you do with the money?" Laura asks me. She's in the backseat, navigating; I'm in the front, trying to get used to driving on the wrong side of the road.

I glance at our cameraman, Austin, sitting in the passenger seat. What I would do with the money is to put it away someplace safe so that if Benjamin ever needs more medical care, we're covered. But so far I've been successful at keeping that subject matter away from the cameras. I try to imagine life as an ordinary father, one who can think about money without his mind drifting to hospital stays and immunosuppressant drugs. What would that guy do with half a million bucks?

"I'd put some away for Benjamin's education," I say. Such careless optimism most parents have, assuming that age eighteen is a milestone everyone's child reaches. "And maybe" — I try to think of something frivolous — "I'd buy myself a motorcycle." Well, why the hell not. That guy, the ordinary dad? He deserves a little speed, a little danger.

"What about you?" I ask Laura. I meet her eyes in the rearview mirror.

"Well, Cassie's education, sure," she says. "Besides that, I don't know. I used to say I'd travel, but I think I've had enough of that." She laughs, then shrugs. "Maybe," she says. I see her look down at the map in her lap, avoiding my reflected gaze. "Maybe I'd think about moving."

I don't say a word. She's being cagey — maybe she means a new house, maybe a new city. Too early to tell, absolutely. But I give her a smile in the mirror, raise my eyebrows just a bit. I want her to know I know what she's up to.

We drive on through the wild, green landscape. After an hour, we've reached the very top of the country; it makes me think of the bit Barbara's always doing about "a scavenger hunt that will cover all the corners of the earth." It does feel like we've come to the end of the world.

We turn onto a twisty coastal highway. The views are beautiful — rugged cliffs and tumultuous water — but I'm afraid to turn my eyes from the curves of the road.

"So what am I looking for?" I ask Laura.

"The Giant's Causeway. We should be almost there."

"And what do we know about this location?"

"Let's see . . . apparently, it's a 'naturally occurring marvel.' It's been called the Eighth Wonder of the World."

"I thought that was King Kong. Or am I thinking of the fifth Beatle?"

But Laura's absorbed in the book. "Oh, here's a picture — wow, it's really something." She thrusts the guidebook through the space between the front seats, but I can't turn to look.

"Just give me the basics," I say.

"Okay. According to this, it's a 'mass of forty thousand hexagonal basalt columns, formed by cooling lava.'"

"Right. That tells me nothing."

"Well, just trust me," Laura says. "It's very striking. You'll see."

"I guess I will."

She reads in silence for a couple of minutes. "It says here there are two legends about its origins. They both involve a giant warrior named Finn McCool. In one version, he fell in love with a lady giant who lived on a nearby island and he built a path of stepping-stones so he could bring her across the water. In the other version, there's a Scottish giant who threatens Finn McCool, and he creates the causeway so the other giant can come across to fight. But then — oh, get this — it turns out the Scottish giant is bigger than he was expecting, and he's not sure he can defeat him. So he builds himself an enormous crib and dresses himself up in a bonnet and booties. When the Scottish giant sees the huge baby, he gets scared about what the father must look like, and he runs away."

"Clever," I say. "Quick thinking."

"Yeah," she says. "But I think I like the love story better."

I glance in the mirror. Laura's looking out the window at the view moving past us. She looks somehow wistful, like she can't even imagine anyone crossing an expanse of water to stand by her side. "I do, too," I say. "I think that's the one we'll take."

When we get to the Giant's Causeway, I can see what she was talking about. It's like a science fiction landscape, some filmmaker's vision of a world different from the one we live in; it seems too carefully constructed, too beautifully precise, to be something assembled by nature on its own. A carpet of stones stretches out into the sea, columns of varying heights but surprisingly uniform shape. They're not all hexagons, in spite of what our guidebook told us – some have seven sides or five or eight – but they're all perfect polygons, packed as tight as pieces of linoleum on a kitchen floor. There are flat terraces and tall groups of columns that spring up like spires, like a city of skyscrapers seen from a distance. I can't imagine any giant going to all this trouble for an enemy.

On our way in from the parking lot, we pass Cassie and Juliet sitting on a bench, being filmed for what I imagine are their exit interviews. Cassie looks okay, all things considered. Laura lingers to watch for a minute, but I take her arm to urge her on. There will be time for everyone to talk after we've checked in with Barbara.

We've stopped at the visitor's center for a map, and we find the Wishing Chair on a list of whimsically named geological formations – the Giant's Boot, the Granny, the Camel, the Giant's Organ (here I pause to make a mental joke on Jeff's behalf) – but we don't need to look too hard, because Barbara is waiting for us about halfway down the slope of rocks with a camera crew and a few members of the production team. Laura and I hold hands to steady each other as we make our way down the uneven path. I hold the parrot cage, and Laura uses the ski pole like a walking stick. Our cameraman and sound guy step carefully behind us, their delicate equipment a single misstep away from smashing to the stones below.

"Do you think they'd met before?" Laura asks as we climb down. "The giant and his lady friend? I mean, if there was no other way to get across the water, then maybe they didn't really know each other beforehand."

"That's true," I say. "Maybe they'd only seen each other from afar. I guess, you're a giant, your pickings are slim; you see a lady giant across the water, you figure what the heck." I pause as we navigate a couple of unusually jagged steps. "Maybe he just knew," I say, trying for a more romantic spin. "Maybe it was all a grand leap of faith."

Laura smiles faintly, concentrates on the stone columns at her feet. I don't know if I've given the right answer, or if she's still worrying about how things worked out for those two crazy giants. But it's not important; it's just a story. The moment that matters is this: a man and a woman of ordinary stature, holding hands on the slippery rocks. A landscape of extraordinary beauty formed without the aid of fairy tales, brought into being by the movements of the ordinary world spinning on its stem. Together we climb down.

Barbara smiles brilliantly when we reach her. I'm actually glad to see her.

"Welcome, Carl and Laura," she says. "You've arrived in second place, but due to a last-minute disqualification, you're now in the lead. Before I check you in, though, we've got one more little task for you."

Austin leans in for our forced smiles, our obligatory "what now?" expressions.

Barbara continues. "I'm standing in front of a geological formation known as the Wishing Chair." She gestures to an indentation in the descending columns, a place where a little bench of stones has been formed by the vagaries of wind and water. "It is said that any visitor who sits here and makes a wish will be lucky enough to see it come true. Each of you will sit in the chair, out of earshot of the other, and tell us your wish."

Producer Eli steps in to give us some instructions that will almost certainly not be televised. "Okay," he says. "I want some drama here. No wishing to win the game, no wishing for a million dollars. If you've got any secret hopes, any conflicts that need to be resolved, anything that hasn't come out in interviews, now's the time."

He gives us a minute to let this sink in, as if he's said something important and deep. "Okay," he says, apparently satisfied that we're on board with his instructions. "Laura, you'll go first. Carl, go stand down by the water until she's done."

I climb down the rocks until the air blasting around my ears blocks out all sound from above. I'm annoyed by this whole thing; they're not usually so transparent about getting us to spill our guts.

And I happen to like wishes — birthday candles, fallen eyelashes, I take all of that seriously. I spent a lot of time as a kid thinking about the best way to phrase my requests if I were ever lucky enough to meet a genie; I'd heard enough cautionary tales to know that you have to ask in exactly the right way if you want to avoid pitfalls. But my genuine adult wishes are not things I like to reveal casually, and to have to come up with some insipid camera-friendly desire seems like a particularly stupid exercise.

By the time Laura's finished and I'm summoned back up to the chair, I still don't know what I'm going to say. Laura passes me without speaking, and I let the production crew pose me in the stone chair exactly the way they want me.

"We want an 'I wish' format," Eli says, "as in 'I wish blank.' Think carefully about what you're going to say. Something about your son's health would be good, or anything Laura might have told you about her and Cassie. And, let me just say . . ." — here he smiles like we're close friends — "if you're going to propose, now would be a perfect opportunity."

I stare at him. It hadn't occurred to me, and it seems to be a spectacularly bad idea, given that I've known my supposed bride for less than a month, and she's not even currently in earshot. I can see the seductiveness of it, though: a moment of high romance and drama, center of attention, caught on film for everyone to see. Some guys would do it, absolutely. I have a feeling Jeff would be down on one knee right now.

"No," I say flatly.

Eli shrugs. "Suit yourself, but make it good. Anytime you're ready."

"I wish," I say, and falter. I shrug. "I wish that no one will be any worse off after this game than they were when they started." The phrasing sounds a little awkward to me, but I'm pleased with the overall effect.

Eli shakes his head. "Nope," he says. "Try again."

"That's it," I say. "That's my wish. That's the only one you're getting."

Eli's implacable. "I'm afraid that if that's the case, we'll have to put you on record as refusing to participate in the task. You and Laura will be eliminated."

Is this one of those moments in life where a person stands up for his beliefs and says, "The hell with the million bucks"? No. It is not. I sigh. "I wish that Laura and I will have a future together after this show is over."

"Good," says Eli. "But try again; I'd like to hear 'game' instead of 'show,' and I'd like to see you look a little more excited as you say it."

Dutifully, I repeat the line. I think of money, and my son. What does it matter? It's true enough. I'm not exactly selling my soul here, even if I feel like I've been defeated in some intangible way.

"Good," Eli says. "You can relax. Remember, you're bound by your contract not to reveal what you've said here today."

I linger in the Wishing Chair for a moment longer. Is it like prayer? I wonder. Do silent wishes count? Before I get up, I give unspoken voice to every true wish I have, sending them out to any forces that might be listening in the cold ocean air.

I start to feel a little better as I make my way down to where Laura's standing, looking at the water. I'm sure Laura didn't want to prostrate herself before the cameras any more than I did, but I wonder if maybe she settled on the same secondary wish. Would it matter for either of us if it wasn't the first thing that came into our minds? No, I decide, as long as I get to hear her say it back.

"Carl," Laura calls. She's standing at the water's edge, on the farthest rocky point that juts out into the sea. The wind blows her hair every which way; the sun is starting to set. She holds out a hand in my direction. "Come look," she says.

I step carefully toward her. Brown stones and blue water, brisk wind and crashing waves. Awkward as a giant, I walk across the stones toward someone I hope will be my love.

THIRTY-TWO

Justin

All the way from Belfast up to the Antrim Coast, I fume and I pray and I try to figure out what to do. Abby drives, which is just as well, because I suspect I'm a little too agitated to navigate the tortuous cliffside roads we're traveling on. I feel furious, terrified, forsaken. I can barely even speak. Abby's keeping her distance; she's been upset with me ever since Trafalgar Square when I couldn't muster any sympathy for whatever schoolgirl-crush nostalgia she was going through. I'm sorry for that, but when you're sunk deep in turmoil, when you've got a sword swinging over your head and you're not sure if it's God or the devil who's going to come to your rescue, it's hard to be concerned about someone whose greatest sin is longing.

But a good husband does what he can to avoid causing his wife pain, and later, after I've figured out a way to bring this crisis to an end, I'll apologize as generously and profusely as I can. Maybe I'll even be able to make her see, without revealing too much, that my disturbed manner today has all been in her best interest. She, more than anyone, is in need of my protection.

I have sinned grievously; that is not in question. I have sinned, and I have repented; whatever punishment I may face is between my Savior and me. What I cannot abide is having some faggot cameraman and some gold-loving Hollywood executives appoint themselves as God's judges here on Earth. What I cannot abide is having my name slandered, my faith questioned, my hard-won grace mocked between commercial breaks. I've never given much credence to anti-Christian conspiracy theories, but I can't help but think that the only reason they want to take me down is because I'm a religious man, because I'm not afraid to speak about the joy that Christ's love has brought into my life. If they had footage of some left-wing college kids, some so-called gay rights activists going at it in a hotel room, they wouldn't be so anxious to sully America's TV screens with it. They have different rules for the faithful. And I'm the one they're calling a hypocrite.

I've been searching and praying ever since London, trying to find some guidance about what the right course of action might be. And what I've come up with is this: I've got to find some way to prevent this show from ever dirtying the airwaves. It's not just for me; it's for the good of every man, woman, and child with a television set. I was an innocent when I started this journey, thinking I could be a force for good, thinking I could use the springboard of mass culture to deliver my message of hope to a wider audience. But I've come to realize that this program and others like it are the basest, most insidious form of garbage.

This is no *Fantasy Island,* reminding viewers to be careful what they wish for; this is a show that tells you that your fantasies and your wishes are the only things you've got. The people behind this show want, more than anything, to encourage dissatisfaction. You may think you have everything you need, they tell you, but you're wrong. Are there dreams you haven't followed? Could you be happier than you are today? (Never mind that some dreams should never see the light of morning; never mind that happiness is a game only fools think they can win.) They can see you, sitting at home under the blanket of all your daily stresses, and they want to teach you how to yearn and strive and despair. They want you thinking that your life is not what you thought it would be, that romance and adventure and a million dollars are out there waiting for you, so close you can see their shadows flickering in the light from the screen.

There are no consequences; you really can have it all. And all you have to do is loosen, just a little, the grip you have on your soul.

It all seems so clear to me now, and I'm ashamed I ever agreed to be a part of this confidence game. But I can redeem myself. Evil is planted deep in this show, and it's my duty to root it out.

By the time we pull into the parking lot of the Giant's Causeway, I've managed to calm myself a little bit. I'm still not entirely sure what I'm going to do, but I feel resolute. I'm going to take some action; I have no other choice.

We get out of the car, and I see Abby's face for the first time in an hour. She looks deeply, deeply sad. Now that I've gathered my own resources a little bit, I feel more able to reach out to her and offer the kind of solace a wife needs from her husband.

"I'm sorry I was short with you earlier," I say, making my voice gentle and soft. "I'm sure this is a rough day for you."

She makes a movement like half a shrug; her face remains the same. "That's okay," she says. "I'm sorry I bothered you with my problems when you weren't feeling your best."

"Don't be silly," I say. "That's what I'm here for." We stand there awkwardly for a moment, the camera spooling away our discomfort for later use. It's clear things still aren't quite right between us, but I'm always at a loss about what we're supposed to do after the "I'm sorrys" are said.

Abby puts her backpack on; her body sinks under the weight. She hoists the parrot cage. "Well, look at that," she says, as the two of us notice for the first time the wondrous spectacle below us.

"God's glorious work," I say. "Here's a cure for atheism, right here."

"I see Barbara," Abby says, her voice a little flat. She's not, it seems, in a very "praise Him" kind of mood. We can work on that. If I can manage to get us through this crisis intact, we'll have a whole lifetime to work on that.

"Let's get down there," I say.

We climb down the rocks; noises of protest come from the birdcage as Abby's steps become more uneven. I consider for a moment what the effect might be if any harm came to the parrot, but I dismiss the idea without too much thought. We'd probably just be disqualified, with any unpleasant bird-related footage edited out.

After a few moments, we reach Barbara and her crew. We stand before her, and I see for the first time what a mockery this all is. This isn't Judgment Day; she has no authority to decide our fates.

"Welcome, Justin and Abby," she says. I meet her eyes and find nothing human there at all. "You've arrived in third place, but due to a last-minute disqualification, you've been moved up to second. Before I check you in, though, we've got one more task for you to perform."

Trained dogs, that's what we are to them. Barbara spouts some pagan nonsense about giants and wishes; they've found another opportunity for us to scatter dissatisfaction over their viewers like seeds over freshly turned earth.

Eli adds his rules to Barbara's and dismisses me to the water's edge. From a distance, the wind shouting in my ears, I watch my wife sit in a chair made of stone. I see her lips move, but I have no idea what she's saying. What on earth might she have to wish for? Have I ever known?

I will not think that way. I will be a better husband, if only, if only. My whole body is shaking; night is falling, and it's getting cold. I keep my eyes on Abby; her wish, whatever it is, takes no time at all to make. A few words, and she's done. And then they're calling me up to the chair.

The lighting crew is setting up to film in darkness; Eli tells me to wait a few minutes while they finish. I sit on the cold stones and let them move me how they want to, while they consider the best way to make me visible against the fading sky. I use the time to pray for strength, for guidance. I try to imagine that the bright lights they're shining on me are coming from within, that I'm so filled with God's love that it's leaking out of me and lighting up the night.

"Here's what we want from you," Eli says. He gives me guidelines for my wishing, as if he can control the things I want.

"And listen," he says, looking me right in the face. "I know you've spoken to Ken. You know as well as I do what kinds of things are going to be revealed here."

I don't even want to listen. I can feel the light inside me; it's bursting out through my skin.

"This is your chance to respond," Eli says. "Now's the time to ask for Abby's forgiveness; that would be a good one. I suppose there are a couple of ways to go about it: you could wish for the courage to live your life more honestly, that's one angle; you could renounce the whole ex-gay thing. Or you could wish for the strength not to sin again, if you still want to go the religious route." He sounds almost bored as he outlines these options for me. This, to him, is all in a day's work.

"I don't know if you can manage it," he says, "but tears would be good, if you want to do the repentance thing. Think Jimmy Swaggart and all those guys; they did scandal well." I stare at him. My veins pump a hatred as thick and black as hot tar. There is evil all around me. "But do something," he says. "I think it's going to look worse if you don't say anything about it. The audience is going to be looking for something."

I despise him with a ferocity that's almost impossible to contain, but I can't let it get in my way. I close my eyes and gather up that hatred; I use it to stoke the fire glowing in my chest. *I will take you down,* I think. *I will take you down.*

The question, as I see it, is this: how can I damage a show like this one? And the answer is simple: do something that will make people stop watching. Reveal this show to be the cancer that it is. I have a few possible weapons in my arsenal, but one in particular I think might be very powerful. I have a secret even Abby doesn't know about; well, I suppose it's clear by now that I have a few. But this one may be my salvation.

It's something that happened during the third leg of the game. We were in Greece, on the island of Rhodes; it was the last part of the Found Object round, and we were racing to the check-in point. We were supposed to find our way into the medieval citadel known as the Old City, after which we had to navigate the maze of narrow streets to find Barbara waiting for us at the Palace of the Grand Masters at the end of the Street of Knights. Abby and I knew all this, but we'd been held up by flight delays, and we were in the last group of contestants to land on the island. When we arrived, we discovered that the producers had added an extra puzzle to the task: there are eleven gates into the Old City, and there were eleven teams left. Once a team had used one of the gates, the producers "sealed" it so that no other teams could enter there. It wasn't immediately apparent which gates had been sealed and which hadn't; there were knights in full armor guarding each one, and the only way to tell which gates were still open was to run around the perimeter of the walled city, approaching knight after knight until you found one who would grant you admittance.

Abby and I were competing for last place with a team of professional masseuses from Seattle; nice enough women, but thinking about it now, I suspect they hadn't proven very interesting on-camera. (Certainly not as interesting as their profession might lead you to believe.) As the four of us raced around, trying to gain access into the city, our cameraman, a guy named Sam, got a call on his cell phone. He spoke for a moment, then hung up and grabbed my arm.

"Monty Hall, man," he said, jerking his head in the opposite direction from the way we were going. "Door number three."

Abby was ahead of us and didn't see this transaction occur. I stared at Sam for a minute, not sure what to do. He didn't say anything else; he just shrugged, as if he didn't really care much one way or the other.

"This way, Abby," I called out, reversing my direction and starting to run. I stretched for an explanation. "We'll have a better chance if we don't go the same way they're going."

I ran right past the first gate.

"What about this one?" Abby yelled after me.

"No," I said. "That's the first one people come to if they're headed this way; I'm sure it's already taken. Let's keep going."

I ran past the second gate, Abby at my heels.

"What are you doing?" she said. "We need to be systematic about this, don't we?"

"I have a good feeling about the next one," I said. "When I was praying earlier, an image came into my mind, and it looked just like that next gate."

She followed me without challenge, a good wife to the end. And at the third gate, we made our plea, and the knight bowed and allowed us to pass through. We found Barbara, and the masseuses were sent on their way.

I've thought about this episode a number of different ways since it happened. Strangely enough, it didn't seem particularly significant to me at first. We were on a television show, weren't we, and hadn't we taken direction from producers and camera crews almost daily? It had been clear to me for some time that the "reality" in "reality show" was meant to be taken with a grain of salt. We got a little nudge in the right direction, and it kept us in the game so we could work toward the money and spread our message of hope a little longer. Who was I to say that was wrong?

But now I see that it was corruption, pure and simple. For whatever reason, the powers that be decided that the religious freaks with their uneasy marriage and their quaint ideas about homosexuality would be a bigger draw than the dowdy masseuses. A quick phone call and a suggestion that we go to the right instead of the left, and they got to keep the characters they liked the best.

I have no proof of further wrongdoing, but I can't imagine this is the only instance of interference in the course of the game. Who knows how deep this runs? They may have orchestrated every elimination, every wrong turn in the last month. For all I know, maybe it was their idea for Ken to approach me on that overheated train ride to Tokyo. (Why that should make me feel like I've been struck in the chest, why I should suddenly feel like weeping as I sit here on this stone bench surrounded by spotlights, I cannot tell you.) I don't know the extent of it. What I do know is this: the game has been fixed, and that's not going to go over well with the American public.

This show is rotting from the inside out, and it just so happens that it works to my advantage.

The camera guys take test shots, measure the lighting. I can feel the brightness inside of me, ready to burst out of my body. The crew members retreat, and I'm sitting alone in the spotlight, ready to make my wish.

"Okay, Justin," Eli says. "We're ready for you."

And here we go. It's showtime.

"I wish," I say, my voice strong and steady, "for the lies to stop. I wish for people to know that the outcome of this show has been tainted. This is not reality; the people in charge have leaked information to players, and the eliminations have been predetermined." My voice is getting louder; I feel like a preacher, inflaming his congregation with the strength of his spirit. "You have been duped," I say, speaking to the camera and to the great big country that lies beyond it. "This show is a hoax, and you should not stand for it."

"Cut," Eli says, raising his hand in the air. "Justin, I think you know we're not going to air that."

"It doesn't matter," I say. I feel triumphant; I've gotten to them. "I'll go to the press, I'll tell them everything."

"Okay," Eli says. His voice is flat. "Three things. One, I don't have the slightest idea what you're talking about, but whatever incident you have in mind, you've got no proof. Two, there's a clause in your contract that prevents you from talking to the media about the show until after it airs. Three, and I think this is the one you're really not getting, nobody gives a shit."

His profanity convinces me that he's bluffing. He's more upset than he's letting on.

"Of course they do," I say. "People are going to want to know that this show is corrupt. I'm going to break this wide open. This is going to be huge; this is going to be your downfall."

Eli's mouth twists, and I think for a minute that I've got him cornered. And then he bursts out laughing. Laughter explodes around me — the PAs, the camera guys, the sound crew, that she-goat Barbara – all of them ridiculing me for daring to speak out in the name of morality.

"Justin," Eli says, still smiling. He sounds almost tender. "Have you ever watched the credits of our show? We have a disclaimer: 'In some instances, contestants may receive additional clues beyond those which are televised, at the discretion of *Lost and Found,* its network, and its producers.' Or something like that, I don't know; you'd have to ask Legal. The point is, people know it's not all real. So what? This isn't the fifties, Justin. No one cares."

I stare at him. I'm starting to feel very cold.

"Now, if that's settled," Eli says, "it's getting late, and I'd like to get this thing finished. We need a wish."

I have ridden amusement park rides whose sole purpose is to throw you off balance. The sudden plunge, the world on its end, the new knowledge that you can't trust your lungs to breathe for you, your legs to keep you upright. I stand here now, and nothing has changed, but the ground has been snatched away without warning. It will be another minute before I know if I'm flying or falling or both.

Juggernaut is the word that makes its way into my mind out of nowhere. *Juggernaut* and *unstoppable* and *futile.* What does it take, I wonder desperately, to get to these people? Are there any lines they won't cross? Shall I spill my blood for them, would that be enough to sway them? I imagine my last words, as careful and poignant as Admiral Nelson's; I picture my body broken on the rocks, a martyr laid down on this false altar they've raised. But no; they would revel in that drama. They would take that image and wave it across the world like a flag. And I have some work to do before I'm ready to meet my Creator.

"Justin?" Eli says. "Today, if possible." He's waiting for me; all of them are waiting for me to take some action. And I understand, suddenly, that there are some circumstances where violence is justifiable. Necessary, even. I glance upward, find my wife's silhouette among the shadows clustered there. And I make my move.

THIRTY-THREE

Abby

I'm not exactly sure what's happening down there. I made my wish, simply "I wish that Justin and I will grow old together," which Eli seemed unaccountably delighted with, though it wasn't anything I'd given much thought to; wishes are something I gave up a long time ago. Then I climbed back up to the top of the overlook, where the other teams were standing, and I watched the lighting crew work to fight the darkness so Justin could have his moment.

I can't see Justin's face from where I'm standing – his back is to me – but I see Eli motion the cameraman to start filming. I don't know precisely what Justin's wish might be, but I'm certain it won't be anything like mine; he's much more likely to see this as an opportunity to wish for all the gay people of the world to find Christ than he is to put forth something as small and humble as a hope about our future. It wouldn't even occur to him. But that's Justin; that's the man I married, and I'm not the kind of woman to start complaining now about problems that have been there all along.

There's a pause while Justin presumably makes his wish, then Eli gestures the cameras off with an abrupt motion. Something's going on; I hear Justin's voice rise sharply, though no one else seems to be yelling. I watch for a moment longer, still not catching any actual words. Then I see Justin pick up his ski pole and swing it in a wide arc. He hits a cameraman in the arm with great force; caught off guard, the man loses his balance, and his camera smashes to the ground. It makes a terrible noise, and several crew members jump in to restrain Justin, but he breaks free and spins around, hitting Barbara full in the face with his makeshift weapon. I cry out, shocked. I don't know what's going on, but this is very bad. I take off at a run and begin moving toward them down the rocky path. I notice that our cameraman, Robert, is right behind me. As I make my way down the uneven maze of hexagonal stones, I look up long enough to see Justin lunge at Eli. He pushes him to the ground and holds the tip of the ski pole to his throat.

A small, helpless noise comes out of my mouth; behind me, I hear Robert say, "Oh, man." I've never seen Justin violent before, although I'm certainly aware of how pent up he can be. How much trouble is he going to be in, I wonder. Is this assault or attempted murder, or what? I'm not sure how much damage you can do with a ski pole. It's not that heavy, and it flexes under pressure. And the point on the end isn't that sharp, is it? But I certainly hope someone gets it away from him soon.

I race the rest of the way down to where everyone's standing. By the time I get there, two of the younger, stronger PAs have their hands on Justin, trying to pull him away. But he's still got the ski pole against Eli's throat, and he's fighting with surprising force. Nearby, several crew members are talking urgently on cell phones. Barbara's got her hand over her mouth; I can see blood trickling down from under her palm.

"You'd better let go of me," Justin says serenely. "I've got this thing on his jugular; I'll spill his blood right here."

"What the hell is going on?" I say to Justin. "For God's sake, let him go."

"No," he says. "I won't. This show is fixed. These people are all cheaters."

"Your husband has no proof of that," Eli says, speaking from the ground. He sounds remarkably calm, but his face looks tense. "He may have misinterpreted a hint from a cameraman."

One of the PAs takes hold of Justin's hair and jerks his head backward. Justin lets out a tiny yelp of pain; in the split second he's distracted, Eli moves away from the ski pole and gets to his feet. The men tighten their grip on Justin, and the ski pole clatters to the ground.

"Okay," Eli says, brushing himself off. "Okay." Now that he's out of danger, I can see he looks shaken. He takes a deep breath, opens and closes his hands a couple of times. And then he's back to normal.

"Let's get the formalities taken care of," he says, his voice brisk. "The two of you are out of the game, obviously. Someone's already called the police, I take it?" He looks around for confirmation; a few feet away, a young woman raises one finger, points to the phone at her ear. I see that Barbara's being attended to by a man with a first aid kit; her makeup artist hovers nearby with a pot of concealer, but she waves him away.

I stare at Justin and try to wrap my mind around all this. Robert moves in for a close-up. "Justin," I say. "I just don't understand this. What the hell were you thinking?"

Justin looks more subdued now; he seems to have deflated a little at the news that the police are coming. "This show is evil, Abby," he says tonelessly. "I have to stop it from going on the air."

"Well, that's not going to happen," Eli says. "Do you want to tell your wife why you're so desperate for the show not to air?"

"It's bad for people, Abby," Justin says. "It confuses people about what they really want. It corrupts. . . . You have no idea how badly it corrupts."

I don't know what he's talking about. Barbara appears out of nowhere. Her face looks swollen and red on one side, though the bleeding's stopped. I notice she's turned the injured side of her face toward the camera. She stands next to Justin with her microphone, looking professionally crisp and cool. All in a day's work.

"Tell us, Justin," she says, and I can hear the smallest note of anger underneath her anchorwoman tone. "Tell us the real reason."

"That is the real reason," he says. "This show damages people."

"Abby," Barbara says, turning to me. "When you married Justin, did your wedding ceremony include a clause about 'forsaking all others'?"

I stare at her. There's a prickling sensation traveling along the surface of my skin. "It was a vow," I say softly. "Not a clause."

"Well, you should know," Barbara says, a killer's smile playing on her lips. Her eyes are on me, but it's the camera she's speaking to. "That we have footage of your husband breaking that vow. With another man."

The prickling feeling intensifies. I feel hot, then cold. I find I have tears in my eyes. Up above, on the road, I can hear the singsong noise of the police car arriving. Why, I wonder, do American sirens sound so different from the ones everywhere else?

Justin steps toward me, reaches for my arm, but I twist away. He's trying to meet my eyes, but I won't let him. "Abby," he says, his voice quiet and pleading. He doesn't go on. It's fine; I don't want to hear what he has to say anyway.

Am I furious? Am I hurt? Yes; I suppose those are the right words. I feel like someone has pushed something sharp into the center of me, leaving me bloody and exposed. Raw. And angry. And foolish. Before me stands a stupid man, and I am nothing but his stupid, stupid wife.

"Abby," Justin says again. "I need your help. Barbara's right, I've sinned, and I need your love to help me get back on track."

"Abby," Barbara says. "Do you have any reaction to the news I've just told you?" When I don't answer, she tries another tack. "Abby, you've lost the game, but what have you found?"

That's not something I know how to answer. I turn away, leave them both behind, and begin the tricky climb to level ground.

I feel overwhelmed in a way I can't quite explain. I feel like I've been standing in shallow water, looking at the calm of the beach, and I've been surprised from behind by a wave so big it lifts me right off the sand. I'm underwater with my eyes open, rolling with the seaweed; I can't breathe, and it takes me a minute to find the earth with my feet. But when I regain equilibrium, I realize I'm in a different place. The pressure of that water has moved me imperceptibly down the shore, and now my eyes are falling on a different view.

I realize, to come back to this chilly Irish evening, that this news is nothing but a relief. This is one of those moments – perhaps the fifth one in my life – when I know, beyond any doubt, that there is a God, and He is with me.

Our marriage has been like a staring contest, I think, or a game of chicken: *I'll do it if you will.* And if Justin had been able to do it for fifty more years, then I would have, too. There's no question about it. The ridiculous tragedy of that, the waste . . . it's suddenly very clear. But there's a corollary, and it makes me feel like I've broken loose from tight restraints: *If he can't do it, then maybe I don't have to, either.*

Back at the overlook, the other contestants surround me. Two policemen in dark uniforms are on their way down the rocks.

"What's going on?" Laura asks, putting a hand on my arm. "Is everything okay?"

"Should we go down there to do the Wishing Chair thing?" Dallas asks. "We haven't done it yet."

I shake my head, shrug them off. "I'll tell you about it later," I say. "Or you can just watch it on TV."

"Can we do anything to help?" Laura asks.

"I don't think so," I say.

We stand as a group and watch from above as my husband is put in handcuffs. The two officers start back up with Justin between them; he looks terrified. I will go to the police station with him, I decide, but it will be the last act of my marriage. I feel free, and also very frightened. I don't know how I'll do without him, without the comfort of the fiction we've written for ourselves. But I feel, for the first time I can remember, like it's okay for me to try.

I imagine now a new ending to my biography, a happier one. Set not at the end of my life, but at some point in the not-too-distant future. *I saw then how it would be,* it will say. *I saw then that I would be sixty, seventy, eighty years old, and still carrying this around, this shame about something that hurt no one at all.* I think that's the way it will go. And though I don't yet see a face, and I don't yet know exactly how I'm going to be able to make it come true, the last line I see is this: *I took her in my arms and kissed her.*

THIRTY-FOUR

Barbara Fox

My father, lover of all things corny, had an expression he liked to use when he found something to be good: "Well," he'd say, "it's better than a whack in the head." But the world is perverse, and no truism is true forever; years later and continents away, I'm here to tell you, Dad, that sometimes a whack in the head is the best thing that can possibly happen to you.

From the moment that troglodyte Justin rubbed together enough neurons to make his muscles lift that ski pole and swipe it across my face, there's been a feeling of excitement crackling through the ranks of the crew. A couple of phone calls, and we sent the news snaking out across the wires — REALITY SHOW HOST ATTACKED BY CONTESTANT — on its way to you. You, sitting at your breakfast table, flipping past the deadliness of the front page and looking for something light to read while you butter your English muffin. You'll eat this up.

But if you want to see it happen, you're going to have to wait. We're not leaking that footage. You want to see a man pushed to his breaking point, you want to see a TV star brought low? Fine; nothing would make us happier. All you have to do is tune in week after week and watch until the show winds down almost to its very end point; then you get your payoff. And oh, will it be worth it.

A man hitting a woman (a public figure, no less, someone you know you've seen somewhere before, though you're never quite able to place her) with a ski pole? That's not something you see every day. It'll shock you; it may even – what do I care? you're in the privacy of your own home – make you laugh. Go ahead, I don't mind. It's not really me being hit, it's that cold bitch Barbara Fox, and after sitting through the whole season, don't you kind of want to pop her one yourself?

Maybe I'm underestimating people. Maybe I'll get nothing but sympathy. That would be fine, too, but honestly, it doesn't really matter to me. What's important is that from here on in – and our venerable executive producer Oliver has taken me aside to assure me about this – the names *Lost and Found* and Barbara Fox are inextricably linked. If we're lucky enough to have another season (and after this, how could we not?), I'll be there. I'm in it for the long haul. And when it's over . . . well, who knows. But I'd like to think that when it's over, it won't mean that I am, too.

It's fantastic. I'd burst right out laughing if there weren't contestants around and I weren't afraid of looking almost human. A journey of a thousand miles, that was another of my dad's clichés. But really, I always wanted to say, who cares how the journey begins? Here's how it ends: it ends with a loose tooth and a bruise across the cheek; it ends with my being able to say that I've found my place in the world.

Finally, like it or not, you're going to know my name.

THIRTY-FIVE

Laura

Our plane touches down in El Paso, and Carl and I are off it in a flash. We've gotten rid of most of the stuff in our backpacks to make this last stretch easier, so all we've got are our Found Objects and our second-to-last clue, which I'm holding tight in my hand:

> There's no Lost and Found, Minnesota,
> There's no Price Is Right, Tennessee.
> But there is one city in the U.S.A.
> Named after a show from TV.
>
> You'll search for the last item on your scavenger hunt
> in a hotel marked by a mountain mosaic in the only
> U.S. city named for a game show.

It's been a long trip for us: sixteen-and-a-half hours from Belfast, with stops in Newark — now *there's* an unexpected site for a Keyword Round; the answer was "canal" — and Houston. And we've still got almost two hours of driving ahead of us before we reach Truth or Consequences, New Mexico. Dallas and Jeff aren't on the plane with us, but that doesn't mean much. There are a lot of different variables on a trip as long as this one, and if they connected through different cities, there's no telling whether we're ahead or behind.

Cassie and Juliet are on the plane with us, as is Abby. (Strange situation; the show decided not to press charges against Justin – exciting footage for them, I suppose – but he had to stay behind a few days to sort everything out. Why Abby didn't stay with him, I'm not sure. I suppose I'll have to wait and find out the details with the rest of America.) In any case, we aren't supposed to interact with any of them on-camera, since they've been disqualified and won't officially show up again until the finish line.

At one point on the first plane, the one out of Belfast, I found myself looking in Cassie's direction, keeping an eye on her, just like I've been doing all along. Carl nudged my arm after a minute. "Is she wearing her seat belt?" he asked.

I laughed, but I could also feel my face getting hot. "As a matter of fact, she is," I said. I didn't have to look back at Cassie to see; I'd already checked.

"And she put it on all by herself without your telling her?" he asked.

"Well," I said. "I believe the flight attendant made an announcement. But, yes, I think she would have done it on her own anyway."

"Interesting," he said, and went back to his magazine. "You must've done something right."

I glanced at Cassie, who was talking to Juliet, looking like any young woman having a conversation with a friend. *Trust her,* I thought, and the words seemed as foreign to me as anything I'd overheard in Sweden or Japan. *It's time to learn how to trust her.* I didn't look back in her direction until the plane taxied to the gate.

Our camera crew – our last camera crew! – consists of Stu on camera and the unfortunately malodorous Raymond on sound. They chase after us as we rush to baggage claim, with our last parrot (presented to us in Newark) swaying along in his cage. Then we run outside to claim our rental car, emblazoned with a blue-and-white *Lost and Found* sign. We load our stuff into the trunk, Carl hops in the front seat with Stu, and I get in the back with Raymond and the parrot. I'm navigating; I've got a map I picked up in Houston, and I've already marked our route. Carl starts the car, and we all settle in for the last leg of our long, long trip.

"So do you think there's any chance Jeff won't get the Truth or Consequences thing?" I ask. Carl knew it the moment he read the clue.

"Nah," he says. "If it were just Dallas, we might be in luck, but I'm sure Jeff knows it. Our dad was big on that kind of trivia."

"Your dad would be proud," I say. "It's absolutely guaranteed that one of his sons is about to win a whole lot of money."

"Pretty wild, huh?" Carl says. "Talk about sibling rivalry."

It wasn't supposed to work out this way, obviously; if Cassie and Justin hadn't both gotten themselves disqualified in the last round, there would be three teams going for the finish line instead of two. Less drama this way, but I'm sure they'll find a way to spin it: brother against brother, etc. I'm surprised they didn't decide to have the finale in Gettysburg.

"A million dollars," says Carl. "Oh, man, we're so close."

"Drive fast," I say. Then, catching myself, "But don't break the law."

I'll admit it – I'm getting pretty excited about the possibility that we might actually win. But after spending the better part of the last sixteen hours thinking about it, I've come to the sad realization that a million dollars isn't really a million dollars. Carl and I would have to split it, for one thing, and then probably about half of it would go to taxes; pay off our house, our car, my credit cards, put some money aside for Cassie's education and my retirement, and how much is left? I wouldn't say any of this out loud, of course, and I'd certainly be very grateful for the money; it would help us out a lot. It's just that *a million dollars* is such a fantasy-inspiring phrase, and the reality of it turns out to be something less than the quit-your-job, champagne-on-tap kind of money I was imagining at the beginning of all this. Maybe this is one of the reasons you see more young people on shows like this; they're less cynical. And they don't have mortgages.

"I-10 West," I say, spotting a sign. "And we stay on that for . . . looks like about forty miles."

"Gotcha," he says, merging onto the highway.

"Only another day or two till you see Benjamin," I say, just to see the way his face softens in the mirror. "Are you looking forward to it?"

He shakes his head. "I can't even tell you," he says.

"I'm looking forward to meeting him," I say, and Carl shoots me a smile across the distance of the seats.

"You think you're up for it?" he asks.

"I think I am," I say. Three-year-olds are easy. Bring stickers, and don't try to be his mom. I can handle that.

Even as recently as yesterday, I would have been afraid to have a conversation like this. I would have been afraid to hint that there's any chance we'll see each other again after the game is over. But today everything's different. Last night, the producers screened our wishes for all of us to see, and it turned out that Carl and I had the very same wish. Apparently, this was what they were looking for all along; it was a secret challenge the contestants didn't know about until after we'd given our answers. We were the only ones who did it right; Cassie and Juliet didn't get to do the task, which is too bad – how I would have loved to see that footage. And I guess Justin didn't quite finish before going ballistic; they didn't even show us Abby's, since she was still at the police station. Dallas and Jeff weren't even close: Dallas wished for a sitcom deal, and Jeff wished for his nephew to live a long and healthy life, which I know Carl was touched by, though it didn't win Jeff any prizes.

Then they showed us ours, and in a moment of giddy synergy, Carl and I both wished for some kind of future together, in whatever shape and form that might take. For this public display of romance, for succeeding at a task we didn't even know we were competing in, we were awarded a trip to a South Seas resort (on which we'll also have to pay taxes, I imagine), to be taken anytime within the next year. The result is that today, as I race toward something that's not quite a million dollars, I feel completely comfortable imagining a day when Carl will do me the honor of introducing me to his little boy. Who knew a game show could even offer such a prize?

We drive through Las Cruces and continue on the highway past brown scrub grass and distant buttes. I've never been to the Southwest, and the landscape is completely foreign to me, but it's thrilling just to be on an American highway again, to see the familiar green road signs and pass billboards for hotel chains and fast food restaurants that are just like billboards I've passed on every other road trip of my life. I feel like I'm finally home.

We pass the miraculous wrinkled mountains of Fort Selden State Monument and the sudden explosion of cottonwood trees that surrounds the water of Percha Dam State Park, and finally we reach our far-more-humble destination: a little resort town that answered a nationwide publicity dare in 1950 and voted to change its name from Hot Springs to Truth or Consequences.

"It's kind of a cool name, if you think about it," says Carl. He booms the name in an ominous voice. "*Truth or Consequences.* Kind of eerie, almost Biblical-sounding."

"Yeah," I say. "If you can keep yourself from thinking about Bob Barker."

"My dad would tell you that Ralph Edwards was the host at the time that the name was changed. He'd be really annoying about it."

"That is annoying. It's a good thing he's not here." I send a smile out to him through the mirror.

We drive into the erstwhile Hot Springs, a low, sprawling city dwarfed by mountains on every side. It has kind of a nice, small-town, isolated feeling, though everything's a little run-down. The sky is somehow enormous.

"So now we just drive around until we find the right hotel?" I ask. "That could take forever."

"Let's find someone to ask," he says. He drives another minute or so until we find a street that looks like it has a fair amount of foot traffic, and he pulls over. I jump out with the clue. There's a café with tables on the sidewalk, and I begin questioning people at random. Soon I have a little crowd gathered, everyone glancing non-chalantly at the camera and poring over my little piece of paper.

"'Marked by a mountain mosaic,'" says a man with long gray hair. "What do you figure they mean by that? Like on the front of the building or something?"

"I have no idea," I say.

"And do they mean it's a picture of a mountain, or is that some artistic term?" asks a middle-aged woman in boldly patterned pants. "Really, they could have phrased it better."

I'm getting antsy here; I glance at Carl, who's watching us from the driver's seat of the car and making a "hurry up" gesture. "I agree," I say tightly. "But does that ring any bells?"

"Well, it's not the Holiday Inn," says the gray-haired man.

"No, I can't imagine they'd send them to the Holiday Inn," says the woman with the pants. "Not very photogenic." She looks at Stu. "Am I allowed to say that on camera, or will they sue me?"

"They can't sue you," says the man with gray hair. "They don't know who you are."

"Oh, they have their ways," says the woman.

"Okay, thanks," I say. I'm about to leave, when an elderly woman sitting at a nearby table calls out.

"The Sierra Grande has a mosaic on their sign, don't they?" she says. "I never noticed whether it has mountains on it, though."

"That's great," I say, leaping toward her. "Where is it?"

"McAdoo Street," she says. She gives me directions, and I thank everyone while Stu works on getting them to sign releases as quickly as he can. We run back to the car, and I tell Carl which way to go. A few minutes later, we pull up in front of the Sierra Grande Lodge; outside there's a sign with a mosaic of sun shining on mountains. And next to it, a square of blue-and-white cloth emblazoned with a suitcase full of stars.

"Bingo," Carl says. He finds a parking space, and we hurry out of the car. I pick up the parrot cage and my backpack, which (much lighter now) contains only the aviator's helmet, the crystal bishop, the sequins, and the Stockholm photos. Carl gets the ski pole and his own backpack, which holds the trilobite fossils, the fake sushi, the rice paper, and the christening gown. We got some strange looks at customs.

"I don't see another car like this one," Carl says, slamming the door. "Do you think they would've given the other guys a different model?"

"I don't know," I say.

We were instructed earlier to run as much as possible – the stakes are high here, and they want that to be obvious to the viewers – so run we do. It's a little silly, since Dallas and Jeff are nowhere in evidence; either they got here before us, and the (not quite) million dollars have already been taken, or they're far behind, and we've got plenty of time. But I'm suddenly filled with nervous energy – and for God's sake, I want to know if we've won – so I have a feeling running is what I'd be doing anyway. The parrot screeches as the cage swings back and forth in my hand.

We hurry inside to the hotel lobby, filled with expensive-yet-rustic decor. It smells good in here, kind of herbal and spalike. And then we stop running and stand there like idiots for a minute.

"Okay, what now?" I say.

"I don't know," Carl says.

I walk up to the check-in desk. "Excuse me," I say, yelling over the noise of the bird. "Do you have a clue for us?"

The man smiles politely, and produces an envelope. I tear it with a flourish. I wonder if I'll ever be able to open mail the same way again.

> *You've lost your fears and found your way*
> *On this monumental trek.*
> *Now bottle up some healing waters –*
> *Barbara's waiting with a check.*

A little clunky, and I don't know that it's fair to say I've lost *all* my fears . . . but there's no time for that. Carl turns back to the desk clerk. "Um, do you happen to know where we might find some healing waters?" he asks.

"Well," the man says, his eyes darting between Carl's face and the camera, "there are many legends about the restorative powers of our hot springs."

"Where are the hot springs?" asks Carl.

"Indoor or outdoor?" the man asks.

"I don't know – indoor?'

He points us to an elevator. "Downstairs," he says.

Waiting for the elevator seems to take forever. We go down to the lower level and follow signs until we find a door marked HOT SPRING. We burst through the door with great pomp, and inside we find . . . no one. Just a rectangular pool, blowing up steam into the air. The walls are painted with colorful murals, and a fountain mounted just above the edge spits a steady stream of water back into the pool. The only noise in the room is a muffled splashing.

"I guess this isn't it?" I say, getting ready to turn back.

"No, wait," says Carl. He points to a basket full of glass flasks. Each one is imprinted with the *Lost and Found* logo.

"Great," I say. "Fill it up with the water."

He sets down his ski pole and picks up a bottle. He opens it and holds it under the surface of the water to fill it.

"It's hot," he says, sounding surprised.

"Well, what'd you expect?" I say. I bend and dip a finger in. It is hot.

"Okay," he says, springing up and holding the bottle up to look at the water level. "This ought to do it." He caps it and picks up his ski pole. We run out of the room.

"Where's Barbara, do you think?" I say. "Outdoor hot spring?"

"Sounds like a good place to start."

This time the elevator is waiting for us; we jump in and go back to the lobby level.

"This way," Carl says, seeing a blue-and-white arrow pointing us toward a back door.

We run down a long hallway, parrot screaming, ski pole clinking on the tile floor. Carl pushes open the door, and we emerge into a sunny courtyard. Barbara is standing at the edge of a large round hot tub tiled in blue. There's no one else around – no other contestants, at least. No way to tell if we're the first ones here or the last.

We head toward Barbara and stop in front of her. For some reason, I feel like we should kneel.

"Carl and Laura," Barbara says. She pauses. We nod.

"Native Americans," she begins solemnly, and oh my God, is she going to give us a history lecture now? ". . . used to praise these waters for their healing powers. Have you brought me a flask of this magical liquid?"

"Yes," Carl says, holding out the little bottle. Barbara takes it and places it on a pedestal to her right.

"And do you have a ski pole for me?" she asks. Carl hands it over, and she props it up against the table with the water.

Item by item, she goes through our found objects, claiming them back like a priestess accepting sacrifices. I know from watching the show in the past that there's no point to this ritual; that it's just to build suspense, and it has no bearing on whether we've won. Yet I can't help wishing that she'd do a little project with these items, build something with all this junk we've collected. Show us there was some rhyme or reason to it after all.

But no. She's just piling it up. Her voice gets more imperious with each demand. "Do you have," she asks loudly, "six sequins from the costume of an Egyptian belly dancer?" Her eyes widen to the size of Necco wafers.

"Yes, Barbara," I say as somberly as I can. I locate the sequins, and she scatters them haphazardly across the display of objects. It's starting to look like a garage sale.

"And finally," she says, lowering her voice to almost a whisper. "Do you have for me a bird known as *Ara macao*?"

"We have a parrot," Carl says as I proffer the cage.

"Very good," Barbara says, setting the bird down at the base of the pedestal. "You have carried these items on a journey that covered all the corners of the earth. And, Laura and Carl . . . you have won *Lost and Found*."

I let out a shriek that's louder than any noise that damn *Ara macao* has ever made. Carl picks me up in his arms and swings me around, gives me a kiss on the mouth for Barbara and the camera crew and the entire American viewing public to see.

The hotel door opens, and suddenly we're surrounded by the eliminated contestants (all except Justin), everyone smiling big smiles and cheering for us gamely. Cassie barrels toward me, and gives me the biggest hug I've gotten since she was ten.

"You did it," she says, yelling in my ear. "I can't believe it. You guys are awesome!" And then, half a breath later, "Can I have a car?"

"We'll talk," I say, holding on to her for as long as she'll let me. "We'll talk."

Barbara reaches under the table where she's displayed our objects and produces a ludicrously oversized cardboard check, which she presents to us with much gravity. And then there are photographs and interviews, and someone comes through with champagne for everyone. Dallas and Jeff, we learn, hit weather delays in Charlotte and won't be in for several more hours. We'll wait for them and film their arrival so that the editors can make it look like it was a lot closer than it was. Tomorrow, Carl and I will sign paperwork to get our money (contingent upon our being able to keep a secret for a few months until the finale airs), and we'll be prepped for the media interviews we'll be doing after we're revealed to be the nation's newest (almost) millionaires.

But tonight it's a party. Cassie drinks a glass of champagne (which I don't say a word about), and I listen to her name all her fantasies for what we're going to do with the money. There's music, and Carl and I dance like a bride and groom. Jeff and Dallas finally arrive, and we welcome them like they're victors returning from battle, and tell them that second place is pretty damn good. Juliet dances with a flower in her teeth; Barbara socializes like a human being; the cameramen, unburdened by heavy equipment, display a collective wit none of us knew they had. Riley and Trent use their awkward charm to try to get all the women in the hot tub; the flight attendants who were eliminated in Egypt get drunk and a little weepy and tell me I'm their hero. Betsy and Jason have a drink together and sink down into old high school stories; it looks like they might part as friends, after all. Abby laughs – have I ever seen that before? The night goes on and on. There's a big, big sky full of stars, and even if a million dollars isn't a million dollars, I think I might finally have an answer to Barbara's question. If only I knew how to put it into words.

THIRTY SIX

Cassie

Of course real life doesn't have neat little endings the way TV does. You know that feeling when you get home from a vacation, and the excitement's over, and you look at your ordinary, familiar little house, and you're like, *Oh, I'm here again*? I think it's going to be a little bit like that. I'm going to get back to school, and all my same problems will still be there. Mia will still hate me, and I still isolated myself from everyone I know, and I still had a baby that I can't stop thinking about. In a few months, the show will go on the air, and maybe I'll be a celebrity for like a minute, but then when they get to the part where I'm throwing things in Ireland, I guess I'll be back to being weird Cassie. Or maybe everybody will suddenly want to be my friend, but it will only be because they've seen me on TV and my mom won half a million bucks. (And, speaking of my mom, did she actually kiss that guy on national television? God.)

I don't know, maybe I'm being too negative. It was kind of a cool experience; it's too bad they don't ask us to write those "What I did for my summer vacation" essays anymore, because I would definitely have everyone else beat. And, hello, we won the money, or half of it, so what the hell am I complaining about?

Mom and I are on the plane home. She's happier than I've seen her, like, ever. She and Carl have plans to see each other in a few weeks. Who knows if that'll work out, but if I'm being honest and

I'm not in a bratty mood, I hope it does. As long as they don't push that "you've got a new little brother" stuff down my throat. And as long as they don't have any kids of their own — is she even still capable of that?

"Hey, kiddo," she says. "It's kind of funny to be on our own again, isn't it?"

"Yeah," I say. "No cameras. I keep expecting Austin or Elliott or one of those guys to jump in and start filming."

"Are you looking forward to getting home?"

"Sort of." And then for some reason, I decide to actually say out loud what I'm thinking, which is not usually my MO with Mom. "I'm kind of dreading going in my room." I don't know why that is; it's not like I haven't been back in there. I did keep living in there for three months after the baby was born, before we left to go on the show. But something about having been away and thinking about it so much. . . . Well, anyway, that's how I feel, and I said it.

I watch my mom out of the corner of my eye. If she says "Why?" and acts like she has no idea what I'm talking about, then this whole conversation is over. But she doesn't. She's quiet for a minute, and she puts her hand on my arm.

"The night you were born," she says softly, "was the most important night of my life. And I'll never forget a single detail."

I know all about that. Every year on my birthday, she tells me what she remembers. *You were born on the coldest night of the year, and everybody said you were the most beautiful baby anyone had ever seen.* It's corny, but I always like hearing it.

"And just because you don't have that baby to raise," she says, treading carefully, "doesn't mean that that night is any less important to you."

I nod. I'm horrified to realize that my eyes are filling with tears.

Mom gives me a sideways hug in the airplane seat. "If you want, maybe every year you could tell me that story. Because, you know, every time your birthday comes and I tell you your story, it's not just for you. It's for me, too."

"Yeah," I say. My voice is all gluey-sounding with trying not to cry.

"We should be getting a picture soon," she says. "Imagine how much she's grown."

And that does it. The tears spill out. It feels awful, it wrenches my body, but it's good somehow. Maybe this is all my mom meant those times when she said we should talk about it. It's not over – putting that baby in someone else's arms wasn't an ending, and freaking out in Ireland wasn't an ending, and maybe nothing ever will be. But with each little thing that's not an ending, it does start to feel like maybe someday I'll have a life that's not all about this. And maybe that doesn't mean having a life where this isn't a part of it at all.

I wonder if things are going to get crazy when the show finally airs; I wonder if people are going to recognize me on the street and write stuff about me online and all that. I wonder if I'll ever even see any of those people again, aside from Carl and his doofus brother.

Before we left, Juliet gave me a big hug and told me I was her best friend and she'd e-mail me all the time, but we'll see how long that lasts. Once she gets home and starts breathing that Hollywood air, things might start to look a little bit different. It's like leaving summer camp – except that when you're at summer camp, you don't usually have someone documenting your every move. (Hey, there's an idea for a show.) Well, who knows: maybe there's some community of former reality stars, and we'll all get invited to the same parties. Or maybe, if the ratings are good enough, they'll decide to do a reunion show. Or maybe we'll all just go back to living our lives.

The plane lands and Mom and I get off, walking slowly, waiting our turn. There's no rushing to be the first ones off, no reading clues and bumping people with ski poles, no picking up replacement parrots. We can say whatever we want. There are no sound guys sticking boom mics in our faces. There's no fanfare, and if that makes me feel the tiniest bit lonely, well, that's just pathetic, and I should get over it.

Back at the Giant's Causeway, when Juliet and I were disqualified and Barbara asked her "lost and found" question, I had some cheesy throwaway answer, something about finding out I was capable of being independent and strong. (Man, that's going to be an embarrassing catchphrase to have floating around school.) And, basically, it's not like I think being on a TV show can change your life or make you a different person in any substantial way. But things do affect us, right? People we meet, places we go? Is it stranger to think you might learn something new in a situation like this than in any other life experience? Maybe I have found something, but it doesn't fit neatly into a little sound bite. Maybe it's going to take me a while to even figure out what it is.

Anyway, screw all the philosophical stuff. We're in a cab heading toward our house, and out the window, I can see us whizzing past all the landmarks of my childhood. There's the park I used to go to when I was little. I remember once, my mom told me it was time to go home, and I wouldn't leave, so she pretended she was leaving without me. She thought I'd go running after her, but I completely called her bluff. She got all the way to the car, and I still wasn't following, so she got in and drove around the corner to a place where I couldn't see her. Then she sat and watched while I stayed there on the swings, all by myself, moving slowly back and forth as the evening got darker and darker. Eventually, she was the one to cave; of course she wasn't going to leave me there all night. But neither of us has any idea how long I might've stayed.

"I can be really stubborn," I say suddenly.

My mom looks surprised. "Yes," she says, smiling slightly. "I suppose you could say that."

"I should've told you," I say, looking out the front window. We're driving past the house where my old babysitter used to live. I don't know who lives there now. "I don't know what I was trying to prove."

My mom doesn't say anything for a minute, and I turn to look at her. Her face is serious, and a little sad. "Well," she says. "You shouldn't have had to tell me." She looks like she might say something else, but she doesn't. And I'm sure there's more to say, I'm sure we'll be adding to this conversation for as long as we're both alive, but for now, this moment in the cab, this is enough.

We pass my elementary school, and the supermarket we always shop at. Everything looks familiar and strange all at once. We're home, whatever that means. I can get nostalgic about it, because someday, not too far off, I'm not going to live here anymore; maybe my mom won't, either. Who knows where I'll end up? Really, when you think about it, I could go anywhere.

We pull onto our street, and I catch a glimpse of our house. It looks like it's shrunk. Our yard is overgrown; that's something my mom wouldn't have thought of, that we should arrange for someone to mow the lawn while we were gone. Who knew grass would keep growing if we weren't there to see it? I'm sure the lady next door is going berserk. She can't stand it when people don't keep their lawns neat. But in a couple of months, she'll probably be bringing her grandkids by for autographs.

Mom pays the cab driver, and we get our stuff out of the trunk. Our backpacks are a lot lighter, now that we've given back all the found objects. They're going to be auctioning all that stuff off to the public after the show airs, but I did talk Eli into letting me keep the sushi. We climb the front steps, and Mom does a lengthy search for her keys. We both have a moment of fear that maybe she left them back in Cairo or someplace. But she finds them, finally, in an inner pocket of her backpack, and she opens the door, releasing all the stale air that's gone unbreathed for the last month.

"You want to go first?" she asks, holding open the screen door and gesturing me inside.

"No, that's okay," I say.

She goes in, and I catch the screen before it slams shut. I just want another minute out here, to stand and look at the cracks in the concrete that have been there since I was born, to pick a leaf from the skinny forsythia branches that stick through the porch railings, the same way they always have. It's like I'm in a museum, standing back at the velvet ropes, trying to read the plaques. But then it starts to seem a little silly to be lingering out here for no reason, and after a minute my mom yells out, "Don't let the bugs in."

I take a breath of the summer air that's not like the air in any other place in the world, and I step forward into what, up till now, has been my entire life.

ACKNOWLEDGMENTS

I'm happy to have the chance to thank some of the people who have played a role in the life of this book. I am extremely grateful to my agent, Douglas Stewart, for his wisdom and encouragement, and to my editor, Asya Muchnick, for her thoughtful reading and sharp insight. I am thankful to everyone at Little, Brown for their hard work and support, including those people whose contributions may not have been visible to me; thanks especially to Amanda Erickson, Heather Fain, Heather Rizzo, Jen Noon, Zainab Zakari, Sophie Cottrell, and Michael Pietsch. Thank you to Shari Smiley at Creative Artists Agency and Marcy Posner at Sterling Lord Literistic.

Thanks to Jennifer Allison, Kate Blackwell, Kitty Davis, C. M. Mayo, Ann McLaughlin, Leslie Pietrzyk, Dana Scarton, Amy Stolls, Paula Whyman, and Mary Kay Zuravleff for reading the novel in its early stages and giving me their valuable feedback. I know this is a better book because of their help. And thanks to Zachary Behr and Shii Ann Huang for taking the time to talk to me about their experiences in reality TV.

Thanks to my wonderful family and friends. Thank you to my parents, Doreen C. Parkhurst, MD, and William Parkhurst. Thank you to Molly Katz, and to my grandmother Claire T. Carney. Thank you to my husband, Evan Rosser, for a million different reasons, only one of which is that he likes most of the same shows I do.

Thanks to my son, Henry, for telling me such great stories and taking me on such interesting adventures, and to my daughter, Eleanor, for being the sweetest baby currently on the planet.

And, finally, thank you to the nice man at the coffee shop who always asked me what page I was on.

CAROLYN PARKHURST is the author of the bestseller *The Dogs of Babel*, which was a *Today* Show Book Club pick, a Book-of-the-Month Club Main Selection, and a *Book Sense* Top Ten Pick. She holds a BA from Wesleyan University and an MFA in creative writing from American University. She has published fiction in the *North American Review*, the *Minnesota Review*, *Hawai'i Review*, and the *Crescent Review*. She lives in Washington, D.C., with her husband and their children.

Reading Group Guide

LOST

AND

FOUND

A novel by

Carolyn Parkhurst

A Tough Act to Follow

Carolyn Parkhurst on the challenges of writing second novel

The day the first-ever review of my first novel, *The Dogs of Babel*, came in, I heard from my agent at about ten in the morning. "It's not very nice," he said, as if a bad review were a matter of etiquette, as opposed to any kind of substantive criticism of my work. He didn't tell me what it actually said; he made the right kinds of reassuring noises and offered to fax me the offending document.

Since we didn't have a fax machine at home, I told him to send it to my husband's office; in due time, I heard from my husband, who confirmed the review's lack of niceness and told me he'd rather not read it to me over the phone. So by 10:30 I knew I'd gotten a bad review, but I didn't know the specifics, and I wasn't going to be able to read it till seven o'clock that night. It was excruciating. Then at 2 p.m., the doorbell rang; it was a bouquet of flowers from my husband. *Wow*, I remember thinking. *This must be one hell of a review.*

It was; and after that there were plenty more – some good, some bad, some mixed.

My point isn't to complain about book reviews; I realize they're part of the deal. You show your work to people, they're going to have their own ideas about it. But there's something very strange for a new writer about seeing your book take on a life of its own. You write more or less in isolation, and when you do seek out advice and criticism, you choose your readers carefully. And then – fingers crossed, if everything goes right – you release it to the world. Suddenly, it's not your book anymore; it belongs to anyone who's kind enough to pay the cover price and take the time to read it. It's both thrilling and disconcerting to discover how varied readers' reactions can be, and after going through it once, I'm not sure I'll ever approach writing in quite the same way again.

The difficulties of writing a second novel are legendary, and since *The Dogs of Babel* was more successful than I ever imagined it would be, the pressure was on from the minute I opened a new file on my laptop and gave it the tentative title "New Novel?" Mostly, I tried not to think about it. I know how easy it is for writers to worry themselves into paralysis, so I tried to look at this new project not as a second novel per se. I told myself it was just one more book in the series of books I hoped I'd write over the course of my career. Still, it was clear pretty early on that that long day of the fax and the flowers had left its mark. Every chapter I wrote, every character I created, I'd wonder, *What are people going to say about this one? What flaws am I missing that are going to be obvious to everyone else?* I don't want to shape my work according to some idea I have about what people want from me; in the end, I wrote the book I wanted to write. But at the same time, I'd like to be prepared for what's coming. Now that I've published one book, I can't help but look ahead to the day when this new novel lands in readers' hands and I finally get to hear what they think of it. And I don't want to be taken completely by surprise.

Strangely, though, the time I spend thinking about the people who didn't like my first book is nothing compared to the time I spend thinking about the people who did. Writing a second novel has reminded me that readers and writers don't always have the same goals. As a writer, I want to evolve, to write something completely new each time; as a reader, when I find an author I like, what I want most is some level of consistency. I've had the experience of feeling slightly suspicious when my favorite authors release books that don't look anything like what they've written before. *Wait a minute*, I think. *We were doing just fine before, weren't we? I liked that last one — why don't you do something like that again?* Maybe I'm just not good at accepting compliments, but when someone says to me, "I liked your book," and then tacks on, "I can't wait to read the next one," my primary response is low-level panic. Because the next one isn't going to be the same, and there are bound to be people who like one and not the other. And even though it was never my goal to write the same book over and over again, there's a part of me that thinks, *Well, why not? It worked the first time.*

On the other hand, what is there to complain about? I like writing fiction, and it's a privilege to be able to do it for a living. Since Little, Brown signed me to a two-book deal right out of the gate, I had the good fortune of writing this book without the uncertainty that attended the first one; I don't know how it will be received, or whether anyone will buy it, but I don't have to worry that it will never see a bookstore shelf. And as with anything else, there's a level of confidence that comes with having done something once before. I had plenty of doubts writing this book, but whether or not I'd finish wasn't one of them; even when I had no idea where the book was going, I had a sense that somehow the plot would work itself out, that somehow I'd know how to bring this story home to its conclusion.

It's been about a month now since I wrote the last pages of *Lost and Found*. The day I thought I would finish, I went back to the coffee shop where I wrote the ending of *The Dogs of Babel*, someplace I hadn't been in more than three years. But it wasn't the same. The day I finished the first draft of *The Dogs of Babel* was exhilarating. For about a year, I'd known how the last paragraph was going to begin — "I remember my wife in white" — and the day I got to type those words, to see them in black and white, occupying their proper place in the narrative, was one of the best days of my life. This time around, I felt more subdued. I took my coffee outside onto the sunny terrace and wrote until I was finished. And then I just sat there. *Is that really it?* I thought. *Am I really done?* I reread the last few pages: yes, that did appear to be the ending. I liked it; I was happy with the book, overall. But for some reason, I was reluctant to let this one go, maybe because I had a better idea of what was going to happen to it. I had hopes for this book, and fears, just as I had the last time, but now they were all more concrete. I knew that before too much time passed, it would be out there in the world for everyone to see; in a little while, it wouldn't belong to me anymore. So I didn't get up right away. I just sat there in the sun, my computer open, my words on the screen, and watched the traffic go by.

This essay originally appeared in *Publishers Weekly* on August 8, 2005.

A conversation with
Carolyn Parkhurst

Lost and Found *takes place in cities across the globe, and I read somewhere that you've never visited many of the novel's exotic locales. What was it like to write about places you didn't know firsthand?*

It was a lot of fun to do the research, but there were times when I worried I was in over my head. I wanted to make sure I got the details right, so I ended up spending a lot of time researching things like the Japanese train system and flight times between different countries. I also wanted to capture the disorientation, the loss of equilibrium, involved in this kind of intense travel. When I was describing my characters' impressions of the places they're visiting, I tried to focus on differences in the everyday: things that are mundane to inhabitants of any particular locale, but which combine to create the sense of being in a strange land.

While the reality-TV frame is a major part of Lost and Found, *you address something bigger about the human condition. Please explain.*

I see the novel as being about the destructive power of secrets, and about the nature and origin of shame; all the characters start out with a secret, something that haunts them that they'd like to keep private, and each one finds that the trial of being on the show brings these things to the forefront in ways they hadn't imagined. The real substance of the writing lay in developing each character's story, learning how each person's voice sounded, and figuring out what each one had to say, seeing their stories intersect and their relationships develop.

Why did you decide to frame the novel around a reality-TV show?

I think there's a lot that's compelling about reality shows – the pressure of being constantly scrutinized, the alliances and backstabbing, the fear of elimination – and I wanted to see if I could translate that kind of drama onto the page. I liked the fact that putting my characters in that atmosphere would provide built-in structure and conflict, and I thought it would be interesting to portray characters who are simultaneously being portrayed by a TV show. It seems that people are often chosen to be on shows like that because they appear to fit neatly into a category that will be recognizable to viewers, and I wanted to explore the disconnect between the complexity of each person's life and the simplicity of their TV persona. And, finally, I genuinely like television and popular culture and thought they'd provide an intriguing world for me to immerse myself in for a while.

What other challenges did you face?

By setting up the game the way I did, I unintentionally caused some problems for myself. Since the show is a scavenger hunt, I had the characters lugging a lot of odd stuff with them: ski poles, aviator helmets, live parrots. I'd write a whole scene and then think, "Oh, man, I forgot the parrots again." And because the characters are being filmed constantly, I had to think about things like camera crews and microphones; I didn't know much about the technical details of those things. I had to find ways to sound convincing but not overwhelm the book with details of logistics.

You are a self-confessed television junkie. While writing Lost and Found, *did your television-viewing habits change? What are you watching now?*

One of the nice things about writing a book about a reality show is that it allowed me to give myself permission to watch a lot of TV:

"Well, I have to watch *America's Next Top Model*: it's *research*." In addition to liking television, I was interested in exploring the subtle ways that TV plays a role in people's lives. As a fiction writer, I believe in the power stories can have over us, and it seems to me that TV is as potent a source for those stories as anything else. When I think of my early years, so much of the landscape of my memories is bound up with television, and I don't think that's necessarily a bad thing. I'm as nostalgic about the TV shows I watched as a kid as I am about the books I loved or the stories my parents told me; all those things played a role in shaping the way I observed the world around me.

I've watched a number of reality shows over the years, ranging from the almost highbrow (PBS's *1900 House*, for example) to the truly embarrassing (I know I watched at least a couple of episodes of *Amish in the City*). Reality shows I've been watching lately include *Project Runway*, *The Amazing Race*, and *Top Chef.* And for scripted TV, I love *Lost*, *Veronica Mars*, and *The Office*.

On the surface, The Dogs of Babel *and* Lost and Found *couldn't be more different! Are there any similarities?*

Both novels deal with the aftermath of loss. Readers learn early on that Cassie has recently had a baby (after hiding her entire pregnancy from her mother, Laura) and that the baby has been adopted; much of their story concerns their grief over the absence of that child from their lives. Abby is a member of a Christian "ex-gay" group, and she's struggling with the loss of her former identity; she's trying to understand exactly where she fits in the world and trying to make her marriage to Justin work. And like *The Dogs of Babel*, this novel explores the question of how well we really know the people we're closest to. Each character is paired in the game with someone they believe they know absolutely, but as we move among the different viewpoints, it becomes clear that none of them understands their partners as well as they think they do.

In addition to being a successful novelist, you are the mother of two small children. How do you balance these two very time-consuming endeavors?

I couldn't do it if I didn't have good childcare. It can be hard to juggle everything, but for the most part, the flexibility of writing works well with having kids; it's easier to balance my time than it would be if I had a forty-hour-a-week job. And I've been surprised to see how much parenthood has informed my writing; several of the characters in *Lost and Found* are concerned with the daily work of parenting, both its challenges and its joys.

Questions and topics
for discussion

1. *Lost and Found* moves between the points of view of several different characters. Which of the characters' backstories were most compelling to you? Which characters did you root for? Were there any characters you *didn't* want to win?

2. At the beginning of the novel, Cassie says, "They picked us because they think we're this big mother-daughter bomb ticking away with secrets, and they're just waiting for us to explode" (page 18). In what ways are the various contestants pressured to reveal their secrets? Are these revelations ultimately cathartic, or do you think the characters would have been better off if they'd been able to keep their secrets private?

3. The rift between Cassie and Laura seems, at first, beyond repair. How do they find their way to reconciliation? What does Cassie learn about being a daughter – and being a mother? How does Laura's approach to her relationship with Cassie change?

4. What is the secret Juliet is hiding? How does her interaction with Cassie over the course of the novel change her perspective? Do you think this change will "stick," or will she go back to being her old self?

5. Carolyn Parkhurst once said that Abby and Justin initially were minor characters, but that she then began to think more deeply

about them, wondering, "Why would this couple feel they needed to change something so fundamental about themselves as their sexuality?" How was that question answered in the novel? Did you think Abby and Justin's marriage had any chance of succeeding?

6. Justin is the more dogmatic partner of the couple, but he is also the one who gives in to temptation. Is he just a hypocrite, or is there something deeper to his personality? Do you leave the book feeling any sympathy for him?

7. What do you think accounts for the current popularity of reality television? If you watch reality television, which programs do you watch, and what do you find most compelling about them? Did *Lost and Found* feel like a plausible portrayal of what might happen behind the scenes? And if you don't watch shows of this type, what turns you off about them?

8. What do you think lies in store for the novel's principal characters after the close of the book? Will Cassie be happy in high school? Will Justin learn to accept himself as he is? What will happen to Juliet? How do you think the winners will spend the money?

THE DOGS OF BABEL

A novel by

Carolyn Parkhurst

"Wonderful. . . . Parkhurst has created two compelling characters to take us through the shoals and delights of falling in love and into the calmer and sometimes more dangerous world of marriage."

— Susan Dooley, *Washington Post Book World*

"A book with a staggering emotional wallop."

— Holly J. Morris, *U.S. News & World Report*

"A delight — original, clever, and populated by winsome characters. . . . *The Dogs of Babel* is a true-love story." — Kimberly B. Marlowe, *Seattle Times*

"A substantial first novel about how abiding love can lead a grieving spouse back from unimaginable loss to a vital new life." — *Elle*

"Enormously engaging on both an emotional and intellectual level. . . . I read it without stopping, and I loved it completely." — Anna Quindlen

"A searing portrait of grief that's also a love story and an engrossing mystery." — Joanna Smith Rakoff, *Time Out New York*

"Miraculous. . . . Parkhurst succeeds magnificently. . . . She illuminates the emotional landscape that faces a surviving spouse who is trying to decide how much of life is about the past and how much is about the future. She can be unsparing about love's limitations. . . . An unforgettable reminder that when you can't change the outcome of events, sometimes understanding is enough."
— Amy Waldman, *People*

"You'll be sucked in by the very first paragraph. Parkhurst has managed to take an absurd topic, strip it of snark, and transform it into a poignant and engrossing story."
— *Daily Candy*

"A captivatingly strange book. . . . *The Dogs of Babel* rises to reach a final moment of pure, stirring grace."
— Janet Maslin, *New York Times*

Back Bay Books • Available wherever books are sold